Praise for

THE ORPHAN'S TALES: IN THE NIGHT GARDEN

Winner of the 2006 James Tiptree, Jr. Award

"A fine patchwork of tales, quilted in diverse colours and textures. Refreshingly original in both style and form, *In the Night Garden* should delight lovers of myth and folklore."
—Juliet Marillier, author of the *Sevenwaters Trilogy*

"Catherynne Valente weaves layer upon layer of marvels in her debut novel. *In the Night Garden* is a treat for all who love puzzle stories and the mystical language of talespinners."
—Carol Berg, author of *Daughter of Ancients*

"Fabulous talespinning in the tradition of story cycles such as *The Arabian Nights*. Lyrical, wildly imaginative and slyly humorous, Valente's prose possesses an irrepressible spirit."
—K. J. Bishop, author of *The Etched City*

"Astonishing work! Valente's endless invention and mythic range are breathtaking. It's as if she's gone night-wandering, and plucked a hundred distant cultures out of the air to deliver their stories to us."
—Ellen Kushner, host of Public Radio International's *Sound & Spirit*, author of *Thomas the Rhymer*

"A work of beautifully relayed, interlinked fairy tales."
—*Kirkus Reviews* (starred review)

"There is an entire mythology in this book, in which the themes of familiar fairy tales are picked apart and rearranged into a new and wonderful whole.... A wonderful interpretation of what fairy tales ought to be. The illustrations by Michael Kaluta constitute an excellent supplement." —*Booklist*

"What Valente has accomplished in this book is far more than a collection of stories; she has sown the seeds of an entire mythos, all her own. The blooms in her night garden dazzle and bewitch, and are wondrous fair." —SFRevu.com

"Valente's lyrical prose and masterful storytelling brings to life a fabulous world, solidifies Valente's place at the forefront of imaginative storytelling, and belongs in libraries of all sizes." —*Library Journal*

"Valente's prose is creative and sophisticated; her imagery is intricate and arresting. Any lover of well-written fantasy will find much to enjoy about Valente's book." —*Green Man Review*

Praise for

YUME NO HON: THE BOOK OF DREAMS

"An internal landscape painted with thoroughly poetic turns of phrase and a slim volume that packs a great deal of punch in its fleetingly short chapters." —*Booklist*

"An allegorical fantasy whose dreamlike threads reach into Shinto and Western myth, mathematics and physics . . . Ayako may be a goddess or a dream or a leonine monster—but, by the end, much wisdom has been learned. Those who admire literary craft and rich language will most appreciate this sublime tale." —*Publishers Weekly*

"It's hard to describe this short novel without falling into a kind of 'elevated' language that misses its more down-to-earth qualities. . . . *The Book of Dreams* has room enough for beauty, awe, and terror, but its roots are primal—basic as the seasons, with their cycles of life and death." —*Locus*

"Though her epic novels have won praise from critics and readers alike, Catherynne M. Valente is still one of contemporary literature's best-kept secrets. . . . Told with mathematical precision and the subtle beauty of a well-structured haiku, *Yume No Hon* is a book not to be missed." —*Reflection's Edge*

"A lovely book. I intend to read it many times." —*Realms of Fantasy*

"Gorgeous, liquid prose...it is short, it is intense, and when you get to the end you are left with the strange feeling that you have somehow read something that is True." —*Emerald City*

Praise for

THE LABYRINTH

"[Valente's] poetic prose simmers.... Readers who luxuriate in the telling of a tale and savor phrases where every word has significance will enjoy the challenge of this fantasy." —*Publishers Weekly*

"Line by line and page by page, *The Labyrinth* contains more beauty than all but a very few books published this year. Each paragraph is an incantation, and the entirety is less novel than dithyramb, less story than dream." —SFsite.com

"If I could not actually speak it, then I would pronounce each word in my head, just like a child learning to read, because without speaking the words I would not hear their rhythm. Valente's writing reminded me very much of Dylan Thomas. There is a lyrical quality to it that demands that it be performed, not just read." —*Emerald City*

"Valente's grasp of language and myth is masterful, and her understanding of human psychology profound. As writer Jeff Vandermeer so pointedly put it in the book's introduction, *The Labyrinth* is 'a small jewel of a novel.' Like any treasured stone, it is worthy of only the finest place on a reader's bookshelf." —*Pedestal Magazine*

"*The Labyrinth* is very much like a classical music piece. Starting softly it sings to the soul, is filled with complexity and poise, reaches a startling crescendo, and then leaves the body luxuriously stirred for quite some time.... The author's sheer use of creativity is what makes the whole story work and in a manner that deserves attention as well as applause. This is original, and a beautiful direction for literature to take. Think mystic, Shakespeare, fables, and allow the gentle escape into a multifaceted world." —*Midwest Book Review*

Also by Catherynne M. Valente

THE ORPHAN'S TALES: IN THE NIGHT GARDEN
YUME NO HON
THE LABYRINTH
THE GRASS-CUTTING SWORD

Poetry
APOCRYPHA
ORACLES
THE DESCENT OF INANNA

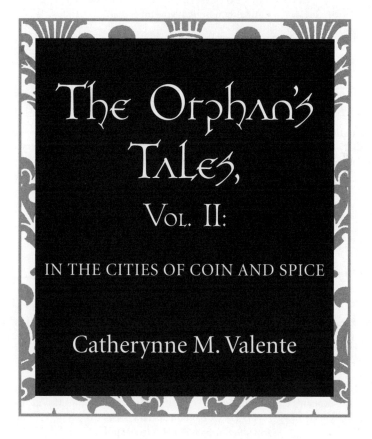

The Orphan's Tales,

Vol. II:

IN THE CITIES OF COIN AND SPICE

Catherynne M. Valente

BANTAM BOOKS

THE ORPHAN'S TALES: IN THE CITIES OF COIN AND SPICE
A Bantam Book / November 2007

Published by
Bantam Dell
A Division of Random House, Inc.
New York, New York

Interior illustrations by Michael Wm. Kaluta
Cover illustration © Michael Komarck
Cover design by Jamie S. Warren Youll

Book design by Glen M. Edelstein

Bantam Books, the rooster colophon, Spectra, and the portrayal of a boxed "s" are trademarks of Random House, Inc.

Library of Congress Cataloging-in-Publication Data

Valente, Catherynne M., 1979–
The orphan's tales. In the cities of coin and spice / Catherynne M. Valente.
p. cm.—(A Bantam Spectra book)
ISBN 978-0-553-38404-8 (trade pbk.)
I. Title. II. Title: In the cities of coin and spice.

PS3622.A4258O76 2007
813'.6—dc22
2007019699

Printed in the United States of America
Published simultaneously in Canada

www.bantamdell.com

BVG 10 9 8 7 6 5 4 3 2 1

For Sarah, who,

when she was older,

wanted the World.

The Book
of the
Storm

In the Garden

THE PATHS OF THE GARDEN WERE WET WITH FALLEN APPLES AND red with their ruptured skin. Rag-clothed winds trailed over grass blanched of green; scarlet swallowed up the thrashing trees until all the many groves stood in long rows like bouquets of bloody flowers with long, black stalks.

It was the girl's favorite time—food was never so easy to find, and the air was filled all through day and night with the flapping and fluttering of wings as crows circled south and geese fled even farther into the warm belly of the world. In the autumn her skirt was always full of pomegranates and grackle-eggs, and though the air was colder, the leaves' color did not lie, and they warmed her like a fire beneath a squat iron pot.

It was from the blazing boughs of a cinnamon tree that she saw through the high windows of the women's quarters in the palace. Her palms were henna-dusted by the perfumed bark, and she sucked the last of the morning's golden yolk from her fingers, now flavored with spice. She kept well behind the skein of leaves as she looked through the arched window, at the woman sitting within, her back straight as an ax-handle, and so still, though hands flashed over her and voices clicked and hushed in her pretty ears. A dozen maids held the woman's long black hair out taut, and slowly, with infinite patience, threaded tiny white pearls onto the inky strands, one by one, as though the woman were a necklace in a jeweler's workshop.

Dinarzad was to be wed.

Surely one or two of the Sultan's daughters were married every year, and the girl paid them much less attention than she did the family of doves that returned to the same birch trees each spring—but she could not help knowing of this one. Gardener and groundskeeper talked of nothing else: Flowers were coaxed and coddled long past their blooming, trees trained to canopies, fruits culled in great piles, like many-colored snowdrifts, and sent wagon by wagon to the kitchens, only to return to the courtyard as pies and pastries and jams and cakes—for Dinarzad wished to be married in the Garden.

It was unseemly, to be married without a roof over one's head, but she had insisted, even wept, and finally it was decided that a roof of trees was not in its nature different from a roof of wood, and the delicate copse of chestnuts before the great courtyard had had their branches lashed and tied and dragged into the shape of a small, narrow chapel. As they climbed their ladders to wheedle and prune the trees into holiness, the gardeners grumbled to the girl that she ought to be especially careful not to be seen, since the Palace was leaking out of its walls for the pleasure of a spoilt *amira*.

In her deep blue cushions, Dinarzad stared into the mirror as she was strung with pearls for the engagement feast, implacable, canvas-blank—and the girl stared into the princess. Still as an owl, she watched the women whose hands were full of the white jewels, watched the decorated Dinarzad like a tall mirror, until the pearl-keepers led their charge away down the stone stairs, her hair trailing behind her like a shred of sky glittering with stars. The girl touched her own hair without meaning to, hair no less black than the other woman's, but tangled and strung through with hazel-husks.

Below her, the tree shook suddenly, and she was shaken from her contemplation of Dinarzad's unmovable face. She glanced down to the apple-smattered path, and saw the boy staring up at her. He grinned sidelong at her, but his mouth was tired at the edges, like a slice of orange beginning to brown. She scrambled lightly down the trunk and gave him a smile small as a secret. The boy was dressed for the feast and obviously uncomfortable in stiff gold fabric and green silks, uncomfortable, especially, with the thin band of porphyry circling his wrist, which marked him to anyone who cared for such codes as the heir to the Sultanate.

The girl did not care. But she allowed that it was a lovely shade of purple.

"How did you get away?" she asked softly. "Surely everyone will want to squeeze your arms and tell you what a fine man you're growing up to be."

The boy snorted like a half-grown bull. "At a wedding, the girl on the dais is the only thing anyone cares to squeeze. It's the same at every dinner until the wedding."

"Who is marrying her?" She did not want to be interested. She told herself she was not.

"How should I know?" He kicked at a rotted apple near his slippered toe. "Some prince or soldier or prince who was a soldier or soldier who became a prince. I can't even remember their names. They all came with chests of opals and baskets of trained songbirds tied together by ribbons of her favorite color and mechanical golden roosters that crowed when you wound their tails—I rather liked that one—and someone chose, though I'm sure it wasn't her. I do know she's not to be his first wife; he has two already, but no children at all. He must have brought something very nice in his barrels—I don't know; he wasn't the one with the roosters."

The boy frowned into the wind and scratched at his collar. "I have to dress like a doll just to watch her eat," he mumbled. "And this thing has no pockets at all—I couldn't even bring you anything."

"That was never necessary, you know," the girl demurred. "I have enough, I've always had enough, even if my enough and yours are as different as an elephant and a minaret."

Her black-rimmed eyes flickered to the earth and back to the boy, and she took him gently by the hand, away from the open paths and into the interior Gardens, past the marble benches and fountains, past the over-picked orchards and the over-pressed grapevines to a clutch of stones so thick with moss that they seemed to be the bodies of long-dead tigers or leopards, whose fur still grew and grew after they had perished. In their long shadows the children were spared the winds, though the girl breathed into her hands to warm her bloodless fingers and the boy's hems were soaked through with dew and old rain. But he did not seem to notice them—he was plucking at his rich vest and looking curiously at the girl.

"You know," he said shyly, "I think I could bring you a dress."

The girl laughed again.

"I have dozens of sisters with hundreds of dresses—they would never notice one gone missing, I know it. It would be warm, and softer than that old rag."

The girl glanced at the frayed fabric that fashioned her skirt, and shook her head. "What would I do with a dress like theirs? You might as well sew my hair with pearls. No, if I am cold, I have blankets of leaves and my birds. I am not one of them, and it would be silly to dress up a camel in lace and bells and jewels. You would do it only to laugh at the poor beast."

They said nothing for a moment, and the boy was ashamed—but he saw the gooseflesh on her shoulders, and the bruised color of her frozen toes. The sky was deepening toward evening, gray and yellow against the wild colors of the Garden, light slowly wandering away from the clouds—and he knew enough of proud young girls not to argue about the dress.

"Is there...is there more?" the boy finally blurted, fidgeting with his bracelet.

"Oh, yes." The girl laughed. "There is always more."

The girl leaned her head against the springy moss and closed her eyes, the stains on them showing full and dark as ever. She began to speak in a half-whisper, like breath leaving a glass flute.

"I will tell you a story from the crease of my right eye.

"Once, there was a long, lonely shore, gray as it is possible for gray to dream of, and the lonely shore ringed a lonely lake, whose water was black as it is possible for white to fear. And in this lake was a dim, wooded island, far off from the shore. There was a ramshackle dock on the shoals, and a ferry, little more than a raft of ash-wood and a long pole, which was dragged back and forth through the silent water by a tall man in a coarse brown cloak—or he might have been tall, if he were not afflicted with a stooping hunch, which the cloak served to hide. To this ferry, and this dock, and this lake, and this island, and this long, lonely shore came a troubled young man who had but one thin and sallow-elbowed arm, and he was the seventh son of a seventh son, so naturally, he was named Seven..."

The Tale of the Crossing

THE PEBBLED BEACH WAS WET AND COLD, EACH gray stone slick with rain and lake and mist. Nothing grew save a thin green mold at the water's edge, no sandpipers pecked at the shore for mites or worms, no cattails knocked against the bitter and scentless wind. Two figures were black against the heavy woolen sky, which leaked a slow, sullen light like wrung sweat. The shapes were featureless save for their curved backs—the one hunched and bone-twisted, the other bent under his satchel. Slowly the one approached the other, until from a distance there was but one great black shape where the two men met and spoke.

The younger man looked up at the ferryman, whose face was scored with lines like a constellation chart, though his eyes and hair were as black as if he had been born only a winter past. Even with his warped spine, he was still a massive creature, leaning against his saw-hewn pole and frowning at shadows moving on the brackish water.

"If you want to cross, it'll have to be now, son. The storm comes through three times a day, and the last gale of the evening is due through sooner than you'd like to know."

The young man frowned and reached into his sleeve with his right hand—for the left sleeve was empty. With his good fingers he pulled a patched purse from the sleeve and clumsily extracted a single coin. He held it against the pad of his hand with a bitten thumb, held it as though it weighed heavier than iron: a small, pale coin, yellowed by many handlings, with a seal stamped onto it, something like a seven-pointed star writhing with spiders. He moved his thumb over it, and sniffed the cold mist. He held it out to the ferryman, staring at him flatly, as though daring him to refuse.

The ferryman did not reach for it. His eyes flickered from the boy's face to his empty sleeve to his fare. Finally, he sighed, a light, rasping sound, like a bird's wings rubbing together. "I know what that is, boy."

Seven snorted. "Is it enough, old man?"

"It is worlds more than enough, and nowhere close to it. But I will take it."

Seven slowly relinquished his coin, rubbing it again with his thumb before handing it over, and climbed onto the ferry, balancing himself as the boards adjusted to his weight. As he settled himself down, he glanced at the hulking figure pulling the pole from its anchor. The ferryman's shabby cloak shifted with his motions, and Seven thought he saw— only for a moment, of course—a  green-black glint of claw flash in and out beneath the frayed fabric, which barely served to cover the man's chest. Seven shook his head and called himself a fool of the fog, leaning back against the makeshift mast, whose sail was so torn and ruined that the ferryman had seemingly given up on it and lashed it to the shaft, useless as a two-legged horse.

The pole guided them smoothly through the vast lake, though it must have been very deep, and the staff seemed not at all equal to its work. For a time they sat in silence, pilot and passenger. Finally, the ferryman swallowed thickly and spoke:

"Where did you get that coin? It is not a thing you should own, a young thing like you."

The lake slid around the pole like old oil. Seven chuckled, and his chuckle was not unlike his rasping cough. His stare was blank and tired. "I am not so young as all that."

"The lake is wider than you think," the ferryman said. "The water warps the distance like a folded mirror. We have time together, you and I, and I am neither mute nor deaf. I am called Idyll, by those who have gotten into the habit of calling me things—and I would know where a boy no grander or taller than any partridge-farmer got hold of *dhheiba*." He spat the last word like a lump of tooth from his mouth, and it lay between them, glinting and garish.

"Where does any man find money?" Seven sighed, looking out over the gray water and the tips of bare trees in the distance. "Ask where an Ajan three-piece comes from, the answer is obvious. Ask where Shaduki silver was minted—you have answered your own question in the asking. Ask after my dhheiba—it must be plain what I will answer. I have been to the city of Marrow, and I have come out again..."

The Tale

of the

Twelve Coins

MY BROTHERS WERE ALL GROWN, BULL-BROAD and earnest as grass, when I was born. I hardly knew them—but my mother held me to her breast as though she had never had another son, as though six other mouths had not pulled at her, as though twelve other little red hands had not clutched at her hair. My father gave me a number instead of a name and returned to his cups.

Of course, as a boy I understood nothing but that my mother loved me and my father did not—my little heart could not begin to grasp that both her embraces and his wine-sopped silence were rooted in the same day, a day that sunk ahead of them like a pit in soft earth. I could not know that for nine months they had prayed for a girl, eaten mashed snake-innards and washed my mother's belly in hidden springs. But another son came, and my parents were always pilgrim-pious and honest as ants.

Among my people a seventh-seventh son is a mark of grace, and grace must be answered; grace must be paid for. On the boy's seventh birthday, he is laid out on the hillside, lashed to the earth by five white-wood pegs, and left to the favor of the Stars. The seventh son pays for the eighth, and the ninth, and the first grandson, and the fifth grand-daughter. A fair trade, don't you think? One child for dozens, dozens, all lined up and waiting to be born while that little boy lies on the mound, shivering in the rain.

It is always done this way, and if any hut full of dirt-farmers were to withhold the sky's due, it would not have been mine.

So my mother kissed me and my father refused to look at me and she had to tie me down all by herself, far off from our fields, her hands shaking as she put the stakes into the soft earth and knotted the ropes as tight as she dared, and I told her she didn't have to, we could tell everyone there had been another son before me, stillborn, and that was good enough for the Stars, one gray, dead baby was good enough, and I wasn't a seventh son at all, I was an eighth boy, and a good boy, and she didn't have to leave me there, where it was so dark, so dark and cold. She cried when she kissed my forehead for the last time, awkwardly lying over my splayed body, trying to hold me. Her tears rolled down my face, onto my lips, and they were all the water I had. She told me that no one knew what happened to the seventh sons—maybe it was something wonderful, something special. But her eyes were dead, and I couldn't look at her while she lied.

After a while, she left, and I looked up into the Stars, which I did not believe were alive—how could I? It was ridiculous. What sort of Stars wanted boys to eat? Or if they did not want us for dinner, to pull their oxcarts or pick their cherries or whatever chores a Star might have to do. The Stars, the living Stars, were children's stories, and I was no child. No one would do this to a child, so I must have been a man. And men are brave, even in the dark, and the cold.

I think I fell asleep—I must have, because I remember waking up, and the smell of burning lamps and burning grass was all around me, and there was a light, a light already fading into a memory of silver, and my ropes were untied, lying limp on the grass beside me. I sat up and rubbed my numb, rain-soaked ankles and legs until, painfully, they prickled into life again, and I was able to stand.

I did not make it to my feet.

A great wind blew through the little valley, and it knocked me to the earth again, a wind so stiff and quick that it slapped my eyes shut like snow-stuck windows, made them water behind the lids, whipped every drop of sweat from my skin until I was dry as a page. I could not open my eyes, I could not see, but hands seemed to clutch at me in the dark, tear at my clothes, carry me up into arms I could not begin to guess at. Dark moved through dark and time passed without speaking to me.

And, though a man would not sleep at such a time, I woke with a raw throat and another child's arm flopped over my face. It was thin and bony, all elbow. As I swam up into myself, I realized I was lying over another body, not less thin than the first. I looked up through a net of limbs, and beyond the limbs were thick bars of glass frosted over with ice. The wind had dwindled somewhat, much as a sirocco will dwindle into a sandstorm, but dwindle nonetheless. It curled and snapped through the cage and every angled limb.

As I struggled up through the mass, some sleeping children moaned and turned over, some wakened ones moved to the side—all were nearly naked, clothed in scraps which might once have been suits and dresses, and none reached up to draw a rag over their nakedness when my movement brushed the clothing aside. I reached the top of the pile of bodies—I thought there were about twenty of us there, shoved into the cage like stacked cow-ribs—and peered out into a world of wreckage.

Please be patient with me—I am trying to describe a place you will never see.

Wind-sprung tears streaked my face as I looked across a kind of central square. There were houses at its pale edges, fountains, even a bell tower, but I could see no wood or stone. Everything in the place was made of what the wind had managed to accumulate—paper and fish-bones and the bodies of unfortunate birds, scraps of fur and broken plaster and apple peels, lemon rinds, date seeds, old dresses, shoes without soles, soles without shoes, frayed rope and shattered pulleys. But most of the detritus of the city, most of the city of detritus, was paper. The fountains shot folios and scriptures and broadsheets into the air, and they were drafted by the gales into construction: endless pages sealed together as walls and stairs and peaked roofs by the unceasing wind. At the smallest break in the storm, I suspected, the whole place would drift into nothing.

The glass cage swung from an iron frame on a dais in the square. Canopies hung in patches over us, shredded cloth stretched through their frames, threads slipping almost to the ground. There were holes and rifts and cuts everywhere, but under their doubtful care, the wind behaved like a willful infant: cowed, but determined to get its own back the minute any back is turned. Folk moved over the rustling courtyard, poring over barrels and boxes and trays—tottering creatures with slender, wispy arms and legs, necks like those of swans, curving up to heads high above their shoulders, and great, distended bellies, swollen as a mother's mound on a woman already full of too much meat and wine. Occasionally, one would peel a blown page from its spidery calves. The moon shone dully through the torn canopies like a bone through punctured skin.

We were ignored in our cage, shivering, clutching each other in a blind search for warmth, for hours. Sometime near dawn I grabbed at an arm for purchase and heard the smallest of cries—and I saw her, for the first time. A little older than I, but much thinner, thinner than a fawn at the bottom of winter's well, and she looked up at me with enormous black eyes, her dark hair cut roughly, like a penitent's, close to her head, in uneven patches and bald spots. Her lips were pale, cracked, as though she had not drunk water in days. Her tiny wrist twisted painfully in my hand. Her gaze slid to the wandering creatures in the square and back to me. I let her go as though she had burned me—and she had burned me, of course she had—those black, black eyes had burned me as surely as a brand. I held out my hand to pull her up out of the well of legs and arms, but she shook her head and cringed back into them. I rested my head against her gingerly; she coughed a little. These were the first times I touched her, and the first sounds I heard from her mouth.

Finally, the sun came gray and dingy through the high and wind-worried clouds, and one of the long-necked things came sidling up to the dais. In one quick motion it unlocked· the door of the cage and stepped aside to avoid the pile of children that tumbled out. Soundlessly, it prodded us, squeezed us, and, with a strength I would not have suspected, pulled us apart, sorting us onto either side of the dais, where others of the city's folk guided us into two shivering lines.

The creature's skin was pale and silvery, as though water moved just beneath the surface; its touch was cool and dry.

I was relieved that the girl was sorted into the same line as I, which was much shorter than the second. We stood side by side, she and I, waiting. The children opposite us were tied together, wrist by wrist, with a rope paler than skin. They looked at us helplessly, teeth chattering, toes blue. Then, their thin-armed guardian towed them over to our side and gave the lead to the last child in our line. It had to prod him roughly, and finally it just put the rope into his hand and closed his fingers around it. The creature who had opened the cage then took the hand of the child at the front of the line and led us all away. By instinct we locked hands together, as if going to a picnic behind our mother's skirts. The girl squeezed my hand gently. We walked out of the courtyard and into the howl, through streets made of little more than rooster bones and petrified branches. It cracked under our feet, and the cracking was the only sound, until we stopped be-fore a tall edifice with a solid, well-made door set into the rubbish-walls. It might have been a church, once, a basilica with tall towers. Now, like most of the architecture of the city, the factory—for that is what it was, I came to learn—was mostly paper. I could read many of the printed let-ters, but they folded into each other or thatched over each other to make an arcane gibberish:

HERE BEGINS THE BOOK OF CLOWN, BURGLAR, CRIMINAL PROSPERITY TO MARROW AND ALL HER MARKET CLOSED BY ORDER GOATFLESH—TWO PORTIONS FOR GOBLETS UNAVAILABLE IN BLUE, YELLOW, RED SILK MEA-SURED BY PROPRIETOR'S ARM NOT CUSTOMER'S WOLF SOUP HOT AND

TASTY CARAT WEIGHT THUS WAS BURIED ONCE THERE WAS A CHILD, WHOSE FACE WARNING: SALE OF INFESTED WHEAT ALL WEALTH TO THE CHRYSOPRASE THIEVES WILL BE PROSECUTED TO THE FULLEST EXTENT—

On and on it wound, around the lintel and over the walls like a frieze, parchment and vellum and plain paper and linen, white and gold and black and gray and even scarlet, bright green mold glinting at angles. The children passed through the door—and it seemed so strange to me then, that a real door should have been shoved into the pages here but nowhere else—first the unbound, then the bound. The silence pressed down like piled stones on our shoulders; it was too much to bear. Just as the last of the knotted ones passed over the threshold, I slipped my place in line, hauling the girl with me, and dashed out, down the steps and onto the wind-racked street of bones and branches.

One of the creatures caught us easily—they are so fast on those thready legs, like terrible ostriches. In a gale-shaded alley it gripped me by the hair. It motioned back toward the factory and tried to guide us with its gaunt fingers. I stood my ground, and my friend moved closer to me.

"Where are we?" I hissed. But my hiss was like a shout in the hushed, empty alley. The thing looked startled.

"You are not supposed to talk to me," it said haltingly.

"We can't obey rules no one tells us about," I insisted.

"You know now. Go inside and don't make trouble."

"We shouldn't have to obey rules we haven't agreed to. You aren't our parents," the girl said, and thus I heard her voice for the first time. It was low and thick and firm as a forest floor.

"She's right," I said. "Tell us where we are. And what is that place where you sent the others?"

It stood, confused, looking from the door, where its companions had already disappeared with the last of the children, to us and back again. It rocked from one stiltlike leg to the other. "I'll be punished," it whined finally.

The girl rubbed her shaved skull. "Look," she said, "has any other child tried to talk to you?"

"Never."

"Then you can't really know you'll be punished. But you'll certainly be punished if I scream and he runs off. If you tell us these things, we will be good, and afterward we'll go where you want us to go." She looked at me, her dark eyes burning like blades. "We promise."

The thing took a deep breath and pulled its meager coat closer over its huge stomach. Its mouth was very wide, almost ear to ear, and strings of bluish hair tumbled down over its cheeks.

It cleared its long throat. "All . . . all right . . ."

The Foreman's Tale

IF IT PLEASES YOU TO KNOW IT, I AM VHUMMIM
of Marrow, third daughter of Orris, who was the grand-
niece of the seventeenth Chrysoprase, which is how our
rulers were titled in the days before the Wasting. From
the degenerated wealth of that long-dead personage,
Orris-My-Benefactor inherited an apple cart and a
fetish stand. In my turn I took proprietorship of these
things, and added to them a meat-pit. Among wealth I
was not wealthy, but beyond the rolls of the Asaad, the
Great Market, I would be envied for the gold at my
throat and the silk at my feet. So were we all, envied and
envying, in the glory of Marrow-That-Was.

When I was a child, the Asaad was the heart of my heart, and in this I was not unique. How high its canopies flew, how bright those draping oranges, those greens, those deep blues! Frankincense bubbled thick and brown in high-rimmed cauldrons, black-faced sheep babbled in their pens, gold was measured out into black purses great and small. How sweet was the sound of creaking cart wheels, the sound of bartering, the sound of coins solid in the palm! The blessed sky over the Asaad was always blue, the polished stones of the square ever shining. For my own part, I was eager to sell our apples, our little figurines, and so proud to acquire the flame-pit and roasting tongs, to add to my family's economy. All citizens took part in the Asaad, or one of the smaller satellite markets, if one could not afford the stall rent demanded in the city center. To shirk one's duty to economy was a crime punishable by scalding irons applied to the arches of the feet. So it was that each morning the entire city—the city that mattered, anyway—crowded under canopies to play out the grand procession of commerce.

My apples were crisp between hundreds upon hundreds of teeth; my jade and onyx and garnet fetishes bought themselves thrice over in luck: bears and snakes and spiders and storks, elephants and crows, and an endless, grotesque variety of Stars. I oiled my hair, the pride of my beauty, with the most expensive attar of emerald—a very intricate process, to press oil from gems, but once, in this place, we knew how to do it. My scalp shone green and black. My neck was short, my thighs round. I was even a bit fat, not an easy thing to avoid in the Asaad, where any taste is answered by twelve more rarified. I preferred date-stuffed serpents with a drizzle of rose-glâce, in my day.

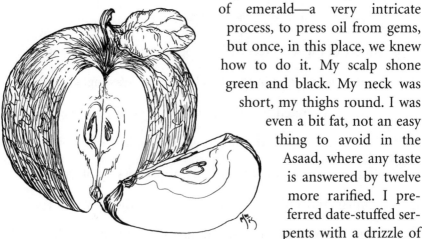

The juice of pepper-crusted dormice and honey-mashed snail shell ground finer than diamond dust ran down my sisters' chins. Little songbirds basted in raspberry sugar and bees' wings made sticky my brothers' fingers. In the fruit-sellers' quarter, pomegranate skins were packed with the tiniest of edible rubies, so small they melted on the tongue like cubes of sugar. Even more complex is the process by which foodstuff is made from the raw material of wealth, but we had mastered this, too, in the days when we knew all things. Once I ate a topaz the size of my father's fist, and its skin split under my teeth like my own apples. The sun was so warm, that day, I thought it would shine through me. My father encouraged me gently, pushed the golden thing to my lips. It tasted of summer-baked wheat and the palest of peaches.

In the Asaad we ate everything we could buy and we could buy anything. Nothing did not answer our hunger, nothing did not have its price.

I first heard of it during the third luncheon shift—the whole market could not cease because we are inclined to be hungry in the middle of the day. We ate in shifts so that commerce never truly paused. That day I reclined on a red sofa beneath a violet canopy spangled with silver crescents, drinking spiced chocolate in a cup of plain gold. I was young then; I could not have expected more. A rind of citrine floated in my drink, and I prodded it with one long, frost-painted fingernail as the quince-seller whispered:

"Have you heard? It's all the way up to the Rhukmini shops now."

A particularly corpulent merchant, who had a few years earlier developed an astonishing and popular hybrid of plum and amethyst, yawned and slapped iridescent blue flies from his own cup. "So? They'll block off the street and we'll go about our business. Rhukmini was a fishmongers' slum, anyway, you old melon-wort, a pale and piecemeal shadow of the Asaad—I call it a blessing. No more lifting one's pant leg to avoid the squid ink and ice-chunked cod blood."

The plum-breeder had taken to the latest fashion of grafting various extraneous limbs to his body—his face was gray, contorting slowly into a small elephant's trunk which sloped over his mustache. He was quite proud of the infant appendage, and made sure all in the Asaad knew it would surely grow much larger by the end of the season. He was a man of considerable size, after all.

"What's happened?" I asked, curious. I smoothed a shimmering strand of hair over my forehead—the heat pooled sweat and gem oil together, and a few green trickles warmed my neck. The quince cartwoman turned to me, her nose rings glittering.

"It's gone," she said triumphantly. "The entire Rhukmini." Second only to our goods is our command of gossip—and she had the upper hand in this other economy. Her short hair was slicked in garnet, and she never sweat.

"Gone?" I was never a conversationalist.

"Well," the plum-breeder cut in, stroking his lazuli-coated mustache with his thumb and his fledgling trunk with his forefinger, "not entirely. There's bits of it left, blowing around. But I daresay no one will be bashing out octopus skulls there anytime soon."

I must have gaped—who would not have gaped? My agate-tattooed teeth (but one art in a city which contained all possible arts) showed behind my thick painted lips. I could see the plum-breeder nakedly calculate whether my teeth trumped his trunk in the hierarchy of opulence, which shifted and slid with each new process, alchemy, or mechanick the Asaad supplied. He seemed to decide his little gray appendage was safely superior.

"Why don't you go down Rhuk-side and see for yourself? I'll have my boys watch your cart; they're as honest as a skulk of foxes, which is to say not particularly, but they sell as well as they steal, and what more can anyone ask of the young?"

I frowned. True, they would steal, but his sons had quick tongues and I was young enough to be curious about the city beyond the canopies, young enough to think the stinking alley full of empty crab claws and squabbling gulls flapping in off the river might be worth the loss of a few apples and knuckles of meat.

I went—who would not have gone?

In the Garden

THE BOY SHIVERED.

"I don't like this story," he whispered. A low wind blew through the Garden, throwing old flowers up into dervishes and clattering one branch against another. "I liked the pirates better."

The girl shrugged. "I cannot change what is written on my skin, any more than I can change my skin itself."

The evening was now full of mist and blue, rolling through the Garden paths like a regiment clothed in starlight. The girl picked at the deep moss and looked toward the Palace, which was as full of light as ever, light and voices. Her fingertips were colorless. She spoke as if from a long way off, and hidden behind a wall of marble and glass.

"If I had not these marks on me, if I were not a raccoon-demon scampering over a Garden rich in scraps, I might have been called Dinarzad, and had pearls strung onto my hair, and married a man who owned golden roosters. It is very strange to think about."

The boy furrowed his clear brow.

"I do not think you would like the man with the roosters."

The girl grinned like a hare who knows it has escaped. "I am not a fool. Most of the time, I am glad not to be called Dinarzad. But the cold is sometimes like dying, and then I think it would not be so bad."

The boy started as though he were a young cat seizing upon a mouse for the first time. "What *is* your name, my friend? I am ashamed I did not ask it before!"

The girl looked down toward the moss and her freezing hand on it like a blight. She made her face very still, still as water, still as stars, so that he would not see her bitterness, hard as hawthorn bark. "How should I know my name? Who was there to call me so, to call me anything but demon, urchin, raccoon? If I have a name I do not own it—someone else must have it folded away in some strange purse, and my eyes will never see it."

Chagrined, the boy followed her gaze to the Palace and they sat in silence for a time. It did not seem right for him to offer his own name when she had nothing to give him in return. He did not want to show her once more all the things he possessed that she did not.

The first dead leaves left their trees and floated down, their stems noiseless against the wet stones. Somewhere behind her, the girl could hear the slow rippling of the pond where the boy had caught her bathing, had caught her under the moon. There were low, wild roses around their cairn of rocks, but they had lost their color to rain and wind, and lay ruined at the children's feet like torn pages.

"If you want me to stop—"

"No!" the boy said quickly, his dark eyes wide. "I do not like it, but I could not bear it if I did not hear it out. Tell me about that awful place."

The girl moved her hand over her eyes, touching that black, soft place where all these things had long ago been written. Not for the first time, she thought she could feel the shape of the letters burning into her. At length she began again, her voice echoing on the green rocks like water splashed into an empty well.

"Vhummim the gem-eater went into the old fishmarket, and the smell there was of old scallops and shattered shells..."

The Foreman's Tale, Continued

THE RHUKMINI HAD BEEN BEAUTIFUL IN ITS way—the sound of silver crab mallets thudding against claws and green clacking of lobsters muffled by their diamond tanks. There had been awnings of narwhal skin, blue as new ink, and carts with wheels of baleen. There had been a little alcove where the curious might sample seawater from every ocean in the world, just to know how the taste of salt differed from surf to surf.

It was gone—not gone, *wasted.*

A terrible wind blew through the long alley which had once been the Rhukmini market, and on it was some memory of the smell of ice floating in fish blood—but truly it smelled of dust, nothing more than dust. The rest was simply ruin, pieces of shell and paper and meat and wire and skin, as if the whole place had been torn into shreds by the hand of some vengeful giant. The wind kept what remained in the rough shape of the old alley, whipping whitefish against one wall and wrapping papers against another.

It was not unlike what you see of Marrow all around you—save that this was new and raw, wet and weeping wound-bright on that old arm of the city. All the colors were still vivid, and I could see smears here and there which might have been cuttlefish or salmon, which might too have been a shopkeeper or a customer in search of malachite roe.

Perhaps I should not have looked closer than this. The alley was clearly marked and blockaded with bleached-pine boards; it was a logical response. A limb has rotted? Cut it off, provide a tourniquet for the tattered stump, and go about the business of living. But I was curious—who among us was not curious? Thus I climbed between the boards and onto the shredded, ruined thoroughfare of the Rhukmini—and fell at once through the striations of refuse and fish skeletons and paper, endless paper, into darkness deep and hard as a closed fist.

Beneath the city, light fell in broken tufts where parts of streets and squares had gone the way of the Rhukmini. It was not as far to fall as you might think. Even so, I could not reach the first fluttering gray pieces of market to pull myself up again. Instead, I wandered—and who could have done otherwise? It was not so far to fall, but it was very far to wander. I could smell my own sweat mingling with the emerald oil of my hair—did you know that emeralds smell of limes and frankincense? They do, they do—I remember it so well, how I loved that smell, the smell of myself adorned.

It was great and black and hollow, the underside of the city. The air was warm, almost hot, and moved languorously around my ankles. Stone pillars snaked and coiled into a sodden bed of dirt—when I think on it now I think they must have been the roots of Marrow, the granite and marble roots of banks and towers and universities, the piled stone roots of tenements, of factories, the golden roots of jewelers' palaces. Each edifice sent down its strange and secret toes into the undersoil, and I wandered through a forest of stone. Despite myself I began to search through the mere for the roots of the Asaad—how much more beautiful, how much richer and brighter, the stone of those roots must be than all these others! It was this thought that kept me from fear in those low, hidden paths, strung with spiders and mold. I would find the Asaad again, and surely it would lift its child up.

But I did not find the tangling roots of the Asaad. I came, after passing through some few threshings of light that sputtered sickly through to the depths of the root-city, to a great snarl of cedar—real wood, amid all that endless stone. The ground was closed tight around the massive red curls, so that I could not see what sent down such tendrils into the dark. And from behind those gnarling crags, I heard a gnashing, a grinding, a crunching, gnawing sound which I shall not forget, for all of my days.

I went toward it. Who would not have gone toward it?

At first I saw nothing in the dusky shadows, the sharp smell of cedar filling my nose like water. Then it was a gleam of white—behind the roots, further back and farther in, a gleam of white flashing in the gloam.

"Is there someone there? My name is Vhummim, daughter of Orris—I have become lost!" I called. My voice was weak and quavering. Whose could have been stronger, more sure?

My answer was a louder gnashing, a louder grinding, like a whetstone spinning.

"Do you know the way out?" I whispered.

"I am the way out," a low, humming voice whispered back to me. "Through me you can find the light again."

It crawled close to me, on its belly like a cringing dog, and peered up into my eyes, a creature made entirely of teeth. Its four legs were a jumble of molars, bicuspids, incisors. Its eyes flashed: wolfs' teeth yellow with age. Great flat elephants' teeth made up its spine, and long tigers' canines curved into ribs. Its feet were hooves of enamel; its jaw hung hungrily open, white and yellow. Its delicate face: row after row of infant teeth, pearly and pale. There was nothing of it that was not teeth—what I could see between the gnashing molars was empty space.

I was afraid then, of course. Who would not have been afraid?

"Who are you?"

It sidestepped, back, forth. The molars of its feet left tracks in the warm, wet soil. "I am Golod, He Who Swallows."

"Will you show me the way out, Golod?"

"You are pretty, and your smell is pleasing." His sharp eyes ground against his enameled eye sockets. "I came to this place to find pretty and pleasing things..."

THE TALE

OF THE

HUNGRY LORD

DID YOU KNOW THAT A CITY CAN DIE AS EASILY as a person? It is true, I promise you. It dies in the same sad, lonely ways that people do: a knife in the governor's heart, a quick poisoning of rivers. And there are cancers that begin slowly, a pinprick in a bookseller's shop in a dust-clouded alley, a lump in a rainspout splashed with yellow leaves. Who would ever notice such a little thing tucked away like that, in a city of pillars and plums and plumes? Or it can become food, as all things inevitably are. It can be devoured, torn limb from street—it can be swallowed. By larger cities, by armies, by citizens too hungry for the meager meat of lamps and botanical gardens and commemorative war statues.

Or by something which has come to like its taste.

I suppose you could call me a cancer, a tumor tucked into the storm gutter, but it would be more apt to call me a creature of appetite.

Would you like to hear about my family? Every time I have come across one of you gem-gobbling peacocks, you immediately tell me who your mother is, or who your father is, or who your great-uncle on the distaff side is. I should offer no less—I had no mother, I had no father. Is not my pedigree immaculate?

There was a man, once, in a wood far from here. This man suffered a great hunger, suffered it the way some men suffer a wasting illness or an arrow in the foot. He was a man of some property, and before he was struck by his hunger, he was not unhandsome, and married well. His wife was lovelier than a year of Aprils, black of hair and eye. He was called Maciej; she was called Malgorzata.

Because of the fortunate match of Malgorzata, Maciej found himself in possession of a goodly number of tenant farmers, which for a time he treated as well as any lord may—which is to say, with neglect at all times save harvest, for at harvest all lords exhibit hunger beside which Maciej's would seem but moderate and mild. But it came to pass that for three harvests the land was cruel and hard, and yielded up barely enough to feed all that tilled it, and the house on the hill had to satisfy itself with selling tapestries and suchlike in order to provide apples and pig flesh and cabbages.

In the fourth winter, there was no crop at all. Wind howled across the fields, bare and bristling as a new monk's head. Maciej and his fair wife stared at an empty table, and so too did all of those who worked that land. It was difficult, as such times are. The last dairy cows had been slaughtered; the last egg chickens had been slurped to the bone. I would not like to tell you what the most wretched of them did to survive.

In the depths of this winter Maciej conceived a great hunger in him, conceived it the way some women will conceive a child. His belly snarled and lurched; he was blind with it, clutching at the very drapes to fill the hole in him. But fortune sometimes smiles on the suffering, and it was a rich, green spring, full of new lambs and new fields planted with seed and breeding pairs brought by sympathetic relatives of Malgorzata, who sent wagons from over the hills. Speechless with relief, Maciej ate, and ate. He paced his halls, his stomach gnawing caverns into itself, devouring apples and pig flesh and cabbages as quickly as he could—but there was no surcease for the unlucky lord! Yet he did not grow fat, for as quickly as he ate he was hungry again, his body burning so hot and bright that at night, the farmers needed no candles: the house on the hill was incandescent with the starving lord.

Finally, when harvest came again and with it the lord's due, Malgorzata thought her husband would be sated. Into his mouth went cider and beer, hazelnuts and venison, apples and currants and sheep shanks. Into his belly went squash and pies and hollering chickens; into his gullet went beef knuckles and mushrooms and pigs by the wagon. When there was nothing left for the farmers to give over to the house on the hill before they starved themselves, fair Malgorzata, black of hair and eye, went to them and begged them to give over their animals to her husband's hunger, which was now so great that mere vegetables and fruits could not touch it. All would be repaid, she promised—had her kin not supplied the spring when the winter was at its worst? They could survive winter; they knew this now.

At first, they surrendered ox and chicken, goat and goose, even horse and dog. All these Maciej ate at his groaning table, to bone and hoof—all save the teeth, which even he could not stomach. These teeth he tossed into a corner of his hall when he had sucked the marrow from their owners, and as the days wore on, the pile grew. His endless feast held no joy for him now: His belly burned and he could not slake it, could not even move from his creaking table. He wept as he ate, for he could not stop, and he hated the taste of gristle and bone—but he could not stop.

Before long their holdings were empty of snorting and bleating. Malgorzata sent to her distant kin for ever larger and more exotic creatures: elephants and tigers and wolves disappeared into the house on the hill, which lit the nights for miles as Maciej sat at his board, eating and weeping, eating and weeping. His jaw crushed leopard and lion, griffin and even the odd unicorn. He did not notice their taste, but he ate them all the same, and the house on the hill blazed.

But even this plenty could not last and the kin of Malgorzata refused to send more. There was nothing further to take from their holdings, and even the draperies had been stripped to feed the unfortunate lord. He had begun to gnaw at the cornices and baseboards, his tears falling from the cairn of teeth as he climbed atop it, trying to suckle at the reliefs of blossoming grapes that adorned the ceiling.

Softly, as was her way, Malgorzata drew him down and sat him at the table which had become the rack on which his bones cried out. He looked up at her with hunger-haggard eyes, red as plague and twice as hollow. He looked at her, ashamed, with hunger.

"It is all right, husband. I have known this day would come."

She laid her hands on the table, smooth and tanned with her days beating blankets in the sun and begging livestock from threshold to threshold. She spread her fingers against the juice-stained grain of the wood.

"A woman may give her flesh as she pleases, and a lady owes no less than her people give. The lord takes equally, all from all. Take only my hands, and swear to me you will replace them."

At first he would not, feigned horror at the very suggestion—but there were her hands, fingers splayed wide and firm on the table, and his mouth watered for her. She did not say a word, but also, she did not withdraw her hands. After a time, he brought out his carving knife, and, weeping all the while, severed his wife's brown hands at the wrist.

Malgorzata did not weep.

He would not eat before his wife's gaze, and crouched in the corner below the mountain of teeth like a whipped dog, sucking flesh from bone. When he was finished, he placed the chewed bones most tenderly in a reliquary of copper and opal, fingers delicately folded on a green cushion.

And for a while, the lord was sated. He was true, too, to his word, and made for his wife new and strange hands—for Maciej was a clever man before his hunger devoured him. He wove together hands of wicker, of hazel and red osier, green and pliant willow. He lashed them to her bruised stumps with leather and bolted the branches to her belt with fine, thin chain that looped and whorled through her skirts, so that she could move her arms as widely as before. To be sure, she moved oddly, her long wicker fingers clattering against dish and cheek, but she was much as she had been, and the house on the hill was quiet and dim at last.

But the time came again when Maciej was consumed. He hid it as long as he was able, but finally collapsed before his lady, the terrible light boiling all through him as he hungered. Fair Malgorzata, black of hair and eye, raised him up and said to him:

"It is better that I lose a limb than that the countryside lose all once more. Take only my feet, and swear to me you will replace them."

This time he did not argue, but brought out his carving knife immediately, nocked and pitted as it was from the joints of so many creatures, and severed his wife's feet at the ankle. As before, he would not eat before her gaze, but crouched in the corner before the mountain of teeth, sucking flesh from bone. When he was finished, he placed the chewed bones most tenderly in a reliquary of silver and malachite, toes delicately folded on a blue cushion.

And for a while, the lord was sated. He was true, too, to his word, and made for his wife new and strange feet—for Maciej was a resourceful man before his hunger devoured him. He wove together feet of wicker, of hazel and red osier, green and pliant willow. He lashed them to her bruised stumps with leather and bolted the branches to her belt with fine, thin chain that looped and whorled through her skirts, so that she could move her legs as widely as before. To be sure, she moved oddly, her long wicker toes clattering against floor and bedpost, but she was much as she had been, and the house on the hill was quiet and dim again.

But the time came again when the lord hungered. And again, fair Malgorzata, black of hair and eye, looked out onto the green fields and covered her face with her wicker hands, saying that it was better that she lose another limb than for the countryside to lose all once more. And she gave over her knees, her calves, her hips, her rib cage, her shoulders. Maciej fed and glowed and wept and fed again, and all the while

Malgorzata's body became a strange skeleton of branches, her chest a hollow cage, her back a ladder of wood. Behind these bars still beat her red, hot heart, and still she had her jaw and some part of her fair face—and both black eyes—though she had given over her left cheek to her husband's need.

Finally, when Maciej starved once more, these things were all that were left, and Malgorzata walked her halls in a body of willow and hazel. He told himself he would not ask such a thing, that the rights of a lord have limits, that she had given more than any man could ask of his wife. But still, the hunger roiled in him, and after so much time the hunger burned for nothing but her. It was the dark of winter, and fair Malgorzata, who had nothing left of her black hair but a stiff fall of twigs, laid herself upon the old table and said:

"It is better that I lose these last than that I live to see my lord ravage his lands yet again. Take my heart and my face which once was fair, but swear to me you will replace them."

Weeping bitterly, his hunger naked on his face, Maciej brought out his carving knife, darkened as its blade was from so much woman's blood, and cut out his wife's heart, and jaw, and fair black eyes. There was no gaze to meet, and he devoured his feast before her wicker frame. When he was finished, he placed the chewed bones most tenderly in a reliquary of gold and garnet, her jaw lying heavy on a red cushion.

And he made for her a wicker heart, and placed it behind her hazel-ribs.

And he made for her a wicker face, and fixed it to her willow-skull.

And he made for her wicker eyes, and set them into her branch-brow.

But her teeth he did not close into the reliquary. He climbed the mountain of teeth and laid them down at its peak, which was by now very near the ceiling.

The lord was sated, and I awoke.

The white bundle of Malgorzata's teeth descended to my heart, and out of the tooth cairn I stumbled, raw and uncertain as a newborn. Maciej stared as I took my first steps, hooves of tooth clicking on the tiled floor. I wobbled, my vision blurred—I saw him clearly, and the wicker body behind him.

I saw him, and I hungered.

The Foreman's Tale, Continued

"I SWALLOWED HIM UP, BONE AND TOOTH. I WAS still hungry, and I turned to the wicker-wight which was once Malgorzata, and we looked at each other, twig-eye to tooth-eye. But I would not devour her. She was my sister, we two things hollowed out by hunger. Instead I leapt from the house on the hill which was now dark, dark as rock over stone, and I took the hunger with me. It is all I am. I am all it is.

"The hunger and I looked for things big enough to feed us. We began with cattle and peasants, but these were not enough. We tried forests but they were bitter, marshes but they were brackish. Finally, we came here."

I quavered, my flesh wet with gem and sweat. "Are you punishing us?" I whispered. "Because we are hungry, too? Because we eat strange things and are never sated?"

The tooth-wight snorted, a peculiar, rattling sound. His movements were like a housecat's, scratching at the soil, opening and closing his tusk-claws, tossing his molar-tail into the air. "Of course not. Does a farmer punish a cow? No, he eats it right up and licks his chops. You are pretty, and pleasing, and we suspect this place is big enough to feed us. We will pass you through us, and revel in your taste. I am no different from any other thing: I want to eat; I want to live."

Golod turned and fixed his oversized jaw on one of the long cedar roots. He ground at it and suckled at it and worried it like a bone—and slowly, the root turned ashen and peeled away from itself in shingles, wisping away to broken shards and pale strips of bark. It kept its shape—and I might have imagined it, I do not say that I do not imagine things, and who would not imagine things in a place so dark and terrible?—but it seemed to me a winding wind fluttered through the ruined root.

"That is not eating," I said softly. "That is wasting, that is ruining, but it is not eating."

Golod leered at me, his wolf teeth gleaming in their sockets. "Do you not also leave waste behind when you consume a thing? It is not my fault that mine is more interesting than yours."

We looked at each other. I knew then that he would swallow me up, and running was impossible—surely he knew these tunnels better than I, he who had chewed them into the lightless guts of the city. I was frozen—who would not have been frozen, about to be eaten like a ripe jewel? Cold emerald slipped down the nape of my neck. I thought of my cart, all my apples, and my little agate god statues, and my new golden spit which turned so quietly and smoothly in the hand. I thought of the topaz of so many years past, and how its juice had trickled down my throat.

"I wonder what you will look like," he said, "when you have passed through me?"

The Tale

of the

Twelve Coins,
Continued

"I PASSED THROUGH. IT WAS NOT LIKE BEING eaten, more like being worried—*wasted*." Vhummim looked at us miserably, her eyes huge and milky in her round, floating face. She stroked her sinuous neck with bony fingers. "Golod put his teeth to me and my skin turned to pages and ash, held together by old, dust-clung air. Down there among the roots of bank and basilica, I became other than myself. My neck grew so long I could not eat, my limbs so long I could not run. Death translates us into what it will—we are the Pra-Ita, those who have passed through."

I stared at her, her withered, stretched throat, so thin

I could almost see through to the wasted edifice behind her. Curling, grasping wind threaded the streets. She pulled her robes aside, gauzy and wispy as dandelion silk, and showed her belly, swollen as a woman long gone with child. But instead of flesh there was a jewel, a great colorless, faceted thing set into her flesh as though she were no more than a ring.

"I speak the tongues of death," she whispered, her voice mingling with the wind. "I am translated, and I do not know myself, save that I have become what I have eaten, and it has become me. Thus went the rest of the city, slowly, the way of the Rhukmini, the way of Vhummim. The Varil's green and blooming docks sank into a river of detritus; the war memorials sighed into crumbling. Finally the Asaad, too, lost all its scarlet and gold, and became nothing but its own shell, money and paper and stiff, dead silk blown together by that endless wind. It happened so gradually that we did not really notice, until we had all passed through, and still we spent our money, still we traded our wasted goods. It is a habit, a compulsion, and it does not need translation. The wind, that relentless, thrashing wind that Golod brought, blows us from place to place, now. The wind keeps us together as long as it can, and then we are gone, gone until there is another valley or cliffside to sigh against, and then it breathes us into our old shape again. This is where we have come, now. It is like any other place to us."

"And the place you wish us to go, with all the strange words on the lintel?" the shorn girl asked.

Vhummim blinked slowly, as though it should be obvious. "It is the Mint. You will work, like the other children. The living work; the dead do not. Be happy that you were chosen for work. It is better for you this way." She closed her dress and fidgeted with the ragged cloth, looking up at us from behind her lanky hair. "If you do not go now, they will miss you at the counting, and it will be bad for you."

"We could just run, you know," I quavered, trying not to think of that flat, heavy door and what it would sound like when it swung shut.

"Please believe I would catch you," said Vhummim solemnly. Her leg cocked up like a stork's, a promise of speed our little legs could not hope for.

We followed her. Who would not have followed?

The door swung shut. It sounded like bones breaking.

The Tale

of the

Crossing,

Continued

IDYLL COUGHED IN THE DAMP AIR, HIS BREATH ricocheting in his lungs like a loose arrow. His fingernails, long as a wealthy woman's, dug into the ash-wood pole as he dragged it forward. A tiny whirlpool formed around its pale shaft as he drew it up—unseen mud clasping, dragging down.

"I would like to disbelieve you, but this is not a place where many men hazard lies. You were in the Mourned City—I envy you. I was there when there were neither ashes nor pages nor fish skeletons piled up into minarets. Are there roses there, still? Have they all gone white and brown, drifting along the dead dockside?"

Seven frowned and shoved his dark hair back from a wan face. Around his bruised eyes were already lines and cracks that would one day be wrinkles, chasms, trenches in flesh. He spoke softly.

"Some days, in the Mint, they blew through the door like snow."

Idyll nodded. In the farthest distance, behind the mist, Seven thought he could make out the spiky, scattered tips of bare trees, cat scratches in a gray sky, and a lonely beachhead. It was still so far off he could scarcely call the water a lake. It seemed to him a vast inland sea, and he trembled without wishing to. The ferryman rubbed at his knee with a hooked and gloved hand that seemed to have far too many knuckles.

"I can feel the storm in my joints now, a soreness like longing. I'll try to get you across before it comes through, but I can't promise."

"What sort of storm? How can there be storms here?"

"The sort that little coat won't begin to hold back. And if you knew much of the local geography, you would have brought better and thicker, and a tongue less eager for questions."

Seven sank back against the ruined mast and drew his knees up to his chest. He rubbed his chin against them and the leaf-stiffened wind reddened his nose.

"*She's* there," he mumbled.

"She?"

"My friend. She's there, in the empty forest, where all those trees are cracking in the wind. She's there, all wrapped in rags. She must be so cold. I can't leave her."

Idyll shook his great head and tugged his cloak tighter around his massive frame.

"Oh, son. I'm sorry. What a lot you have paid me for nothing."

The young man dug his fingernails into his palms and coughed into his sleeve, the nettle-sharp wind tearing his breath into scraps.

"You don't understand. You couldn't possibly understand us—we always save each other..."

The Tale

of the

Twelve Coins, Continued

WE WERE COUNTED JUST INSIDE THE GREAT hall, before our ears could adjust to silence and our eyes could adjust to darkness. The Pra-Ita were all around, their huge heads bobbing silently as crows pecking at grass. My head throbbed with the sudden cease of the wind. The bald girl stood just behind me in the long, gray line and clutched my hand.

"My name is Oubliette," she whispered, and she whispered it like a blessing, as though her name could hold me close and comfort me. I squeezed her cold fingers.

The numbers spilled out of the Pra-Itas' mouths like

water unwanted, and we were led, child by child, to the center of the room, our little hands placed on smooth bars and handles we could not quite see in the dim light, things which seemed like soft-toothed gears, things which seemed like trays, things which seemed like long tables. Beneath our fingers, we began to understand, lay a machine, and as our eyes softened to the shadows, we saw it whole for the first time.

In the middle of a peeling gray floor stood a peeling gray frame. It hunched like a broken turtle, a high, arcing shell through which nameless things passed, lumpish gray heaps disappearing, passed solemnly as relics between children no older than we, and tipped into the rusting, ash-ridden structure. Smokestacks tottered high into the vaulted ceiling and spat pale fumes into the air in weak, spiraling puffs. Pistons drove into the depths of the machine and emerged again, dark and wet. A terrible crunching, stamping sound filled the room, and at the far end of the shell, the contraption contorted into a twisted, enameled mouth, built in the image of a thing which had once walked, a thing made entirely of teeth.

Out of this mouth ran a long board, and onto it slowly spat coin after coin, dull and yellowish white, clunking dully onto the black wood.

Perhaps once, in the long past of Marrow, when they knew all possible things, the machine, the Mint, had moved of its own accord, but now small hands pressed and pulled and shoved at its every corner, turned its every gear, drew up its every dowel and thrust it down again. Furtive dark eyes gleamed around the shell and in it, dozens of children adding their limbs to the apparatus so that it could move, so that it could press out coins at a stuttering, halting pace. Thin hands sat on our shoulders like owls' feet, and thin fingers curled around our chins, holding our faces fast toward the creaking thing.

"The living work," came a whisper which seemed to be Vhummim, her breathy, weary sighing—but who could be sure among all those long, stretching throats?

Satisfied that we saw the machine and knew that we would soon be among those dark eyes and pale hands, we were led, all in a line, the newest children of the Mint, to a long narrow room, barely held together by the clawing wind whistling through page-turned rafters. All along the walls lay little beds, turned down neatly, their coverlets thin as a cough and fluttering lightly as the gales rushed by outside. The Pra-Ita urged us all toward them, and like good boys and girls we each filed in, found a bed, and curled away from the door, the machine, the terrible long-necked creatures. On each pillow was a sliver of glassy stuff—I licked it under my blanket, then pushed it eagerly into my mouth. It was candy: something like raspberries, something like black tea, something like sugared bread crusts. I savored it, its juice running down my throat. Then I remembered Vhummim, and her city before it was my city. I spat it out into my hand and stared in the gray half-light. It gleamed and shimmered, scarlet, pink, rose.

They had given us rubies. Shaved and slivered down enough to feed a dozen children. I looked over my shoulder at the Pra-Ita clustered near the door, watching us suckle the gems in our hungry mouths. They moaned quietly, miserably, watching us eat. I was too hungry to refuse to give them what they wanted: I pushed the cherry-colored stone back onto my tongue. It sat there like a scald of light. I shuddered and turned away again until I heard the door shut like hands clasping each other in prayer.

We were alone. In the morning, I was sure, our shifts would begin. When the darkness came wheedling through the shivering ceiling, I crawled out of my bed and found among the dark little heads one which was bristled and shorn: my friend, my Oubliette. She opened the corner of her pitiful blanket to me, and I climbed in beside her. We clutched desperately at each other, each trying to steal the other's warmth—there was little enough to steal, and finally we simply lay in each other's arms, trying very hard not to be terrified.

"Did you see what went into the machine?" I asked.

She shook her head.

"Did you see what came out?"

She nodded.

The room was filled with the sleeping and soft weeping of other children, mewling like lost pigeons. I didn't know what else to say. She didn't cry, like the others, she just stared, and everywhere she stared seemed to shiver under her gaze.

"What happened to your hair?" I said finally, quiet as a thief with his hand on a coffer.

As if in answer, she took my hand in hers, both of us cold to purpled fingers, and drew it around her waist to rest against her shoulder blades. What I touched was not flesh, not flesh, but bark, and wood, and hard, twining vines with berries like knuckles. She was a child in my arms, yes, the front of her skinny and hard-used but still pretty and certainly a girl—but her back from neck to ankle was a gnarled and hollow tree, half dead, petrified into gray and sallow stone. The only warm and living thing I felt with my arms meeting around her was a thick, long tail, a heifer's dun tail, ending in a soft tuft of fur. She would not look at me.

"Now you see what I am. I am wicked, and ugly, and that is why the hungry ghosts took me..."

THE HULDRA'S TALE

MY MOTHER USED TO SIT ME ON HER LAP AND tell me where we came from—so many times that I cannot now forget even a word of the tale.

It is said that once there was a heifer so lovely that her skin was as red and flowing gold, her eyes as polished wood, her swishing, flicking tail brighter than a whip of fire. This cow was not quite a cow, as all beautiful things are both more and less than their bodies. In the folds of bark which enclose us all it is written that once she was a girl, nothing but a girl, with hair so long and shining that it caught the eye of Aukon, the Bull-Star, who put his white-hot hooves to her form and shaped her into his own image so that he could love her as he wished to.

Perhaps this is true, perhaps it is not. But as lovers sometimes do, once he had finished with her he wished to keep her all for his own, and the poor thing was left a heifer lowing at the sky—though she was the loveliest of all heifers who ever ate grass and drank water, it was not much consolation, I am sure.

"Where will I go? What shall I do?" the heifer cried.

And answers came, though not those she would have wished for. For though she knew it not, Aukai, the Heifer-Star, the Milk-Star with her black eyes, had seen what her brother had done, and set upon him. A terrible struggle occurred between the two huge creatures. If you have seen bulls battle over a mate, it was nothing to this. Aukai burned brighter than temple fires in her fury, and finally pinned Aukon against a hillock and chewed from him, with her wide, flat teeth, the flesh which made him a bull, leaving a lonely and broken ox lowing weakly in the night, light leeching from him into the mud churned up by their grappling. In disgust, Aukai spit her brother's silver-dripping testicles away in a broad field, and thought no more of it. It is said that ever after maddened monks castrated themselves in her honor, doing penance in place of her heavenly brother. Perhaps this is true, perhaps not.

Yet a Star is a strange thing, and its ways are stranger still. In the place where the ruined flesh had fallen, a great almond tree grew, with broad white flowers and green fruits. And it came to pass that the cow who was once a girl wandered by the great tree in the height of its flowering. And the tree, too, being only somewhat less than Aukon himself, looked on her and loved her still. With whipping branches he dragged her, hoarsely braying, into his hollows and his crooks, and there stroked her skin with pale and papery twigs until, after many months, her wide flat teeth, not sharp, but sure, chewed their way free of him.

Perhaps this is true, perhaps it is not. Love rarely waits for permission. She ran far from the howling tree, who reached for her with long, snapping vines and needles—and in her running she gave birth to the first of us who are called huldra, who are girl and cow and tree jumbled together by some inattentive hand. The heifer looked on her first daughter with horror—how far she had come from the girl she was! But who would love this terrible child if she did not? Already her udder swelled and stretched. The wretched infant clutched at her mother's

stiff golden hair, and the heifer sank to the earth to nurse. As the years
went by she dropped children like pinecones from her flesh, and occasionally birthed one in the usual way of cows—poor creature, who bled
children everywhere she went, and each one mongreled and mottled as
we all are.

"My poor girls, my pitied boys," she said when we sat around her like
a herd, flicking our tails at flies like buzzing sapphires, "I know in my
heart that it will be for you as it was for me, and you will be loved always, yet only by those who do not share your shape, and care nothing
for your say-so. I have given you nothing but sorrow and a dun tail."

Perhaps this is true, perhaps it is not. Perversions are often written
over with elaborate stories, and who knows what strange nights' revels
ended in the huldra, who are tree and human and cow all together? I
would not have liked to have been there.

But the story is not wrong about us.

I once had a golden ball, you
see. Am I telling this tale
poorly? Would a grown
woman tell it better? My
mother knew how to tell a
tale properly. Perhaps she
would have mentioned
the ball in the beginning.
Perhaps she would not
have shown her tail so
soon. Perhaps a good
child would not admit that
she owned such a thing as a golden
ball—it has never done a girl any good to have
one, in all the history of the world. But I am not a grown woman, and I
loved my ball.

My sister was not given one, nor my cousins. What you must understand about a golden ball is that by giving one over into eager hands,
parents acknowledge a certain wickedness in their children that must be
occupied by something other than flesh or sweets. A mother does not
give such a gift to the daughter she bathes in milk and perfumes in
asters and daisies. She gives it to the scraggle-haired, mud-kneed child

who plays by herself at the side of the old well. It will keep her from young men and candies that glitter like fluttering eyelashes, and if she or it or both together should tip over the side of the well, as has been known to happen from time to time, well, at least no daisy was wasted on her.

I once had a golden ball, you see.

One day, when I was turned barkwise to the sun, the miller's boy came up to our ash-wood fence. He said the things you might expect a miller's boy to say: He had never seen a girl with roots in her knee-pits before, I was pretty as a cherry without a pit, and wouldn't I come just a little closer? I shrugged. I was heifer-strong; there was nothing he could do to me. I came close up to the bars of the fence, and he said my eyes were the darkest he'd seen—then he kissed me quick on the mouth. He stole my first kiss, did just as folk have always done when a huldra is in sight: take her without permission, without a care. It is because of this sort of thing that we were solitary creatures, living in our high-up huts, cradled in oak branches, so that the tree in us may rest, and speak rarely to those who are the same whether their back is turned or no.

I bolted for home, but as I ran I thought of little but the kiss. His lips tasted like flour and honey just scooped from the hive, and I told my mother so when I scrambled up the ladder of rope and found her ladling out grass soup for my supper. The next morning, she gave me the golden ball, and told me to run along and play. I stared at her, stricken. No word passed between us, though she had the grace not to hold my gaze. Her tail swished nervously behind her, dark brown across our branch-lashed floor. I took my ball quietly and went out into the fields, to play.

It was a little sun I kept close to my chest, so that it warmed next to my skin. I wrapped my long black hair around it and unwound it again. I called it little names which seem silly now. I polished it over and over with the tuft of my tail and kept it near me while I slept. It gleamed against my cheek like a slap. And I tossed it into the air by the old, vine-strangled well, smeared with flowers which once were red, sitting among the tall, seed-topped grasses like a huge, embittered toadstool. I could smell water in the old thing, algae-jeweled and wriggling with tadpoles, but I could not see it. Up and down I tossed my ball—it caught the light, burned it, scalded it, and my eyes were filled with tears as I stared into that little round star. I was never alone: It rolled and lay still and sparkled as well as a friend.

The day then came when the summer sun itself was a golden ball, and I lay like a dandelion in the grass, and slept with its hot palms on my face. Did I dream? I don't remember. But when I woke my ball was gone, and in its place was a little red-eyed creature who came nearly, but not quite, to my knees, staring and stroking my hair. It was a hedgehog, quite respectably large and furry, golden from hunch to nose—his quills jangled and clinked when he moved, a little glistening sound. He wrung his burnished hands and stroked his golden whiskers, and his eyes—were they garnets? Were they not?—glowered under lashes like wedding bands.

"Good afternoon," I said, after a long while. Perhaps I should have said something prettier. A grown woman might have known what to say. The hedgehog bowed. I think if he had had a hat, he would have removed it.

"Good afternoon," he replied, in a high, rough voice like that of a flute scoured with river mud. "I have been watching you sleep. You do it very well."

I laughed. "My mother always hoped I would show a talent for something. Perhaps I shall become a sleeper by trade."

The hedgehog did not laugh. "My name is Ciriaco," he said, as if his name could hold my hand and put me at ease.

"And have you seen my ball, Ciriaco? I am fond of it, and it seems to have rolled away somewhere as I slept."

The hedgehog looked at the long grass uncomfortably. He wrung his hands even more wretchedly; he made a soft and sorrowful rasping noise in his shimmering throat. Slowly, the animal bent until his nose brushed dirt and his quills ruffled along his back, passing a glimmer of prism between them. And then, with a little hop, and an even littler tuck, he snapped up into the air and landed in a thatch of clover as a round, smooth ball all of gold. Perhaps a grown woman would not have squealed and clapped. But I was not grown.

"How did you come to live inside my ball, friend hedgehog?" I cried.

Ciriaco rolled forward slightly, then back, and unfurled himself again, patting dust and pollen from his golden hands as he rose to his full, though not terribly impressive, height once more.

"Your tail is very soft," he whispered, blushing to his tiny ears. "It has been a great comfort to me..."

The Tale
of the
Golden Ball

IN THE KINGDOM OF THE HEDGEHOGS, THERE are mountains with mouths. They open and close; they twist and sneer. Out from our hedgerows each pearl-handled morning, boar and sow trundle up the black paths, slick as tongues down the side of the crags. We do not speak to one another—it is not done. In the old days, it seemed as though the earth rose up with the sun to swallow the mountains again, so many little brown bodies made the ascent each day, silent shoulder to silent shoulder. We did not sing work songs, or tell tales of the brave hedgehogs who went before us, caged hummingbirds clasped in fear-tightened paws, into the dark.

The dark took them; the dark will take us. No more needs to be said.

I worked in the upper shafts, where gold ran along the rock walls like calligraphy. The Kingdom of the Hedgehogs possesses miners of all kinds: iron and copper and silver and gold, diamond and sapphire and emerald and tin. When we were born, our parents, rheumy-eyed from days on the mountain and pulverized silver shot into eyelashes, placed plugs of each substance into our tiny, clasping paws. Whichever we gripped tightly and waved about with the first and last glee we ever took in the fruit of the mountain, this we would cut from the earth for the rest of our days. Each family was possessed of a little wooden box full of gleaming slugs—and if a child should choose differently from his parents, it was the last he saw of them, as he ascended or descended among the shafts.

My parents were higher than I—diamond-diggers in the ethereal heights. My brothers and sisters were lower: a few coppers, a few irons, and one sorrowing tin-cutter, my sister who lay in our mother's arms for a single night before bucketing down to a tin-mother whose pup had gone up to the sapphire shanties. So it goes.

And if a child should not choose, if his paw was weak and clammy, or if he greedily grasped all metals alike, he was given to the mountain, and left to die or eat dirt as the hedgehogs before the mountain had done.

Such was the rhythm of life in the Kingdom of the Hedgehogs. We carried in our little glass-blown lamps; we carried out barrows of ore. We slept, we ate, we dug and chiseled and chipped.

I had a water drill I loved. It fit my palm very well—the years had worn paw-holds into the handles.

You may think we were joyless. Beauty cannot seed in joy. Diamonds are crushed from black rock; beauty is carved out of the dark by hedgehog quills. Our mountain was parceled out slowly to all the courts and all the crowns of the world. Slowly, over centuries, it shrank and shrank. We were satisfied by this: that dark may be chiseled into light, and that a jewel touched by a hundred paws might sit one day on a beautiful girl's innocent head.

In my day the mountain was still greater than anything else on the blasted plains, and I knew nothing outside of it. One day, we would take the last of the mountain to the last princess, and we would be free. So went the tales before the soldier tumbled onto us like a loose slate slab hidden behind a cord of gold.

It was in the upper shafts, my rose-throated hummingbird buzzing softly by my side, scraping her green wings against the twig cage, that we found her.

She had short hair, brown as fur, and an iron cap-helmet dragged down over it until it covered her brow. Behind her was a massive barrel, and she leaned against it, sleeping. She had no armor, no plates or chains or any of the other sorts of things that can be made out of the mountain-molten we bring down. She had a spear and a wide, round shield. And the circles under her eyes were like caverns without water, and in her ragged leather uniform her body floated thinner than lime dust. Her face was a mass of blisters and scars, stretching over her bones like a star map spread over a broken table. We did not confer with each other on her strangeness—it is not done. In my memory, I seem to think I prodded her foot with mine. She started awake, clutching her spear.

"The pass is fast, don't fear, don't fear!" she cried, shrinking from the dark. We never shrink—but we have pity for those who do.

"Of course it is, it is our pass, our mountain. We have no need of you to guard it—come away, girl, away from the dark." I touched her hand with my paw, but she drew it away and curled her lips back.

"Duty may not be shirked," she hissed.

"Who gave you this duty? Surely not us, yet we are masters of this place."

She pulled up her shield to cover her, not unlike a blanket, and spoke echoes into all the chambers of the mountain.

"I am she who is called Widow, who was given this post in the long night now forgotten, and who will not now abandon it..."

The Soldier's Tale

Do you know what *vesicant* means?

I didn't think so. What good can such vocabularies perform for hedgehogs snuffling in stone? But I know—I know now.

The farm where I was young was thick and furred with wheat. I had two brothers, and they had me, and we had nothing else in the world but a father whose knees knocked hollow in the wind. I seem to remember plow horses and mules and chickens squawking in the dust, pigs and roving deer and great shaggy cows. But if ever I saw them, I was too young to do much but pull at the tail of one or the ear of another. In my youth the livestock of our country slowly dwindled to nothing at all—there were no blights or famines, no locusts or one-eyed witches poking fingers at the fields, but there were strange tales of a far-off kinswoman in need, and there were letters sealed in green wax, written on vellum so thin I could see my hands through it. But I could not read them, only pull at their edges like a mule's flicking tail.

"Kin may not be denied," my father grunted, and off went our dappled horse and our last milk cow.

My father took the plow onto his own shoulders with straps and brass buckles and with much pain. Grimacing through many red and screaming welts on his broad back, he tilled our fields. We grew up, my brothers and I. We were often hungry, though not too often. But I sometimes think that if we had not once had plow horses and mules and chickens squawking in the dust, pigs and roving deer and great shaggy cows, we would not have given so much to have them back again.

One evening when the blue lay deep and even as water on the wheat, a lone man came striding up our walk with a sword at his hip and velvet in his coat and a warm helmet on his head. He led a cluster of horses behind him, stamping in the dust. He was recruiting for a King who lived so far from us that his name was to our ears as an oar presented to a mountain-dweller. This King was in need of soldiers for his conquests, which the man assured us were innumerable and glorious. This is what all Kings say. They are words a monarch learns before *mother* and *father*.

I learned the word *mercenary* from this man.

The recruiter offered his horses in exchange for the strongest and wisest of our sons.

"In a land without horses, what use is a boy?" he reasoned.

My oldest brother thought this was very exciting. That is what oldest brothers always think. My father looked at the horses, and at his son, and at the clear, cold sky.

"Kin may not be denied," he grunted.

And my brother vanished down the walk, asking to try the recruiter's sword a bit before he could get one of his own. We were glad of the horses, and my father released the straps and brass buckles and laid the plow onto better-muscled shoulders than his own. He had some peace, and so had we.

One afternoon, a year hence, when the gold lay hot and breezy on the wheat, another lone man came striding up our walk with a sword at his hip and velvet in his coat and a warm helmet on his head. He led a cluster of cows behind him, lowing in the dust. He was recruiting for the same King, who had conquered much, yet lived still so far from us that his name was to our ears as snowshoes presented to a desert hermit. This King was yet in need of more soldiers for his battles, which, we were promised, were mighty, clamorous, and righteous. This is what all recruiters say. They are words those tasseled creatures learned before *hunger* and *thirst*.

I learned the word *impressments* from this man.

The recruiter offered his cows in exchange for the second strongest and second wisest of our sons.

"In a land without cows, what use is a boy?" he reasoned.

My older brother thought that his destiny called him with long, bright horns. That is what older brothers always think. My father looked at the cows, and at his son, and at the hazy, yellow sky.

"Kin may not be denied," he grunted.

And my second brother vanished down the walk, his back straight and tall, his gaze on the path, never speaking to the recruiter at all. We were glad of the cows, and my father and I tasted milk for the first time in years. It was sweet and thick—I learned to strain cheese and in the silence of an empty house, we set to building a butter churn.

One morning, a year hence, when the silver lay pale and wet on the wheat, yet another lone man came striding up our walk with a sword at his hip and velvet in his coat and a warm helmet on his head. He led a cluster of chickens behind him, pecking at the dust. He was recruiting for the same King, who had conquered much, yet lived still so far from us that his name was to our ears as a feather bed presented to a scalebound fish. My brothers, this man said, were dead and cold, and on a field without wheat, rain was filling up the hollows of their ears. Yet they died with honor, and we ought to have been proud.

This is what all soldiers say. They are words we learn before *left* and *right*.

I learned the word *attrition* from this man.

The recruiter offered his chickens in exchange for another son to fill the ranks.

"What use is a boy in a land without eggs?" he reasoned.

But my father shook his head and said: "You have taken both my sons from me and given me only meat in return. I have a daughter left, who may choose to go with you or not, as is her liking, but of boys there are no more to take."

The recruiter frowned. "My King does not approve of women fighting."

My father shrugged, a half-dead smile on his chilblained face. "Then you have no business here."

"No," I said very quietly. "I want to go. I will cut my hair and bind up my breasts and wear a heavy helmet—but I will go where my brothers have gone, and I will fight where they would have fought, and it will not be as though we were together, but it will be near enough to it that I can sing to their shades under the branches of I cannot say what trees."

My father and my recruiter stared at me, the one grief-ridden, the other appraising. "Kin may not be denied," I answered my father's gaze, my own cast toward the earth.

They cut my hair together—in those days it was very thick, and I lay against a stump while they took turns hacking at it with a rusty ax. I bound my breasts by myself, for modesty's sake. The recruiter put his own helmet on my head—it had a chin guard, and sat heavy as guilt on me. I vanished down the walk. I asked the recruiter if he thought I looked like a boy.

"You look fit to make widows," he said, laughing cheerfully, and thus I took my soldier's name. We walked toward the hills, and the sun rose high in the sky.

It was not a full year before I took my first breath in the thick of the Five-League Fog, before my chest swelled up and burst like a drum struck with a knife.

In the Garden

THE BOY'S FOREHEAD WAS CREASED LIKE A WELL-READ PRAYER BOOK. He studied the moss, his shoulders stiff, and picked nervously at his fingernails.

"My father has sent many such men out into the world, and they have come back with all manner of soldiers trailing after them like baby quail. They all look very fine in their uniforms, and I have been promised a scarlet cloak of my own when I am grown."

The girl's face remained smooth and implacable as still water. "It is only a story," she said.

"My father's wars bring aqueducts and roads and bathhouses to barbarians."

"I am sure that is true."

"One of my tutors is from a conquered land. He tells me that he loves the Palace, and his thick, silken robes, and his children are happy."

"I would not doubt such a man. You do not need to tell me these things."

The boy frowned more deeply. His palms itched. The sky was a deep gray, stitches of night blue showing through the rough linen clouds.

"Sometimes I climb the persimmon tree to watch the officers muster," the girl confessed quietly. "They are handsome, and so tall. I did not think boys could grow to be so tall. The helmets blind me in their rows."

"One day I will wear one, and a long, curving sword besides, and no one will bring roosters for me."

The two children were quiet for a moment, and the dull disk of the sun cast fitful shadows on the stones, like hands which cannot quite grasp. The girl watched the boy play with his purple bracelet, watched him avoid her eyes. As grackles and lost, bewildered seabirds wheeled and cried over their dark, bent heads, the girl thought it best to simply continue, as a soldier will when he has forgotten all save the hill before him, and his own heavy feet.

THE
SOLDIER'S TALE,
CONTINUED

HIS SKIN CAME OFF IN MY HANDS.

I never saw the King—I did not expect to, yet a tiny part of me, the part which imagined him leading his troops with raven plumes blown back from a silver helmet, was disappointed. The King cloistered himself in his castle, it was said, surrounded on all sides by rivers, one white, and one black. It sounded like a child's story, and in the days to come I wondered if there had ever been a King, if we were not simply marching and fighting and digging and eating horrors of worm and centipede and mud to keep starvation at our backs because someone, somewhere, had once simply dreamed of a King with a golden crown.

I am sure that someone, somewhere, has told that King's tale. I am sure it was grander than mine. I am sure it was an important tale, full of history and pageantry and grave consequences for the whole countryside. I am just a soldier. I do not know those tales.

At first I worried that I would be discovered—but after a few weeks in greasy mud and fog colder than the ice scrim on a pail of milk in the morning, one soldier looks much like another. I was never questioned. I was set a watch, and given a wooden sword. The men laughed like a treeful of crows and said that I would have to earn a real one. In fact, I wore more or less my own clothes, and kept my recruiter's helmet, though many tried to barter for it. The King, it seemed, felt iron and leather could be best used elsewhere. I was told to guard twelve barrels bounded in iron, and not to look inside them. Simple—yet all I remember now when I think on it is his skin, wet and loose, sloughing off between my fingers.

We were encamped in the wide steppes which through the ministrations of hundreds of soldiers had grown thick with their autumn crop: mud. It clung everywhere: hair, eyes, fingernails, knees, throat, nose. It smelled of leaves and mushrooms and dung and us, for we could no longer tell our own smells amid the mud. The barrels were stuck in slime, green climbing the wood. With my ridiculous toy sword I stood before them, muscles corded with the care of cows and horses that had once been brothers, and peered into the night. A terrible tea was concocted from wheat seeds, caterpillars, and mud, and I drank it down at the end of every watch before feebly asking if I had not, through faithful duty, earned a real sword. One by one soldiers, bearded and bare, bald and hairy, chuckled and told me that I could not have a real sword until I had killed someone—what was guard duty when no one threatened my guard?

Yet we fought no battles, and I killed no one. Mold began to grow between the pommel and the grip of my plank sword. I waited; we all waited. My recruiter rethreaded his tassels in gold and went on to the next village. I asked after my brothers—but who could recall two boys now dead? I waited; we all waited. Once, only once, did I ask the only officer whose cloak still showed color, what was in the barrels. He paled and his mouth twitched as though he might vomit on my barely shod feet.

"It came from the King's man, before you got here. Suffice it that I know and you do not—be happy, and do not pray to trade lots."

I was a good soldier; I guarded my barrels. It was half a year before anyone came looking for them. Before his skin came off in my hands and I sucked in my last breath of clean air.

It was very black at night, like the inside of a great dark heart. Snuffles and snores and the occasional weeping rattled through the mist and the mud, the endless clammy damp. He came crawling like a centipede, this way and that, his helmet cracked wide across the crown, his cheeks hollow under coarse stubble. He must have been hiding among us for days, waiting for my watch, the skinny soldier with the wooden sword. He lunged at my barrels—I caught him full on the chest, hacking at him with my stupid, useless stick. I slammed it into his eye a few times and he grunted, groaned, our breathing fast and heavy as we grappled in the mud, our weight pressing us knee-deep into the sodden earth. He punched me hard in the stomach but I did not let go, though the breath went out of me like a soul ripped free. We fell together into the barrels. I collapsed on top of him, and his sweating bulk cracked one of the vessels beneath him, grinding its shattered planks into the sludge. I scrambled up—and his skin came off in my hands.

My father used to tell stories about people who lost their skins: selkies and leucrotta and suchlike. Underneath, they are always something different, even beautiful. A girl in a seal suit is wet and pale and shimmering under her gray, rubbery skin. But this was not like that—there was just blood and fat and sagging skin, and he melted in my arms, slipping away like a coat shrugged off in the summer. The smell was thick and acrid as burnt cat meat.

A greenish white paste oozed from the broken barrel—pale steam already rose from it, curling and wafting, as though deciding which way to drift. It clawed the air before me and before I knew it I had breathed it in, long green trails of smoke filling up my chest, rubbing at my skin. Blisters rose before I could blink, fat and rippling on my arms. My eyes burned, something seemed to burst in me like a tiny sun, and I stumbled away from the man without skin, away from the ruined barrels.

My superior came running across the field of sleeping men, lugging water in two wooden buckets. He threw them onto the wreckage of bubbling flesh and pale, pasty sludge; hissing and spitting, the slime vanished into the earth, leaving a ghost smoke floating over all those dreaming heads, smoke that would leave them scratching and weeping, but well enough in a day or two.

"You idiot!" he mumbled, gently leading me to a thin little stream and dousing my head in the clear water. "It has to be diluted, it has to be mixed by someone who knows how—you don't just drop a person into it, and you sure as sword rust don't breathe in the raw stuff!"

"His skin came off in my hands," I moaned, coughing harsh and sharp, trying not to rub at my blistered arms.

He shook his head. "Of course it did. You smothered him in the Five-League Fog. The King's man sent it, that old horror in his collar and robes. It's to be used when we go into the mountains, when we take them for the crown. But cut with water, you silly child! Cut, and blown out fine as ash through bellows! You're lucky to still have skin on your bones and eyes in your skull!"

As the shallow morning light dripped over the hills like white oil, he helped me to wash in the river, and he did not even remark on it when he saw my bandaged breasts, my ruined, reddened hips. That is how I learned what *vesicant* means: it means a thing which burns, which gets into you and raises up blisters like accusations—his skin came off in my hands, but my skin burned for years after, like a sentry torch.

The Tale

of the

Golden Ball, Continued

THE SOLDIER'S HANDS SHOOK AROUND THE EDGES of her shield. She extended her arms slowly, letting the bowl rest against her chest. Under the ancient guards, they were covered in the same old blisters, huge and bruise-colored, hardened into burls, snaking over her flesh like a ruby chain.

"I breathed too much of it, whatever it was. It was only meant to make enemies double over weeping, and I had enough to suffocate a leopard. As we climbed higher into the mountain passes, it became plain that I was not going to recover. The blisters did not recede; I could not stop coughing. But as we began to fight real battles, as I finally came to have a sword of metal, it also became plain that I could not, any longer, be wounded. The blisters were good as diamond clothes—nothing could cut me. We took a village on those steppes—ah, the screaming of horses!—we took a village and a woman with her face tattooed like a demon spat three arrows into me without making a dent in my skin. I put my sword through her sister. Somewhere in the distance I saw a helmet with black plumes, and one of the cavalry said it was the King. I didn't believe him.

"After that, the men were spooked as horses in sight of a snake. Finally it was decided, before the rest descended into the valleys, that I would be left behind. I would guard the pass. I would, should the chance happen by, requisition from the conquered all the ore I could, to send below, to the troops who are ever in need of arms." She licked her dry lips, her eyes darting between us like a deer's. "I have been here a long time, years— maybe years. It is hard to tell, in the dark. Sometimes I hear my brothers calling from the shafts. But I am not their sister anymore, and I cannot go down to them. The blisters are all of me, I float in their shell like a fog."

I frowned. "We own this mountain, but we do not dredge up ore for you or your wars."

Widow laughed softly, full of regret as a pail of rainwater. She snatched up one of the other hedgehogs quicker than a cave-in, dredged him in his wheelbarrow of gold flake like a piece of meat through flour, flipped her shield over in her lap, and rolled him around the edge, into the shape of a ball. From a spigot in the barrel she drew a few greenish white drops and smeared them into  his fur, and kept up her steady rolling around the hard, bronze edge.

Onto the stones of the upper shaft she rolled a perfect golden ball, and then she reached for me.

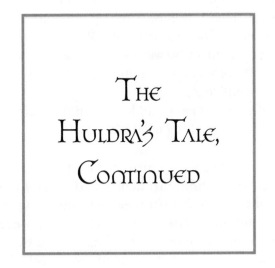

THE
HULDRA'S TALE,
CONTINUED

CIRIACO STOPPED, HIS LITTLE GOLDEN MOUTH snapping shut like a treasure house door. I sat in the now-long shadows near the well, my mouth dry, my hands clasped in my lap.

"She rolled us all, in the Five-League Fog and in our barrows—she was so much bigger than we, and so much stronger than she seemed. For all I know she wanders still in the passes. Now our skins are hard as hers, and we were used as hard as she. She sent us down the mountain to the valleys, and we served a King we had never heard of. His name was to us as milk to a cattleless land." The hedgehog glowered and picked at his quills. "Did you know there was a war here, in this very place, a long time ago?"

"Don't be silly."

"There was. I was here; I fought. We were pressed into service as cannonballs. We learned new words, too. I was shot into the side of a bull elephant, and his blood swallowed me up. And after, when the fields were full of violets and blood-spattered balls, mothers began to take us home and give us to girls who were not sweet as cream and honey, but clever as bees. There was a war; I am a veteran. Does that make me sound brave to you? Does it make you like me?"

Perhaps a grown woman would have been more circumspect. "You are a golden hedgehog all my own! How could I like you better than I do?"

His red eyes flared and dimmed in the late afternoon light. The grass seeds and dandelion dust had settled around him in a floating halo of white. "That is fortunate, for I am going to marry you. That is what I am owed, after all my loyal service—even ordnance should come home to wife and biscuits. I have been your toy. I like you; your hands have always made me blush. I have waited as long as I can, until you were grown enough to smile on me. After all the amusement I have given you, do you not think some recompense is due? This is what I demand, and this is what shall occur."

I laughed from my belly. I laughed as only children without fear may. "I like you, Ciriaco, but I am not going to marry you! Even if you were not a hedgehog and I were not a girl, I am only a child and very far off from fitting a wedding dress."

"I am the mountain," he growled. "I am owed. I have not forgotten who I was before the war—I must be fitted to a princess, an innocent girl whose fingers have yet known no rings. It is the way of things, and I will not be denied just because I am not a pretty ruby crown or a bracelet of silver and sapphires."

"Hedgehog, I am not a princess. My parents are grain merchants. We eat well and dress well, but it is a pretty poor kind of royalty, even among the huldra. Princess of bread and beer!"

"That is princess enough."

"I'm sorry, poor beast. I will not marry you."

I had hardly spoken when they came: gold and copper and silver and tin, ball after ball rolling through the grass, iron pitted and pocked, quartz streaked in grime. They opened up into hedgehogs, their red eyes slitted and sharp, glaring at me from beneath furrowed and shining brows. I stepped backward, as though a pail of water had been overturned at my feet.

"There are few enough of us who are left," rumbled Ciriaco in his yellow throat, "but enough to keep you safe and still. Your parents will not miss you—they gave you a golden ball, after all. Most probably they expected you to go missing long ago and are even now wondering why you do not get on with it."

I clenched my fists. "I am not wicked," I insisted.

"Then why have they left you all alone to amuse yourself with abandoned war relics? Why does no one call you in to dinner? Why does no one cry, 'Oh! Where has my pretty daughter gone?'"

I twisted my tail in my hands. "I am not a favorite—that doesn't mean I am wicked, and it certainly doesn't mean I shall do whatever my talking toy tells me to."

Ciriaco growled, a sound like clock hands scraping together. At this the two hedgehogs nearest me, a cast-iron fellow and a sow of copper, leapt forward, drawing a handful of quills from their backs like young men drawing their swords. They each seized in cold, stubby hands the long ropes of my hair and with a little roll and a little flip, pinned my curls to the earth, driving their quills in like tent stakes. I tugged and wept but could not pull free. Ciriaco raised his eyes to me, moist and scarlet.

"If I say I love you, will you soften?"

"No, my own golden ball, I am only a child. I will not be a wife."

The other hedgehogs, smooth and ordered as a little army, began to tear into the earth as I struggled, pinned by their quills. They tore up strips of wet brown sod with bits of grass and yellow flowers still clinging to it, and began to build.

"I shall build us a house, Oubliette, a house for living and loving and cooking and dying, and you will live in it whether you like it or no," cried Ciriaco, and he danced with a terrible joy while his family worked, their backs shimmering in the last of the sun. His golden feet tamped the soil, and the sod bricks grew around me. "I shall be no one's ball again!" he sang.

Indeed, through the night they built up the house, and closed me into it like a rafter. By dawn only my eyes and mouth were left naked—and out of the cracks between the soft bricks flowed my trapped hair, with more quills than I could count wrapped up in the dark strands and plunged deep into the field, each lovingly contributed by the hedgehog architects. From a distance, all anyone might see was a humble sod house, with bits of old tree bark showing through the walls. The sheaves of hair stretched from the house like an awning, and Ciriaco reclined in their shade.

The other hedgehogs shrugged and rolled once more into gleaming balls. In the swelling morning, they trundled off through the now-bare field.

"I love you, Oubliette," said my golden ball. "Put your hand to my head again and I will put a quill ring on it, and we will be happy in the house I have made for you."

I cried quietly, my tears running muddily through the bricks. "Please, please. Let me go home."

"You are home—you are the very substance of home."

So it went. He asked to bend his quills into a ring every day, and every day I felt mud climbing my nose and refused. He was right, you know. No one came crying: "Oh, where has my pretty daughter gone?" No one looked for me. Perhaps a golden ball is nothing but a ball of yarn to lead difficult cats skipping away from their mothers. Perhaps I am wicked in some way I cannot guess, some way which a hedgehog or a miller's boy can see, but a girl may not.

Finally, Ciriaco left me during the evenings, satisfied at last that I could not pull my hair free, nor escape his house. He rolled away and out of sight, burrowing into leaves and blossoms for warmth, leaving me to frost and hardening sod. I felt as though I too were bounded in blisters like diamonds, clapped up in a cold moun-

tain. My tears froze on the fringes of grass sprouting from the walls when winter came—and when winter came, and the house was dusted with snow, like a new grandmother's hair, my rescue came shambling into the field where I stood, my knees bent and burning.

The Tale
of the
Twelve Coins,
Continued

HER BREATH HAD MADE THE SMALL SPACE BE-
tween us warm.

"I don't think you're wicked," I said quietly, my voice
filling the space as surely as a limb.

"If I were not, someone would have come for me, in
all that time," she reasoned. "If I were not, I would not
have been given a golden ball and told to go off and
play. I would have been kept close to the trunk of my
mother's body, and wrapped in her tail, the way I
wrapped my ball." She turned her head away from me.
"If I were not, the ghosts would not have taken me."

"But you've done nothing wrong. Your mother left

you to the mercy of a ball—mine left me to the mercy of the Stars. But I did nothing *wrong*. We are not wicked, we're not!" I curled my fingers into my palms. Oubliette only shook her head.

"How did you escape, finally?"

But she sealed up her mouth like a letter. Light sifted flour-thin through the shredded walls, and long gray fingers curled around her neck, around my waist. They pried us from our beds, plied us into clothes of paper threaded with dirty string, pleaded silently with us to eat what they had brought: handfuls of aventurine and garnet. We sucked them down—they were hard and chewy all at once. Our teeth split their skin, and they tasted like licorice, licorice and beets. The same grasping fingers pulled us from our meager food and pushed us down that long corridor which led to the machine, which led to the Mint.

The workday had begun.

I tried to keep close to her, but it was impossible in the press of so many children. I could not see where she went, the one head floating shorn and strange among the others. Little voices rose and fell, paper trousers rustled—it was a little like school, save that we were all so afraid, so afraid. The Pra-Ita did not speak to us, but placed our hands where they wanted them, pushed our fingers as they meant us to move.

I was stationed at the edge of the great, arching thing. Already it hummed with moving bodies, lurched and swayed as though it were it-self alive. It was Vhummim herself, to my surprise, who cradled my arms in hers. Her blue-white hair brushed my face as together we reached for shroud-covered baskets. Her diamond belly pressed against my back as we drew back the shrouds, and her wheat-stalk arms caught me as I fell away from the thing that she meant me to haul up out of the straw—for under the colorless gauze were the tangled limbs of chil-dren, glass-pupiled and sightless, gaping at nothing.

"It was better for you," she wheezed, wretched and worrying, "I told you it was. To work, and not to be minted."

"You make *money*? Out of us?" I felt as though I might vomit, but kept the hard, chewy gems down.

Vhummim's eyes creased with embarrassment. "We didn't notice," she whispered, "when we wasted to nothing. We didn't notice, for a long time. Our markets were so busy—we could not cease trade because of a few ruined districts. Or even more than a few. Our economy kept our heads to the ground. And even after, we kept up our markets, oblivious. We only truly saw what had happened when gold and silver no longer shone for us, no longer warmed the fingers with their very touch." She cringed away from me—as though I stood in a place to judge her! "It meant nothing to us. Our jewels had no taste, our coin no weight. What does a ghost treasure? That which lives, that which is hot and hard. There is nothing more valuable than bodies, and we trade now in bone, we trade in it and mine it from the unwanted, we mine it and mint it and it goes to the new Asaad, where you first entered the city, and it buys pale shadows of what we used to love: apple cores and broken stone and skin with no meat, glistening and thick. It is called dhheiba, this new money, and we prize it as we once prized silver, as we once prized the taste of topaz. I am sorry, but all things flow to the Asaad, and so must you. The living work."

I stared at the child whose arm flopped out of the basket, white and cold. It was a boy, with yellow hair and green eyes. His neck was bruised, as though he had been seized by long, inexorable fingers which squeezed and squeezed.

"See?" said Vhummim. "We spare you this task, at least."

I considered struggling and running from her, but she was surely stronger than I, and faster. She moved her arms along mine again, sinuous and silken, and gently lifted them to grip the boy by the torso, provided the strength, this first time, to heave him onto the machine, where other children, longer employed than I, dully dragged him along to shining blades which quartered him, eighthed him, and further, and further. The meat was cleaned from the precious bone somewhere in the belly of the Mint, and far down the machine, round coins emerged, stamped with the spider sigil, clean and white.

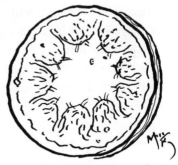

I worked for hours with Vhummim guiding my every gesture like some grotesque pantomime. I stopped looking at them, all those boys and girls—I just closed my eyes and reached into the baskets, closed my hands automatically. I could not look, I could not. Finally, a horn sounded from somewhere far off, and we were ushered away from the great hall and toward a trough brimming with sapphires. I shoveled them into my mouth as I once had brown beans. They tasted like pastry and milky tea. The diet of jewels had begun to disturb my stomach, truth be told, and I wished, fervently, for bread. The Pra-Ita watched us eat, as they had before, and stroked their necks obscenely. They led us without sound back to the barrack beds, and I understood, as my arms ached under the thin blanket, that this day was now every day of my life. I wept into the pillow, trying not to feel the heft of thin arms and legs still in my hands.

Oubliette climbed in beside me, shaking, her eyes wide as a wolf's, her teeth chattering. I held her so close to me I thought I might break her—but she clutched me with as much desperate strength, as much hopeless terror. We spoke in quick-fire shots, like arrows loosed one after the other, breaking each shaft before it in mid-flight:

"Did you see?"

"Yes—did you have to—"

"Yes—did you do it?"

"I had to! Did you—"

"Yes—did you throw up?"

"No, but I wanted to. Did they tell you—"

"No!"

I told her all Vhummim had told me, and her tears were hot as boiled water on my hands. We shuddered together in the dark. Neither of us spoke for long moments, stretching out like wool around a spindle. At last, because I could think of nothing else to comfort either of us, I murmured against her bristly scalp:

"Tell me the rest?"

She began to talk to me, her voice dim and hushed as rain against a broken fence...

THE HULDRA'S TALE, CONTINUED

IT SIDLED, DID MY RESCUE. IT APPEARED UNDER the hoofprint moon, washed in white, the distant grass brushing its knees. My rescue approached hesitantly— it sniffed the air, stuck out its tongue once or twice to taste it. It took a few steps, then stopped to watch me, then a few steps more. The moon was very high by the time it was near enough for our eyes to connect like copper key and copper lock. My frozen tears shattered as I smiled.

It was a unicorn.

I have heard that unicorns are pale and perfect, all white and silver like a bride's veil—those are silly tales, told by sillier uncles and grandfathers. They are dark, dark as race-horses, brown and jet, with the tails of lions, and a boar's cloven hooves. They have little black beards that hang from their chins like unchewed grass, and their horns are not pearl and gold, but twisted bone, the stuff of antlers, twisted round in yellow and red and black. Those horns are thick as my own arm, and sharp as shears—but the horn of this unicorn was severed a little above the base, and the stump had bled, scabbed over, bled again. It was a mass of hardened, blackened blood, and only hints of horn gleamed through.

The mutilated beast sidled closer to me and though she drew back, much as a wild horse fearing that the hand that holds the apple has a mate which conceals a bridle, she nuzzled my cheek with her nose, soft as a mule's.

"I smelled you," she said. A unicorn's voice is a low, liquid thing, like pomegranate wine.

"I wonder you could smell anything buried in sod." I laughed. A unicorn is fearful to see, but it is not a hedgehog, and my heart was lighter for that.

"I smelled your innocence, like baking bread. It called me over the wood and the field."

"I am wicked, not innocent."

"Do not tell me my business. Innocence is a technical thing—I do not care what menial vices you think you have committed. I misjudged purity once, so you ought to believe I am careful enough these days."

"Can nothing be done?" I asked shyly, trying not to look at her ruined forehead.

"Like innocence, a horn once squandered cannot be regained."

I tried to shift my weight inside the house of sod, for my legs were stiff and heavy. Often in those days I wondered if I would grow in this hunched position and become a bent-back long before I became the kind of crone who ought to have one. The unicorn moved her dark eyes over me.

"You are in pain," she said distractedly.

"Yes. I'm afraid you cannot lay your head in my lap."

Her nose wrinkled. "I do not want to! Why should I want to lay my head in a child's lap? I am too old for such games!" Her eyes slitted in anger and could I have run, I would have, for her snorting and pawing were awful to see.

"I'm sorry. I ought not to believe dusty old tales—enough are told about my kind that I ought to know better."

She calmed somewhat, and moved nearer to me again. I looked up at her through my pinioned hair. "But I *am* in pain, unicorn, and should you help free me, if perhaps your head were to fall—in sleepiness, no more!—into my lap, who should blame either of us?"

She gnashed her yellow teeth a little. "If I free you, you will only run away and I will have to chase you, and then I will be sleepy indeed."

"I will not run."

"You will! You do not like me; you only want to use my teeth and my horn and such for your own ends—that is how all of you are. I am nothing but a shop to you, where you may reach onto the shelf and take anything you like."

"Then tell me a true tale—tell me how you lost your horn, and keep me company, if I am innocent enough to pull you over the fields like a plowshare."

A Tale of Harm

I AM NOT INNOCENT. CONSIDER THIS: IF A UNI-
corn is innocent, if she is the core and pivot of all possible purity, why should she seek it out? Why should she
care if some other creature is innocent, if she herself
runneth over with virtue? Why should she, time
and time again, though she knows better—she must
know!—be lured from the deep and shadowy green-
wood by the simple presence of a girl in a white dress?
Ridiculous. We want it because we have no idea what it
is, except that we know its smell, its weight, its outline
against a gray sky. We want it because it is new. We go
toward it hoping that we can touch it, that we can

understand it, that we may become innocent ourselves. You might chase down a cooling cake, but not if your belly is full. So it is.

The science of innocence is complex and technical—I shall not worry your little ears with such talk. Suffice it to say the hymen is irrelevant, as irrelevant to us as trousers. The word *innocent* means *without harm*—did you know? Your mother ought to have taught you what a dictionary was. There is some debate, when unicorns gather, as to what, exactly, the definition ought to be: one who has not been harmed, or one who has done no harm. The smell is different, of course, and everyone has their tastes. I have always held that those who do no harm are the most rarefied creatures—which is why we draw back in such horror when the huntsmen come. Suddenly the dove who opened its little wings to us is a dove no longer, but a thing which has caused harm, great harm, which has brought arrows and knives, and smells like burning crusts, scorched flour.

It should be clear that whatever interpretation is supported by the majority of the herd, it is a thing we have no part of. We do not have this horn for hanging laundry upon, or water-divining, or lock-picking. It is for gouging and puncturing, it is for ripping the flanks of deer and punching through the shells of turtles. It is perhaps for piercing, even, the skins of innocents—I will not say that the first unicorn to discover one ran her through immediately, and the scent of her blood was so sweet and spiced that we have sought it ever since. I will not say it, but it may be true. We are carnivores, we are horses and more—we mate and maul and shatter trees with our hooves, we fight each other with tangled horns, we race with such speed that the earth is torn to strips beneath us. We harm. We are not ashamed of it; it is our nature. But like all things we are drawn to that which is our opposite. And we are harmed in our turn—oh, doubt it not, child.

And yet our horn is not a dead, mute knife: It is our secret self. When the wind blows it plays the slivers of space between red horn and black like a flute of flesh, and the most terrible and radiant songs are heard— but only by us. It is for mating, and for mothers with colts at their teats. I remember that my father knelt in a storm and let his horn sing me to dreaming once, when the forest was full. The voice of his horn was high and sad and bright as lightning, and I loved him. But he is gone now, and no storm can move me.

They used a boy.

In the green and bramble, his smell was sweet as plums and

peppermint leaves. How do they find us? I suppose it is simple enough to track an animal, to find its drinking places, its sleeping places, its loving places. And by a pool clear as air they sat a boy down in the softly blowing dandelion seeds, a boy with large, calm eyes and the most hesitant beginning of a brown beard, told him to be very, very still, like a good boy, and he might see something to tell his children about.

I did not want to go. The scent of it is horrible and wonderful, and we all of us try to ignore it, to bend our heads into the roses and blot out the smell, to pretend that golden beehive up in the poplar is of much more interest. But eventually it wins out, the sweetness and the longing, the almost-memory of a thing which we are not, could never be, the curiosity, to touch such a foreign substance, like ambergris or the tails of crystal fish—to kneel in the lap of grace and be touched, for only a moment, by something which smells of violets, and thick salted bread, and wholeness.

He held out his arms to me, and it blew off him like steam. I ground my teeth, but I went to him, foolish as a virgin, and knelt near him, knowing that next would be the bridle and the whip—but I could not help it, his innocence wrapped me up soft and golden and if I could but lay my head in the lap of that purity, I would know what light was made of, and warmth, and grace. He would not hurt me, the scent said; he was not capable of it.

He held out his arms to me, and slowly I sank into him. His hands went to my pelt, my mane; he gurgled a childish pleasure, and I opened my mouth to breathe him in. But the breath that came was not my own, for he sighed gently upon me, as though blowing out a candle. The secret music rose up, and I started in his embrace, for it was the sorrow-and-blood song, the marrow-and-grief song.

"What are you doing, child?" I cried.

"I wanted to hear the sound the wind makes out of you." He shrugged, his brown eyes warm and delighted.

"But how did you know of it? It is ours, our own thing, and not yours to play."

"My mother and father taught me everything about you, forelock to withers, so that when I found myself with your head in my hands, I would not hesitate..."

THE
POISONER'S TALE

MY PARENTS NEVER WORRIED FOR EMPLOYMENT.
They were poisoners, the best of their breed, and when they had a son, they called him Bryony, after the black herb that makes the palms itch until the owner claws them to gleaming ribbons. They resolved that I would be a prodigy among poisoners, and set about my training as soon as I entered the world.

My mother drank tiny slivers of mandrake, powdered finer than hummingbird wings, in her morning tea, and it passed to me through her milk. She rubbed my lips with hellebore, just enough to taste—brackish and foul, if you'd like to know, like river water after a storm. My father made fried eggs with translucent crescents of night-shade sizzling in oil, salads of oleander and monkshood, pies of yew berries and rosary peas. All these things they fed me, tiny portion by tiny portion, so that when I was grown, none of them could hurt me, any more than blueberries might hurt another boy. They delighted in finding new things to wean me with: cherry bark that causes a plague of gasping until the breath is entirely gone; foxglove that inspires riots of excited murmuring, nearly poetry, before a convulsive death; thorn apple, which grants extraordinary visions, then a black blindness. Once my mother bade me hold a sprig of mistletoe and one of hemlock in each hand and eat a needle of one and then the other, while she wrote down my descriptions of stomach seizures.

There were more exotic venoms—the saliva of a rabid wolf, harpy milk, basilisk bile. But we always found the simplest poisons to be best. You cannot imagine what can be made from a buttercup.

It was, in its way, a happy childhood. I was loved, I ate well—and pinkgill is not at all an unsavory mushroom when used judiciously, and eaten by those whose bellies are staunch and steadfast as ours. We lived in a rickety, bare-roofed house on stilts near the long blue river, which was cold as a corpse's cup and prone to flooding. Poisoners are paid well, of course, but if one displays one's wealth, then one is often asked its source, and we thrived on a discreet business. The riverside was a poor part of town, where folk slopped their garbage onto the current and cursed their chickens in braying voices, and so we chose it, and my parents practiced their art on me with tender attention.

Curiously, however, the layering of poison upon poison in my blood did not prove entirely benign. My skin grew stretched and thin, like a snake's, and quite as untrustworthy. When I was just a boy, my father was teaching me to mix bilewort, holly seeds, and elephant ear to make a draft that would plant the seeds in the subject's stomach, resulting in a very festive arrangement bursting from their mouths a few weeks after application. When we finished, he spread a bit of the stuff on my tongue, like a sacrament—for my parents believed sincerely that death was a sacred covenant between poisoner and condemned, and like all sacred things, required due reverence. We give a person the world distilled, and thus deliver them from it. What more profound act can there be? I closed my eyes, prepared for profundity. The brew tasted dry and dusty, like flowers left too long in a white vase, but there was a sharp tang to it, an arrow of sourness that flashed bright across my throat.

I looked at my father, surprised, and held out my hand: A little holly sprig sprouted there, its berries vermilion against my skin. It grew smoothly from my palm, the child of some combination of oil and seed or root and blossom that I had suckled in over the years. We laughed nervously and trimmed the miniature bush down to the skin. Eventually, it scabbed over, but from then on I was occasionally plagued with effusions such as these, twisting out of my flesh like new limbs.

And so I became both source and practitioner—but I was not allowed to actually sprinkle the food or mix the draft, no matter how I might long to experience the exchange of one world for another. My education was purely alchemical.

"If we let you loose the venom from your own hand, it might spook the unicorn," they said, grinning, knowing I did not understand.

But I observed many poisonings while I was beardless and giggling, concealed behind door or hollow wall, beneath hanging tapestry or bed. Shall I tell you of my favorite, while we have the time? You must be curious—we are so alike, you and I.

The Doge of a far-off country, a place full of red rocks and red roofs and stoops dusty with sage and sap, was possessed of two daughters, the one devilish and heartless, the other sweet and good as milk. Such men are often afflicted thus these days. In this city of red rocks and red roofs, which was called Amberabad, the first child of the Doge was called Hind, and she was the sort that liked to dance with men and eat iced cakes and read books with pictures she ought not to see. The second was Hadil, who liked only to please her father. As they grew, alike in beauty and poise, the Doge frowned into his cups and weighed their differences. He was a complex man, and decided to teach them a lesson, though perhaps a switch to the back of one and a stiff drink to the other would have sufficed. But he was, as I have said, a complex man.

Now Amberabad was a prosperous, though small, city, which sat like a fisherman with his legs dangling in a salty spit of sea. A tiny inlet fed blue water into the center of the territory, and all along it grew weeping cedars, at which the young men would laugh, calling them the future wealth of Amberabad. For the present wealth of Amberabad was amber, which is so plentiful in those parts that one may walk along the narrow, rust-colored beaches and pluck wet, glistening stones from the sand. Some even fish for it, with fine nets of nettle and flax, drawing red-golden gems like salmon from the frothing water. The city smelled richly of resin, and strangely of burning jewels, and cast its shadow in pale yellow streaks on the earth, for Amberabad was a city in the sky, suspended between the trunks of the great seaside cedars.

Long garlands of chicory, milkweed, and tightly budded roses wound around the delicate bridges that led from tree to tree as in some cities streets will lead from ministry to cemetery, and in others canals will lead from market to haberdashery. The people of Amberabad are exceptionally fleet of foot, and hardly any of them fall. The Doge's palace is, rather predictably, built out from the widest part of the trunk of the greatest of cedars, and all of its rooms are enameled in amber, studded with carvings of blossoms, women, soldiers, horses at full gallop, and any number of heroic scenes. All the rooms are red and gold with this gleaming material, and with the soft, furry planks of cedar which show through the occasional strategic gaps in the walls.

In these rooms walked the sisters Hind and Hadil. Hadil wore long strings of amber beads, lacing over her body in complex patterns, close at her throat and looping wide over her wrists and waist, crisscrossing her modest, high-collared chest. Her eyes were bright and gold as sap, her hair as deep a red as the most costly resin. Hind too wore long strings of beads, but hers were cast from amber pitch, the strange black ruin left behind when amber is burned to make that costly oil which her sister so resembled. These black beads whorled round, loose at her throat and close at her wrists and waist, crisscrossing her barely contained breasts.

In these rooms Hind tried to coax her sister to read the books she read, which had woodcuts no girl should see, and to eat cakes which would make her spidery figure ample, and to leave open the amber doors of their room so that men from other cedars might swing across the milkweed garlands and sing to them through the hinges. In these rooms Hadil tried to rein her sister close, and close up the hinged doors when the night streamed darkly in, and crumble the cakes onto the sill for passing birds, showing her sister instead plain brown breads and raw roots. She tried to train her sister's wanton eyes to prayer books which had no woodcuts at all, but only psalms and hymns, which Hadil would sing on the balconies of her high house until her voice became known as the Bell of Amberabad. In these rooms neither sister yielded to the other, and they sat sullenly upon their red couches, the one chewing her roots, the other her cakes.

"Why will you not play with me, as a sister should?" Hind would cry.

"Why will you not pray with me, as a sister should?" Hadil would whisper.

And so their father called upon us, and we traveled in our little caravan to this city, which, my father said, was over-fat, nearing the time for a fasting, as he usually said of the opulent cities where our arts were most appreciated. He was something of an ascetic, my father, tall and thin and imperious, his sparse hair gone slightly green from the same little drafts of poison to which I was happily accustomed. The Doge was unspecific in his letters as to the shape of the lesson, only as to its intended content. Thus we pored and pondered until we had devised what we thought an acceptable tutorial.

It was a very complicated boil: shattered oyster shell and quartered toad, lily of the valley and autumn crocus cut carefully from the insides of my cheeks, jack-in-the-pulpit and poached rhubarb leaves, smoked and reduced and thickened with cane for weeks. At the last, pearls were dissolved into the brazier, and toad eyes pierced and allowed to dribble into the mire. We baked them into sweet candies, with a light flavor of anise and dusky peppers, and presented them to the girls at a banquet, posing as cooks. I watched from behind my mother's voluminous chef's skirts, a little kitchen waif gawking at the finery.

They sucked them down happily, Hind greedily chewing and Hadil making small kissing gestures with her pink lips as the anise puckered her cheeks. It was some time before the effect would be seen, and we were invited to stay and enjoy the food we pretended to have prepared. I was sitting between my parents with an antler fork in one hand, poised to mouth a sliver of sheep's fat, when Hind turned to her father and said:

"When you are dead and I am Doge, I shall invite all the woodcutters and poets to this place, and they will write odes to the beauty of Amberabad and her two daughters!"

Hadil blushed. "When you have gone and I am Doge in your place, I shall cover my face in mourning white, and no images shall be made of anything at all for a full year, so that we may remember only your kindness, and your face."

Hind looked at Hadil with disgust. "When did you lie down under the surgeon's knife and let your heart be cut away? Can you not even once smile with me and be my sister? Stuff your pinched face with your damned bitter roots and choke on them! May you—"

She did not finish her curses. Out of her mouth came a single pearl, large and white and shimmering. Hadil cried out in surprise, and from her rose-scented lips came a slim green frog, hopping unconcernedly onto the table. Another followed, and another pearl from her sister, and another frog. The table leapt with green and clattered with white, the Doge's beautiful daughters holding back their curled and perfumed hair with both hands as they vomited up jewels and amphibians.

The Doge scowled. "I told you to teach them. Teach the one that goodness is not enough, and the other that cold cruelty is too much. What is this? Precious jewels from the corrupt daughter, slimy creatures from the virtuous? You will get no payment from me."

My mother, always the orator, bowed low. "Your Grace, forgive me, but you do not see as we see. From the mouth of the child you judged wicked comes nothing but cold stones, lifeless, shellfish waste. In a seaside kingdom such as yours, they are too common to be called valuable. Beautiful, yes, and they have their worth, but they are just pretty rocks. Out of the other comes frogs, which you may consider ugly, but are food and clothing and curatives and poisons. They are eminently useful creatures in any clime, and she will never be hungry, nor anyone who comes near. Yet those who come near will as often as not cry out in disgust and speak not to her sweetness. Tell me I have not taught a lesson they will remember!"

The Doge laughed, and so did I. Hind hiccupped, and a pearl formed at the corner of her mouth. She stifled tears as one of her sister's frogs caught the jewel with his tongue and swallowed it.

I have heard that, swollen with pride in her frogs, Hadil became an inefficient Doge, caring only for her amphibian subjects, ordering every frog to be escorted across the road and hoisted on silk cushions, lest the poor beasts suffer. She kept up her singing until no one could stand to step out of their homes, as she added songs for her father's shade and songs for the betterment of frogs and songs for the salvation of her lost sister. Finally, there was no hour left in the day when the Bell of Amberabad did not endlessly drone from its high balcony.

Hind, I have heard it said, went into the world, dropping pearls behind her and thinking no more on politics.

Perhaps we had too great a love of preaching. But we were clever and delighted each other and practiced our arts with a precision nearly unknown in these degenerate times. And I will take their place when they have gone. I will be greater even than they, for I need no wild wood to give up its savages to me. I am the wild wood, and to produce both pearls and frogs from maidens I need but to extend my hand.

A Tale
of Harm,
Continued

BRYONY PUT HIS HAND NEAR MY NOSE, PALM UP,
and from it twisted up a thorny rose, cloying in its
scent, which interfered with his own.

"You understand why I could not give the girls their
candies. I did not, not then. But when I was older my
mother and father showed me their books, and I read
about you, about the unicorn, about the song that the
wind plays on your horn. They told me that my gradu-
ation from their little academy would come when I had
caught you and made my poisoner's cup, for no poisoner can afford to be felled by his own leafy thralls, and
it is known that your horn makes all poison as harmless

as water. 'There is a unicorn in this part of the world, and her name is Nevinnost, and we have saved you for her,' they said. 'Go and become a man.' This is why I have knelt by you, and held your head, and let you smell me all you like, the last wafting fragrances of my innocence, for I am eager to do harm in the name of the world distilled, eager to join my parents again in their stilt-house."

"I should have expected it."

"Yes, you should have. I hope I have been a soft bed for you, Nevinnost. I hope the scent of my skin is all you hoped for."

With this he drew a long silver chain from beneath him, and wrapped it round my neck. I recoiled—his smell had changed, slanted into acrid and burning, charcoal and soot and rinds of sour lemon roasted on white embers. He smiled and the stench worsened; my nose clogged with clanging, warring drifts of him, smoke and ashen logs, vinegar and limestone and his stinking, cloying rose. As I struggled, they came. And surely you have heard this part of the story before: how the huntsmen came with their green hose and their brown arrows, and held me to the earth while Bryony sawed my horn from my head with a blacksmith's blade.

The wind made a sound like shrieking when the red whorls snapped and shattered. I bled—the black whorls bled and the ground was wet and slippery; I scrabbled against them but the blood-mud held me fast. Our horn is flesh, no less than your nose, and the blood spurted from me like a string of black pearls onto the velvet lap of the poisoners' son.

The Huldra's Tale, Continued

THE UNICORN GLARED AT ME, DEFYING ME TO tell her how foolish she had been to go near him, or that she was no kind of beast to have lost her horn. Perhaps a grown woman would have done this, but I could not.

"Nevinnost, I am sorry for what he has done. A boy once took a thing from me, and in its place I was given a golden ball, and now you see what has become of me. I am like you."

Her gaze softened. "I am not a unicorn if I have not my horn. I am only a mule with a beard and a very odd tail. You are still a girl. Though I am sorry for you. A golden ball is no thing to give a child."

"Please help me. I can help you, if you will release me. I will not call a huntsman. I will not call the awful hedgehog who bound me here. If I am innocent, you are safe."

"All things are innocent until they are not," she snorted, but bent her dark leg and pawed at the quills which bristled from my pinioned hair in untold numbers. She dug at the soft soil, bit at the slick metallic quills, but her teeth could not catch on their surfaces, and they were driven too many and too deep for her to reach. Finally she just stood before me, her brown flank glistening with sweat. The night sky was beginning to lighten in the east, a long, jagged strip of cold blue against the cold black, and I knew Ciriaco would be coming soon.

"My hair," I whispered. "Chew it off, and I will be loosed. If I am innocent then all parts of me are innocent, and you may taste of it, in my hair, in my curls, a thing which your treacherous boy would never give. Take my innocence, and set me free."

Nevinnost hesitated, sidling to me and away just as she had done when she first approached, neighing softly and reaching out her long, bloodied head to me, then drawing it back. Finally, she began to graze at the black strands, just like grass, and in the dew-frozen morning, she severed my hair at its roots, murmuring as she did, in pleasure or in pain I could not tell. But she was somewhat overzealous, and she chewed my hair right to my scalp in her hunger and eagerness. I did not mind. Long after I could move again I let her keep at her meal, leaning forward when she could not reach me.

"You taste like the moon, so cold and so pure," she whispered in my ear, and began to kick at the sod bricks, by now turned to iron plates by the frost. I tumbled out of the house that my golden ball built—for I still and always thought of him as mine, and my ball—at Nevinnost's feet.

"You said you could help me," she said, still in a half-swoon.

I turned and clawed in the hard soil around those unnumbered quills, gold and silver and copper and iron and quartz and diamond and emerald and sapphire. I dug deep and as I dug I wept and grunted and cried out, all those months walled into the sod tower rushing from me like frogs from a good girl's mouth. My fingers were hooked and grimed, but finally I held out to her a bouquet of dirt-clung bristles, in every metal imaginable.

"It is enough," I said, sobs hitching in my voice, "for a new horn."

Nevinnost bent her head and nuzzled me very lightly. "My horn is a colored cup on a table far off from here. I cannot take another while it still lives—what would it say? But should it break, in lands I will never see, perhaps, perhaps, I shall know what wholeness is."

Very slowly, she sank to the ground and lowered her ruined head onto my lap. Blood had begun to ooze again, just a few drops, from the scabs on her severed horn. She closed her eyes and breathed very deeply through her soft nose.

I lay beneath her, feeling her weight, heavy as guilt.

THE TALE
OF THE
TWELVE COINS,
CONTINUED

OUBLIETTE RUBBED HER SHORN HEAD ABSENTLY.
"She took my innocence, what there was, into her, and
then not only was I wicked, and ugly, and at the mercy
of anyone who decided he loved me, but I was a grown
woman, too, and bald as a vulture. I had hardly stumbled out of the field where Ciriaco had built his house
of sod and child when the city blew in, and the Pra-Ita
seized me up, knowing, as my ball did, that no one
would come looking for me."

"I don't think they know—they just gather whatever
the wind scours up—"

"They know."

I could say nothing. Instead, I slipped out of bed and hopped quickly around to the other side, the floor icy beneath my soles. I climbed in again, behind her. Gingerly and gently, I put my arms around her—I was a man, and ought to know how to do this—and pressed my skinny body against her bark-back, holding her and rocking her like my own child.

"You are not ugly or wicked or at anyone's mercy," I whispered. "Though you *are* bald."

She laughed a little, but as she warmed beside me, I felt her crying, quiet as pages rustling.

We worked at the Mint for seven years.

She kept her hair short, cutting it with the side of a sharpened gear. It was short and ragged, but thick, dark, over her head. When I asked about it, she shrugged and said: "My hair is hers now."

I cannot begin to tell how often the wind carried us, or to what crevices of the world. Sometimes it seemed that beyond the tattered borders of the city, it snowed. Other times I seemed to smell a sage-and-stone desert. There was never a lack of materials for the Mint. Mostly, we did not have time to look at those borders, or anything outside the walls of that place. We worked. We ate—opals and garnets and pearls and chalcedony and hematite and lapis lazuli and malachite dark and green. Vhummim was right: A topaz tastes like a peach. Once, when the quota for the day had been exceeded, we were given diamonds. They tasted like frozen lemons.

Occasionally, we slept.

They watched us whenever we ate, stroking their long necks in time to our chewing. The dead city traded and bustled, but ate nothing, drank nothing. They watched us like a play, and salivated. Some of us grew up—many did not. Like any machine the Mint was fickle and thirsty. Fingers were crushed and arms were torn from sockets; not infrequently an entire child fell or was pushed or jumped—ah, so many jumped!—into the gears and stamps. The first time it happened, I cried out, and my cry in that huge, silent hall was like a knife through the air. Everyone stopped, turned to stare. But they stared at me, and not the child who had swooned into the coin stamp and left a bloody stain on the boards. I had cried out; I had called attention to myself. They hissed at me to be quiet, and the Mint ground on.

By the time I was fourteen, only Oubliette was older than I. And by then, we thought we were strong enough, and clever enough, to escape. Gems are not nutritious, but the Mint gave us a dim and sallow strength, turning and twisting as we had to, shoving the stamps down, as she did, or shoveling dead children onto the boards, as I did. We did the same work for seven years.

And we shared a bed—not as lovers, you understand. I think I would have married her, eventually, except that marrying her would have been

like plowing a river with a perch-drawn plate: I wouldn't know how to begin, and what would be the point? When I looked at her body I did not see breasts or hips or even a tail and rough gray bark. I saw money. I saw coins piled up in a basket. I saw the money her bones could make. This is not the stuff of husbands. Some things you cannot put behind you and forget as though a golden curtain had closed on them. We shared our bed for warmth and company and if we had not I think one of us would have gone headlong into the gears long before. I scratched her bark and burls; she rubbed my neck. We helped each other return to ourselves when the work was done. After a while, we stopped sneaking about, and just filed into a common bed at shift's end. The Pra-Ita said nothing. There was always a new child for an empty bed.

On that night of all nights, as I cradled my tree-girl in my arms, she spoke, quieter than a single drop of water dripping from a roof:

"I am going into the machine tomorrow."

I started, turned her to face me, her dark eyes wide and calm. "What? Why? Why would you leave me here?"

"Hush, I'm not leaving you. I have found us a way out. I am going to crush my arm in the stamps tomorrow, after the shift bell. I will creep back onto the floor and put my arm on the boards. I will let the great glossy stamp sever it. I will make with it the dhheiba we need to buy our way out. An arm is not so much; I have another. But I will need your help to run the rest of the Mint—the scrapers and scrubbers and cutters and board-runners. I think if we are quick we can do it."

"An arm's worth of coin is not enough to tempt anyone in this place. They have hundreds of arms at the end of any reach."

"It will tempt Vhummim. She likes us. She watches over us. It will be enough."

I was silent for a long while, and the other children, young and new, snuffled in their gray beds.

"It is a good plan, Oubliette. But not for you. I will put my arm beneath the stamp, I will let it cut into my shoulder, and you will remain whole."

Her thick eyebrows furrowed and she scowled at me. "Why? You know you are an overgrown, scruffy-limbed infant when it comes to pain."

I held her face in my hand, cold skin on cold skin, her clipped hair bristling against the tips of my fingers like quills.

"My arm is bigger. We will get more money."

She said nothing—what could she say to that?

"You will cry out."

"I will not."

We held each other all that night, and she kissed—the only kiss she ever gave me—the spot where my shoulder joined my arm.

In the Garden

THE BOY HAD LEFT HER.

He always left her. Each morning, and the morning after that one. She did not mind, really—it was difficult to speak for so long, to remember so much of what was written on her eyelids, to be close to another child when she had been alone for so long. She had not known how that could tire her. And so it was that when he had gone from her, she often went into the placid Garden lake, to let the cool water, rippling like a dress pulled up above the knees, wash him away from her. The hard, round pebbles under her bare feet were comforting—she had always had them, and the lake, and the reeds, and the knocking cattails, and the moon and the stars, to stroke her to sleep. She thought of the boy, how eagerly she waited for him whenever the red sun sank below the pomegranate trees, yet how often she was emptied, when he was gone, like a painted vase whose water has been flung out onto the flagstones. It was so easy to miss someone, she thought, when you have never missed anyone before.

She knew her stories so well, she did not lose them when she spooled them out to him—she told herself this over and over. They were still her own, her own. But when the words of the tales passed her lips and wound into his ears, they seemed to become so solid, to grow limbs and hearts—bodies winding into each other like snails winding into their shells. When she had been alone, and whispered those tales into nothing more than the surface of a little pond or a thatch of blackberries, they had stayed thin and wispy, shreds of a gown which did not quite fit her fluttering in the wind. She was happy to see them grow solid—she told herself this over and over, too.

Waist-deep in the lake, she turned her face up to the starlight, and the falling shadows of dwindling ash leaves. The leaves were all gray in the dark, their reds and golds seeped out like tales. She ducked her head under the water, once, twice—she had long ago stopped praying that the black marks would come off when she did so. She would be looking for him again by the next evening, she knew, but now she felt as though all her self was laid open, like shining tendrils, like snakes let out of their basket to wriggle in the world, and she gathered them in again, in the silver light.

When she came up for breath and cleared the lake from her eyes, a figure was walking nearby, cloaked in white and not her boy at all, some distance from the violet-bordered water.

It was Dinarzad.

Her hair flowed behind her like the shadow of a much taller woman, and her feet were bare on the grass. The girl feared Dinarzad had gone mad—proper amiras did not go about thus. But she seemed calm, did not weep or tear her hair, but touched the trees lightly, as she passed, as though looking for something. Finally, she saw the girl in the water, half submerged like a lamia or a mermaid, and froze near an orange tree which was still glossy and green in the forest of bare branches. The girl said nothing—when one approached a strange animal for the first time, she knew, sudden movements would frighten it or enrage it, and if she did not want a terrified goose on her hands, surely she did not want a terrified princess.

Dinarzad opened her dark mouth and squeaked. She tried again, her voice clearing like a winter sky.

"I wanted to hear . . . I wanted to listen—"

She bolted, a doe caught before an arrow. The girl watched her go, not knowing what she could do to make the woman stay. She had never tried to make the boy stay, once the tales had begun. He was naturally faithful as a sleek hound.

*   *   *

And so it was not surprising when he found her near the moss-drenched stones the next night—it was only as much as she had come to expect from him, expect and anticipate, though it cost her. He brought her a round cheese and a slice of pastry. They whispered and ate as they had always done until the sky had gone as black as it might, and she could begin again in secret and in safety.

"I want to hear more!" the boy said excitedly, clapping his hands. "Dinarzad didn't speak to me all day—it was like a holiday! Tell me how they escaped!"

The girl smiled softly and breathed deeply, opening up her tales again, herself, like a reliquary full of sacred bones.

"Seven was certain he would not cry out when the stamp pressed down on his shoulder—he would be brave and stalwart, stoic and true..."

The Tale of the Twelve Coins, Continued

I SCREAMED. OUBLIETTE PUT ALL HER WEIGHT on the stamp and it slogged into my armpit, mashing skin and bone and blood together. It did not sever on the first try, and I whimpered, I groaned like a woman in labor as she loaded up the stamp and brought it down again. I think I may have fainted away, for I remember waking to her tightening a strip of one of the corpses' dresses around my stump. She held the tattered shoulder to the hottest parts of the machine, which glowed a baleful red, and I probably screamed again. It was a wonder we were not caught—but then, the children often cried out in their sleep, often screamed, often wept. Perhaps I should have let Oubliette do it after all. She would not have screamed.

I remember staring at the ruined arm, which was once part of me, once my own, and would be no more. Those were my fingers, fingers that had gripped pens and bucket handles, cow teats and apple cores. Those were the lines on my palm, that foretold who knew what future. It was my body we put through the Mint, laboriously, my blood we smelled as it wet the innards of the machine, as we turned the gears and moved the pistons with her two hands and my one. It was my body I heard crunched under the final stamps, and my body I saw emerge from the mouth end of the machine's arc, the mouth which had been shaped into a tooth-wight's grin.

Twelve coins, pale and round, of clean, gleaming bone. All we had in the world, out of my own flesh, like a wet fruit cut out of its skin.

During the midday meal, we found Vhummim watching one of the girls devour translucent tourmalines as though they were the first cherries of summer. She stroked her neck. She stroked her diamond belly beneath her rags. We smeared our best smiles on our faces and called her to us.

She did not seem to notice the arm—so many of us were mangled there, another injury was no foreign thing.

"We want to leave, Vhummim," Oubliette said firmly.

"I am certain that you do, little one. All is not as it was, when Marrow was the center of the world and no man wished to leave it before his pockets were full of lapis and his arms full of women. But you must know I cannot help you."

"We do not want your help," my friend hissed. "We are citizens of Marrow now. We have paid our taxes, we do our civic duty. And we have the right to trade, just as anyone."

Vhummim cocked her head, her bluish hair falling into her face like waxen icicles. "You have no money to spend, precious ones. No dhheiba. What could you possibly buy with air?"

Oubliette drew out our purse. I was still half faint and ashen; I did not trust myself to handle the coins without dropping the whole lot to the rubbish-floor. One by one, she fed the coins into her palm until it was piled high, and held it out—six, only six coins in her shaking hand, to buy our lives back. The grain merchant's daughter knew to hold something in reserve, in case the ghost drove up the price. Vhummim licked her lips with a colorless tongue.

"That is not enough to buy your ruby breakfast," she said, but she did not look away. She and Oubliette locked their gazes for a long time, a kind of silent bartering I could not enter. Finally, the foreman spoke, her glassy eyes drooping in her skull.

"In the days when we ate all possible things, the rarest transactions were the most prized, even if they were no more than a twig traded for a feather—if the seller of the twig were a man with one eye, and the seller of the feather a woman with a beard, it was called a success. No worker has ever made this offer, and I will accept it, in the name of the old Asaad. But you will leave under the vault of night, and I will boast of my trade only after you have long gone, lest it be judged less rare than I think, and I am punished."

We agreed, and she took the coins in her long, spidery fingers, closing them over the bone reverently, with a strangely kittenish moan of pleasure.

"It was like this," she murmured, "before, in the time when all possible things were bought and traded, and the silk was high and red over the Asaad. The feel of economy was like this, light and thick and sweet. I remember it, I tasted it long after I could taste nothing else, the memory of Marrow the lost, which was called Shadukiam in days now dead and cold."

She closed her eyes and looked up through the ragged roof, her gray throat ululating in grief and longing.

The Tale

of the

Crossing,

Continued

A WIND HAD PICKED UP ACROSS THE WATER. THE
surface was dull and flat, gray as a maiden's eye, and
moving quickly, wrinkles forming and traveling around
the little ferry.

"I suppose Marrow seemed a fit name, considering
their new vocation, better than their old one, at any
rate," Seven mused.

Idyll chuckled and shifted under his cloak. He
stroked the hunch of his back with one hand thoughtfully. "Shadukiam was a place of wonder once, boy—
those roses blowing through your door once covered
the whole place in a dome of flowers. There were silver

towers, and diamond turrets. There were women in purple and men in scarlet. It smelled of algae and gold. Do not speak of what you do not know."

"I know enough of that stinking, windblown hole!" Seven said hotly, his breath fogging in the icy air.

"Because you know a corpse does not mean you knew the man."

They lapsed into a woolen silence. Seven pulled up his collar around his face with one awkward hand and scowled into the breezes whipping his cheeks. He could see the clouds bunch and knot in the northern sky, not dark, as rainclouds ought to be, but pale. They were simply gathering, a great snarl of white, like cotton wound sloppily round a spindle.

"The storm is coming," Idyll said quietly. "She's early today. I don't know if we'll make land by the time she blows through."

"I have weathered storms before, old man."

"No doubt, a brave thing like you. But lake storms are a breed apart."

"I *am* brave," Seven grumbled. "If I were not brave, I would not have come here. I would have drunk steaming cider by a hearth instead of this, built a house, had children. I am going to save her. She saved me. We kept saving each other, even after the Mint. What else can I do?"

"Nothing, son," said the ancient ferryman, his voice relenting to softness. "No one who crosses this water ever had another choice." He poled the silt-stuck bottom of the lake, and somewhere far off, a bird keened, a gull or cormorant. Seven thought the trees were closer now, that the silver line of a beach gleamed below them, but he felt sick with the rocking of the ferry, and his eyes were rubbed raw by the wind's fingers. The sky was so blank he could not see the sun, and he thought he smelled a coming snow. Idyll's cutting voice sank into his thoughts.

"Tell me, how many of those awful old things do you have left?"

"One," the young man said. "I saved two. One to get me to her, the other to get us back. I saved enough for this, for her. That's all that's left."

"And that leaves four to fill out your tale, before the storm screams in and there is no more room to talk beneath the white winds."

Seven nodded and coughed roughly. "Four. Four coins for a cripple and a monster to ply the road—that's all there was outside of Marrow, once Vhummim had punched through the fish-bone wall at the edge of the city for us. Roads, paved and dirt-packed, cobbled and painted and bricked. We followed one, we might have followed any of them, but we followed that one, and now I am crossing a lonely lake to her, to her, my sister and my friend..."

THE TALE

OF THE

TWELVE COINS,

CONTINUED

WE CHOSE A ROAD, AND FOR THE FIRST TIME IN
seven years, a golden sun, hanging in the sky not unlike
a ball, shone on our skins. It turned us red. We swam in
blue rivers and splashed each other. We ate blackberries
and walnuts cracked with flat stones. We did not work.
Yet when we swam and I saw her naked flesh shoot by
under the cold, clear water, I still saw nothing beautiful,
only dhheiba, lurking beneath.

We wandered for a long while, she and I. We might
have searched out our homes again, or homes which
would suit us now, but we had, by mutual agreement,
done with cities. We kept to the green orchards like

foxes, and sucked at sweet owl eggs. Autumn was beginning to swell the apples before we saw anyone on our road, and I am sure we looked quite feral by then. Oubliette's hair was even growing long and shaggy, crow black, framing her face like rough hands. We had no mirrors or shears, and my hair was longer than hers. We were in quite a state—though happily gorged on apples and rabbit haunches, as we were between us quite clever at catching them. After agate and jasper, soft meat and crisp fruit were miracles to us, and we sought them out, starving. And so, when we heard the cart clattering down the lane, we were still in rags and shoeless, but fatter than we had ever been.

The cart had two great wheels, which towered over the thing itself, painted blue and spangled with silver stars. A little wagon was suspended between the wheels, with a peaked gypsy-roof and round windows. Doors opened in each side, and it seemed spacious enough; maybe it was even pleasant to sit inside and watch the spokes clack by. It was drawn by a lithe man clothed all in green—hose, doublet, fetching little cape and hat, all greener than apple skin. He had hair the color of egg yolks that stuck out from under his cap and a thin, affable face. His feet, from the knees down, were the spindle-swift legs of a dun brown gazelle, and his green hose ended just before the fur in a brass buckle, old enough to have gone slightly green itself. Oubliette and I stared, our mouths gaping.

"Well, good morning, little ones! How does the glabrous day find you?" he said, curtseying as well as his legs allowed. He did not let go his long blue poles, and his voice was like a thrush's chirping song. He smiled—his teeth were small and bright and sharp as a fox's.

"Good . . . good morning," I said. Oubliette held my hand tightly.

"You are fortunate to have crossed paths with us, my wastrels! I can see you are in need of civilization, and art is the midwife of the civilized soul. We are performers and minstrels, singers of songs and players of scenes, catamites and castrati, the finest and brightest and best-dressed of all of these. For a coin we will show you the world on our stage, for two we will teach its ways to you. I am Taglio—juggler, dancer, eunuch, acrobat, and scenery-wrangler, and superlative knight of the cart!"

We introduced ourselves shyly, but neither of our hands went to the hidden purse. We could not afford to spend my body on this colorful man, no matter what he promised. He beamed at us with sparkling green eyes. As we looked closer, we saw that the silver stars were simply bits of tin suspended from the wheels. The paint had worn in places,

from a startlingly dark and vivid cobalt to pale turquoise. The effect was very pretty all the same, and the stars made a tinkling sound in the breeze.

"Wouldn't you like to have a little dance?" he trilled, hopping from one hoofed foot to the other. "A little scene—'The Princess and Her Faithful Cat,' perhaps? 'The Huldra, the Bull, and the Tree'?" Oubliette looked stricken, and Taglio hurried on. "Or something more grown-up, as befits two upstanding young things such as yourselves? 'The Murder of King Ismail'? 'The Rape of Amberabad'? 'The Siren's Seraglio'? Or perhaps just a song, a card trick, a coin from behind your ear? We are flexible, we are amenable, amicable, and amiable, as all must be in times such as these. We too are hungry for sparrow pies and blueberry cordials, and barter our talents for such reasonable fees."

A large red paw emerged from one of the blue windows. It stretched lazily, extending its scarlet claws and retracting them again.

"Who is that, Taglio my pet?" a low voice came from behind the bird-skin curtains. It had a growl to it, but was not unpleasant, like rubbing fur against the grain.

"That will be my mistress and my partner, the other half of my 'we,' my menagerie, my muse, my terror, my darling!" said the green man, finally setting his long poles onto the dappled ground and gallantly opening one of the moon-round doors of the spectacular cart.

Out of the blue stepped a Manticore.

I know this now, because she has since carefully shown me all the parts of her body and explained their origins and uses, but then she seemed an outlandish vision, and I could not have named her for a hundred bone coins. She was a lion, of sorts. Her pelt was red as leaves, and oiled to a glossy shine—but her head was that of a woman with enormous blue eyes, the same blue as the cart, her aristocratic face framed with stiff, wiry hair the same shade as her fur. Haloing her head like a mane, it flowed back over her muscled shoulders like a genteel shawl. As she exited the cart completely, her tail came into view—it was that of a great serpent, mottled green like old copper, scaled and scabrous. At its tip was a scorpion's barb, hard and shiny as a beetle's carapace.

"Grotteschi the Red," Taglio crowed, "actress, beast, mezzo-soprano!" The Manticore inclined her head modestly, her ruddy cheeks high and lovely. There was something strange about the line of her jaw—it did not close quite right, like a child's broken music box, but it was wide and generous, her lips like a swipe of blood. In her jaw were three rows of sharp yellow teeth. "Will you not hear her sing? It is worth five times anything you might pay to listen, I swear by my Absentia." Oubliette crooked a quizzical eyebrow, and the gazelle-man grinned. "A eunuch is lacking in some things, and flush with others. That which I do not possess are naturally absent from me, and thus, in polite company, I refer to them as my Absentia. We must all be allowed our little eccentricities. If you will sit yourselves down on the grass—a cushion fit for lords and ladies of twice our collected ranks!—I will tell you the tale, should it please you. The first taste is always free."

The Manticore rolled her bright eyes.

"How can they decide if they want the whole show if they do not get a taste of us?" he protested.

"Go on, then, and don't complain to me when it's mice for dinner again," the red beast retorted.

Taglio smiled his sharp, glittering smile, tapped the earth with his hooves in a shuffling two-step, and began.

The Tale of the Eunuch and the Odalisque

SING, OH, SING, OF THE GRACEFUL GASELLI! Nimble and fleet are their boot-black feet, and sweet are their whistling songs! No shepherd more steadfast than we, no firefly so quick on the wing, no melodies lighter, no lyrics brighter than ours—than ours!—on the sheep-spotted fields of home!

We are the bringers of grace, we are the players of the goat-horn flutes, we are the fire-tenders in fields where hay has been bundled and wheeled. But light up your camp and find us gathering near, stamping our hooves on the grassy ground, stamping our hooves to the beat of your drum, stamping our hooves to the sound of your wine-sped violas! But kindle a flame and see us creeping in from our sheep and our cattle, creeping in from our milk and our meat, creeping in from the dew and the damp and the pinwheeling, heart-reeling ergot on the rye, the wheat, the golden, gleaming grain!

And if in the morning you find your wife has gone missing, if in the morning you find your brother run off, if in the morning you find your number one or two less than the night before, it is not our fault, we are but animals, and follow our bestial nature, as you do, as you do, else there would be no fires and no wine, no songs to thresh the mind, no whirling, no wheeling, no slaughter-sheep bleating—and what would our lives be then? Yes, we take one or two, but what do we give you? Fire and wine and songs in the mind and whirling and wheeling and lovely girls bleating—we give as good as we take.

Yes, sing for the Gaselli. These are my people, and we are well sung. We hunt the campfires out in the low dells, and do we dance? Do we sing sweeter than any twanging country harp? Bet on it. Are we lissome and lithe, are our faces fair, do we kiss like poets imagine they do? And are there one or two gone in the morning? Bet on that, too. By our green you shall know us, our green coats and our green skirts, trailing behind us so that only those who know to look will see those boot-black hooves a-gleaming. And what befalls those lucky one or two, who in the damp, ashen dawn are nowhere to be found?

All creatures under the Stars must eat, my dears.

We are shepherds—to eat the sheep we tend would be an abomination, would it not? To eat cattle and goat would be obscene! How could you even suggest it? What perversion you describe! Be off with you, now, else you shall feel my hoof!

But wait. Perhaps there was a Gaselli with hungers like the ones you expound. Perhaps there was one who did not like the taste of girl, even less the taste of wiry Gypsy boy. Perhaps he thought lamb and roasted cow smoky and rich and sweet, perhaps he thought goat salty and soft to his neat, white teeth. Perhaps his name was Taglio, and perhaps he stands before you. And it is not impossible to imagine that after years of secret meals and pantomiming at the revels, pretending to gnaw a bone or lap a wound, he was caught gorging himself on a little lamb who had died of the cold. But this poor Gaselli begs forgiveness! What it was that caught me at my feast is hard and hard to believe.

It was a cow. This does not strain the mind, I am sure! But it was a cow the size of a barn, with eyes like the forked spaces between flames, depthless and black and glittering fair! Her flanks were dun-golden, smooth and muscled, showing girl white, sow white, wool white skin beneath. Her hooves were bronze, her udder full and firm as a moon, her nose flared trumpet-wise, the breadth of her chest enormous. Yet she moved, I swear it so, without sound over the grass, graceful as a trained horse, and her hooves burned the earth where she stepped, sending up sighs of steam.

There was a light about her, I tell you true. It was not a glow, but a light that hung within her, like the shape of a second cow. I fell before her, on my knees.

"O Great Heifer of Heaven!" I cried, for my poetry had not left me. "You have come to punish me for devouring your children! But they were sweet, and I am weak!"

She regarded me calmly. When she spoke her voice vibrated in my bones. "I eat. Why should you not?"

"Because Gaselli eat dancers, not the flock. We are to eat drunkards who cannot find their way home through the mere—not a poor, defenseless cow who never knew where home was to begin with."

"I know where home is."

"I daresay you are not defenseless, either!"

"I have not my brother's horns, but it has never been a worry to me. I have not my brother's heart, either. I shed my hiding place to taste the salt-sweet grass and listen to the lowing of beasts, for these things are as cool water poured over my forelock when I have been cloistered in the stone and the dark for so long. He never cared for the grass."

Sing for the Gaselli! But also sing to them—for we are beloved of tales, and they are beloved to us. I knew her then, and scolded myself that I had not known her before. Had I not myself told tales of Aukai, the Milk-Star, who makes oxen of bulls with a snap of her jaw? Had I not told of the mad castrati-monks to frighten the calves in their crèches? I fell to my knees, my own small, furry knees, below her great, shining face—beauty beyond any dancing girl with a red shawl and blue stockings. Her light filled me—I could hardly see for the glow of it!

Perhaps it is not right to explain how a man is moved. Perhaps he ought to keep the logics of light and blood and heaven locked tight within him, with a chain and a snapping dog before it. Perhaps it is enough to say that a man with graceful feet and a tongue more graceful still was struck dumb by the radiance of a cow, pierced with shame for all he had eaten in her image, cut through with adoration of the smallest shadow cast by the flick of her tail. How can even the most quick-fingered of minstrels convince his catgut harp to tell what ecstasy is? I am the most quick-fingered of minstrels, and I cannot.

What did I say to her? I swore things. I babbled like a lost sheep. I would join those who cut themselves in her honor, for her love. I would do the penance her brother refused. If she would but touch me I would die at her lowing. It is hard to recall now. Ecstasy slips the mind. But before she could reject me—might she? I could not let her!—I drew my sheep's shears and did his penance and mine there on the long grass. My blood mixed with the blood of the flock, and with her light, her milk-light, lying on me like a forgiving hand. The pain was a ripping, a gouging, keener than horseshoe nails pounded into me, and my green trousers were a sudden red—but her light was with me, and filled me, and the silver singing in my head was greater than any shear, the silver, woolen singing which stopped up all but itself, the silver, wild, and woolen singing which I shall not forget for all my cart-drawn days.

Below her I lay in a sop of blood. She watched me, calm as a cloudless sky. She blinked.

"What sad, strange things you are." She sighed, and lumbered away over the low hills, scalding the weeds as she walked.

Perhaps I was hasty. Perhaps I was foolish. But I never liked the Gypsy girls anyway. Faith is always embarrassing in the morning. The other Gaselli recoiled—if I had been a secret deviant before, I was unmasked. I left them with little remorse. Let them revel and eat and revel again. It did not interest me. But I found, in the wide world which does not smell entirely of wet sheepswool, cowhide, and goat-hair, that the opportunities for a eunuch are limited.

I did not wish to be a spy, which is the chief activity of my, if you'll excuse the expression, breed. To be a spy is no better than to be endlessly dancing in the midst of a throng you intend to devour, and I had had enough of that. I had no patience for the intrigues of a chancellor or advisor to any sort of king or treasurer. And when it came to it, the chief activity of the monks of Aukai seemed to be to rattle their Absentia in little cedar boxes and brag about how long it had taken them to faint from the pain. That did not seem to me to be the most sacred of pastimes. It seemed logical enough, therefore, to choose what was left to me, and travel south through the orange-blossomed jungles to the lands ruled by those who kept harems. I had been a shepherd of flocks which looked and smelled far worse, after all.

And so I came to shepherd the Raja's women, who were varied and beautiful as a herd of horses, swift and sleek, red and brown and black and golden, their hair dipped in frankincense and braided up in pearls, their skin kept firm with bamboo switches, and bound up in yellow silk, for this color marked them as the Raja's, no less than a chair or a shoe. Of course, my clothes, too, were yellow, and I mourned my lost green, but I belonged to the Raja, too, down to my name and my boot-black hooves.

I was happy—I soothed the new ones when wars brought them trembling to my care, the older ones taught me to play cards and juggle, the ones in between told me tales I had never heard before. There were so many women, in truth, that the Raja could not possibly visit them all, and thus he was not much a part of our lives, a specter only, looming in the distance. And every night, there was lamb to eat, and chickens, and goat, and quail eggs, and deer flanks. No one even suggested that I might eat a girl.

Immacolata was not a concubine, or a wife, or even a war prize.

She was an odalisque, which made her like me. She was a virgin who served the harem. She did not guard them, but dipped their hair in frankincense and braided it up in pearls, hardened their skin with bamboo switches and bound them up in yellow silk. She painted their breasts with bronze paint when they were called up to the bedchamber, drying their tears and working the most wonderful calligraphy on their skin, like the tracks of jeweled spiders. Her own silks were red, red as the blood of my body that night under the Star, and she moved among the others like a scarlet ship in a golden sea. I will not say I did not watch her on those tides. I did not cut out my heart on that long grass.

One day she came to me—she came to me, a yellow-bound fool, to me!—and drew me aside, to a long golden couch, and sat me next to her. Her hair was a river of smoke, curling away from her stark brown eyes and amber skin. She was all the colors of expensive teas, dark and golden and burnished. There were no pearls in her braids.

"Have you seen the new wife?" she asked, her timbre low as an iron horn.

"No—I did not know we were due."

"I have seen her. She is not kept with us. But if you would leave this place as I would—"

"Why would I want to leave? I chose to wear yellow and play cards with the old wives."

Immacolata looked at me as though I was mad. Her eyes widened, and I could see the oily gold with which she lined her lashes. "I thought you were like me," she said quietly.

"I am!" Foolishly, I clutched her hands. She snatched them away.

"No, no, I wish to leave this place more than anything, more than I wished to be a bird when I was a child, or to learn the craft of tea-making, when I was grown..."

The Tale of the Tea-Maker and the Shoemaker

I DO NOT REMEMBER BEING MADE OF TEA. MY mother told me this story, and then my father told it to me, and it was the same story, so I am sure that it is true, or at least that they have agreed upon it.

Saffiya was a shoemaker, and she lived in her cobbler's shop, which had a copper bell over the door and a knocker in the shape of a sole. She was not a beauty—but among her shoes no woman would shine. She made shoes of blue silk and shoes of black leather, shoes embroidered with scenes of leafy forests and flowers as intricate as a fingerprint. She made huntsman's boots and soldier's boots and soldier's boots and boots fit to withstand a Quest, and she made dancing slippers: shoes of gold and shoes of silver, shoes of fur and shoes of glass. She made tiny shoes shaped like cups with woolen sides and iron soles for her cloven-hoofed customers, and long, knitted socks for the serpentine. She made three-toed shoes for aviary custom and gently shaped iron into horseshoes. She had even made, as an experiment, a large and generous single shoe, with space to wiggle the toes, in case a Monopod happened by. On this great shoe she carefully stitched scenes of wine-making in expensive violet thread, dyed with the saliva of a certain snail. Her most famous shoes, which none had yet been able to afford, sat in the window like a relic in a shrine. They were made of raw black silk and green thread, and had soles which were so fine they would not dare to whisper on a floor of pebbles. It was said that they felt like the dreams of Saffiya when slipped on the feet. Among her shoes she was plain and hardworking, her hair the color of leather laces, her eyes the shade of well-worn soles.

Elpidios was a tea-maker, and he lived in his teahouse, a small place with a grass-thatch roof and long rows of tea plants before and behind. He was not a beauty—but among his teas no man would shine. He made green teas that tasted of warm hay and sunlight, black teas that tasted of smoke and sugar, red teas that tasted of cinnamon and blood, yellow teas that tasted of frankincense and dandelion root. He made delicate white teas that tasted of jasmine and snow. He made winter tea from the last dried leaves and twigs of the harvest, and this tasted of bread and grief. He made teas from cherry blossoms and chrysanthemum petals, rose and lotus, orange peel and magnolia. Some of these tasted light and sweet, like clouds drifting from the sun; others tasted spicy and dark, like thick cakes. His most famous tea, which none had yet been able to afford, was brewed from white tea leaves, violets, and a single red leaf. This was the tea that tasted of the dreams of Elpidios, and he priced it dear. Among his teas he was plain and hardworking, and his hair was the color of oolong, and his eyes were the color of wet leaves.

One day it happened that the tea-maker found himself in want of shoes, and the shoemaker found herself in want of tea, and these two met. She fitted shoes to his feet; he fitted tea to her throat. For her he made his dream tea, and held his breath while she drank. For him she took down from the window the slippers of black silk and green thread, which would make no sound on the floor of his teahouse.

She sipped the deep red tea and exclaimed, "Why, you have been dreaming of me!"

He slid into her shoes and exclaimed, "Why, you have been dreaming of me!"

And so it was.

Now, the years went by and though Saffiya stitched her shoes and Elpidios steeped his tea, they had no child of their own. Saffiya was not greatly troubled, as she had plenty of baby shoes to make without adding any of her own, but Elpidios longed for a daughter, and his teas began to taste bitter and brackish, and he no longer made the dream tea at all. Finally, he went to his wife and said:

"The ways of the world are marvelous and strange. Let us take my finest teas and fashion them into the shape of a child. We will place her in one of your shoes for her cradle, and let her lie under the light of the Stars. Who knows what may happen?"

"Husband, this is not the way of making a child."

"Let us try. And if it remains a pile of brown leaves with no life in them, I shall forget that I ever dreamed of a child, and begin to brew my tea of white leaves, and violets, and a single red leaf once more."

Saffiya was mild and even-tempered, and she knew that madness must play itself tired if it is to pass. She made a sweet green shoe with crimson teaberries on a snowy hill embroidered on its sides. It had a little heel of cherry-wood. On the tongue she sewed with infinite care a living chrysanthemum with sixteen petals. But when it came time for Elpidios to reveal his tea doll, he refused.

"There is one leaf missing," he said, and departed for the highest hills with a sack on his shoulder. He was gone through the fall and into the winter, and Saffiya began to worry for him. Perhaps she should have made sturdier shoes for him, she thought. She drank a pale tea of dried birch bark and strawberry leaves he had left behind, and stroked the sweet green shoe. But at length Elpidios did return, smiling his old smile. In his hands he held a slender leaf, the color of the moon shining on an open well. He told his wondering wife that he had heard of a place where a tea bush grew that had been touched by a Star in the first days of the world, and that he was certain now that their child would wake.

So together they placed this shimmering leaf in the center of the tea doll, and placed the doll in the shoe. In the long rows of tea they laid the sweet green shoe, and waited.

For many days nothing happened. Saffiya assured her husband, for by now she had begun to hope, that all children take time to grow. Elpidios paced in his teahouse. Finally, they heard a crying in the tea rows, like a kettle boiling. The tea-maker and the shoemaker ran out into the long leafy paths and found there a little girl wailing in a sweet green shoe.

But I do not remember being made of tea. I suppose no one remembers what the world looked like from inside their mother.

We lived happily and well, and I drank the dream tea every day, and found how often my father had dreamt of me. I grew to wear the sweet green shoes on my own brown feet, and found how often my mother had dreamt of me, too, when my father was in the highest hills. I learned to make green teas and black teas and red teas and yellow teas, and white teas like melted ice. I learned to stitch forests and flowers and fashion shoes of gold and silver and leather and glass. In time, my parents died, as parents will do, and though I was younger than I would have liked when this occurred, I dried my tears. I made both the famous tea and the famous shoes, and I believed myself complete.

But as they were not beauties, I am not. Even when the procurer came with a sword at his hip and velvet in his coat and a warm helmet on his head, I was not beautiful enough to be stolen for the Raja's bed, only for his prison of silk and bronze. None of the girls in our village were spared service of some kind or another, and I was made a slave to slaves, maid to the wives and concubines. I paint on their breasts as once I drew patterns on the silk for stitching. They are unhappy, and I do not know how to soothe them, for I am unhappy, too. But I make for them the dream tea of my father, the tea of white leaves and violets and a single red leaf, and hope they taste my dream of a life outside.

I served this tea not long ago to the newest wife, with her fifth child already at the breast. She sprouts children like berries, this one. She is very beautiful in her white veils, and her black eyes are so deep they seem to have no pupils at all. Her hair falls past her waist in long black curls, and it shines most curiously in the candlelight, like the skin of a salamander. She fixed those depthless eyes on me as she sipped my father's tea, holding her golden cup with both hands.

"I am sorry for you," she said, and her voice moved against me like a stone crushing millet. "But if you would not waste to less than an old brown leaf in this place, come to my bedchamber on the third day of the new moon." She set down her cup and put her hands to my face, the light in them terrible and wonderful, like a judgment, like a promise. I was weeping before I knew it, the nearness of her bright and awful and endless. "I swore to him not to incite the harem," she murmured, "but an odalisque is not a wife, and I can see the leaf your father placed in you, glowing still. Because of it we are sisters, and I cannot abide a sister's suffering. Tell the eunuch who keeps you that Zmeya commands you to attend her."

She kissed my cheek, gentle as a thrush singing.

The Tale of the Eunuch and the Odalisque, Continued

"YOU DO NOT UNDERSTAND," IMMACOLATA SAID. "For you, this is a pleasant world, no different from an open pasture speckled with sheep and horses. But we are not sheep, and we are not horses, and we did not ask to be shepherded, nor corralled for the use of the biggest bull."

Her last words stung like a crop—had I not done the penance of a hulking bull? I hung my head.

"I will take you to Zmeya's chamber."

Immacolata seized my hands and her hair brushed against my arms. Her red silk rustled against me. "Come with me! There are better things in the world than this, I swear it. Why would a eunuch care so to deliver bound women to an intact man? You owe him nothing—come away with me! I have watched you; you have watched me. Let us not pretend otherwise." She cupped my face in her hand. "I know you are Gaselli, yet you have never hurt us, never."

I tried to protest that this was no act of chivalry, but she stopped my  mouth with a copper-ringed hand, cheap baubles empty of stones and thrown away by other women, which left green bands on her fingers. Before my widening eyes, she turned one of the pronged rings inward and pressed it into her neck so that blood welled bright as her veils and trickled into her collarbone. I did not understand—but she pressed my face to her neck. I opened my mouth to assure her again that I did not want her flesh, and her blood slipped between my lips.

She tasted like tea. Of all the dancing women in their shawls, she alone tasted sweet.

I took her gift, and her hand. When she walked with me to the great harem door, the bells at her ankles sang—and no one marked our passing from that place.

The Tale
of the
Twelve Coins,
Continued

"I TOOK HER TO ZMEYA'S CHAMBER, AND IT IS true what they say, that Zmeya was a great snake beneath her woman's skin, but we did not trouble ourselves much about it, I being half gazelle and Immacolata being all tea bush. Deliverance was as simple as an open window. We went into the wild together, Immacolata and I."

Oubliette's eyes were wide. "What happened to her? Why is she not with you now?"

Taglio grinned his feral grin and danced a lazy step or two. "The first tale is free, the second must earn its way in the world."

"We have nothing to give you, I'm afraid," I said sorrowfully. "You must see us as we are—poor in all things save blackberries and road dust."

"That is a tragedy true, my young master," the eunuch said with a sigh.

"Where are you headed?" I asked.

"Over hill and dale and mountain, river and desert and possibly those blighted hills and dales again—to Ajanabh, where we have heard artists of our caliber are welcomed," thrummed the Manticore's voice. Grotteschi's warm, spiced tone seeped into me, and I shivered. Oubliette and I exchanged looks. Perhaps we had not done with cities.

"We cannot pay you for a song or a scene, but if you would accept company, we would travel with you," I said nervously, overexcited as a groom.

Taglio frowned. "Much as we might enjoy little ones, they are expensive to maintain."

I breathed deeply. "We cannot pay for trifles, for songs and bells and flutes, but if you will take us in, that is a great enough thing to pay for."

Oubliette gripped my arm. "What are you doing?" she hissed. But I smiled at her, a smile I hoped promised games and warm afternoons and songs with new friends, and no more dank barracks, no more paper blankets. I tweaked her tail a bit, as I did when she was grumpy. She relaxed, but her grip did not lessen. I squeezed back, and she drew a single dhheiba from our purse. The Gaselli and the Manticore recoiled, but could not take their eyes from it. I felt the weight of it in my hand, my own flesh. Was this what Vhummim meant, about the thrill of the rare trade? I felt sick.

"That would buy an army of children twice your size," the green man breathed. He took it solemnly, and closed it away in his belt. I did not let it go easily, but I let it go.

"Can you sing or juggle or act? Can you balance on a branch? Do you have any interesting deformities?" Grotteschi tore at the uncomfortable silence and peered at us, a buyer canvassing horses.

"I can juggle," Oubliette said, blushing in the face of the great lion. "I once had a lovely ball, and I learned well. And—" She turned slightly, so that her bark-back was clear, and flicked her dun tail with a flourish.

The red lion's face softened, and Taglio's mouth opened slightly, in shock and recognition. The gallant little man sank to his knees before my friend and put his hands to her face.

"Oh, poor child of Aukon! You should have said so from the first," he whispered.

In such a way we joined the pair of them on the road we chose, which led to a lake and a cold, gray wind.

Though we asked to walk with Taglio, panting to hear more of Immacolata, he insisted that Oubliette ride with the great scarlet Manticore and not trouble her little feet. I would not leave her side—I would never leave her, never—and reluctantly, we slunk off toward the jangling blue cart, and climbed inside the waiting door, making room for ourselves in the coil of Grotteschi's thick, mottled tail. We inched closer to the beast to avoid her green barb. But the tail flesh was warm as a sun-baked brick, and we were soon quite comfortable. The feel of it beneath our backs was soft and firm, but we could feel her pulse, low and thick as a huge drum.

She turned her remarkable blue eyes onto us. The shaggy red hair around her shoulders thickened on her neck and chest, curling below her chin so that she really did seem a maned lion, king of the pride, save for her woman's face. She licked at the stiff, wiry fur.

"You want to hear of the odalisque, yes? Of the tea-maker's girl. You would rather walk out there, on the hard ground with the moon slapping your heels with her bony hands, than in here with me. Taglio thinks he can tell stories, but the songs of the Manticore are famed by those who survive them, and I knew her, too."

Gingerly, Oubliette reached out a hand to stroke Grotteschi's brilliant fur. The serpent-lion purred and hissed all at once, and her eyes softened.

"Listen, darling, infant things! And tell me I cannot sing as well as a gazelle..."

The Manticore's Tale

SING, OH, SING, OF THE SUN-MUSCLED MANTICORE!
Thundering fleet are their scarlet feet, and great are
their echoing roars! No hunter more patient than we,
no serpent so sour-tailed as we, no snarling leaps
lighter, no long teeth brighter than ours—than ours!—
on the scrub-spotted deserts of home!

Ha! Let us have none of that. Do not sing of us. We do
not want your songs. We will sing, and you will listen.

* * *

The desert is wide and white and dry as an old bone. We worry it, we gnaw and tear and peel it bald. And we sing when the moon is jumping on the sand like a skinny white mouse, we sing and the saltbush weeps. The oases ripple under our breath, the blue and clear water where the rhinoceros wrangle, where the cheetah purrs and licks her paws, and the Upas trees waver green and violet in the scalding breeze!

They will tell you the Upas is a death-bower. They will call it the hydra-tree of the desert, and warn that if you sleep beneath it for even a night, you may wake, but to no morning man has known. They will say that three hundred soldiers all in bronze and feathers camped beneath an Upas once, to drink from the clear stream that flowed beneath its branches, and that by the time the sun touched their toes all were dead and cold as dinner. This is ridiculous, a fairy tale. But I suppose it is yet not entirely untrue, for the Upas is our mother, and we are enough of death for anyone. And if soldiers camp under an Upas when she is blowing her seed, it is no fault of the hungry kittens that tumble out if they find their supper plump and laid out on the sand.

Look, passersby—though not too closely!—at the radiant Upas, lover of the Sun in his golden bedchamber, her red branches thick and strong as a haunch, thorny and pitted, her green needles far too glossy and stiff to grow in the thirsty desert. Look at her fruit, nestled in the shadowy forks of her knotted trunk, how scarlet and purple, how thick and full of juice! Touch one at your peril, for these gleaming berries are not fruit but eggs, and it is we that grow within them, in the crimson sacs which wax in the blistering scrub-light, full of the peculiar Upas yolk we drink and drink, which fills our tails with enough poison for a lifetime, until we rip that silk-thin skin and tumble out headfirst into the water, or soldiers, whichever seems most convenient.

I remember the Upas milk. It was sweet, like blackberries and blood.

In the fruit sac we know all things: how the Sun preened on the face of the oasis pool, how one Upas, though neither the tallest or most beautiful thing in the desert, opened up her branches and grasped the reddening beams for her own. Her wood warmed and the pool rippled—the Sun would not have noticed if his mirror had not been marred. He would have been angry, and scorched the tree for her theft, had not the first Manticore fruit burst open before him, and if he did not think the little cub with her needle-teeth and her whipping tail and her sky-bright eyes was the most lovely of all imaginable things, and immediately set about teaching her to sting and roar and sing and kill, all the things he knew. The Upas smiled, and told her sisters how to follow her lead.

After we fall, it is harder to remember these things, to know they are true. But we do our best to love our parents and turn our prayers to the sky and the sand.

It is only unfortunate that we are more or less helpless when the Upas blows us free. No more fierce than little red kittens or infant snakes, blind and wet and mewling. Our tails do thrash quick and sharp in those first hours, indiscriminate, for we have not quite learned to control it when the oasis, littered with palm nuts and antelope ribs, catches us in green-gold arms. This is when the wranglers come, if they are clever, with their silver tail caps spangling in the desert light.

I would like to tell you I was reared in the open flats, the white and worried bone, that I tore open leopards and antelope and rhinoceros, that I remember what that tough gray flesh tasted like, and that horn. I would like to tell you that the Sun and I ran together, bounding red-pawed over the saltbush and the pale weeds, that in the warm red rocks I rolled with my legs in the air, scratching and roaring and eating as I pleased. I would like to tell you that the echoes there taught me to sing. I would like to tell you I was happy, and that the Sun was high in the sky.

But the wranglers came with a little silver cap, something like a thimble with buckles and straps, and armored in polished metals splashed with the last desperate strikes of countless kittens, lashed the thing to my barbed tail. My thrashings were dull thuds and sprays of sand, but nothing more. I howled—it is not only the province of wolves. I howled and that did startle them, for the voice of the Manticore is terrible and piercing and sweet, the sweetest and most terrible of all possible voices, like a flute and a trumpet playing together. It is barbed as surely as a tail. I howled and keened, thumping my useless limb against the ground pitifully. They took out wax stoppers and closed their ears to me, and into an amber cage I went, clapped in an amber collar, and gagged in leather to keep me silent.

Tell me again how the Gaselli sing. Tell me that no melodies are lovelier than theirs.

The heights of the amber city made me dizzy. The platforms spiraled up and up those impossible cedars, and on the spindly bridges I nearly fainted away, so far below did the ground sway and wobble. They pulled me up with squeaking pulleys and moving flats drawn up with wet ropes. I retched into the muzzle and choked on my own bile. The green branches cut the clouds as I rose and crumbled against the lifting floor and sobbed against the straps which bit into my face until I tasted my own blood with every lurching inch upward. I hitched and gagged, bewildered, as afraid as any lost beast. But I was close to the sky, so close, and the Sun beat my back fondly.

The amber cage had an amber lock, and there was a girl with an amber key. She kept it on the beads that slung around her like chains, dangling right at the base of her throat. In those days any number of creatures were brought from every hovel and height in the land to delight this creature, whose clear, calm eyes took in everything with equal regard and due. She was dutifully amazed at my fur and my tail, dutifully frightened at my muffled roar, dutifully patted 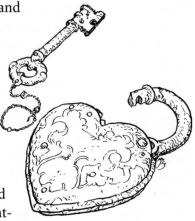 my head, and dutifully passed on to the next wonder of nature brought up the trees for her pleasure. She took no joy in any one animal over any other, and her voice was genteel and grateful when she thanked the wranglers for bringing her these miracles and grotesqueries. By the latter, she meant me, and thus I was given my name.

For some weeks she came, dutifully, to visit her menagerie, escorted by wranglers and noble nursemaids and occasionally her father. She played with the pygmy elephant and the wobble-kneed young Centaur whose legs were bound in her absence so that he would never grow to shame her with excess height. She had a Djinn whose smoke had gone out and a fish in a great glass bowl which owed her yet two wishes. Their games were odd and solemn—she sang to them and sat them to tea with amber cups they could not help but break, and scolded them for their manners. She forced their struggling heads onto her breast and all exclaimed it a miracle that her gentleness of spirit and purity of heart could charm the most savage of monsters.

She did not charm me.

After attempting to get me to drink from her dainty cups and sing with her while she did her sewing, she declared with great sadness that the beast she had named in jest was truly a grotesque beyond salvation, and that I should be sent away, for I was surely, in my unfathomable heart, unhappy there. I knew this meant the slaughterhouse or simply being shoved off the platforms into the narrow spit of sea, but what maiden knows how the world is skewed to spare any testing of her virtue?

When she and her escort had gone, a small, dark shape remained, silhouetted against the door frame of the wretched zoo. It came into the light, and I saw that it was a girl like the other one, and lost interest—save that she came and knelt by my cage, and, loosing a strand of black beads from her throat, put her own amber key into the lock, and opened the amber door.

"Poor Grotteschi. Do you see these beads? When amber is burned to make resin, this horrible black stuff is left over when the golden oil pours dutifully into the catch. No one wants it. It is garbage. I, too, am what is left over from her, what is thrown away when she has passed over it, what remains in the corners when she has swept by."

She put her hands to the muzzle's buckles and let it loose. By then I had grown, I was the size of a small horse, but the muzzle had never been changed. My jaw would never close quite right again. She did not mind my teeth. She rubbed my chin and my cheeks, wiped at the hardened blood with the hem of her dress. Her name was Hind. She was a good girl, and I slept in her bed from that night on.

Even when I was fully grown, she slept curled between my paws and demanded iron supports for her pitifully delicate bed. Together we snuck into the libraries at night, and she taught me to read from the books kept on the highest shelves, which I could reach for us, stories of lost girls and lost beasts and grotesques like us. She brought me cakes from the kitchens, covered in icing, so much thicker and richer than the mashed and rotten meat of her sister's zoo. When she became more beautiful even than her sister, I used to sing at her window to the men who gathered there to play their flutes or harps. They scattered when faced with my superior songs, and I padded back to Hind and her black beads. I was happy. The Sun was high in the sky. Happiness, when you look back on it, seems so brief, but then, with her, my whole life seemed to pass by under the flitting cedar shadows. Until the day she ran into our room and slammed the door behind her, her chest heaving under those black beads, her face flushed with tears. I ran to her, and she buried her head in my mane. Finally she drew back and sobbed horribly, a long, broken howl—I remember when I howled that way.

A pearl fell out of her mouth.

The Tale of the Twelve Coins, Continued

GROTTESCHI'S VOICE HELD US FAST. OUT OF HER misshapen jaw came a strange, lilting tone, low, rasping, but sharp and keen as a plucked harp string.

"Someone had poisoned her," she moaned, "having no business in Amberabad but to vex my friend, because her father did not like her books or her cakes or her pets. What kind of a person fills their larder by punishing other people's petty complaints?"

Oubliette and I shifted against her tail, and I glanced over at my short-haired friend under my eyelashes.

"You're telling the wrong story," I whispered. "What about the tea girl?"

Grotteschi stared at us, her eyes bright and amused. "What an impatient couple you are. I was getting to it, you know. So spoiled by my friend in green! You like his story better, because it has a harem. Young boys always like tales of distressed women in silk."

Oubliette elbowed me hard. "I like this story. Be quiet," she hissed.

The Manticore rolled her eyes.

"Very well; a performer must always play to her audience." Oubliette dared to creep closer to the red lion, resting gingerly against her ribs. "Hind begged me to take her away. She promised that she knew how to use the floating platforms, and we could run from Amberabad to another city, where her affliction of pearls might be of some use to us. And so the girl strung with black beads packed her cakes and some few of her precious books and climbed onto my back, proudly astride, as her father had told her over and over not to do..."

The
Manticore's Tale,
Continued

WE DESCENDED TOGETHER THROUGH THE BRANCHES
and clouds, onto the long road, and she clung to me all
the way down, her long fingers gripping my mane so as
not to fall while I bounded off the last amber plank. I
faithfully kept my tail from curling tightly upward, as
the recalcitrant thing is wont to do, so as not to hurt
her. We stepped onto the thick grass and my friend
laughed to feel it, solid ground beneath her. We went
into the world, in search of this other city, and it was on
the road to that fabled place, which was called Ajanabh
then as it is now, that we met the oddest couple
trundling along the seaside paths.

I am sure there is no need to describe my Taglio to you. Was his hair longer in those days? Were his eyes brighter? I cannot tell. He did not wear green then. Immacolata had shredded her red silk, but kept it knotted into her hair as a reminder of her bondage, braided bright against the brown. They were beautiful. Taglio played his pipes and Immacolata had become a kind of tinker, though her tea bags were never far. They made a meager living through sleight of hand and the odd set of tongs played for a hunk of bread and a chunk of cheese. They told us their tale, and that they did not know where they were going, only away from where they had come, and they had been already years on that hungry road. Hind, being fond of pets, asked them to go along with us to the city of spices, which was so far from where we stood that it might as well have sheared off from the map of the world and gone drifting on the underside of the parchment.

"I am lonely for company," Hind said. "Though my red beast and I love each other, I think she would be glad of another beast, and I of another woman. In Ajanabh there must be spices for your teas that you have not yet dreamt of. In Ajanabh there must be meats roasting that you could not begin to name. Come with us, and tell us tales, and eat our cakes, and read our books, and become as beloved as you may."

When she finished her speech, her hands were full of pearls. The couple stared at her.

And so we traveled. With Hind spitting her pearls word by word, we were rarely hungry. Taglio taught her to juggle and pantomime; Immacolata made us tea over countless campfires. They were happy—there are many ways to be happy, and they had theirs. They pulled coins out of each other's ears and made countless cups and shoes vanish, only to reappear to gales of high-pitched laughter, like owls hooting in the wind. I envied them, and so did poor, lonesome Hind, who had no more pretty boys at her window, only me to sing to her. Every evening the red-braided girl would take the Gaselli behind clusters of trees or reeds and let him taste a single drop of blood from her throat. Her neck was a pattern of tiny scars, like a star chart. Hind watched this in silence, standing alone near the fire with her hands clasped tightly together. Whatever she thought of their ritual, she kept to herself.

Slowly the sea became long, grassy valleys, and in one of these valleys we stumbled into a shantytown of brilliant and varied colors, tents breaking the low morning fog like the masts of ships. It was something like a circus, performers of all kinds rubbing the sleep from their eyes and stretching their legs, strapping on stilts and polishing trumpets, practicing violin scales and barker calls, elongating any number of legs into graceful steps. A hundred voices trilled octave to octave, a hundred lines of tragedies and comedies bellowed out from a hundred obese contraltos.

As we descended into the cheerful maelstrom, Hind clung to me, unsure of so many strange folk. Immacolata stroked her hair. A woman nearly collided with us on the path through the tents, driving before her a massive boar which walked on its hind legs, a little yellow cap on its head and yellow ribbons hanging garishly from his bristly neck. The woman was rather short, slender as a cracked whip, dressed all in goatskin, fur hanging gray and coarse from her arms, her waist, all the way to her tiny ankles. Her eyes were a keen, narrow gold, and her hair was blue as drowning. She held a long churchwarden pipe in one hand, its mouthpiece glittering green.

"Watch where you wend, friends, or my pig is like to trample you. It takes all his concentration to keep in a straight line," she said, her voice thick and raspy with smoke.

"Excuse me," said Immacolata, always polite—and it had long ago been agreed that Hind was not to talk to strangers, as we would not want to be robbed of her by someone who fancied having a girl who dispensed endless jewels from her mouth. "But where are we? What is this place?"

The woman drew deeply on her pipe and blew green smoke at her boar. She looked up at the tea girl's scarlet ribbons, and her eyes narrowed further. "How long have you been away from Varaahasind, my little decadent?" Taglio started as if slapped. The goatskinned woman laughed and coughed and laughed again. "Don't worry—who would I tell? As for the rest, this isn't any place, silly things. By tomorrow we'll all be gone, each to our own corners of the yawning, grassy world..."

THE
PIG-TAMER'S TALE

MESINYANE HAS A TUSK PIPE AND A PIG CALLED
Femi, and my pipe it is a hollow tooth, and my pig he is
so named, and thus you may be reasonably sure that
Mesinyane tells you these things.

I am here because this is where we go, who travel and
perform and live on the world but not in it. The wind
blows us together, to exchange news and tricks and
techniques, to whisper to each other what cities can afford us, to trade tightropes for horseshoes. The blue of
my hair is paint, the shade of my eyes a cheap glamour
purchased from a mixer of oils and unguents who had a
green cart and great, long fingers. I am dressed up no

less than my boar. We do all these things, trade and dye and dance and learn and part—it is a happy vagary of our lives. Word is passed horse to ox to magician to singer, and we wind our way, eventually, to an agreed-upon dale. This is a Vstreycha, a congress of fools, and I came to it from Varaahasind, where I was born in the house of my father, who was also a fool, but the kind who lets the milk curdle in its pail and the beer lose its head to the breeze, not the professional kind.

When I was grown, and our hut of pigskins was low and warm in the jungles outside the city—we were too poor to live on the terraces, near the palace with its perfumed queens! I often used to dream of catching a glimpse of one of those women, strange and exotic as chained leopards. But we lived on the outskirts, where the banana leaves cast green shadows, and my father Femi slept behind the stove.

This is not so odd—certainly it was warm as a held breath in our forest, but it is a pleasant thing to sleep on the bricks behind the stove, warmed as they are by the bread baking against the side of the iron, and sweat away bad dreams and the occasional cough. I often wished to sleep there, but my father held his post like the last soldier on a hill.

"Father," I would say, "go to the well and get us some water so that I can make us fish stew."

My father Femi would roll over on his bricks. "Why must you pester me so, Mesinyane? What did I have a daughter for? Get it yourself."

And so I would go and pull the water from the well with buckets of baobab wood, and the stew would be sweet anyhow, with green onions and pink tails floating in it.

"Father," I would say, "go and cut us some camphor wood, so that I may build up the fire and warm your bricks, so that the hut may smell of cinnamon, not yesterday's fish stew."

My father Femi would roll over on his bricks. "Why must you pester me so, Mesinyane? What did I have a daughter for? Cut it yourself."

And so I would go and cut the camphor wood and bring it in to dry, and the hut would smell of thick and spicy things, and the bricks would warm beneath my father's back.

"Father," I would say, "go to the market and fetch us two black roosters so that I may roast them up for us, and stuff your pillows with the feathers."

And my father Femi would roll over on his bricks. "Why must you pester me so, Mesinyane? What did I have a daughter for? Get it yourself."

And so I went into the jungle, where the banana leaves are high and their fruit not yet ripe, where the cacao flowers are wet and pale. I was muddy to my knees by the time the road smoothed out through the coffee plants wavering white and green and red. My arms burned with shoving the forest aside to let me pass, and my face was full of the pricks of mosquitoes. But I could see the first rounded terrace tops, and my mouth watered for the chickens to come.

But my legs are small, and by the time I found a little butcher's shop with cockerels hanging in the window, all was dark and every door shut against me. My feet were torn and bloody, my shoes worn through to nothing, sweat clinging my hair to my scalp as though I had slept all the day on my father's stove. I looked up and down the narrow street, full of clothes shops where I could afford nothing and bakeries already puffing the smoke of tomorrow's bread through their roofs. The palace hunched in the distance, and the high wooded hills hid the moon from me. There was nowhere I could see that would open its doors to a goat-furred urchin, so, with rather fewer sniffles than you might expect, I settled down against the brick wall of the butcher's shop to await the old red sun's return.

I could not really sleep, but fitful dreams ran over my eyelids, leaving their tiny footprints. Sometime after the moon had finally grunted and sweated and hoisted herself up over the treetops, I saw through slitted eyes a figure walking from the palace toward me: a man who was white all over, the white of milk or cheese or chalk, and he wore very little, his long, muscled legs showing bare, his chest slung with a barbed harpoon and nothing more. His hair was long and straight, and in his arms he held a woman, stiff and dead, her beautiful limbs frozen and unmoving, crystalline snakes wrapping her arms, her skin clear as the glass of a poultry-seller's store. I had never seen anything so radiant and lovely as those two, and I think the man looked at me as he passed, but I cannot be sure. He cast a flitting light against the alley walls, shadows spitting angrily at the stone.

I could not help it—I was curious as a mouse who has not heard that someone, somewhere, has thought of a thing called a trap. I followed them, creeping close behind. I followed them all through the night, in which they floated over the ground like the moonlight that so rarely penetrated the banana canopy, and into the day, in which they still gleamed, as though their skin was hungry for light, always light. I followed them through the cacao flowers wet and pale and the coffee plants wavering white and green and red, I followed them through the baobabs with their roots like elephant trunks, I followed them past my own house.

Now, I loved my father as best I could, and I did not think he would want to miss such a thing passing by our very own door. So I rushed in and shook him awake on his stove.

"Father!" I cried. "There are Stars stamping flat the banana leaves outside our door! Come and see!"

My father Femi rolled over on his bricks.

"Why must you pester me so, Mesinyane? Did I have a daughter only to nag me and pelt me with lies? Go see yourself if you like, but leave me alone!"

"Father, I do not lie! Come and peek out of the door, just peek, and if there is no pale figure striding by you may lie on your stove all day and night and I will say nothing about it!"

My father grunted and slowly rolled back and forth, working himself up to standing. He stumbled off of his stove and went to the door, placing his eye to the jamb—and indeed, a slim, cream-blanched ankle was disappearing beyond a clutch of palm fronds. My father's face contorted like an acrobat's leg—as if in a daze he wandered out of the house and after the creatures. I knew that he was not so thick as to be unmoved by our little plot of land alight with gods! The two of us, small and quiet, followed them through the night and into day.

But it was difficult to keep up. Sleeping on a stove does not really prepare a man for marathons through high brush.

"I'm thirsty!" whined my father Femi. "What did I have a daughter for! Fetch me some water!"

"There is no clean water to be had, Father. Be patient, and perhaps we will pass a stream."

"But there is rain pooled in the leopard tracks here!" he said, pointing at some broad, deep pawprints.

"It is not safe, Father Femi. Remember what your wife, my mother said: 'Drink from the feet of a beast and win those feet for your own.'"

After a long while, as the jungle became thinner, and the mud turned to pebbles underfoot, and still we only saw the burnt leaves and steaming mist of their passing, my father Femi cried again:

"I am thirsty! Find me some water, girl! What did I have a daughter for?"

"There is no clean water to be had, Father. Be patient, and perhaps we will come to a lake."

"But there is rain pooled in the tiger tracks right here!" he said, pointing at more deep, broad pawprints.

"Remember what your wife, my mother said: 'Drink from a footprint and it will not go well with your own scraggle-toes!' "

"Your mother is off whoring herself to the Raja," my father snapped, "eating sugar pies and lamb fat and sleeping in silk every night!" His face was red as a boil. Tears leaped to my eyes.

"She didn't want to go! The procurers came and you wouldn't beat them back with your fists or your club or your bricks, you only slept on your stove and refused to budge! 'What did we have a daughter for?' you said. 'You get her back, if you want her so much,' you said!"

We walked after the Stars in sullen silence after that. High red berries glittered, and I was thirsty, too, but I obeyed my mother. Finally, my father wailed, a long, wretched sound.

"I am so thirsty the sides of my throat stick together!" he moaned. "There is water in the boar-prints—let me drink, cruel Mesinyane!"

I turned to him and planted my hands on my tiny hips. My face was flushed and sweat-stung, my arms itchy from biting vermin, my feet a bloody ache. We were losing their scent, even as he dawdled. "Fine!" I cried. "Drink from the hoofprints, Father, drink your fill, if you will just be quiet and do as you're told!"

Happily, my father Femi set to scooping the coppery water from the deep pig-prints. "Perhaps, when we catch them, the Stars will give me a new stove, with smooth bricks which do not leave marks on my back," he chortled. I crossed my arms over my chest and waited for him to finish.

As I watched him gulp down the rainwater, mud trickled down his chin, and before it could drip back again onto the churned earth, my father Femi's chin was considerably hairier and broader than it had been before. The filthy water frothed suddenly between two yellow tusks, his thick hair twisted into a forelock, his eyes grown tiny and beady. Before my eyes my father twisted and grew until he was a great, huge, lumbering boar, and though I didn't mean to, I laughed at him squealing in the forest, still thirsty even after all his slurping.

THE
MANTICORE'S TALE,
CONTINUED

"AND HERE HE IS, THE OLD BEAST, WITH NO
stove at all anymore!" laughed the pig-tamer; and gave
her boar a little slap on the rump. He moaned, and
through his snorting he seemed to say:

"Why must you pester me so, Mesinyane?"

The blue-haired woman grinned at us. "We lost their
trail—I have an idea where they were going, but a Star
lost stays lost. I decided to make the best of it, and
worked out this little act, which keeps me out of huts
with stoves and in thick shoes. But I had to dress him up
in ribbons and hats—folk don't believe it's a tamed

beast if it doesn't have the right costume. All tamed things are made a bit ridiculous in the process, you know."

Immacolata was ashen, twisting her red ribbons with a shaking hand. "It was Zmeya, wasn't it? She's dead, somehow, she's dead!"

"That's the story we tell—and you'll find that story told quite a bit in the Vstreycha. After she ate up her wicked husband Indrajit, the king-dom fell into the hands of the harem, who knew best what goes on in the palace, and through a complicated chain of ears, what goes on everywhere. The old perfumed queens run things in the city of pigs these days. They make sure the tale spreads far and wide, of what wronged wives may wreak. It was bad there for a while though," she mused, "while they made their way to the throne. There was a terrible spate of poisonings. Some of us here do poison from time to time, if work is hard. I've heard such things from them—they love to see Father Femi and his pretty bows. Maybe one day we'll trudge back to the jun-gle and let Mother see what became of you, eh?" She prodded the great pig and he moaned again.

"Where do you think they were going?" whispered Immacolata.

Mesinyane shrugged. "Fools are a keen old pack of crows. There is a fool for every scrap of knowledge in the world, I'd bet, and they talk to each other. I think they went to the Isle of the Dead; I think he went to bury her, to do as much as one Star does for another in the way of fu-neral rites."

I thought I saw tears in the odalisque's dark eyes, but I could not imagine why. She had known the woman for a moment, and so what if she was a Star? The Sun was my father, and he never slept on a stove.

"Can I offer you supper?" said the gold-eyed pygmy cheerfully. "I have a nice rasher of bacon back in my tent." She grinned, and her teeth were small, small and sharp.

Once Mesinyane had filled us with bacon and rhyming songs about the laziness of pigs and men, we wandered alone through the Vstreycha. Taglio and Immacolata learned many new tricks with their cards and silks, and they purchased a ramshackle cart with a particularly moving rendition of "The Rape of Amberabad," which we shall perform for you, if you like. It was a favorite of Hind's and of mine, especially the part when the red ship sails up the harbor—which we made with fluttering blue gauze—and the three-breasted captain cuts the palace into amber coins for her hold. They bought this broken cart and Taglio painted it blue to match my eyes, and Immacolata fixed its silver stars in their firmament. Finally, we found an amber-seller in a tall black hat with a long golden feather flopping on its side, and Hind asked eagerly for news of home, of her frog-spitting sister, of her father with his silly lessons. I told her she should not care, but she only smiled sheepishly and pressed the bearded fellow for gossip.

I told her to let it lie, I told her, but she could not. Do I go whining back to the desert when an Upas dries up her sap and lies down by the water? No, I do not. But she could not let those who did not love her nearly so well as I lie still behind her as they ought. And so she heard from this man in his ridiculous hat that her father had died, and the Bell of Amberabad chimed in mourning, day and night.

Hind twisted her black beads. She looked at me, stricken, and buried her head in my mane. I pressed my broken jaw to her face, and her tears were hot as Upas milk.

"It is all right, my girl," I whispered into her hair. "They are gone now and you are free of them. I will sing for you at any window you indicate with the smallest of your fingers, and we will be happy. There are many ways of being happy. We will find ours."

Hind looked up at me miserably, scarlet strands of my hair clinging to her face. "No, Grotteschi. I must go home. I will not be forever the wicked sister. I must do as much as any woman does for her father, for her sister."

I crouched down in the small mound of pearls that had spilled out over her toes, my paws dark against them, and made my voice soft as fingers stroking old drumskins. "I will never go back to that place. My jaw aches when I think of it—I will never touch amber again with these paws." Hind wept silently. I could not look at her. "Are you leaving me?" I growled.

She flung her arms around me, and her beads were hard on my cheeks. "Find me in Ajanabh," she whispered, pearls streaming over my shoulders like tears. "I will go there, when all things which should be in the ground are buried. I will go there, and you will find me, and sing at my window, and I will come out to you."

When the first silver streaks of dawn began to stream across the valley, she was gone, and so was the Vstreycha. A few tent spikes remained, a few pearls rolling loose and dirty. Taglio might have consoled me, and

I went padding about the wreckage of the makeshift camp to find him, to find his boot-black hooves and his smiling face, which was dear to me, if not quite so dear as a wicked sister and her loud laughter.

Immacolata and her Gaselli were down in the depths of the vale, by a freezing stream which gurgled blue and frothy through the tall weeds.

"I am going," said the odalisque quietly. I don't think I ever heard her raise her voice, in all the time we walked paw by foot. She was calm as tea in a cup.

"She knows you care for her; you do not need to do more," said the eunuch, his head low.

"I will repay her gift to us. I have heard the story from three fools and a tragedian of her death, of how she killed the King, and how her brother carried her body off from the palace. Where did he take her? What can she have in that cold, dark place where Stars go? I will not let her languish—she did not let me!" Finally Immacolata's voice did break, and she struck her fists against the chest of her ersatz lover. "What did you give to the Star?" she wept. "I will give her no more than a little leaf. What did you give? What did you give?" She ripped her scarlet ribbons from her braid, long strands of hair coming with them, her tears terrible, like water boiling to a white scrim on the bottom of an old pot. "I am not like you! I don't care about religion. She saved me, she saved me when you only watched and guarded the door. She said we were sisters! How can I let her go into the dark alone? I cannot abide a sister's suffering!"

"I am sure she has enough of wild followers and grief-stricken siblings."

"She saw the leaf in me. She knew this day would come. Drink my tea and you will know what I dream of. Wear my shoes and you will know what I dream of. I dream of my sister, alone, weeping!"

He held her then, stroked her torn hair. I could not hear what he said against her skin, but I saw the sharp gleam of blood again, and I saw him dry her tears. She stood back from him, an old, familiar smile on her face.

"I have one last thing for you, who has as much of my blood in him as his own."

"I do not want anything else. I only want you to stay."

She tried to laugh, but it came out poorly, a broken cello string. "Please, my love, don't. She needs me." The odalisque shook her hair back. "I am made of tea, remember? It will be as though I simply steep, in endless water. And because of that, I can do a thing which would amaze anyone in the Vstreycha. Come close, my dear gazelle, and jump through my ear."

"What? Don't be ridiculous!" Taglio recoiled. She only laughed.

"I am only tea—can you not leap through a tea bush? So you may leap through me and come out the other side." She went to him, put her  hands on his face, kissed his eyelids. "Taglio, dearest shepherd, dearest sheep, in this way you may enter me, and it will be as though we neither of us have lost anything in our lives."

He pressed his head into her, and I could hear his sobs, the sound of them like planks of wood splintering under a bronze ax. But he drew back, and to my never-ceasing surprise, took a running start, and leapt into the ear of Immacolata.

The Tale
of the
Twelve Coins,
Continued

"HE CAME OUT OF HER CLOTHED ALL IN GREEN, as he was before the harem, as the Gaselli always were. His buckles shone brilliant, his cap was soft as a mule's nose. But he looks at the green now and sees no pretty dell and unguarded campfire. He sees her leaves. Mourning clothes, he calls them, the green of young tea plants. He has never taken off the clothes of her body, and in this way, I think, he dwells within her always.

"They waded into the stream together, then, hand in hand; waist-deep in the rushing, icy water, Immacolata turned to her eunuch and smiled, tears spilling down her cheeks like cream onto a rich table. She reached up, behind his ear, and with a little flourish, produced a shimmering silver leaf out of the air.

" 'You must find the Isle of the Dead, and take this seed of me to her. I know you will do this for me; I know it as well as I know the lines of my palm and the hairs of my head. Go into the world, and take me out of it. This is my heart—carry it with you. I will dream of you in the dark, and you will taste it in my tea, and feel it in my shoes.'

"With that, Immacolata dissolved slowly into the water, like sugar. She drifted apart, each brown leaf wafting slowly onto the stream. The current held her for a moment, a great circle of leaves with green-clad Taglio in the center, and then carried them off and away."

Oubliette and I gawked at the Manticore, our mouths hanging open as though we had gone simple. And as we sat curled in her tail, the great red beast closed her sparkling eyes and began to sing, low and soft, like a wooden flute and a diamond trumpet playing together. She did not lie about her songs—we wept openly under the strokes of her voice, the lost, sorrow-bound notes moving against us like hands, telling us how beautiful Immacolata was as she drifted downstream, and how it pierced Grotteschi to hear Taglio keen and scream as he did on that lonely bank.

Finally, she closed her misshapen jaw, and we came slowly to ourselves. "We had both been abandoned by our best-loved beasts. It seemed right to carry out their wishes together, and we went first after the Isle of the Dead."

"Did you find it?" I said, breathless.

"No," she said shortly. "And it is my turn now. We are going to Ajanabh and I will sing for my girl at every window until she comes to one, her black beads tumbling out, and calls me up to her."

The great beast glared defiantly at us, setting her jaw as best she could, daring us to mock her. We nestled in quickly against her, and there were no more stories that night. After a time, all of us slept, even her, her scarlet fur buffeted by snores.

I woke in that awful cold that seeps in sometime between midnight and dawn, as if the sky had frozen, and its black edges crept into your clothes through every seam. Even in the cart with its warm curtains I shivered, and turned to Oubliette for warmth as we always had—but she was gone, an empty space in the coil of Grotteschi's tail where she had been. My stomach seized—in all those years I had never woken to an empty bed, she had never been anything but there and heavy and warm in the night. *Don't leave me, don't leave me,* went the refrain of our life together.

Carefully I moved the coils of the Manticore's tail from my legs, gingerly lifting the beetle green shell of its scorpion tip from the door frame, and crept outside, into a cold that stung my face like birch branches. Taglio rested next to the long blue bars of the cart, his green clothes clung with dew, ice stuck to the bottom of his boot-black hooves. Oubliette lay asleep, curled against him like a cat, her face clouded with dreams but not frightened—I do know the look of fear on her face, I know it so well. I wanted to go to her and sleep against her as I used to, to tuck my head into her shoulder and breathe together, to hold her between me and the dark. But perhaps she was not entirely mine any longer, perhaps she had not snuck out of the cart on a whim, and I should not disturb her.

I crawled under the cart handles and drew myself up next to Oubliette anyway, her familiar body, her familiar smell. Taglio stirred, and extended his long, slender arm over both of us.

"I couldn't find it," he sighed. "That's what you want to know, isn't it? How I could stop looking, how I could let her go. I tried so hard, but the paths that go to the Isle are hidden and dark and I could not find them. I am a shepherd, I know only well-tilled fields and plots of earth where folk have lived back and back and back to their greatest grandparents. I couldn't find it, and Grotteschi deserves her chance, too. Someday I will start the search again. Perhaps in Ajanabh, there is a mapmaker who knows the way, or a poet who has heard of how it is done."

Gently, so as not to wake Oubliette, he pulled a small box from his jerkin, an intricate box of tea wood, with a sweet green shoe carved on its lid and inlaid with beryl. He opened it, and there inside lay a silver leaf, glimmering dark and pale.

"But I keep her with me, always and always," he said, and closed the lid again.

And so we traveled together, ever wending toward Ajanabh, which proved to be farther than I could have imagined the ghost city could carry us. I had never dreamed the world so wide. We walked, we rode, we performed to keep bread in our bellies, lacking anyone capable of spitting out pearls for our daily use, and Taglio caught the occasional gamey rabbit. Oubliette went with him to hunt, and she became a wild thing, rarely speaking, growing lean and tall, her movements sudden and sharp.

In our little show, she danced.

There was a red curtain in the cart, and when there were more than a few villagers with pennies clutched in their turnip-pulling hands, we strung it up high, and pulled Grotteschi's tail through it, slung with a thin green sock to hide the barb. She shuddered when we pulled the cloth over her, every time, but she did not protest—it was our best act. We had others: Grotteschi often sang, and as she sang she turned her face to the sky and wept, and this never failed to fill our baskets with food and money, for the Manticore's song seemed to grip folk by the wrist and empty their pockets by force. Taglio danced—but he often frightened folk, who knew how the dances of the Gaselli usually ended. More often, he tied a ribbon to his Manticore, and terrified them with his tamed monster. More often than not, Grotteschi devoured the ribbon in disgust afterward, and we were always short of them. But Oubliette's dance was the best thing we knew how to do.

With her sock in place Grotteschi's tail was a very convincing snake, and she and Oubliette performed a strange and sinuous dance while Taglio played his pipes or his fiddle of almond wood. As the years went on and the road grew little shorter, I learned to play his fiddle, and we accompanied the beast-dance together. It was always an alien, affecting thing, when Oubliette danced. Though she wore a long dress, some villages called it obscene—but it was only that she danced so desperately, faster and faster each time, and never twice the same. She danced as though she could dance her way out of the sod tower, and the golden ball, and the ghost city, and the hedgehog's love.

What she danced, while Grotteschi writhed her tail in undulating patterns, flicking it and swelling it and coiling it in lazy circles, was a story we learned in the Vstreycha, a story we never found unknown in any hamlet or within any burgher's wall, of a woman who was also a snake, who was also a Star, and how her husband betrayed her, and how she took her revenge. By the final notes, Oubliette would be concealed behind the curtain, and only the great green tail remained.

My friend grew obsessed with this story, with her dance. She hardly spoke to anyone anymore, though at night she still could not sleep alone, and clung to Taglio or me or even the furry flank of the red lion.

Once, when she was strapping knives to her calves in order to hunt deer, I tried to kiss her—just once, just to see if I could. She recoiled and looked at me with bruised black eyes.

"Why?" she said, her voice long and deep now, a grown woman, finally. "Why would you do that?"

"I don't know," I said, and it was true.

She brought back a fawn that night. Its spots were white and eerie in the moonlight. In the morning, she was gone, and Taglio's little box was empty.

The Tale
of the
Crossing,
Continued

"I FOLLOWED HER. I HAVE ALWAYS FOLLOWED her. She is there, on that island, I know she is, and I am going to save her. We save each other; it's what we have always done. I was made to save her; she was made to save me."

Idyll frowned into the sky, black and boiling with the oncoming storm. "How did you spend the last three coins?"

"Why do you care? Isn't it enough that you have one of them?"

"Call it an interest in numismatics." The old man chuckled.

Seven covered his eyes with his rough, knuckle-split hand. He forced back tears, though his throat threatened to strangle his words. He could not make his voice steady; it was ragged and broken, the sound swallowed up by the great glassy lake and the rumbling sky. "I spent them to get here! I spent them to find her! I spent them to get farmers and astrologers and idle princes and dairywomen to tell me where she had gone, mapmakers and poets and river pilots and necromancers to tell me how to follow after her. I spent them to get her back—what else are they good for? What else could they buy? I spent them to buy her back, I spent them to cross the lake, I spent them and they're gone and all I have is an empty sleeve." He broke into fog-softened sobs and the old ferryman might have comforted him, indeed leaned forward to do so, had not a thin, reedy wind blown by, a wind like the last gasp of a man frozen to death on a barren snowfield. The wind blew aside Idyll's shabby brown cloak, and Seven saw what was beneath it—he meant to scream, or cry out, but all that his lungs could manage was a groan and a slack jaw.

Idyll's skin ended at the base of his throat. The rest of him was all bones, great, long, yellow bones, and his skeleton was more than a man's, for the thin fringe-frames of huge wings arched up from his spine, the substance of his senescent hunch. He had fleshy hands, and feet, wrinkled skin sagging and dry, but beneath the cloth he was as naked as it is possible for a man to be, and through the gaps in his bones, Seven could see the choppy silver waters of the lake.

Through those same spaces ran two black lizards, chasing each other up and down his barrel–rib cage like squirrels around an oak tree. They chattered and hissed as they passed, flicking their tongues at his clavicle, his pelvis. Their eyes were white, like the eyes of blind men, and once in a while, one would pause briefly, as though he had found a walnut, and gnaw on one of the ferryman's vertebra.

Idyll looked chagrined. He pulled his robe back over the racing lizards. "It's not so bad, really. I've gotten used to them. But I suppose that they require an explanation as surely as a bone coin..."

THE
FERRYMAN'S TALE

THERE ARE SOME WHO SAY THE MOON IS DEAD, that only the dead trace their lineage there. They are wrong, and if you would believe the scripture of such creatures, you would surely believe anything.

The Moon is ever fertile. She cannot turn to look at herself in the ocean's mirror but that a peony with crystal edges blooms from her navel. When she speaks, oysters fall from her mouth, oysters and tadpoles with wiggling tails. In the dark of the world before there were eyes to open and call it black, she was whole, and perfect, and did not change her shape through the month.

But in the dark as in anything else, there were drifting winds and currents, and these blew gently against the ribs and shoulders of Moon, causing her to slowly spin in the sky, her arms outstretched as a child will do when she floats upon a clear and blue-green inland sea, letting the little kissing waves push against her body.

When the Stars left the sky—folk do not lie on that score, at least—their going left sucking holes in the dark, and winds issued from them as from a burst balloon. Poor Moon was battered on all sides by these whistling winds, and she began to spin faster and faster. As she spun in the sky like a dervish, the winds were so fierce that they began to peel off slivers of her flesh, pale and translucent and shimmering. These slivers drifted dreaming to earth, feather-slow and fragile as petals.

Finally, Moon had nothing left for the empty sky to peel away. The little black core of her rested at last in a lightless hollow, no bigger or brighter than a speck of soot. But as all things will do when they are allowed some respite, Moon began to grow again, for she cannot help her fecundity. She turned this way and that, and peonies bloomed from her navel, chrysanthemums exploded from her palms. Oysters and tadpoles fell out of her mouth. Pine boughs snaked around her waist. In her hair saplings writhed and danced in blind ecstasy. It was not long before Moon was full and vast again, as she had been. But the Star-sparse sky had become like a river flowing between a few sharp rocks, the currents more fierce than they had ever been, and no sooner was she round and bright but they began to peel off her flesh again.

And so the Moon waxes and wanes, from a swell of light to a speck of soot. Poor, lost little Moon, who gets only the briefest moments of respite. We are sorry for her, we feathers, we petals, we sloughed-off children. Moon skins the Hsien are, cast away like plum skins. We are the drifting shells the black winds blow from her, silver-dim as the shadow cast by a foxglove at moonrise, clear and hard as frozen glass.

Once we waged a holy war against the rotting heretics who cling to a false Moon, but they do not mourn for their dead as we do. Attrition is a terrible thing when you must bear it alone. Long ago we gave in—if they wish to amuse themselves with morbid fairy tales, we will not spoil their games. We persevere, knowing the truth, even in the face of their perversion.

I am sure that I have given the impression of maleness to you— it seems to suit the work. But we are not male, and neither female. The petals of the Moon have no sex, no children, no marriage. More of us drop each month from her flesh, and if they survive, like turtles sent across the sand into the welcoming sea, then we are replenished. We are not equipped for children; we are tiny moons, and moons do not couple, do not increase the number of aggregate moons. Neither do we eat the five cereals as men do, but suckle wind and drink dew. We age slowly as stones, and it is difficult for us to die, though it does happen, as it is possible to smash a quartz-riddled rock.

Thus it is that I am old enough to be able to tell you that I raised the Rose Dome of Shadukiam over the diamond turrets of the city in the days before it withered into Marrow. I was an architect then, and I was sought out by the city fathers to cap their walls with flowers, flowers which would not fade, nor wilt, nor fall. It was thought by some that a walking sliver of the Moon would know something about permanence. I was promised a wine vat filled with opals and silver as payment—they were always decadent, nothing has truly changed.

In those days Shadukiam was a spiky forest of scaffolding. They were still cutting slabs of earth away to plant buildings like saplings in the wet black soil—how the city of metal and merchants began obsessed with growing things! The diamond turrets were only lately erected, their facets still tapped and chiseled by workmen with no fear of heights. The roads were tamped with feet, not rolling stones of gold and silver. The Asaad was canopied in wool. How we match, you and I! I remember the city before it was Marrow; you remember it after. This is history before history, boy, and I was there.

*   *   *

I instructed some few of my siblings to make their nests on the sparkling turrets or the platforms below them and await me, while I flew into the world to seek out an imperishable rose.

In the Garden

THE GIRL HAD WATCHED THE BOY DISAPPEAR INTO THE PALACE LIKE a bee buzzing into the mouth of an alligator. She had followed as close as she might, wanting to extend—just a little longer!—the time in which she was not alone, not cold, not silent. While he went into that shadowy, many-towered place, that place she would never go, the girl paced out the square that was to hold Dinarzad and her husband with her little feet. The scaffolding was half up, the chestnuts bent forward and around, their bare stick-limbs thatched and wired with gold to make a canopy thick enough to shield Dinarzad's veiled head from the eye of heaven. The girl wondered what the eye of heaven might see through so many branches and layers of silk. The sun was not quite up, but she and the boy had either become much better at their little game, or Dinarzad had become much less vigilant. Her friend was safe in his warm bed, she was sure, piled with fox fur and wool. Perhaps the dew wet his hair at the brow, perhaps not.

The peacocks wandered around the Garden, their green-violet tails dragging in the flower beds, their blue heads popping up behind clusters of late-fruiting berries. The girl and the peacocks had always been wary of each other—they did not know how to sing, and she did not know how to affect an ostentatious display. Peacocks are not entirely wild, and she was not entirely tame. But on this day of all days, she made peace, and tightened her throat enough to make a squeaking peahen's cry. A cobalt bird ventured out from its briar, and after nipping her fingers once or twice nestled its head in her hands. She longed for the lake, but she longed more for her birds, her geese, the untamed ones that dipped into the Garden for flowers and glittering insects and then went on when the winter came. The long emerald feathers brushed her cheeks as the creature gesticulated, and she laughed, low and piping, an owl's evening cry.

"Is there anything that does not do as you say?" came a voice behind her.

The boy emerged from the chestnut chapel, and the peacock started, hissed in his direction, and huffed off, its tail held in high indignation.

"Many things. Gardeners, sisters, Sultans."

"Well, you have yet to learn their mating cries. I'm sure you'll get it eventually."

The girl grinned sidelong. "You should be in bed. You will get us in trouble again."

"There is another banquet today, for my sister's new family, her suitor's mother and father and thirty-seven brothers and sisters, if you can believe it. I haven't even tried to count the cousins." He gave a short, sharp laugh, like a bow twanging. "They killed a giraffe! I had never even seen one, but they brought the spotted thing in through the back gate, so that they can all feast on the neck. Do you think a neck will taste good? I'll try to bring you some, if you like. But truly, no one will care if I've run off again—they're used to it by now, and she can hardly throw a fit in front of her new relations. They'll be dancing and eating until their feet or their tongues wear through—one or the other."

The girl began her pacing again, wiping her peacock-warm hands on her skirt.

"Would you tell me a tale in the daytime?" the boy said shyly. "Does it not seem strange even to ask, to talk by first light instead of last?"

"Is there anything that does not do as you say?" the girl asked archly. He blushed.

"You know my cry. I do not know yours," he mumbled, not meeting her gaze.

A thin kind of sunlight, not so very different from moonlight, seeped through the clouds as through a cheesecloth, tipped the trees in wet light, and slanted down the edge of the girl's long, straight nose. Her hands were cold with morning, the Garden paths damp and shivering. She drew him away from the newborn shadows cast by the chestnut chapel, and into a thorny, bloomless bramble, not unlike the first one they had shared, save that this was bare and brown, the thorns overhead dripping dew. The boy settled himself with sure habit, and reached for her hands to warm them as he would have with one of his younger siblings. She let him rub the skin of her fingers until they tingled red and hot, and began again.

" 'It seemed obvious to me that you could not raise a rose that did not know deep in its stem and roots how to wilt and die,' the ferryman said. 'But, I reasoned, you might freeze one in its blooming...' "

The Ferryman's Tale, Continued

THERE ARE MOUNTAIN PEAKS WHICH NO POOR, earthbound creature can see. Clouds hang from them like prayer flags, veil them and shroud them, and we would not see them either, if the sky were not for us a road, and if we could not see that the road keeps going past what you would call the summit, peak, tip. To these hidden places I flew, extending moon-blown wings as far as I might. Their tips frosted, their shadows on the snow were fitful and pale. From my chest hung a long leather strap, which held a sackful of what would pass as money on the ceiling of the world. I was so close to the sky I could smell its sweat, and if the Moon, our poor,

besieged mother, had not been resting in her coal-
dark core, I would have—would I?—been able to
touch her as she spun.

In time, I came to a peak beyond which the road
does not extend. I do not say that there is no
higher crag, but it is the summit of the
Hsien, as those rocks far below were the
summit of men. Perhaps some other thing
laughs at my peak, calling it but a valley, a
respite from heights. I do not know; it is not
my place to know. I flew as high as I was able,
and my wings burned with the effort. I walked in the
snow shoals ringed by sharp stones, ringed by crags like
the prongs of a crown. The peak of a mountain takes
many shapes, and this one was as a circle of land with granite
teeth all along the edge, cut with many frozen rivers and ponds,
which had once flowed with water when the mountain-table was lower,
in the history before history before history.

Along these old, hard rivers were tiny houses all of glass, or ice, or
both—I suspected that they had once been made of glass, and broken in
the harsh winds of the country, but froze again so quickly
that no one noticed the shattering. Perhaps this had
happened so many times that there was nothing left of them but shatter, held together by
surprised gasps of ice. To these houses I
shuffled in snowshoes made of wicker and
my own feathers. When I reached the center of the town, I sat myself down in the
snow and waited, my wings twitching in
the drifts, drawing quick, lively patterns in
the white. I was prepared to wait a good
while, but hardly a week had passed
before the shattered door of one of
the houses cracked open and a
small, green thing shambled out to
me.

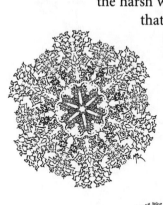

I had come to the kingdom of the
Kappas, and one of those reluctant, recalcitrant creatures was even then shifting un-

comfortably from foot to foot before me. She was very much like an upright turtle, though even upright she no more than passed my knees. Her shell was green as a girl's eyes, her limbs mottled as moss, leathery and lithe. Her hands and feet, between which there was little enough difference, were large and webbed, like a duck's, but her wrists and ankles were thick, knotted with muscle. She had a few thick yellow teeth in her face, which contorted into something of a beak under a fringe of brown hair cut like a monk's tonsure. It fell flat and frosty across her forehead, and bald in the center, where the turtle-girl had no skin, but a deep hollow in her skull, which was filled with still blue water—save that considering the snow and wind, it had frozen solid and now shimmered silver and safe in the bones of its owner.

"I am Yoi-who-was-born-in-the-evening," she said, her gravelly voice like feet scraping the bottom of a lake.

"And I am Idyll, who was born, well, at night, I suppose. I have come to beg a treasure from you, but I have not come without barter." I opened my sack at last, the heavy old thing, and drew out a handful of green fruits, long and glossy. Yoi sniffed at them and her black eyes widened.

"Cucumber," she whispered.

"You are very wise, Yoi-who-was-born-in-the-evening. I have culled cucumbers for you from the world over, slicers and picklers, yellow and green and white as a ghost's nightclothes, sandwich quality and rough, hardy breeds good enough to be boiled in stew. Gherkins the size of your thumb and rare hybrids, tiny as peas. There is even a southern varietal whose blossoms are red as a heart, and the meat of the fruit blushes orange."

The Kappa's mouth watered, though her saliva froze at the corners of her lips.

"And what is it you wish to trade for?" she asked.

"A rose which will live forever, and never fade or wilt or drop petal."

"Does it seem to you, Idyll-who-supposes-he-was-born-at-night, that roses bloom in this place?"

"Are not the Kappa great tenders of plants? Are your reputations undeserved? Surely in your shattered houses there are many wonders, or the world is much deceived."

The little turtle sighed. "It is possible that we still possess what you desire, the rose-which-was-born-in-a-lizard. But in these times of still and cold it is rarely our habit to part with our hard-won graftings. Even cucumbers—precious, delicious cucumbers—do not grow so well here. But such is the choice we made..."

The Tale

of the

Lizard's Lesson

I WAS NO ONE'S BELOVED DAUGHTER. I UNDER-
stand that in tales told off the mountain, in stories told
around hearths like burning hearts, it is always a King's
son or a merchant's best-taught boy who is spirited
away to some black kingdom or ventures forth to find a
wife or a slab of gold. But I was nobody in particular: I
was born in the evening. The water was violet and so
was the sky, and I hatched in a nest of unripe berries
and brambles, and ran toward the water with all my
brothers and sisters, praying that no kestrel or osprey or
alligator would snatch us out of life just as we came into
it. Many of them never felt water on their webbing.

We wallow in our pools and rivers, we Kappa. We are drawn to the water, to the deep of it and the loam. The water in our skulls calls to the waters of the world. We love our pools, their catching of star-which-is-born-in-the-water and cloud-which-is-born-in-the-reeds in the perfect mirrors of their surfaces. And should a terrible, naughty, wicked thing who was born in a house stumble into that perfect water, and splash about and churn up mud, we certainly ought never to be blamed for biting them soundly.

The pool of my birth was a little pond, greenish brown, with a few reeds sprouting like hair on its banks, and three matronly lilies which grew close together, drawing their yellowed petals around them like woolen shawls. She was not a grand pool, or a tempestuous river, splashing her way through a century of rock, just a circle of water in the dark of a wood, neither deep nor wide. But she was mine, and no kestrel had snapped me up before I sank into her evening mire with gratitude, and I loved her. I scrabbled in her shallows to keep her free of weeds. If a farmer came to draw her waters into his bucket, I gnashed my teeth at him and narrowed my black eyes to slits. If a miller's daughter came to bathe in the deeps, I pulled her hair with my thin fingers and bit her where her spine joins her hips, and soon enough she shrieked her way home.

This is how we lived, connected, each in our pool, connected each by each, born-in-the-evening to born-in-the-morning, by rivulets of rain trickling from pond to creek to river. And we kept our water still and balanced in our skulls, for we do not like to lose it—for days after, until we are full again, we swoon and dream and are blind, while the water swells up again. Soon enough all manner of beastly things managed with their dry brains to discover this, and they made endless sport of bowing to us. We are polite, ever polite—manners are our provincial pastime and native dialect! We may bite them when they trample our homes, but how can we then refuse a bow? We are compelled to bow in return, and then I suppose it is very funny for them to watch us stumble and fall about like drunk turtles.

I taught my three lilies to give fruit. We are very good at instructing the world to bend and bow to us—it learns *such* things from us, things it would never have thought to try on its own. I brought peach plants as exempla for my lilies, and by patient tutorial coaxed sweet, small berries from them, though they were reluctant, as all old women are, to try new things. The lily-berries-who-were-born-at-noon tasted of paper and crystallized honey and dust. Because of the lesson I taught the lilies I was allowed to follow the trickling streams from pond to pond and join the grafters and seed-splicers of the Greater Kappa, who spent their days in contemplation of the infinite lessons we had yet to give, and in charting those we had already completed in illuminated catalogues. The vaulted ceilings of the Greater Kappa were whorled with leaves and vines, and if, whilst sketching a theoretical pumpkin tree and its symbiotic attendant in the margins of a treatise on the unassuming apple—always keeping one's posture pleasantly straight and one's water in one's head—a turtle was hungry, she had only to reach up and pluck a sweet, wet cucumber from the window frame and her belly would be satisfied.

With a basket of lily berries I entered those green vaults, nervous as a child on her first day of school. I was given a desk below a window of cucumber flowers so sheer I could see through to the valley outside, all a-blossom with hypotheses.

When I had been there for three years and produced only a few modest successes: the blue lime-blossom, the oolong-melon, and the lemon-macaque, I was sent into the field with Yazo-who-was-born-at-the-bottom-of-winter. We were to return in a year to teach our own variant on the humble, workaday rose. She was a year ahead of me, but considered a tragic mistake. Her first lesson, the pomegranate-ant, had seemed to promise so much, yet she had done nothing but catalogue since she arrived. Therefore she was punished by being partnered with an untried turtle, and I was cautiously prodded to work harder by being yoked to the puzzling genius who refused to work. We were decades from our greatest collaborations: the Upas-which-was-born-by-the-water, the Ixora-which-was-born-burning, and but a year, give or take, from the rose-which-was-born-in-a-lizard.

Yazo was pretty, her face an unusual yellowish green, her tonsure glossy and black—but her hair was messy, her eyes always tired.

There were little holes in the webbing between her fingers, small as needle pricks, but I saw them. As we walked out from the seeded doors of the Greater Kappa, I shouldered her pack as well as my own, so as to save her the effort. We are polite, ever polite, as I have said.

"Yoi-who-was-born-in-the-evening," she said, after we had been walking in the fields for a time, following the curve of the river which flowed through the central room of the Greater Kappa and out again into the world, "do you suppose that when our water spills out, and afterwards fills up again like a basin emptied in the morning and filled at night, we are the same Kappa, the same dear turtle that we were before?"

"I do not know, Yazo-who-was-born-at-the-bottom-of-winter," I stammered. "I have never considered it."

"I have spilled out my water once a month since I entered the cucumber vaults," she said softly, dreamily, looking out over the warm water and drifting milkweed-mayflies.

"What?" I cried, aghast. "Why would you do such a thing to yourself? It's terrible, obscene!"

"Perhaps I am teaching myself a lesson," was her only answer, and we walked in a stubborn silence which would not give us up. I looked again at the holes in her webbing and her frazzled hair, her peculiar skin. I saw why the other Kappa did not like Yazo—she was ragged and strange and possibly mad. But still, I did as she said.

And what she said was that we were bound for the Kingdom of Glass Rain, a far-off prairie land whose folk had discovered a novel way of ferreting out the answers to things. In need of answers, we turned our shells to the grasslands, and I thanked the Stars each night that the journey was not so long as a month, so that I would not have to witness Yazo's scarification.

The Kingdom of Glass Rain was indeed full of wild grasses, which blew over the flats like waves rolling in with high tide. They were green and gold and their stalks were silvery gray, and the waves were very beautiful. All ringing the dell were red rocks and squat, flat-topped hillocks, streaked in pale swathes of yellow stone. It was cold; the sky was high and brittle, and the long roofs of the capital, tiled like, well, like a turtle's shell, glinted clear and sharp in the distance.

We were received, in a manner of speaking, at the gate of the local academy, which was a thick, dusty cedar door carved in a complicated pattern of interlocking lizards. I say "in a manner of speaking" because we were not at first sure that anyone at all was there, just inside the shadowy threshold, which smelled of hay and eggs and old cedar, polished by a hundred hands.

"Please," a voice said, small and gentle, like a shivering cat pawing at the kitchen window. "Who is this who wishes to enter the breeding house?"

But there was no one standing where the voice seemed to be born. Only the beginning of a long hall filled with hushed voices and the sounds of clacking claws on glass.

"I am Yoi-who-was-born-in-the-evening, and this is Yazo-who-was-born-at-the-bottom-of-winter, of the Greater Kappa, who have come to ask answers of you." I aimed my speech where I thought it should go, but the voice sounded again, farther off to my right.

"I am sorry, I know you cannot see me, and that it is disconcerting. My name is Ostraya, and I am the Princess of Glass, and I keep this house. If you have questions, I am she who will breed the lizard who will have your answer."

We were somewhat nonplussed by this, as you might imagine. "But where are you? Why can we hear you and yet see nothing?"

The voice laughed a little, as if at a very old and no longer particularly funny joke. I felt a weight fall on my hand, cool and hard—a hand of glass.

"The Glass Rain took me..."

The Tale

of the

Glass Princess

IN THIS COUNTRY, WHEN WE SPEAK OF THE GLASS
Rain, we do not wax poetic. It is not a quaint local figure
of speech. We speak of the spring, new and green and
grass-scented, which brings clouds so white and pure
that they have no scent at all. The clouds crawl in
and let loose their bows—and the Glass Rain comes
upon us.

The drops are slivers of glass, a broken mirror falling
from the sky. They pile on the grass, cutting it low, like
terrible, hard snowflakes. They scream as they fall. They
slash the air and catch the cloudlight, they flash and
flare. For weeks after, the roads crunch and chatter

beneath our feet. When the clouds come, mothers hurry their children indoors, bankers seal themselves up in vaults, cobblers barricade themselves behind row after row of iron-toed shoes. All crouch and listen as the rain clatters and shatters and shivers to pieces on the tile roofs, and falls off the eaves in a rainbow of reflected storm colors.

I was caught outside.

My mother is the Queen of Glass, and I can hardly begin to tell of her beauty. Even as a child, there were times when I could not speak for awe of her, her silver hair and silver eyes, her lashes like spun sugar, her lips so red that apples envied her. She was the breeding mistress then as I am now, and her fingers were ever bandaged, for lizards are tempestuous, willful creatures.

In this country, lizards are not plentiful. We brought them when we were nomads, so many generations ago we have given up trying to remember what land was first our home. But bring them we did, and bred them in warm burrows where they cooed and hissed happily over clutch after clutch of eggs. Who first noticed the markings on their backs? Who can say? A woman, a man, a child? A King, a Queen, a pauper, a knave? There is a book on a golden podium in my mother's hall which says, with many pictures in costly scarlet ink, that a cook with wooden shoes once sought a novel way to cook cabbage. One evening he produced the most amazing dish for the royal banquet, towers and turrets of shaped cabbage, stuffed with raisins and goat meat, with cabbage trellises draping over cabbage rivers steamed in black wine. When the cook was asked how this extraordinary display came about, he produced his pet lizard, which had, in the markings on its back, a complex and magnificent recipe carefully filigreed in scale and spine. From that day forward, lizards were culled and read, and though not all of them had recipes written upon their backs, many had stories, and equations, and formulae, and prophetic utterances, and laws we had never heard of. The recording of the lizards' markings became the obsession of a generation.

And then it was discovered that if one bred the lizards, new and marvelous markings resulted. If the lizard which showed the method for creating a beautiful copper spoon were bred to one which showed a new technique for mining tin, eggs would hatch with fat babies carrying the instructions for beating out a bronze sword, or schematics for a water drill, or an epic poem dealing with two statues on opposite ends of a square who fell in hopeless love, one of copper and one of tin. Thus was born the Lizard-Calculus of the Glass Country.

This is what the book on the golden podium in my mother's hall says. I do not know, but it makes a very pretty story, and I was encouraged to eat cabbage each day as a child.

However it began, this is now the pastime of our aristocratic classes, the breeding of lizards, one to the other, and certainly most extraordinary things have resulted. I am not surprised you come to us for answers—what answers have we not given, when asked? Why, we have learned that it is even possible to distill food from rocks and jewels! We have bred the very algebra of government on the back of an iguana! Yet though we have bred lizards with rain hymns to those with a map of the glass molecule sketched in orange against black scales, and those with storm predictions to those with plans for a glass cathedral blazing red on green, we have never discovered a way to hold back the Glass Rain.

When I was young, my mother kept me always at her silver side, against her silver hip, in the crook of her silver arm. For her, "Queen of Glass" is only a title, or a way to talk about her wonderful features, her customary silver crinoline, her glassy, wet scent that drifts after her like pine trees dripping dew to a moist forest floor. For me, it is simply what I am.

She let me out of her sight only once, when my favorite lizard, a huge, fat fellow with a map to the Antipodes subtly drawn in brown on his dry, parchment-colored hide, broke his braided silk leash and went bounding across the grasses, his whipping tail held high. I tore after him, my mother in her glittering dress and glass parasol calling after me, calling my name across the green. But I could not let him go—he was meant to be bred to a sleek little black female with a yellow navigational chart glinting on her belly. We had high hopes, and besides, he always slept with me at night, and he would be lonely out in the cold. Soon I was quite far from my mother, though I could still hear her high, even call.

The storm came quickly that day, and none of the lizards had predicted one that season. The white clouds rolled in like horses stumbling and with a terrible crack, like a knife thrust through a mirror, the Glass Rain fell. I felt it—I must have felt it. But when I think back on it now I cannot remember any pain, I cannot remember hurt or skin slicing open or the edges of the rain meeting the edges of me. But meet they did, and thousands of slivers of glass fell screaming into my skin, piercing my shoulders, my hands, my scalp, my cheeks, my legs—ah, there it is, I remember, the legs hurt when they went—in so many places and so quickly that I was rooted to the spot by the glass that had poured so suddenly into me, like water filling up a vase.

In fact, it was so quick, and so many slivers fell that day, that when the storm had passed, I stepped away from the prairie and onto the road again, and to my surprise, a girl of glass stepped out of the girl of skin.

So much glass, so quickly! More of me was glass than flesh in that moment, and so it has been ever since.

My mother was frantic. She culled lizards from every kingdom, even fresh stock with nothing at all on their backs. Clutch after clutch of eggs were laid in the hopes of finding a cure. She sent letters to every doctor and wizard and witch, begging them to turn her daughter to flesh again. They even—I hesitate to say it!—fed some few of the breeding lizards which seemed to have glass-lore on their backs slices of my old skin, which had been gingerly carried from the field. It did not matter. I remained glass. They tried rolling me in pollen, or clouding the glass with oil and paint, or mud and grass. But I am made of rain; it all slides away.

Finally, on a day when it was so clear that roaming squirrels were blinded, a drifting snow fell on those fields, and walking with my sorrowing mother, her silver hair limp and strung with flakes, I felt my skin frost over, forking lines of frost shooting over my cheeks, my arms, my belly. My breath fogged in the air, and the sun shone through my hair just as it would through a real girl's curls.

My mother threw her arms around me and her warm fingers stuck to me, but she only laughed and wept and called me her darling. We strode through the fields, and she picked crocuses for me, and gave me honey cakes to eat. We talked of the lizards, of the Rain, of silly things which we always talked about when I was only a voice and a weight on the couch—but they seemed brighter and more important, now that she could see my frost-fringed eyes close when I laughed.

But it cannot snow all the time.

On those few days when the sun and snow join hands, my mother and I go walking in the high and brittle grass. When all the other days dawn snowless, we weep, and tend the lizards in silence, and I try to spare her the pain of hearing my voice without seeing me. I am the ghost of her daughter, and I am sorry, I should not have run off. That silly old lizard. I should not have done it.

But in secret, I think glass is very beautiful, and I among all possible village girls may stand in the Glass Rain and look into the clouds as they weep their hard, cutting tears. They cannot hurt me anymore. And I became the breeding mistress in my mother's place, long before I ought to have inherited it—the lizards love me, and they can bite all they like. My glass fingers never feel it; their teeth leave no mark. I am good at it, better, even, than my mother, and it was I who discovered the way of rendering jewels to food, for which I was much praised.

But my poor mother, she cries out for me at night, and cannot see that I am there.

THE TALE

OF THE

LIZARD'S LESSON, CONTINUED

"I AM A GHOST-LIBRARIAN," THE VOICE SAID. "A shade who carries lizards to and fro, opens and closes pens, but no more. I will become a glass crone with wrinkles like prisms, but I will never be Queen. I will haunt my wretched, mourning mother and make sure the eggs are dry, and that is all."

We gawked a little, I admit. That is not very good manners, but perhaps we can be forgiven.

"What is it, then, that you wish to barter from us, Yoi-who-was-born-in-the-evening?"

I cleared my throat. "It is a matter of roses, Ostraya-who-was-born-in-the-rain," I said, shyly.

"Oh! Roses are very interesting, are they not? Did you know that if you feed one nothing but sugar water and a mash of honeybees, it becomes sweet and thick enough to be fried for sandwiches, like boar meat or fish? We have lunched on rose and leek sandwiches for most of this season!"

We expressed some interest in this, and were shown the parent lizards for that recipe, one grafting process so complex there hardly seemed to be a lizard beneath the markings, one anatomical diagram of a large pike. They lolled about in their pen, proud of their children, their thick legs and flamboyant tails, and knew nothing of what was on their skins. We were shown by invisible hands all the lizards which had a thing to do with roses, and spent many months there in contemplation. Yazo was beside herself, her breath thick and fast, her water jostling in her skull. I kept away from her when she spilled herself, and the days after when she could not remember who she was. It was too disturbing, and I did not know how to ask again how she could torture herself so.

Only once did I stumble upon her at that grisly ritual. I had a theory regarding ink and yolk production I wanted to share with her, and I admit that contrary to manners I burst into her room to find her on her knees on a white mat, with a silver bowl before her. I grimaced, and would have left her, but she turned her black eyes to me, and the green bags beneath them were so terrible and deep. I knelt at her side.

"Yazo-who-was-born-at-the-bottom-of-winter, please do not do this. It is an obscenity; I cannot bear to witness it. Do you not see your webbing? Your hair?"

"I am teaching myself a lesson, Yoi. Myself and all Kappa. Of course I see it." She brushed my tonsure fondly. "I am sorry it distresses you. But you must understand—the others think that to lose one's water is only a matter of a few days' bleary eyes and stumbling into things. It is much worse. No one will believe it, and so I show them in my skin. When I am far gone enough, they will understand that we must find a place where the water can be kept safe, and never spilt out for the amusement of a village oaf." She coughed and took my hand. "I do not even remember now how to grow the pomegranate-ant. I have done nothing of note because I cannot remember how. One day I will not remember when I was born. But that is all right. Then they will see."

I helped her. Forgive me, I helped her to bend forward into the bowl, and listened to the blue water splash in the silver, and looked into her skull when she had finished, empty and dry, the color of old weeds. I laid her in her bed, and sang to her while she slept insensate.

In only another month, while Yazo was stumbling in the dark and crying and even I could not reach her, I asked Ostraya—I had a little glass bell which let her know I wanted her—to bring me the glass lizard, which is to say the lizard which first carried on it the way of making glass, of blowing it into shapes. I held under my arm an enormous red female who would absolutely not stop licking her eyeballs. She was a rose-lizard, the very simplest one I could find. On her back was nothing more than a minutely fine, infinitely detailed image of a rose, perfect in every petal and thorn. It was red—red on red, the rose itself a deeper and bloodier shade than her skin. Ostraya was quiet for a long while, but I could hear her breathing and knew she was not gone.

"He is an ancient fellow," she said finally. "And a miserable, hoary old monarch besides."

"If it is too much to ask in the Glass Country to see this beast, Ostraya-who-was-born-in-the-rain..."

But she brought him, in a wicker basket on his own blue pillow, a gray and green and crusty bull, his crest flopped over as though exhausted with the effort of staying upright for so many years. His eyes were milky and filmed; his throat emitted a constant rattle. But he was covered in instructions, and so I felt generous toward him.

He bit me, of course, when I placed him in the pen next to my scarlet female. Lizards are vicious.

By the time Yazo was herself again—though she looked strangely at me when I used that phrase—the red lizard was getting her nest ready and looking very pleased with herself. We waited, and waited, and ate rose and leek sandwiches and rose steaks and rose roasts and poached rose until we had to say, very politely, to be sure, that rose was no longer quite to our liking, begging the pardon of all our estimable hosts.

When we departed the wide prairie, we had passed through the warm season and into the cold again. The next Glass Rain was still weeks off, according to the latest lizards. We had in our packs a very curious young thing with coral skin and a stark black lesson snaking across his back, and even Yazo was talkative.

"It was very clever of you, Yoi-who-was-born-in-the-evening. I will tell everyone that it was you and not me who discovered it," she chirruped, skipping down the breeding house steps like a child.

We walked out of the womb-warm hall and into a clear, freezing day.

The sun streaked through heavy clouds and played chasing games with the grass. And very lightly, it began to snow. We laughed and stuck out our tongues, feeling very strange indeed to feel snowflakes falling into our skull-water. We turned back to look at the bright, tiled roof all covered in white, and saw at the door a beautiful, sad-eyed young woman, all of glass. Her hair fell in crystal rivers to her waist, and her dress was crisply cut, frosted at the elbows. Her hands were slender and tipped in blue, her cheeks jeweled and clear, a little glass mole on the side of her transparent nose. She waved us farewell, her mouth a wide, sparkling smile through which the sun blazed.

At her feet was a huge, fat lizard on a glittering leash, his glass belly rippling, crystalline and swollen, his fringe sharp enough to cut, his tongue hanging out of his mouth like a glass bookmark.

THE
FERRYMAN'S TALE,
CONTINUED

"OUR LITTLE CORAL BULL WAS A SENSATION IN the Greater Kappa. His lesson, which became our lesson, was enough to catch the breath of all the turtles with their feet tangled in cucumbers. How to make a rose which would never die or wilt, which would lose one petal in a century, whose gloss and shine were like glass, which would last until all the glass of the world were turned back to sand."

"This is the rose I seek."

The Kappa gestured toward the glass houses. "It is there. I told you we chose this place—we chose because of Yazo, darling Yazo, Yazo-who-was-born-at-the-bottom-of-winter. By the time we had become famous, by the time the Upas and the Ixora grew tall in the thesis-fields, and the corral was full of rolling Manticore, fat and furry as kittens, and fluttering Firebirds, she had almost no skin on her. Her webbing hung from her fingers in shreds, her eyes were sunken, her hair had all fallen out. She did not know her name—but I told it to her every day. I woke her and whispered in her green ear: 'You are Yazo, who is beautiful, and was born at the bottom of winter, and my friend.' Everything I did, the great grafts and splices that made my name—I told everyone that she was the senior of us, that she was my collaborator, my indispensable partner. Her name rose with mine, even as she forgot it entirely, and nothing I said in the morning mattered. She prodded our kittens listlessly, and did not notice if they nipped her thumbs. But she did what she meant to: She proved to them the danger of losing the skull-water, that it was more than a few days of blear and blight. She pleaded with us to move the Greater Kappa to a safe place, a place where horrid villagers would not be forever bowing to us, and laughing at our spill, where we could be sure that we would not lose ourselves as she did."

Yoi led me to the houses, whose shattering traced lines over every pane of glassy ice. Shapes moved inside, but she did not invite me to enter.

"The Greater Kappa is all around you," she said gently. "These are greenhouses. Here on the roof of the world our water freezes and does not flow out—by her we are saved, and the best minds of the Kappa are preserved against the depredations of the average vicious child."

"I am glad for you," I said, putting my hand on her little shoulder, where the rim of her shell met flesh. "Though your houses seem to be in disrepair. Perhaps I can help with that, if you give me what I need."

She snorted. "We do not need your help."

Pushing the door of one of the larger houses open, I was thrust into a world of green, green plants and green turtles, and a sea of heads glittering blue, liquid water rippling bright. Hundreds of eyes turned to me, and regarded me with calm.

"The cold took the houses, but in most cases, ice is as good as glass. Here it is warm, here we may be intimate with each other, and let our skulls thaw. Here we teach our lessons as we always have, and our catalogue grows. But we keep ourselves to ourselves, and the world comes no more begging bouquets at our door. Until you." Her expression grew grave and sad. "But the cucumbers—for some reason the cucumbers detest the climate, and they refuse to grow. We have all the blossoms we could want, but their taste is inferior to the fruit."

"I have brought you so many varieties, surely you can breed a cucumber with a heart of ice. All I ask is my rose." I kept my wings folded neatly back and stooped under the ice roof, trying to be as small and familiar as it is possible to be as a swan among turtles.

"Yes, well, you must wait," huffed Yoi. "We hardly keep mature specimens on hand for the pleasure of whatever outlandish flying thing finds its way to our doorstep. But we would enjoy the cucumbers now, of course." She grinned, finally, and her teeth were small and brown and neat, like a wooden model of a child's teeth.

I handed over my sack amiably, and the Kappa scurried forward like cats to cream, sorting those to eat from those to dissect, and chewing greedily at the unfortunate fruits which were deemed too common to breed. And as they ate, Yoi beckoned each of them away from the feast and to her, touching the water of their skulls and whispering. When the meal was done, I was sent away, told to meditate on the wonders of succeeding generations of plant life, and wait. A glass house was provided for my comfort, an empty cottage at the far corner of the village.

"Why do you have an empty house, if you do not expect visitors?" I asked as I was gently but firmly pushed toward the door by a dozen webbed hands. Yoi answered me, her face downcast.

"It is Yazo's house, who died the day we came to this mountain. We keep it in her honor, and you must treat it kindly."

It was a long while to wait. I wrapped my wings around myself in the low-raftered house of Yazo, slowly opening and closing them in imitation of the poor, lonely moon. This is the Hsien's way of meditating, and when her light shone through the shattered panes, my skin was covered in her, covered in long lines of blue like a mother's arms. I considered many things, though not often among them was the nature of succeeding generations of plant life. In my mind, lightened by the nearness of the moon, I designed the Dome of Shadukiam, shaped it petal by frame until it stood erect and perfect within me.

When it was done, Yoi came to collect me. She wore a little black cap which I took to be a sign of respect for her absent comrade in whose house I trespassed. She did not explain it. I followed her up the snow-pat street and into the greenhouse where I had first seen rippling water in the depths of her tonsure. Within were countless Kappa, all respectfully standing at attention, their hands clasped together.

In the head of each one floated a flawless rose, pink and white and red, without blemish or brown. Yoi slowly removed her cap, and beneath it, too, was a large and spotless flower, as true a scarlet as any I have seen before or since. I must have looked surprised, for she laughed, a small, musical sound like wooden drums pattered upon by rain.

"How did you think we grew things? In the soil like farmers? Every lesson I have taught, from lily-berry to Ixora, was grown first in my own head. Where else should I trust it? Take these things, Idyll-who-supposes-he-was-born-at-night, and do not let our work be forgotten in the world below."

One by one the Kappa reached into their skulls and plucked their flowers, careful not to spill a drop, and one by one they piled them into my sack, until it was brimful with roses.

"Farewell, Yoi-who-was-born-in-the-evening," I said, and as I ducked out of the glass house, I saw the smallest of cucumbers budding from the walls.

And so was finally built the Rose Dome of Shadukiam. As I had constructed it in the house of Yazo-who-was-born-at-the-bottom-of-winter, so it blossomed over the infant city, its colors reflected in the cart tracks of the mud streets. My siblings and I flew back and forth over the apex, nets full of immaculate flowers suspended from our shoulders, sewing them to the superstructure with infinite care, with a thread of diamonds and iron. And the stalks which arched so high and bore their roses with grace long enough that no one can now speak of Shadukiam without her roses? Glass, all of glass, perfect and pure as ice, perfect and pure as a young woman's face.

And once in a century, there would be a strange, soft rain as each rose lost a petal and the petals would drift to streets that were mud, then stone, then silver, not unlike a Hsien peeled off from the face of the moon.

All this completed, I went to the city fathers of Shadukiam and asked for my payment, my opals and silver. I considered briefly that I should have asked for better, but agreements are agreements, and living stones rarely break theirs. Imagine my surprise when the Shaduki governor glowered darkly and mumbled that he could not possibly render my payment when the flowers that crowned his city were clearly no roses, but some monstrous abomination of a flower that only a specter like myself would know where to find.

"Did I not do just as you asked? Did I not find for you an imperishable rose?"

"Well—" The little man shuffled, twisting his bracelets in anxiety as I flared my wings, towering over him. "Even on this point we must disagree. They are not strictly imperishable, are they? One petal in a century, it's quite a lot of work for city sanitation on those occasions..." He sweat red and redolent under my nose.

"I have worked wonders for you," I whispered.

"Even so," said he.

"I will bring down the Dome on your heads; the shattering of the frame will be heard all the way to the sea."

"Again," said the wretched governor, his hems weighted in gold, "we must disagree."

It is difficult to subdue a Hsien. One might as well try to keep the moon still. But they gagged me and bound me and there were so many of them, so many, like ants, and the blood they drew from my scalp was white and thick, like molten bone. They bound me and dragged me up to the highest of the diamond turrets, which were clearer and sharper in those days than they have ever been since, and with so many hands they impaled me on its tapered tip. I saw the glittering edge of the turret slide through me, dripping white, shredding through my skin. I shrieked owl-shrill, but there was no help, only their laughter, which perhaps you know well enough, my boy. My siblings tried to release me, but they were kept away by volleys of arrows so thick they seemed to be flocks of ravens flinging themselves at the Hsien. For nine days I lay there bleeding on my roses, and they kept vigil, watching me die. I screamed, I cursed, and all of Shadukiam listened as though I was a great bell tolling out their hours.

I bellowed out any number of dooms, any number of hideous wishes to the alabaster ears of my mother. Maybe she could not see me, up there on the roof of a city. Does she see the grackles, the sparrows, the doves? She did not see me. But I seem to remember now, in that history before history, so long ago, that as the ninth sun set I sobbed weakly and begged her to let that place die, too, to let it become as dead and gray as her own dry kneecaps, to let it starve, since it would feed no one but itself.

I seem to remember this, and I am sorry.

The Tale of the Crossing, Continued

"WITH THAT NINTH SUN I PERISHED THERE, AND I cannot say what became of my body, no more than any man can. I came here; it is the first thing I remember, the lonely shore and the ferry. And the bones and the lizards—we are all translated on these shores, and I am sure I don't understand it, but there is a kind of poetry in metamorphosis, and if I could but see my lizards, I should be very interested to know what is written on their backs. But I was angry at first, and the little things scratched so terribly, and my journey on the lake was much farther than yours. When the storm came, I seized the pole from the ferryman in a frenzy of itching

and impatience, a nice old woman with no teeth at all and two parrots'
heads squawking out of her palms. I tried to steer myself, and fell into
the water. I'd advise you not to try it. When I spluttered and gasped my
way back onto the raft, the old woman was gone, and I have been the
ferryman for all the years upon years that have piled up since in this
place."

Seven blinked and chuckled a little. "That's quite a story."

Idyll shrugged. "Almost as good as yours."

A few drops of rain spattered onto his broad face. And, as is the way
of storms, once the first drops had squeezed from the sky, the rest came
tumbling after, and soon the pair was drenched.

"This is your storm?" Seven
asked shakily, trying not
to think of the crea-
tures scurrying be-
neath that pitiful
scrap of cloth. But
the ferryman shook his
head.

"Best let me shelter you,
boy. We aren't going to make
it across before they come
through."

Idyll held out his arms, and
shuddering, Seven fell into the
embrace, his teeth chattering as
bone arms and flesh hands
wrapped him, as the cloak stuck to
his skin like wet grass, as two pon-
derous wing-frames, their hollow
bones whistling in the whirling wind, tore
through the cloth and closed over his body. He
could feel the lizards moving, and tried not to look
them in the eye. But the backs—he saw their backs, and on one
was a terrible song of wind through broken windows, and on the other
was a complicated algorithm concerning cloud patterns, and together
he thought they might say something about the staying of rain.

Suddenly, the wind began to shriek—truly shriek; dozens upon
dozens of throttling screams rolled past Seven's ears, men's cries and

women's keening, children's hitching sobs. Clouds whipped by him, sharp and hard, slashing his cheeks. He felt warm blood dripping from his chin. The rain was nothing, he could not even feel it, but the terrible shrieking and the hard clouds, they clutched at him, trying to reach him through the cage of Idyll's arms. The ferry pitched and bobbed on the raging water, spray flinging itself against the two passengers. Wisps of gray cloud snapped from the wide wings like laundry on the line. Seven gripped the ferryman's frame and shut his eyes, buffeted and battered by the voices in the wind.

And as quickly as it had come, it was over. Seven stood on the ferry, his face bleeding onto the boards, Idyll slowly folding his wings up again under his cloak and picking up the long pole once more.

"What sort of storm did you expect in this place, Seven? They come through every few hours, like chariots rounding the last corner. Everything is plainly itself here, nothing more or less. You bear up under the Storm of Souls, and cross the Lake of the Dead." The old man's mouth twisted into a mocking smile. "Are we not courteous, to name ourselves succinctly? Are we not kind? Be glad I have not yet tired of my work. Be glad the Moon is patient, or I would have pushed you overboard and had my peace."

Seven sat heavily against the mast. He wiped at his bloody face.

"But you are not dead, my friend," Idyll went on. "You are as you are, and untranslated. How did you ever find your way here?"

The boy shrugged. "There is a lake here, there is a lake there. A lake, and a cave, and a grove, and if you pay the maid who lives there," he cleared his throat, "if you pay her enough, she will open the cave and the grove and the lake, and let you pass."

Idyll snorted. "Strumpet. I shall have to have a word with her." Seven smiled weakly. "I find it curious," the ferryman continued, "that you have never once asked whether I carried her across, your tree-girl, and how she came, like you, or like me."

There was a long pause. "I know she came. I know it."

"I suppose you will see soon enough."

And indeed, it was not long before the mist cleared and a long silver shore spread out before them, glistening gray pebbles washed by weak gray foam. A small, paint-peeled dock jutted into the still-sulking water. Lashing the ferry to it, Idyll squinted into the murky forest that began just beyond the beachhead. He did not step onto the dock.

"This is the Isle of the Dead," whispered Seven, gripping the dock post with white knuckles. The ferryman burst into laughter, a short, shocking sound that echoed across the shore like an ax blow.

"There is no Isle of the Dead! The geography of this place is more complicated than you could possibly imagine! Why do you think these docks are needed, and a ferryman? I am no mere psychopomp—I am the lake-pilot. I know all the waterways, all the Isles. There are as many as there are whales in the sea, and more, whales and sharks and tortoises together. Perhaps whales and sharks and tortoises and anemones. I know them all, I know the navigable paths, I know where to take each wretched soul that comes to my dock. You wanted to go after her? This is where she came. This is where I brought her, and she paid as dearly as you, never think she did not. She wanted to come to this shore alone of all the others. This is where I take the Stars, it is the Isle of Lost Light, and I would not take you beyond it—you are not qualified, and neither are they."

Out of the Garden

DINARZAD FOLDED HER HANDS IN HER LAP. ON EVERY FINGER WAS a ring of gold and tiger's-eye, and so her hands seemed to look back at her, baleful and fiery and sad. The braziers flickered and warmed her shoulders, and through veils the color of a peacock's head she watched the banquet which seemed to whirl around her like dishes around a mute centerpiece, or dancers beneath a tall, elaborate lamp that has no choice but to shine. The ivory circlet cut into her skin, and in the morning her forehead would be red and chafed. The man beside her had a thick mustache, and had brought her as the sixteenth in his parade of gifts a tiny bird of paradise carved from a single huge pearl, with a tail of trailing sapphires and topaz. Its eyes were dead and shimmering, and when you pulled the tail, some mechanism deep in the bird's throat chimed like a clock. She thought it was meant to be more like a crowing or singing, but to her it seemed nothing more than a clock marking the time. She pulled its tail. It chimed. She delicately placed her napkin over it, so that she would not have to look it in the eye.

She was thinking about the girl in the Garden.

It was the pirate ship that she remembered when she thought of the girl's stories, the pirate ship and the sad, broken Papess. She thought she understood that, how to give up and give in to the inevitable. She knew what inevitability felt like, how it tasted. It felt like the mustached man's hand on her knee. It tasted like his kisses. She wished that she could cut her hair like a Sigrid, so that they would stop stringing it with jewels and brushing it straight. She wished she could cloister herself away from inevitable kisses.

She wished she were an orphan with endless tales to tell and no one to love her enough to bring her birds of pearl.

But she was not her brother, she could not bring herself to sit at that girl's feet and listen to her openly, she could not bear the possibility that the girl was not a bird of pearl, that she could not simply pull her tail and hear the chime she longed for. But she did long for it.

"And where is the little Sultan tonight, your brother?" said her suitor amiably, his voice like thick liquor, flowing over her and into her skin whether she willed it or no.

"He is hunting in the country, my lord," she said, not lifting her eyes under the deep blue veil. "After all, when he is not so little a Sultan anymore, he will not have time for such noble pursuits. He took our father's ebony bow and went to shoot a lion in my lord's honor, as a wedding present."

She wondered at how easy the lie was. *Is this how you tell a tale?* she thought. *You open your mouth and chime, let whatever seems lovely pour out, and hope it sounds more like singing than the tolling of a clock?* She warmed to her story and lifted her eyes demurely.

"My brother is most impressed with my lord. He prefers you infinitely to the younger man who brought all those ghastly roosters. He is most interested in the mechanism of your birds, which he feels is superior to the golden clockwork of that other man."

"Why, I should be happy to show him how it is done!"

"I am sure he will be most grateful, my lord—how generous of you, to marry his sister and show him such wonders! He will surely reward my lord beyond measure. My brother is a prodigy in the ways of diplomacy—he spends his nights in contemplation of the movements of nations and governors, and in the perfect halls of his mind he moves them as deftly and surely as *shatranj* pieces. He thinks so often and with such intensity that I have with my own eyes seen steam pour from his head as from a kettle. He will be a great Sultan, when he is grown, and he will always remember the delightful singing of my lord's birds."

"Your voice is sweeter than all of my birds chiming at once."

"But not, I think, sweeter than those of all your wives chiming together."

But there she had gone too far, and a shadow passed over the oiled and perfumed features of her bridegroom. She coughed and summoned up a maidenly blush, lowering her eyes to her plate again. The gold was streaked with goose fat, and she had no appetite. Somewhere far off on its own long table was the spotted carcass of the giraffe neck, which was so rich and marrow-sweet that she could not stomach it. A few sapphires peeked out from her napkin. She pulled the strands, and shuddered at the sound.

When the night was over and her neck ached from keeping her head bowed, she went to the tower room and folded her cloak in half, then in quarters. It was red, dyed over and over until it was so dark that to call it red beside other reds was to call the sun bright beside a lamp. It was lined with deerskin, from some country so far off that the deer were shaggy and thick-pelted. Its lower hem was trimmed with black wolf tails. It was the simplest, least ornate cloak she owned. She pushed it slowly into her brother's pack, and with it the little pearl bird.

"I don't know where it came from," the boy said. "I certainly didn't bring it. You told me not to."

The girl ran her fingers over the fabric soft as ink. The wolf tails flopped over her small hands, and the deer fur ruffled back from the hood. "It's all right if you did."

"I didn't! I brought quail eggs and cinnamon candies! They were having goose tonight—I didn't feel right about that."

The girl considered it for a while, and decided that if he could not work out the clickings and whirrings of his sister's mind, it was far beyond her to do so. She unfurled the coat, and the boy helped her heft the thick, heavy thing over her thin shoulders. The prickle of the deer fur on her skin was strange and thrilling, something akin to the slick tang of the cinnamon in her mouth. She smiled a little, and her teeth were cold in the air. As she arranged the folds around her by the side of her lake, which was strewn with leaves and duck feathers, the little bird fell out into her hands. She looked at the boy curiously, but he shook his head. She pulled the string of sapphires and topaz, and the pearl bird opened its intricate mouth, letting loose a loud, clear chime, like the tiniest church bell in the world.

The girl laughed.

THE TALE
OF THE CROSSING,
CONTINUED

SEVEN STEPPED OFF THE DOCK ONTO THE WET beach. Idyll was already punting away from him, the flash of lizard tails peeking out from his cloak every now and then. The young man walked up the shoreline, gingerly, trying not to look down—for the beach was strewn not with gray pebbles, as it had seemed when he saw it from the lake, but with thousands of closed eyelids, glistening silver and wet, which opened wherever he stepped, their irises pale and accusing. They wept constantly, and their tears mingled with the lake foam in salty waves. He clutched his empty sleeve and did not look down, though his stomach lurched with each wet and yielding step. He was relieved when the coast of eyes gave way to gray loam and skeleton leaves, and the forest spiked up around him, bare and thin-branched, birches and larches and gnarled oaks with no leaves clattering in the lackluster wind.

But he did not know how to find her. He wandered in the wood, and no bird called, no deer chewed acorns, no mouse scurried past. There was no sun, and he could not tell where he went—but he went on. He was frozen and numb with a damp that crawled over him like a pair of lizards.

"What have you done now, you silly old cripple?" The voice came from nowhere; the wood wound ahead of him in its patches of gray and white, empty and still. But he knew the voice—oh, how he knew it.

"Oubliette, where are you?" he whispered.

One of the trees, an old twisted ash, turned around, and it was his Oubliette, her hair brown and fog-plastered to her neck, her eyes wide and sad, her dress, what was left of it, pale and clinging. He ran to her—who would not have run? He ran to her and she put her arms around his neck, her brow on his mangled shoulder.

"Why did you come after me? How will you get back, you stupid boy?" she said ruefully, shaking her head against him.

"I came to save you," he said, surprised and confused. "It's what we do, isn't it? We save each other."

Oubliette pushed him away. "I didn't need you to save me! Do you know what it cost me to get here?"

"Do you know what it cost me to follow you?" Seven exploded.

She turned again on her heels, and her tree-side whipped around, pitted and petrified—and smooth, not tail at all. He had not seen her because she was all tree now, her sweet tufted tail gone. "I paid him in flesh, the ferryman and his awful lizards. I assume you did, too? You spent the last of our dhheiba to get here? To *save* me?"

"Not the last."

Oubliette's eyes blazed, her skin suddenly less than gray, flushed with anger. She threw herself against him, almost knocking him to the forest floor, and kissed him with such ferocity and brutal strength that he could not breathe. Her mouth was hot in the freeze and the fog, her teeth cracking against his. She drew blood from his lip and tore away, her mouth still stained with his, scarlet in the gray.

"That's what you wanted, wasn't it? The grateful kiss of a rescued maiden? Her pretty hand in yours? Doe eyes batting stupidly at you? Just like a miller's son!"

"No! No! Oubliette, I never wanted you like that, you know that!"

"Well, why not?" She laughed, desperate and shrill. Seven looked at her, his eyes full of tears, his back bent and broken, his sleeve dangling.

"There are some things you never get over," he whispered. "What do you see when you look at me? Tell me what you see; tell me you see a man. Tell me."

Oubliette cringed, her mouth twist-ing into an ugly grimace. She was so much older now, he saw. Her jaw was hard and sharp, her face her own, entirely, without the smallest hint of a child haunting it.

"Bone," she hissed. "I look at you and I see bones. Bones and coins."

"I know." Seven reached for her again, and she let herself be held, shaking like a caught deer. "You saved me, my friend, my only friend. I had to save you. *I had to.*"

"I *chose* to come here. I wanted to come. I went to the lake—"

"I know! I went, too! Did you see her?"

"Yes! She was beautiful, so beautiful, and her face was so dark—"

"Were you scared?"

"No, well, yes—were you?"

"Of course! Did you do it?"

"I had to! Did you—"

"Yes—did you throw up?"

"No, but I wanted to, when she cut me to fill her bowl—"

"All that red! It was like—"

"Before. Yes."

The two looked at each other, half smiling.

"Do you want to talk about it?" Seven said against her wild-smelling hair.

"Not really," she snorted, wiping her eyes. "What is one entrance to the underworld? It's always the same, the blood and the hooded lady and the cave. You give what you can, you go into the dark. The dark took us. No more needs be said."

"There is always more. Tell me, like you used to, when I warmed your bark with my belly and you kept your hair so short."

"You were always tiresome and greedy." Oubliette sighed, but she was smiling a little. "I went to the lake . . ."

THE TALE

OF THE

DANCING GIRL'S
DESCENT

TAGLIO KEPT HIS ABSENTIA IN A LITTLE BOX, too, did he tell you that? He showed me once, and he wept over them, shriveled and black, knocking in an orangewood box like the rattle in a snake's tail. He wanted me to see them because I am a huldra, and so in some roundabout sense he had mutilated himself for me. For my grandmothers, for my celestial aunt. I wrinkled my nose—it is embarrassing to witness another person's faith laid out like that, reduced to something small and dry and lifeless, a reliquary full of toenail clippings. I think he always liked me better than you. He had never met a real huldra. We were abstract; the story of the

Heifer-Star and her brother was real. I was proof of his religion, I was as good as a Star, and I slept against his stomach between the cart handles. He looked at me and told himself he was right, that the dull, phantom ache between his legs was sacred.

I don't know anything about that. I am only myself. I have always been made of wood and girl and cow, and that is no more a divine revelation to me than a man's thumbs are to him. You never thought I was proof of the existence of a god. But I felt sorry for our green gazelle—do you remember his little cape?—and I let him tell me I was holy. It seemed the least I could do. We hunted together while the Manticore taught you to pick pockets and sing scales. He was so quick with those teeth, and I became as quick as he. It was so hard to stay by you—I looked at you and shivered as though the hollow walls of the Mint were still all around me. I looked at you and knew I should have taken the burden, I should have lain under the stamp. It was my idea; it was wrong of me to let you do it. I looked at you and remembered everything. With Taglio singing little rhymes to the rabbits until they were close enough to snatch, I forgot.

And I forgot when I danced. When I was Zmeya, I was beautiful, and strong, and immune to all hedgehogs. When I was Zmeya I could not be touched. I did not have to be a tree-girl who had lost a kiss to the miller's son, or her hair to a unicorn, or seven years to a factory. I was her, and I was green, and I writhed. And as the music became quicker, as you joined in with Taglio and played his little flute, I understood less and less that I was not her. On the hunt he called me holy; in the dance I knew I was divine. If it seems silly now, at least I have the consolation that many others had gone before me in madness for love of her, for love of the snake and the sky. I cannot explain it better. I danced her so often that I felt her in me, I felt her far off in the dark, coiling around herself in the fog. What damage does the telling of a story play upon its teller? I told her story hundreds of times. I could not bear to remain outside of it.

The day after you kissed me—I was not angry, don't think I was. I never thought of it again. Taglio and I went after supper. We were on the track of a fawn. I lay on my belly in the moss and birch leaves and watched its spots flash in and out of the wood. He lay beside me, and we whispered to each other while our prey chewed twigs.

"You look like a snake lying there. I am sure it is not an accident, and I am sure you are about to leave us," he hissed accusingly.

"Why would you say that?"

"You are barely here. I can almost see through you. You would speak to no one, and only dance, if you did not like to hunt so well. If you did not like me so well. And I have begun to wonder if you do not like me only because I once saw her."

I turned my head slowly, so as not to start the deer. "Don't say that. You are my cart-knight."

"For now. But you left us days ago—I felt you go. Now there is only this stranger in your place, lying to me and telling me she is you."

I looked at the mash of old, broken forest beneath me. "You do not want me to stay. That is why you say such awful things."

With equal slowness, he cupped my head in his hand. "Darling huldra, bull-born and borne to me by a fortunate wind—go. I will not be the one who keeps you, and we will soldier on without your moods and your scowls, much as we love them. Find whatever you are already looking for."

"I will go," I mumbled, "to the Isle of the Dead and do what you could not."

He blinked, as though I had cut into him with my hunting knife. I saw his lip tremble, in anger or grief or hope, and a long while passed when we did not mark the fawn at all, but wrestled in our gazes. Finally, he drew from his vest a little brown box, and drew from it a silver-black leaf.

"Don't fail us," he said, and as one, with the leaf clutched in my hand, we sprang out of the brush and took the fawn down in one single red stroke.

How do you find the land of the dead without dying? Everyone has a story of that place. It is gray and lonely, it is a raucous circus, it is a place of judgment where the soul is weighed against a feather, it is nothing at all, I do not care, little girl, go away and don't steal milk from my cow. You could ask a thousand folk and hear a thousand tales.

Or you could go to an astrologer and by turning your back amaze him into drawing you a map to an almond tree which is almost a legend, but which is in actuality your petrified, mistletoe-infested grandfather, and tell him that if he does not tell you the way, you will cut him right down and not even weep, for he never should have touched your grandmother at all.

You could brandish an ax to make your point. It would have to be a very sharp one. The tree might ask how he would know the way. You might say that he is neither living nor dead, being mostly Absentia and almonds, and surely able to tell you how to slip into the in-between places. The tree might grumble, but only one or two swings of the ax, only one or two showers of wood chips would probably induce him to shout and wail and holler out just exactly how to find a lake with a woman living near it, at the mouth of a cave.

The tree who is some part of your grandfather might then whip his branches around and try to catch you, slapping at your arms—but it is too awful to think about, and you would get away as quickly as you could, and would certainly never tell anyone about it.

There is a lake here; there is a lake there. It does not seem much like any other lake, save that its beach is littered with thin slivers of glass like rain-drops. Over that sharp shore I walked, with my good, solid shoes well bought, and my steps echoed across the wa-ter like shouts. So I should not be surprised that she was awake and waiting for me, a black cowl drawn over her face, so that I could only see a long hoopoe's beak, long and thin and curved, pointing out at me. Her black skirts spread out over the ground in drooping folds, on and on, down the beach and into the black water, and it seemed that there was no difference between the cloth and the lake.

"Let me pass," I said.

"Pass what?" she said, and her voice seemed hollow in that clacking beak.

"Pass through you, to the land of the dead."

"You may try to pass through me, but you will find I am very thick, and made more or less of bone and meat, and therefore I am afraid you will find it tough going."

I blinked at her, and she threw off her hood, revealing a middle-aged woman, neither thin nor fat, with the beginnings of gray hair creeping through brown, and skin like an old blasted oak. Her eyes were narrow and dark. She reached behind her head and loosed a clasp, pulling the beak away from her face—she was only a woman, with a mouth and a nose and teeth like any other.

"Didn't you like my joke?" She laughed. "One doesn't get many opportunities to chat in my line of work. The least you could do is chuckle a little. Maybe even giggle. Don't girls still giggle out there in the world?"

"I'm out of practice," I grunted.

"So am I, dear. Maybe it was not a very good joke."

"What do I have to do to get through?" I am afraid I was very short with her. Perhaps you did better.

She sighed. "You might listen, instead of talking so much..."

The
Mourner's Tale

I OCCUPY A STRANGE PROFESSION. IT IS ONLY slightly stranger than my previous employment. I was once a mourner by trade, an avocation which harpies take particularly well to, having a screech like no other creature.

Did I forget to mention? Well. Don't look under the cloak.

We know what a lament is better than any who walks on five toes. When we are required, we live with a corpse for weeks on end, we live with our lament until it has shape and heft, until it has the weight of the corpse, and in the putrefying gases we detect the virtue or degeneracy of the subject. Decomposition does not lie. We lament not when we are told to, but when the lament is finished, be it days or years hence. When we can hold its hand and walk down the street of a city, showing it the grocer's where the deceased bought her carrots and turnips, the butcher where she cut her meat and in secret met her lover, the gallery where just once, a portrait of her hung, then the lament is grown and done. It nods sadly and passes through all these places to a grave, where we screech and sing and tear our hair, where we rend our breasts and howl grief into the ground.

Once, in Irsil, which is poor and sad in all things save retired soldiers with broken swords and useless plowshares, we took fifteen years to rear the lament of a certain general. We walked it through the shanties and the porches where old officers told their bloody tales to the wind, and they followed behind, falling in like ranks, to hear how the old man was mourned.

It is necessary work. I was good at it. I suppose that is what got me here.

One cannot, among the mourning harpies, be truly considered adept without the hoopoe's beak. We can crow and keen and split your ears into bloody halves with the anguish in our throats—but not all of a lament is sorrow. Even in the old general's scar-kneed life there was sweetness—there was a woman in a village who looked like his mother, and he married her, and we did not refrain from commenting on that, for a lament has no shame—but there was a moment before he left on campaign when the woman who looked like his mother showed him twin babies, a boy and a girl, and he could not breathe for the sweetness of their cheeks, and we sang that, too.

But it is hard to sing of sweetness with a harpy's mouth. We are made for rending. It is hard to simply weep.

We must go and get it, the beak, and we may not steal it, but must sing the hoopoe's lament when it dies, and if its chicks deem the lament sufficient, they will give it over. In such a way the hoopoe ration the grief of the world.

I was past thirty by the time I went to get my beak. Not a few of the others were unsure that I would ever be ready to wear it. I am sure you wonder at the hoopoe—are these not tiny, colorful, but shallow and flittering birds? How could a beak like a dove's wishbone ever produce such funeral songs as I speak of? But I say to you that once there were great hoopoes the likes of which you have never seen in these fallen days. Their rose-orange wings were like those of an albatross, and their beaks were trumpets, and we were the wind blown through them.

I went into the mountains. I will not bore you with the details of a Quest. They are all much the same: One goes forth, one obtains, one returns. But when I found a huge old mother hoopoe dying in her nest, I crouched down among her flame-headed chicks, their feathers tipped in black and white speckles, to hear the life of the bird I would lament. She turned her old downy head to me and this is what she said:

The
Hoopoe's Tale

MY EGG WAS HARD TO BREAK. THE YOLK WAS
golden and ropy. I opened my eyes in such brightness.
My mother pierced her breast with her beak, and fed
me on her blood, which tasted like flying. She called me
Orange as the Sun.

The tide came in, the tide went out. I ate worms and
beetles.

I sang very loudly and so did another hoopoe whose
tail was black and strong. I made a nest of hazel and
down and bits of a strange, sweet red wood that a raft-
builder had left carelessly behind. I laid three eggs that
year, and four the year after. I pierced my breast with

my beak, and fed them on my blood, which tasted like flying. I called them Pink as a Fat Worm and Speckled as a Shadow and Red as Mother's Blood and other things. There were a lot of them. It is hard to remember.

The year after that I laid one, and last year I laid five. So it goes.

The tide came in, the tide went out.

A hawk chased me once. She made a dent in my skull and another in my beak. I clipped out one of her eyes.

A cat mauled the hoopoe with the black tail and my last eggs were from one with a blue crest.

Now I am old, and I have no blood in me for more children.

It was a good life.

The Mourner's Tale, Continued

I HELD HER OLD WITHERED HEAD IN MY HANDS
like a browned apple, and her thirteen chicks gathered
around, Pink as a Fat Worm and Speckled as a Shadow
and Red as Mother's Blood—and also Blue-Bottomed
as a Jay, Rosy as a Burned Farmer, Sour as a Hungry
Badger, and all the rest. I raised up my head and sang of
that diamond egg, the struggle to shatter it, the light
of the morning sun on that shimmering yolk, the taste
of Mother's scarlet blood! I sang of the beauty of the
black tail, of the smoothness of infant eggs, of the flow
of blood from Orange as the Sun's breast, the sting and
the pain of her children's beaks on her breast. I sang of

the frightful, bitter-voiced hawk, and the great battle which lost the bird of prey a precious eye. I sang of the wicked cat and the lost mate. I sang of new love with a blue crest. I sang of all those eggs, all that blood, and an empty chest singing out at the end of its days.

I flew down the mountain with Orange as the Sun's beak in my hands, slightly dented from the hawk fight—but the dent made the sweetest, most broken and sorrowful notes of any beak. I tied it onto my face and began my trade.

Some years hence I was approached by a clutch of women weeping like hoopoes for their comrade, a corpse they carried on a bier made from the prow of a ship. She had white hair and a smile on her lips, and I listened well as they told me her life. I took the body to my accustomed place, hidden away in a forgotten and empty land by a little lake where I would not be disturbed for the years it would surely take to bring up this woman's lament from infancy. But they had paid me well, those women, and I settled into my task, combing the fading corpse for its tale. It smelled sweet, and nothing at all like a corpse, like roses and incense, much as you may mock me to hear such things said. I learned much from her slow rotting away to nothing, and though her body is gone, I am still fashioning her lament.

Before it shivered away to dust, I happened to catch a glimpse of the great bier in the water, and to my surprise, the skeleton had the head of a decrepit old fox, whose fur might have once been red.

"I STAYED HERE SO LONG AND FOR SO MANY
years that the other harpies forgot all about me." She
drew aside the long folds of her cloak and beneath them
I saw that her harpy-body, covered in brown feathers,
had grown entirely into the earth. There was now little
difference between feathers and leaves, and her legs
were gone altogether. She grew up out of the dirt like a
stubby sapling. She chuckled and closed it again. "I told
you not to look. I have been here so long the ground
came up to greet me, and we have gotten along very
well. I chew dirt like a shrub, and the strange roots of
this place ensure I have time to finish her lament. The

cloak grows like foliage, and my face has set into something like bark. But even in my work, even as the dirt came up to hear my lament in its youth, I began, in my songs, to catch wafts of other bodies from the cave, the beginnings of other laments that cried out to be raised properly. I understood—though slowly, for have I not already said that I was a slow student?—where I had made my nest. Once in a very long while folk interrupted my work on the fox-girl's lament to ask passage into the cave. At first I told them I hardly cared where they went, but as I guessed at the true shape of the cave, that it was something like a door, I thought it only right that tolls be exacted."

"What sort of tolls?"

The harpy grinned. "There is only one kind of toll the dead accept: blood. It's always blood. The hoopoe, the Gaselli, the Stars. Pierce your breast with your beak and pour out your blood for the hungry."

I moved my hand to my chest. "What is in there? What is the Isle of the Dead?"

"Who can say? I am planted, I am not dead. Is it where the Sky went to escape her children? Is it the underside of the Sky? Is it just another country, with other laws and customs? No one tells Wept, she is just the keeper of the gate."

"Is that your name? Wept?"

"I have done it all my days, and never for myself. It is my name; it is my nature."

I pulled my calf-knife from its sheath and she pulled her bowl from the shadows. I paused, and cut into the skin of my back, letting sap puddle in the metal bowl, golden and thick as yolk. Wept raised her eyebrows and smiled widely, as a child will when shown a new thing. She pulled her cloak aside to let me pass, and I felt her feathers on the wound as I went into the dark.

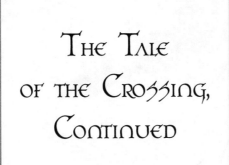

The Tale
of the Crossing,
Continued

"Yes," Seven breathed. "I had only blood to give her, of course. And she told me no tales, but I remember her face, and her bowl. But why?" he pleaded. "Why did you leave me? I would never have left you."

She looked at him with blank eyes. "I stole a leaf," she said simply, and took his hand, leading him up and into the forest, far past the lapping sound of the lonely lake against the lonely shore.

It was not a town. Nor exactly a village. It was certainly no city. But there were houses, low gray things slick

with old rain, as though someone had once lived there, long ago. It was very dark on this part of the island, and there were pricks of light in the mire, almost, though not entirely, like Stars. One of them spun very quickly, faster and faster until a woman seemed to step out of it. She was flushed with color, all the color that the forest might have had, nearly too vivid to look at. Her skin was like a snake's, scaled and thick and a screaming, writhing green, shot with black and blue and scarlet. Most of her undulated serpentine and boneless, her torso longer and more flexible than a woman's ought to be. She wore yellow veils that whipped and snapped at her heels, but covered nothing in particular, not least her green skin, which showed dark and shining through the gold cloth. Her hair was long and black and glassy, and the bangles around her arms were jeweled in a hundred kinds of agate. Her eyes were black as the bottom of a well, and her blue-black fingers were long, grasping. Her legs were clamped together, as though by sheer hope they might squeeze into a tail, but they stayed stubbornly separate.

She was pregnant, her verdant belly sloping out of her veils like Vhummim's diamond.

"I brought her the leaf," said Oubliette, by way of an explanation Seven did not at all understand. "Immacolata's leaf. I danced her for so many years, I loved her, I didn't want her to be alone. I owed it to her, to both of them, to find the cave and the lake and cut off my tail. We are not...unhappy here, together."

"I am not alone," the woman said, her voice throaty and deep, echoing through the wood. "No one will let me alone..."

The Tale
of the Leaf
and the Snake

I LOOKED DOWN OUT OF THE DARK, WHERE light held hands with light. I remember the looking, and the first searing step out of the Sky, how it hurt so, and how I cried out for my mother as I fell. They caught me in their green, my limbs so raw and full of light, slashed to ribbons, bleeding out of the pits of my knees, the hollows of my elbows, the nape of my neck—all the places where a hole can tear. I bled and I wept—we all did. We wanted to burrow into the world, but we didn't know how it would hurt.

And the snakes were there, their green and their white and their black, their red and their gold. Their sheltering hoods, their comforting tails. I looked at them, how they stopped up my wounds with their little mouths, how they warmed me with skin that had baked on flat rocks in the sun, how they hissed and sang their whispering songs. I looked at them and I wanted to be like that, I wanted to be able to move like that, to undulate, to hiss and sing and have colors like that. They were as beautiful to me as anything had been since the dark, and while my brother was sharpening himself into a harpoon, I lengthened, and stretched, and arched my back, and coiled until all of me was a coil, long and green and grinning. And where I first slithered, stepping lightly into a snake's body, I crushed beneath me a tea bush with delicate leaves, and thought no more of it than a woman who breaks a twig underfoot while running through a forest.

I was not there when the Manikarnika died, but I heard them cry out. We all did. I slid over the hills and away with the rest—I did not want to be alone. So many of the smaller Stars saw my coils and, delighted, shivered into their own. We cloistered together, we ate sparrows and mice whole, or capons and honey, as was our liking. Our shapes changed with the hour; we were fluid as rivers. We were not alone.

I knew his face when he came. Of course I knew it. Even a Star dreams. I have been dreaming a long time, and I watched the glittering cord of that man's life spool out until it intersected with mine, and how the sparks lit the grass at my feet! I looked at this man and thought: *Oh, how we are going to hurt each other.* But Stars, you know, are fixed in their courses, and we can no more change the throttling paces of orbit than a rabbit can shorten its ears. I saw his cord lashing and snapping in the dark, and could do nothing.

A moth told me the day I was going to die.

I sat in my room, and my children were all around me, playing with toy swords and real ones, depending on their age, lolling about, their skins flushed green with relief—their father had left us alone for a day, and we could relax into serpents, let our scales show through. We had each other, and no one would disturb us.

I sat at the window. The wind came through off the tea fields, sweet and brown at the edges. My son was mending the hem of my dress, his mouth full of pins. My daughters played Chaturanga, their shoulders warm as diamondbacks in the sun. Some other of my boys chased a white kitten I had brought them, their eyes bright and hungry. We were not alone, not ever. I wiped the youngest's nose, and told her to keep her tongue in her mouth—the pink and forked thing licked in and out feverishly. These are the things a mother does—did not the Sky once wipe our noses and tell us to stand up straight, did not the blackness of our mother admonish us to raise our voices and be curious, be bold, to look after one another when curiosity and boldness failed? Did she not tell us she loved us, that we were never alone?

In the dark at the beginning of the world, she said those things. And I said them to my children, though the words often stuck in my mouth, and I did not expect to say them, when I burned incandescent beside my brother and not beneath that snapping cord, that man whose breath stank of frightened women and into whom my light leeched, and leeched, and leeched. I did not want children. They were a poor substitute for what I lost—did the Sky feel the same? Is that why she left us? But I looked at them that day and knew that they came from me, that he chewed a hole in me and they swelled up so bright, so bright! And they are why I did not leave. Perhaps I do not understand my mother—but I think that is not unusual.

I sat by the window and my hand was green as vines on the sill. The moth landed on my forefinger, nailless now and scaled. His wings were pale brown, with circles like marks left by cups on old wooden tables. He was not special. Perhaps neither was I. I wore him for a moment like a jewel before he turned his furry head up to me and spoke, his voice susurring and small, twigs rubbing against dry leaves.

"If you will not eat me, I would tell you a thing."

"Why would I eat you, little moth?"

The insect paused, his feelers twitch-ing. "You are a very large snake. At least, some of you is."

"And you would make a very small meal."

"I am grateful..."

The Tale

of the

Birds' Tears

WE KNOW BECAUSE OF THE BIRDS.

In Amberabad, there was a moth with yellow wings like a wolf's eyes, and she drank the tears from the eye of a sleeping hunting hawk. The tears were cloudy and sweet, like dandelion milk.

In Muireann, there was a moth with black wings like the back of an otter, and he drank the tears from the eye of a sleeping pelican. The tears were blue and clear, like the ice from a frozen river.

In Shadukiam, there was a butterfly with wings like spun glass, and he drank the tears from the eye of a sleeping parrot. The tears were red and glimmering, like the petals of a rose.

In Ajanabh, there was a moth with gray wings like dust on a book's cover, and she drank the tears from the eye of a sleeping mynah bird. The tears were yellow and dusty, like saffron.

In Al-a-Nur, there was a butterfly with blue wings streaked in white, and she drank the tears from the eye of a sleeping swan. The tears were bloody and dark and salty, like a thing not to be touched.

Near a castle in the center of the Eight Kingdoms, there was a moth with great flapping wings that cast delicate shadows, and he drank the tears from the eye of a sleeping goose. The tears were gray and slow.

In Jinnestan, there was a dragonfly with a body all of black and green, and he drank the tears from the eye of a sleeping alerion. The tears were sharp and piquant, as though teeth had been ground into them.

In Hoaka, there was a moth with gray wings like blown ash, and he drank the tears from the eye of a sleeping ptarmigan. The tears were rosy and thin, like a girl's perfume.

In the city of Lament, there was a very small moth with the whitest wings you ever saw, and she drank the tears of a sleeping hoopoe, and the tears were soft and fine, like the hair of children.

In Irsil, there was a butterfly with no wings at all, who with her very last strength drank the tears from the eye of a sleeping sparrow. The tears were spicy and thick, but they did her no good.

In Kash, there was a moth with wings all flaming and smoking, and he drank the tears of a sleeping phoenix, which were molten white, like a blade not yet born.

In Urim, there was a moth with wings like mourning veils, and he laid them over the eyes of the dead. He drank from the tears of a blood-cold kingfisher. The tears were red as apple skins, and blue as moon-light.

In Nahara, there was a moth with wings like a church window, full of brilliant greens and reds and blues. She drank the tears from the eye of a sleeping loon. The tears were black and thick, like an ebony sill.

And in Varaahasind, there was a moth with brown wings like a hundred other moths, and he drank the tears from the eye of a sleeping peacock. The tears were blue and green and gold, like the skin of a snake, and his name was Fahad, and he came to this window, his belly full of tears.

What do the birds dream that makes them weep so? We might have asked, but they are quick to eat, and not to converse. Instead we flutter over the face of the world, in every dusty pocket and lantern halo, and drink their grief, and taste their mourning in the draft. Eggs that fall from the nest and break on the grass, terrible strands of yolk flung from blade to blade, not enough seeds in the winter, falcons with claws that snatch, fish which are too clever by half—ah! We have known these sorrows! But once in a long while there are the flavors of other miseries floating there. It took all the tears I have mentioned and more for us to taste the whole of it. We brought them, clinging to a thousand proboscises like diamond necklaces, to the cistern at the center of Ilinistan, the City of Insects, which is a place you are not permitted to know. There is flame there which does not burn the wing, and webs which do not tear, and rivers of sugar water trickling through mossy stones. There hives make honey for joy in its gold, and not for the hungry mouths of men. There ants may rest, for winters do not scour us, nor is any sweet thing rare.

There are so many flowers there, my lady, you cannot imagine.

And in the center of Ilinistan, there is a cistern, where the ants and the beetles and the termites hollowed a stump so smoothly and perfectly that anyone might be proud to write upon its walls as though it were the finest paper, save that the stranger should be promptly devoured by spiders for the offense. And once in a long while, the drinkers of tears commune there, to understand the sorrow of the birds, who are also not permitted to know the way to Ilinistan. So we let our tears fall, one by one, blue by white by red by green by yellow, into the cistern, until it is full to brimming, and we can look in its waters and see the shape of the thing that the birds mourn.

In the cistern, oh lady, oh Star, oh lost and lonely thing, I saw your face, and knew that your course would pass under the ground, where only the worms go, to whatever pale, blind city they call their own, and which I am not permitted to know.

The Tale
of the Leaf
and the Snake,
Continued

THE MOTH REGARDED ME FOR A MOMENT.

"Will you not weep, lady? Do you not care?"

"I am more interested, friend Fahad, in the existence of a place which I am not permitted to know."

"He will come for you this evening, this very one."

"And he will find us dressed in our very best, as befits children awaiting a visit from their father, and a wife her husband."

I put my hand, very gently, to the moth's wings, and stroked the fine hairs. "Stars burn out, little moth."

*   *   *

But surely you know this story. Surely you danced it, or sang it, or heard it at your mother's breast. I am so common, these days. Everyone speaks in my voice.

I did not burn out. Oh, Mother, why did you not let me? You could have stitched me together again, as though the hole was never there, and I could have forgotten what it felt like to tear myself out of you, what it felt like to have children tear themselves out of me, what it felt like to dribble light into a man's mouth night after night. What my children looked like as they faded to nothing. What I looked like, too.

I did not burn out. I came to the lakeside, where, I suppose now, all things come. There was a sorry little dock in dire need of new paint, and a low tide, frothing gray water and sandpipers fishing for fleas. What sort of fleas do they find, I wonder? I walked the shore, and my elbows were damp. I was stuck between woman and snake, my body twisting out of one and into the other—did my mother wish to indicate that I should have made up my mind? I have already said I do not understand her. She probably had nothing to do with it. I walked the shore and I could see the ferryman coming, I could see his raft and his ruined mast, I could see his pole. And when he moored at the dock, I stepped forward, to climb aboard.

But the air thickened like cream around me, and there were hands on my chest, pushing me back. Dimly in the fog I could see the faces of my girls, my loves, my little Stars, their beautiful eyes burning up the air. They put out their hands to me, and I took them as I used to—they were cold, but women's hands are often cold. How many times do I remember breathing on them, rubbing them red again? They would not let me pass. They opened their mouths in unison, and I saw that their tongues were cut out. They pressed on me in unison and I staggered.

And in the throng I could see two, one with no eyes, and one with no ears, who cried out louder than any. They pushed and wept and their laments were like stones thrown after an unwanted child. They pushed me back from the shore, and the ferryman watched, but made no move. They pushed me back, and back, and back, to the wet green jungle and the red towers.

I opened one hundred and forty-five pairs of eyes.

They pushed me into those bodies, those bodies who had eaten me, chewed me to gristle, and still held me in their swilling bellies. It felt strange to move one hundred and forty-five pairs of arms. They seemed to pinwheel all around me, I could not keep them steady. I looked with my eyes into my eyes into my eyes, I was in all of them, and I could smell pig's flesh, always, always. They swallowed me down; I lived inside them like a child. And in the core of each of them, under the pig's heart and the pig's squealing lungs and the pig's starving stomach, was the little white blade of the pig's tooth. Only my husband was empty of that tooth, and him I could not bear to smell, or hear, or touch.

But the rest were a smoky labyrinth of pig and man, and I writhed through it, flashing green at their boiled and festering pinks.

I am tired, the boar's tooth said.

I am sorry for you, I answered.

I was only hungry. I didn't mean to eat all those maidens, all those boys, all those horses. But I was so hungry. What beast is blamed for its hunger? Only me. He cut me up like breakfast and pulled all these creatures out of me, and now I am hungrier still, I eat for a hundred and forty-five, my belly growls in one hundred and forty-five skins, and I am so tired.

I am sorry for you, I said in the depths of those hundred and forty-five. *He cut me up, too, like supper, and pulled children out of me, and I am tired, too.*

If I were myself again, I would eat him, and be sated.

Would you like me to help you?

Yes, oh yes.

But surely you know this story. Surely you danced it, or sang it, or heard it at your mother's breast. I am in everyone's mouth these days, just as I was then.

My brother saw to my body. It is in a cave somewhere, I think—sometimes I smell dripping water, and old stones, even now. I came again to the lakeside, and this time no one put a hand to my chest, or a wail to my ear. It was empty, and the wind wheedled the stones. No one came for me. I was alone. The dock had been painted. The sandpipers seemed fat. My hair was wet this time, wet with belly and tears. I waited a long time, but the ferry came, dragging dark water behind it.

I came from the lake to the Isle. I came from the Isle to the thing which is not a village nor a town nor a city. I huddled in the low gray houses, cold and alone. It was not pleasant, but it was not unpleasant. At least he was gone, and I only moved my own eyes, and not one hundred and forty-five pairs of eyes. I called out for my mother, but she did not answer. I called out for my children, but they did not answer—though a low scratching came at the ramshackle door.

I opened the door, my own hand so bright against the gray. I do not know what I expected, but what I saw was a young woman whose body was covered in diamonds so that she had no skin which was not jewels, no pink or brown about her. Her hair was a river of ice. Around her were fourteen slips of light with no faces, like candles lit in a chapel.

"I'm sorry," the diamond girl said, and her voice was so familiar to me, though I had never heard it. "They never grew up, you know. They wanted to find you, they are drawn to you, Mother-moth, but they don't really understand, they don't really speak. They are just light, light which knows it was once something else, but which cannot quite recall. But you called them, and I brought them. They did want to come."

My children glowed around me in a ring, and little Diamond, bright as a burning pyre, smallest of the Manikarnika, folded me into her arms.

There are so few of us who ever died, this is a sparse and lonely place. But we are all together, and some reflection of our light floats around us, like lamps shining in a pool. My girls are here, my Grass-Snake-Stars and my Copperhead-Stars and my Cobra-Stars, my loves and my oracles, and we wander as we used to, our little cloister. I am never alone.

"Who built the houses?" I asked Diamond once. She shook her head.

"They were here. How should we know how to build houses? I think—" She blushed, and the diamonds in her face flushed into rubies for a moment. "I think Idyll built them for us. Surely there must be days when no one dies."

I would like to say time passed, but I cannot be sure. I would like to say, "One day I met two men walking between the birch trees." But what is day? What is night? It is always dark here, some anonymous kindness, to remind us of the cradle of the Sky. And so all I can say is that it happened sometime, and somewhere, among the white trees, in the dark. Two came walking hand in hand. They were both bright as I, but I did not know them. Their skin was red and deeply grained, like wood, and when we clasped hands in greeting, their fingers were hard as a raft's planks. They wore sailors' rags over identical bodies, and their eyes were wood-warm and gentle, lined a little at the corners—but perhaps that was just the grain of their skin. Reddish hair flopped over twin foreheads like thready bark.

"We are Itto," they said in unison. One's voice was deep, and the other's high, like a child's, but beyond that they were the same in every fashion. "We were the Twinned Star once, and in this place, we have been made to walk two by two. We do not find it unpleasant."

They spoke always together, and it was only strange to me for a while. He had been translated into twins, as I had into my half-snake self, and their skin had gone the shade of their raft. They told me the tale of their raft, and their death, and their fox-girl, and I held them while they cried for the lost craft and the lost world—we are all so lost; we are all so broken, the least of us would hold the smallest as they wept. I told them the tale of my husband, and my children, who still followed me like confused will-o'-the-wisps. The two young men looked at me with chagrined, resigned eyes, as though they expected no more than this, and held four red arms out to me. I did not know what they meant. I told them of the boar-men, and how the voice of the boar-tooth sounded, and how the women stopped me at the shore. They folded me into their wooden arms on the floor of the forest, and I lay stiffly against them. I did not cry—snakes do not—but I was grateful for them, for their circuit of arms and because they had not sought me out, to show me their love, to make certain I was not alone, to show me some ill-got devotion, to disturb me in the dark. I softened against them, and they stroked my hair. I told them how I was just once alone, on the lakeside, the second time, when no one came for me.

My children lay around us in a ring, like glowing, insensate mushrooms.

"I am not a raft," I said, and the twins chuckled.

"We are not a King," they answered.

It was difficult to tell them apart unless they spoke, which was not often. One of them became my lover, and his deep voice sounded in my bones. The other was harder, more raftlike, and he was simply kind to me, his child's voice rare and thin. He helped me molt, and once, when there was almost something like a moon above the Isle, he came to me, having cut himself on the hinge of my door, and touched my lips with a light-smeared thumb. It tasted of salt, and wood. The other twin was with me always, and his kisses were red and dusty and gentle. They tasted like the sea. We walked in the wood, and once in a while red fruit appeared on the trees like ambassadors from some far-off spring, and we all ate together. I was not alone. I am not alone. Who could think I have ever been alone?

But a girl came with a bloody stump where her tail should have been, telling me how lonely I am with her huge, needing eyes, clutching a leaf in her hand. I knew the leaf in a moment—I had seen it in the tea-woman, the distant child of the leaves I had crushed when first I fell. She brought it to me as though it would mean something to return my own light to me, like a child's doll which was discarded long ago, one eye missing, one arm empty of stuffing. I placed the leaf against my skin and it melted back into me where it belonged. I thought no more of it, and offered the girl my house, my red fruit, though she would not eat, the ungrateful thing. But perhaps it did mean something after all, because it was only afterwards that my belly grew.

I cannot tell if it was the light of one twin or the kisses of the other or the leaf itself or the girl who brought it that filled me up with child again. Perhaps it was all of them. Perhaps none. But I am not alone, even in my own skin.

The Tale of the Crossing, Continued

"HOW IS IT EVEN POSSIBLE IN THIS PLACE?" Zmeya cried, cradling her stomach in her arms. "What will come out of me, that was born with the dead for midwives, a dead mother, a dead father?"

Oubliette looked down in shame. Tears were hot on her face, steaming into the air. She glanced up at Seven ruefully. "I'm sorry," she said. "I wanted to save you. To save her, the tea girl. I was just silly."

Zmeya's face softened, shades of green playing over her cheeks. "Oh, I don't blame you, poor thing. You are so lost, too. Can I help but tease you for those great hungry eyes, for all those things you said when you came here squeezing your little leaf? But why would you not eat at my table?" The Snake-Star moved forward to hold the huldra's head in her hands.

Oubliette laughed and wiped at her tears. "Anyone who has read a book in her life knows not to eat the food of the dead," she answered. The two women embraced briefly, as though they did not want to embarrass their visitor. Seven felt the weight of how much she had seen and done without him pulling at his sleeve.

"Why do they love you like this?" he demanded. They started back, away from his frayed voice. "Why does everyone fling themselves at you, just praying you'll catch them? Immacolata, Oubliette—they gave up everything just for you!"

Zmeya looked at him over Oubliette's bent head. "I don't know!" she hissed. "Who knows why you do anything? You look at us and call us gods and sacrifice your seventh sons on altars we know nothing about! You build up towers we never asked you to build, and with your other hands you slaughter us and tell us that wood is too fine for the likes of us, and rape us until our legs crack! How should I know why some few of you fail to mutilate us? But if those few fling themselves at me, what can I do but catch them? Who will do it, if I do not? If I turn them away like bad children who ought not to trouble their betters?"

"They are not your children to catch!"

"Tell them that. And then tell me to turn away a girl who cuts into her body for my sake, tell her that she is not welcome, there are already too many sisters here, we have no room for more."

The one-armed boy turned to his friend with eyes that pleaded and prostrated. "Was I not brother enough?"

Oubliette glared at him. "There are some things you never get over," she spat. "You left Taglio and Grotteschi without a word. Were they not family enough? Have you thought at all of them, how they might miss you, how they might wish you had stayed, if they are closer to Ajanabh, within its gates, if Grotteschi is even now singing at shuttered windows?"

Seven said nothing.

"That is how often I have thought of you," she finished.

In the Garden

THE TWILIGHT WAS THIN AND WISPY OVER THE LAKE. THE GIRL'S SKIN was warm under her cloak, but the boy trembled.

"When you finish the tales," he said, "when your eyelids have poured out all their ink between us and the Garden is black with them, will you leave me as Oubliette left Seven? As Seven left the Gaselli and the Manticore? Will you go off into a place I cannot touch and never think of me again?" He swallowed hard. "Or will you remember that there was once a nice boy who was not afraid of you, and walked in the Garden with you, and listened to you, and did not interrupt more often than is polite? Will you sit at a table of blue crystal with parrot wings for legs with fabulous monsters all around, eating lunches of leek and rose and think to yourself: I wonder whatever happened to that boy, where he is now, if he is married, if he is fat, if he has kept the Garden well trimmed?"

He could hardly look at her; his hands shook like brown cattails.

The girl scowled at him. "When I finish the tales, when my eyelids have poured out all their ink into your hands and I have nothing left for myself, will you run back to the Palace like a good prince and leave me to my fate, just as Hind left the beast who loved her? Will you go into rooms at whose doors I am not even allowed to knock and never think of me again? Or will you remember that there was once a nice girl who did not ask too much of you, and walked in the Garden with you, and told you stories that made your head swim with all manner of strange fishes, and thought so much for your safety that she taught you all the secret places that were once hers alone? Will you sit with a Sultan's turban and crown on your head, a Sultan's bangle at your wrist, at a golden table borne up by the backs of perfumed slaves and think to yourself: I wonder whatever happened to that girl, where she is now, if she is married, if she is fat, if she has made friends among the demons?"

Neither of them spoke for a long while, the air between them heavy and sad as old rain. The girl clenched her teeth against the reassurances that yearned to come. They were soft and sweet and untrue. She did not know—how could she know?—what would happen.

"I think," the boy said, "that I would bring supper out to these stones, out to this lake, for fifty years, for all of my reign, in hopes that you would come back, with fresh ink on your eyes, and new marvels to tell. I would take down all the Garden gates, and someday there would be an old, white-haired man with green apples and roast dove in his napkin, sitting by the water and asking himself whatever happened to that girl."

She smiled, and touched his hand. The bird of pearl sat between them, unconcerned.

"We have the whole night," she said. "The moon is not even up. Shall I finish the tale of that awful, lonely Isle?"

"Yes," the boy breathed.

THE TALE
OF THE CROSSING,
CONTINUED

THE CHILD WAS LONG IN COMING.

Seven joined Oubliette in one of the long, empty gray houses. There were two windows, and two long beds, and a low, rough table, but she would not let him eat the apples and plantains and pomegranates that were laid out there.

"Who left us this?" Seven asked.

The huldra shrugged. "They tend to credit Idyll for anything strange and bright that does not come from them. But who can say? The second bed is new, as well. Maybe no one. Maybe it grows from the table like a spring of holly from a holly bush. Maybe this is a house-bush, and it blossomed up a new bed for you, and supper." She crooked a smile, and things went easier between them then, though they both wondered how long they could last without eating the rich red meal that each evening sat shining on the table.

They slept separately for half of a single night before Oubliette crawled in beside her friend like a wary cat.

In what passed for mornings on the Isle, one of the Itto twins might come and take them to see how the wispy lights of Zmeya's children wheeled along the forest floor, playing like butterflies or finches. Diamond might come with one of her sisters to bring sticks of fire to each of the houses' hearths, should the houses have hearths that day. They were odd, intractable shacks who might offer a fire grate once, and, if rebuffed, withhold them from everyone for weeks. So when hearths appeared, the Stars hastened to please them with sparks and crackling logs. Yet no matter how often Seven and Oubliette politely told their house they were not hungry, or did not care for fruit, there it was the next evening, fresh and new and sparkling.

Sometimes Zmeya herself would come, with a kind, distracted smile, and her teeth were sometimes green and sometimes red, and her face was soon enough famil- iar to them as any neighbor's who often comes to borrow sugar or soap. Once she took them far into the Isle, into the bare forest, and showed them a little clear pool. She placed her finger on the water and it swelled up with brown leaves, tea leaves swirling thick and fast in the shape of a woman's face, a woman's face the color of the sole of a shoe, the color of oolong and lemon peel. The face wept sweet brown tears to see Zmeya, and more to hear the mortal pair tell of Taglio, and how he fared in the world. Oubliette and Seven thought that thin, warm voice was the loveliest thing they had ever heard.

At other times, Zmeya would take them walking down by the shore, and showed them a firm stone path among the blinking eyes which Seven had not seen, and they would watch the horizon for a sign of the ferry. There were algae on the lashes of the eyes, but the sandpipers did not come out that far, and only once or twice did they hear an owl, or a thrush, or the weird, whooping cry of a tiny hoopoe.

The lake was vast; the other side could not be seen, and when it rained, which was often, the water and the sky blurred into one great gray globe. Seven repaired the dock as best he could with no tools and one arm, which is to say not very well, but the effort was appreciated. Oubliette painted it with a mixture of boiled bark and beach-tears. It glowed ghostly in the water, and after a time, as was surely inevitable, the raft appeared within the great gray globe, and the ferryman brought a woman to the valiantly mended dock.

She was not yet a crone, but tending toward it as a weather vane will veer toward an easterly wind. She had long gray wings where her arms ought to have been, and her feet were webbed and yellow. Her hair was dark, streaked with wide bands of silver feathers, the thick black strands clearly losing their battle against the bird. There were well-grooved lines at her deep, wide eyes, and at her mouth, but she was thin and nimble as a goose in flight, and her cheeks were whipped and flushed by the lake gales. Her gait was businesslike and brisk, her fingers long and purposeful, pushing back her fog-damp hair from her forehead. Her gaze went immediately to Zmeya's swollen stomach.

"I see I am needed," she said. Her voice was rough, as though she had been talking without cease for years on end.

Zmeya covered her belly with one long, green arm. "How long," she murmured, "do you think it takes a child to grow inside a dead woman?"

"As long as it pleases, I expect," the stranger said with a bemused grin.

Idyll glanced at Seven and Oubliette, and opened his mouth as if to say something, but closed it again. Finally, he grunted:

"The dock looks better. Shoddy joint work, though."

He slowly poled away from the shore and into the mists. The water lapped behind him, a sound like an infant crying far away.

"Well," said the newcomer, "that's done with. Now, Mistress of Snakes, Pig-Slayer, Star of the Jungle! Your brother is worried about you..."

The
Midwife's Tale

IN MY YOUNGER DAYS, I WAS A GOOSE.

This is nothing to gawk at. Geese are quite common in my country, which lies as far to the east as the ice floes lie to the north. When we moved through the sky, we were like a hand passed over the face of the sun, and the forests were in shadow. My name was Aerie then, and it remains.

But that was a long time ago. Now I am a woman, and my flock is gone, and my brother was King, for a time.

Perhaps you have heard this story. It is not so common as tales involving ravenous snakes, but some few minstrels still sing about the goose-girl and how she and her brother killed a tyrant.

My brother did not love a lonely chair in a lonely castle, and went long ago to join the Patricides in Al-a-Nur, where he is at peace, and wears a red habit. I was not there with him when he took his vows, though he sent men to find me to all the corners of the world, to beg me to come home. But that place, that castle with its rivers and its secrets, was not my home, and I hid when I heard them call. They told him that they found geese and girls, but not both, and with a bent head he went out of the world, and out of our story.

I went to find the thread of our mother's tale and tuck it back into the stitching. Thus, I found a Quest after all. Perhaps it runs in the blood. I chased the tale into the high mountains tipped with snow like wise men's beards, and down to the sea, laid before me smooth as a dress. The world is wider than anyone guesses. It took years, and along the way, I had something like the education my great-grandmother might have given me. I learned the ways of the grass-and-leaves witch; I learned how to make love potions and cold cures and gout-softeners for those who could pay me, and to look up at the sky to tell a young girl whether her husband would have light or dark hair, and to deliver her baby when the time was right for it, and to bury her when the time was right for that. Silver came again to my temples, a silver like feathers. I did not mind the time, or the distance. That is what an education means.

Finally I went where I ought to have gone to begin with, to a burnt-out ring of trees and old huts half reclaimed by the golden grasses, where a wildcat hide was still hanging on a branch, and goose feathers blew like ashes through the paths that led from hut to hut. How many times the flock must have come to this place to mourn themselves! The blackened dome-frames smelled of horse tallow and scorched wood. The sun was bright and hard as I walked through the ruins, the old red sash of Leucrotta skin flapping against my hips. The place was not even big enough for anyone to plunder, and I wept for my mother for the thousandth time.

When the sun had drained itself into the western hills, I heard a colt snort in the distance, and found, not far off, a small black horse chewing the long, dry grass. It was not special—it was not the great black Mare I longed to see—but it was not afraid of me, and it nosed my pockets for apples. Ascertaining that I had none, it trotted off, and with a horse-woman's logic, I followed after. Soon I was at a dead run, streaming sweat just to keep her in sight. Often she would wait for me to catch up and then canter off again, and in this way we came, at length, to a great hollow cave. By the time I came to the crevice in the cliff wall, the colt was nowhere to be seen.

The cave was as empty as the razed village. How I wanted to see the Mare! Even the horrid Fox! But the chamber was empty, and the walls were smooth, with no little door to let me pass, and no wolves came to greet me. If the Sleepers still lay within, there was no longer any path to them. I sat on the earthen floor of the cave and called out. My voice hardly even echoed.

My old bones were so weary, and I had come so far. I will admit to tears.

I fell asleep there on the dirt, my fists clenched like a baby's against my mud-streaked face. He was crouching above me when I woke.

"Why are you here?" he said, and his voice echoed—oh, how it echoed. He was a man whose skin was like paper, whiter than paper, paler than any mortal skin, like snow over snow. His hair fell long and straight to his waist, and over his shoulder was slung a large and barbed harpoon of bone. His eyes glowered golden, and his bent legs were covered in silvery tattoos, a whipping, curving tongue I could not read. Now, I know my grass and I know my leaves and I know my stories. Laakea the Harpoon-Star could hardly stare me in the face but I would know him. "Why do you come to this place?" he demanded. "It is not for you, not anymore. Go home," he spat. His scorn burned me as surely as a flame.

"I...I came because of my mother, to find the Wolf-Star, and the light..."

"You do not have claim to that light any longer. It is all used up. Go back to your love potions and leave us alone; we are not a fountain at which you may casually drink."

"Where did she go? The Wolf? The Sleepers? Where is the Mare?"

His face colored angrily. "The last girl came and went. This place is spent. It had a life, like any tree or beast. It was born when two sisters died here, and fed their gifts to a third, and ended when a horsewoman touched a Fox without permission. The Mare, as you call her, has probably already forgotten it existed. And Liulfr—my kin, not yours—went back to the Sky, to put those bodies in their graves, to do what Stars may do for sisters, and cousins, and kin. Go home. There is nothing for you here."

"But I have looked for this place all my life!" I spread my empty, grubby hands.

"I do not care! Why do you awful creatures insist that we care for every little thing you do?" The Star let out a terrible wail, his beautiful face contorting in grief, his head thrown back, tears streaming from his eyes like lightning. "One of you killed my sister! If I could I would tear all of you apart for one glimpse of her whole again!"

"I did not kill your sister," I growled.

"It does not matter. When you look into the Sky, do you see our faces? No, you see a multitude, all the same. So it is when I look at you. My sister's body lies within, where the Sleepers were. She is more holy in her smallest blink than the lot of them, and she deserves this place no less than they. But I will not let any little girls drink from her like a cup."

"I...I didn't mean that. But I was young when I began, and now I am old, and if I do not take the light soon, I will die, and my family will perish in the dark."

"It is not yours to take. It never was. This is not about your family; it is about mine." He paused for a moment, his alabaster jaw set hard. "If you are unafraid of the dark, would you pay for the light your grandmothers took? I will give you, one last time, the light you seek, if you are willing to barter for it."

"Yes, anything!" Well, that is a foolish promise, but foolishness is not only the province of the young. He knelt before me, and I did not know what to do, but his eyes were huge, vast pools of gold and pleading.

"Find her. Find her and tell me where we go. Tell me what happens to us, tell me she is at peace. Tell her I love her. Tell her I tried to protect her. I cannot bear to think of her alone!" His voice broke and he was as miserable as a child lost in a dark wood. "Tell her I miss her so."

With that he drew his harpoon and thrust it into my heart.

The Tale
of the Crossing,
Concluded

ZMEYA'S EYES WERE FULL OF GREEN TEARS. "I miss him, too," she said.

"He put his harpoon into me, and more light poured into my chest than my grandmother ever knew. It burned me through and through, like scalding oil poured down my throat. I felt it screaming in me and called out my mother's name, I felt it screaming in me and called out my brother's name, and my grandmother's, and all the names of my flock. The silver came bubbling up out of my mouth like blood and he drew back the blade."

Zmeya was nodding. "He never gave up more than a

cupful of his light. He still burns where he walks, as we all did in the earliest days."

"It was enough so that I seemed to the ferryman a Star, and he brought me here, where I aimed."

"How much did you pay him?" Seven asked. Aerie blinked. "Idyll. What did you pay him to ferry you across? How much did you bleed for the harpy?"

The witch-woman laughed. "Coins are for the living, boy. For those who shouldn't be here, and for carrying back those who shouldn't be there. Blood is for those who have no business on this lake. There are other ways of getting to this place—namely, by dying. Laakea offered to cut my throat as quickly as possible, but I knew a faster way. I loosed my Leucrotta-sash from my waist and fell down as dead as when my brother snapped my neck. And here I am, half-goose, as I always was. We have an agreement—I will ferry back to him what he seeks, and he will tie it on again at the new moon." She looked the Snake-Star up and down again. "So, seeing that you require my more mundane skills, I hope it pleases the child to come out sooner rather than later." She crouched down and spoke directly to the heavy bulge in the serpent-skin. "Do you hear that, little one?"

We showed Aerie the island, and cautioned her not to eat the red fruits if she meant to go back. She and Zmeya talked at length, cloistered together like novices, their heads bent, long wings folded around long scales. The serpent asked how she could possibly be with child; the goose asked if she had pains, chills, aches in her feet. It happened that they were conversing in this way when Zmeya cried out, her voice in the mist like eggs cracking, and fell against one of the gray houses, clutching her stomach. The house yielded hurriedly, cupping her back in its wall. The Itto twins came running, their red feet throwing up pebbles, and caught her up in their arms, whispering to her and stroking her hair and cooing against her neck. They cradled her against them as she pressed her cool snake's cheeks to theirs. Fourteen wan, wispy lights peered out from behind the thin trees, frightened and flickering. Aerie only shrugged and set to her work, her wings nearly as deft as hands.

"It did not hurt like this, before, with the others," Zmeya said, shuddering.

"You are dead. Your body does not want to give up this hot little clutch of life. It wants to keep it."

Seven and Oubliette looked on from a distance, and it seemed to them a terrible birth. Zmeya's shrieking shot out over the shacks, bleak and rasping. Her feet kicked out on the ground, and a sickly light spilled from her as blood might from a living woman. Finally there was a child in Aerie's wings, with great black eyes and a shock of dark hair, her skin gray and wet. Zmeya held her and smoothed her daughter's hair. The fourteen lights looked curiously over her shoulders. One of the Itto twins put out his ruddy, grained finger, and the baby gripped it, her fist sure.

"What will you call her?" Aerie said. "Names are so terribly important, you know."

"I shall call her Sorrow," whispered the serpent after a long while. "I shall give her now a surfeit of sadness, and hope that it will pay in one stroke for happiness in all her days. Perhaps she will have more days than my other children."

The fourteen lights dimmed a little, but not much.

But it was not to be. The child was sickly, ill, her cheeks hollow. No matter how the serpent tried to nurse her hatchling, her breasts would not fill. No light came filtering through the branches to illumine her, to feed her. The babe's breath was hot in the air, her wails bright and cutting, the only living thing on an Isle of shades and Stars, and interlopers halfway between. The child had no light that anyone could see, and her little lips trembled in the cold, showing her pink gums, no more than a cold, hungry little girl. Sorrow could not be fed, and she slowly wasted, becoming thinner and thinner, while Aerie waited for the new moon.

"What is wrong with her?" Zmeya begged for answers.

Aerie sighed. "You are dead. You cannot feed a child with your hard, cold flesh. You cannot expect the child of dead Stars to glitter and gleam. She will die here, the only thing ever born in the land of the dead."

And Zmeya wept, bitter and keen. The lights around her flashed in grief. "Please, Aerie. Take her. Put her on the raft and when your sash is tight around you again, go quickly to the mourning beast by the glass-strewn lake which Oubliette and Seven sought, and take her from the cave—you can have a cave, at last, all your own. I cannot watch another child fade to nothing."

Aerie pursed her lips. "You did not want her, you know. It would be no worse than if you had never had her at all."

Zmeya drew herself up, her face grave. "Do not try to shame me, woman. A hole was chewed in me, and out she came, and she deserves a chance to step down out of the dark, as I did. She is my girl, delicate and small as a Grass-Star, and I love her, I do love her."

One of the Ittos, the one with the child's voice, touched Sorrow's damp hair. "She is ours, too, and we love her, and she ought not to perish here where no one can see what sort of beast a snake and a ship can make. Take her."

"What is it you would have me do? I am too old to rear a child to grown. I do not think Laakea is the fathering type."

Zmeya considered. "He would shut her away so no one could ever harm her, and she would never see the sun. Care for her yourself, I would ask you. Or if you cannot, find a family whose child is dead, and bear her into their open arms. Or take her to a family with linens in a new crib and jewels in their hair, with hearts which are fierce and sweet, and put her in their cradle in place of their daughter, like a magpie with her secret eggs. Find the mortal girl a home in some far-off kingdom, take her to a childless creature who might love her like its own young, but take her, take her away, and let Sorrow grow up happy and whole and fed, warm by a fire and in sight of the Sky."

The twins stood on the mended dock and cupped their scarlet hands around their mouths. They made a long, desolate sound, like foghorns on a lonely bay. Seven and Oubliette held hands, and Aerie flared her wings in anticipation. The ferry parted the fog not long after. Zmeya bundled her daughter onto the raft, her tears splashing on the infant's face.

"What is it you think you're doing?" Idyll asked. "I do not bear passengers without payment. And I am not fond of being summoned like a maid."

The assembled throng looked from one to another. "What payment can there be on this Isle?" the deep-throated Itto asked helplessly.

Slowly, Seven drew out a single yellow coin, of old bone, smoothed

by his fingers. It bore a faint spider sigil. Oubliette looked at him, her eyebrows raised. "Is this child worth so much to you?" she asked.

"No," he said simply. "But I ate the apples the first night I was here. I am sorry I lied, but you would have kept me from it. I know you will never leave her, and now I cannot, either. I do not wish to. I will never leave you. In any gray city, I will stand by you, and you will not be alone."

Oubliette threw back her disheveled head and laughed. "I ate the plantains that night, too, that first night you were here."

Seven squeezed her hand, and gave over the coin to the ferryman without looking at it, without weighing it in his palm. Idyll frowned and turned it over in his hands. His forehead was creased with concern and disapproval, but he allowed the child to be tucked into his bony arm. Zmeya and the twins held each other up in the midst of the fourteen lights, and they kissed their daughter over and over.

As the ferry drifted off from the shore of eyes, Aerie smiled faintly, and pressed her cheek to the serpent's.

"Don't worry, my dear, I know just where to take her. And I will tell your brother that you are beautiful still." She looked around, and back toward the beachhead and the distant houses. "And not alone in the least."

As they watched, the goose-woman's waist cinched itself in, a thickening band of red appearing like a bloody fog—and by the time it seemed solid enough to touch, she was gone. The ferry drifted beyond the mist, leaving them alone on the dock, grim and grieving as a funeral.

In the Garden

THE BOY CLASPED HER HANDS IN HIS. THE MOON WAS SO HIGH AND bright that it scrubbed their faces in silver like an industrious nursemaid. A stiff wind lashed the poplar branches, and the cattails rattled their woody cacophony. The girl sat in the midst of her wood, as red in her cloak as the first sun of winter.

"What happened to the child?" he cried. "Where did Aerie take her? Was she beautiful when she grew up? A warrior like all Zmeya's other daughters?"

The girl laughed, her smile broad and glad in the night, starlight dancing on her lap, her dark eyelids rippling slightly, like the surface of the little Garden lake. The boy blushed, and the girl thought that she liked that best of all, when he could not contain how much he wanted to hear her speak, when he broached his etiquette in eagerness. The blue night shone on his cheeks in patches, and his breath was frosted in the air. Somewhere behind them, a fish jumped and splashed down with a tinkling noise.

"If you will return to the Garden, and to me, I shall tell you, and things even more strange and wonderful." She grinned.

The girl pulled the bird of pearl from the folds of the black wolf tails and tugged on its sapphire tail. It chimed out the midnight hour, long and clear and sweet.

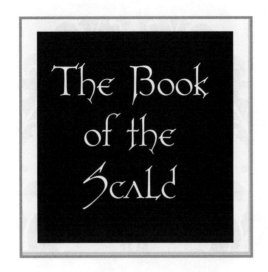

The Book
of the
Scald

In the Garden

IT WAS SNOWING IN THE GARDEN.

This was not unheard-of—surely in the books of the Sultan there was a woodcut of ladies in fur collars cavorting in the snow, little bell-strung dogs leaping at their feet. Some few flakes had even fallen when the girl was young, but certainly not this, not a blizzard which sunk men into ice to their knees. Frost had not gilded the leaves of the lemon trees in so long that even the oldest of noblewomen doddering in her bed could only dimly recall what color her dog might have been, and the sound of his jangling bells. Yet the lake had frozen into a reed-rimmed mirror, and the pine needles were sheathed in ice, glittering cold and quiet. Children cavorted; dogs leapt. New woodcuts were hurriedly pressed.

The chestnut boughs were frozen in place, and the wedding was set for the longest night of the year, so that the feast could last as long as possible. Beasts from far-off places were brought to the Palace to be roasted, and the boy sniffed at plates of rhinoceros, crocodile, camel, bear, and hippopotamus. He wondered glumly what would be served at his wedding. He was tired of being clucked over by seamstresses who seemed only to discuss how much he had grown; and how broad his chest would be in a few years. Needles glittered in their mouths like ice.

In all the delight at the snow, the Garden was blazing with candles and colors, as the Palace yearned to touch and taste the stuff for themselves. The kitchen maids stuck out their tongues to catch flakes, and young men brought frozen oranges to their lovers. Skirts of violet and emerald swished over the paths; shoes of clattering horn and oiled stag-skin spoiled the perfect white with footprints, like ink scrawled haphazardly upon a page of new paper. Among all of these the boy sometimes thought he saw the girl— but there were so many black-haired girls in the Palace, and each time he rounded a hedge or a clay bowl of winter lilies or a bare plum tree, following a stream of dark curls, there was only a pretty, rouged child with jewels on her forehead. He could not often bring himself to even apologize.

But he was sure she would come again. He knew it. The flat sky filled with drifting snow and it melted on his scalp, but he felt no cold. She was there, in the Garden, somewhere, and so he was happy enough, sure that just around the next drift she was waiting for him. When she had disappeared before, he was sure she had abandoned him, but now—had he not heard the tale of Seven and Oubliette? Did he not know himself as true a friend as the one-armed boy? Did he not know her as wild and lovely as the huldra? His faith only faltered a little, like a larch bending in a stiff wind, as the winter wore on, and the snow did not melt, and she did not appear. He chased drafts of black hair like rabbits, and the night of the wedding drew nearer, and she did not appear. Dogs leapt; bells jangled.

Finally, the night before the wedding bloomed lightless, moonless, starless. The only lights in the Garden were high braziers and candles, their flames reflecting blue and white on the sparkling, freezing ground. The boy walked through the chestnut chapel, where everything from altars to aisle was draped in cloths to keep it safe from the frost. And so it seemed that the deepest snow of all lay on Dinarzad's dais. As he passed it, he thought he heard the chime of a little bird, and, his heart leaping, he dashed into the snow to follow it, through bloomless rosebushes and the black husks of pomegranates, through blazing, icy persimmons and knobbled acacias, all the way through the center of the Garden and through it, to the far edge, farther than he had ever run before, to the great silver Gate which ran all around the Palace grounds like a river. The bird chime led him on, and the boy's breath was quick and fast, his brow wet, by the time he reached the filigree Gate, which showed an endless scene that circled the Garden and back again on itself, a scene of a great battle between men and monsters, in which the men had stern eyes of silver and pearl, and the beasts had craven expressions wrought in iron. Braziers capped the Gate every so often, and the wood beyond was dark and deep.

On the monsters' side stood the girl in her red cloak.

In that moment the boy loved his sister for slipping that outlandish thing into his pack—the girl's lips were pale and her eyebrows white with snow, her long hair strung with flakes like pearls. She held the little jeweled bird with its long blue and gold tail in her hands and did not smile, or raise her eyes. He could not be sure if she was crying, but her breath was warm and misted on the air.

"I do not know any more stories," she whispered.

"What? But you swore to tell me more!"

"There are no more that I can tell."

"But if the tales are over—"

"I did not say they were over. I said I did not know any more." The girl picked at the pearly beak of her bird.

"I do not understand."

The girl looked up, and the rims of her eyes were red beneath the sweet, inky black of her lids. "I told you long ago that I read the tales of my eyes in cast-off mirrors, or in pools and fountains. I told you that it was difficult, that I could only read one eye at a time, and that I read them backward, slowly, as such tasks will go. I told you stories from the creases of my left eyelid, and my right. I told you all the stories that I could read in those mirrors and fountains and pools. I have told them all. All that remains now are the tales which begin on one eye and end on another, which cross creases and lashes and twist over each other—these tales I do not know, I cannot tell. I cannot close my eyes and yet still read them in the water, or in the glass. They are hidden from me."

The boy opened his mouth, and closed it again. "But I want to hear more!" he cried.

The girl smiled, a long, slow smile he had never seen before. "Will you tell me a story, my prince? Will you read from my closed eyes and let me rest my throat, let me hear the last things which are written upon me?"

"But...I can't do it. I can't tell them the way you can. I'm not like you, I don't know how to tell a tale, I don't know how to speak in all those voices."

"It is all there, already. Please. I want to hear them. I want to know what is waiting on my skin, waiting to be told, waiting to be heard. I have told you so many things—tell me a story, if you are my friend."

The boy was blushing furiously. By the firelight he laid out his own cloak on the stiff, ice-scrimmed snow, and gave the girl a tiny vial of orangewine and a slice of hippopotamus, which they agreed was not entirely pleasant, and tasted something like chewed mud and riverwater with a honey glaze. Finally, the boy leaned forward, until their noses were almost touching. He could see, as once before, the lines and letters of her eyes, and the closer he looked into the black, the more the words swam up to greet him, submerged alphabets and sigils. He became dizzy; he closed his own eyes, and righted himself like a little ship tossed on a violent ocean. He looked again, and the letters were still there, floating, serene. His voice was high and quavering as he began, unsure and frightened to his marrow to appear foolish before the girl.

"On a blasted plain where the Stars do not look there blew hot winds like bellow-gusts, and scrub sage crawled over white rock." He read slowly, as if first learning his letters. "On this plain hung a great iron cage in a great iron frame, and the wind shrieked through it like a woman cut open on a slab..."

The Tale
of the Waste

THE MOON WAS A MOUSE SKULL IN THE SKY. THE blue of the air was dense and deep, the color of the ocean floor, yet it blazed with heat, and golden stones quavered against the horizon. Three long shadows were cast on the thirsty earth, whose dark cracks forked out in all directions like vines searching for the smallest trickle of water. Three long shadows lay black and sere on that fractured desert. The iron cage threw its bars down to the dirt in disgust. There it met the curious shadow-shapes of a woman and a leopard sitting with her ears bent forward, alert and interested. The woman held her cat on a long silver leash which swung back and forth in the wind. She was wrapped head to foot in heavy black veils that whipped and billowed behind her—only her eyes were naked to the air, yellow as withered lemons, her irises sickly red.

The cage was filled with smoke.

It blew out of wrought bars that had been bent into a crosshatched orb hanging by a chain thicker than a man's waist from its frame. Black and acrid and stinging, it whorled and eddied and spun, caught and caustic. Within the smoke flashed two red-orange eyes, baleful and fringed in fiery lashes, tipped in fiery brows. The circuit of smoke snapped its tail around twice and a body rose partway over the soot, like a mermaid peering through her own scaly tail. Her face was full of fire, and her hair was the root of that exhalation of smoke—it blew and curled away from her dark and flaming features. But the smoke came too from below her waist, for her flesh ended there very much as a mermaid's will, and nothing but blackness and red sparks striking snaked out where her legs might have been. She was naked, humiliated, her breasts tipped in angry fire, her navel a glowering, ugly ruby, everything that might once have been hers piled up beneath the cage like a funeral offering.

The two women watched each other for some time, like two vultures on a long and lonely branch. The leopard did not stir, except for the occasional wave of her tail across the blighted ground.

Finally, the leopard spoke.

"Who has put you here, friend Djinn?"

The creature thrashed her smoke again, obscuring her blazing eyes. The moon was setting behind her, dry and transparent against the blue, as if it too had been sucked dry.

"That's a nice trick," she hissed, her voice like the snapping of green branches as they first catch flame. "Doesn't the tall one talk?"

The leopard yawned, her whiskers flaring, her pink tongue lolling out before the great cat remembered to put it back.

"Her throat is afflicted, if you'll pardon her. Her name is Ruin, and I am Rend, and we travel together because it suits us to do so. We did not know that these parched wastes were a prison. We did not expect to find such a thing here."

A tendril of smoke unspooled out of the cage toward the veiled woman in something like the shape of a slender hand, three of the fingers circled in flame like a rich woman's rings.

"Please!" cried the leopard. "Do not touch her, you mustn't touch her."

Ruin's tired eyes were soft and sorry, and she raised a hand out of her black robe by way of explanation. It was withered nearly to the bone, the skin as cracked and peeling as the desert, the nails blackened and split. Pieces of her skin were slowly stripping away, blowing back from her crooked fingers in the hot air. She folded her veils over the hand again and looked down in shame. The smoke recoiled and the Djinn drew it back into the hanging cage.

"We would share our food, if you give us reason to pity you, and our water, which is more precious than amber, but you mustn't touch my lady. She is not well." The cat looked wretched, her eyes black and round, her spotted fur twitching under the predations of sand mites.

The Djinn considered, her eyes narrowing. She rubbed her nose with one painted hand—for the palms of her hands were stippled in glowing patterns, swirling in and in on themselves, the incandescent ink tracing scarlet loops where the lines of her hands might have been, if she had any.

"I am Scald," she said at last, "and across six seas and nine deserts, I was one of the three Queens of Kash, and I had a crown of embers."

Rend pawed the soil. "Why are you caged, Scald?"

The Djinn was quiet, her clouds dark and thoughtful. "Across nine seas and six deserts, I laid siege to the city of Ajanabh . . ."

The Tale of the Cage of Ivory and the Cage of Iron

In the city of Kash, there are six Palaces, six Thrones, and six Crowns. Three Queens and three Kings there are, each in their house. I was the Ember-Queen, and my coal-buttressed hall stood at the end of a long boulevard which was lined with Ixora and the Palaces of my sisters, the Tinder-Queen and the Ash-Queen. So too my brothers' fastholds, the Hearth-King, the Kindling-King, and the King of Flint and Steel. When I call them my brothers and sisters, of course I by no means wish to indicate that they are any relation to me—cut this thought from your heart. Monarchs are members of a wide and varied fraternity, and this is all my connection to them.

We are the inheritors of the Kingdom of Kashkash, who was the first of the Djinn. He spun all of the rest of us out of the smoke of his beard, and the black curls flowed over the face of the earth. In the sacred fire of his heart we were first conceived, the immaculate flame. His stare burned forests in their shade and caused even human women, icy of heart and eye though they are, to swoon before his majesty. As his wispy children cavorted around him on the plains of the world, he exhorted them to follow him, dancing before them, as he led them into glory and might.

He told us that we had no need to build cities as the rest scrambled to do, but that cities would build themselves around us, for what man did not need fire? Thus he stood at the center of Shadukiam in the days before it knew that name. The whole of the city swirled up around him, all those roses, all those diamonds! Djinn followed him wherever he bade, into that glittering city and out again, and still his name is holy among us, incandescent, radiant. He was beautiful. He was loved, for in his beard were wonders lesser Djinn could not dream of, lamps and jewels and scrolls of flame and cloud, which he would pluck from his body and distribute like bread. He danced on the minaret tips of our first real homes and cried poetry to the blood-riddled sunsets, cried ho! For the thousand-year holocaust of the Djinn! And far below the rabble screamed their adoration. Of how many Kings in those days did Kashkash grant the wishes? How many maidenheads did he burn clear through? We named this city for him, and even human virgins anoint their foreheads with ashes in mourning, all these centuries hence.

This is what we tell to the world, with horns of brass and carnelian. So I was told; so I believed while I grew, a child in the city of Kash, wishing for golden bells for my belt and sweet honey for my supper. Thus we have told the world for century upon century. In my own time, my smoke-hair snaked and spiraled so long and so far that I had to carry it at my hips in two baskets of woven silver, and the other children laughed at me, until their parents admonished them—for such a mark meant that I would be Queen, just as the great beard of Kashkash marked him as King. I was taken away from my little house, taking with me three sets of golden spoons and a very nice samovar, and was initiated into the strange world of royalty. I was ten years of age, but among my people this is a respectable middle age. We do not age, but we die out rather more quickly than other folk. We flash and spark and die. Those who are pressed by seals and trickery into lamps and suchlike live longer, nigh on forever, as a coal will live if not struck alight. And as a coal is not alive, so a Djinn confined is not. This is the choice we make: Once in the open air and burning, ah, we never last long. Thus at ten I was no child—but my crown was young as a weeping orphan without a breast.

The Ash-Queen and the Hearth-King, Kohinoor and Khaamil, escorted me into the Alcazar of Embers, each of them carrying one of my baskets. I thought they were terrifying and beautiful, with burning gems set into their black skin and burning gold rings in their noses. Kohinoor was tall and thin as a hermit, all black smoke without a single spark in her, while Khaamil was smaller and fatter, lovely folds of flaming skin undulating, cradling a huge topaz in his navel. He had but one golden eye, the flame in it dancing like a dervish. The other socket was empty and burned black.

In the center of a red tile floor lay a banked and glowing bowl of coals, the symbols of my office. The Queen sat me down on a purple cushion—I balanced gingerly on my smoke, so as not to burn the tassels. She spoke firmly and kindly as she was able, being a woman of no small position, and too busy to care for an upstart new Queen. They had both of them been fonder of the old Queen, who had simply gone up in flames at a family dinner the previous winter, to the mild surprise of all present.

"Now, young one," said Kohinoor, firmly putting me in my place, for she was nearly fifteen, a daunting age, "it is not appropriate that you should reign and remain ignorant of our history. Thus it is our duty to tell you how things were in the old world, and how they came to be. However, we have a luncheon appointment with the Kindling-King, and he is serving blackened basilisk, which is our favorite, so kindly pay attention so that we are not forced to repeat ourselves…"

The Tale of the First Djinn

NO DOUBT YOU VENERATE KASHKASH AS YOUR grandfather and best-loved household god. Stop. At this very moment.

It is necessary for the glorification of the Djinn, and also so that we may not be endlessly ensorcelled into various kitchen items for the purpose of granting the wishes of fishmongers' daughters, that the name of Kashkash be adored and feared. Do not rub that lamp, darling, lest Kashkash leap out and swallow you whole! Do not clack your spoons together, sweetling! Kashkash will come billowing out of the handles and gobble you up! It is, however, not sensible to expect others to adore and fear what we do not, and so the secret history of the smoke-fiends is known only to a select few, of which you are now a member. It keeps the Djinn in terror of their monarchs, and the world in terror of the Djinn.

Shut your mouth, dear, it does not do to attract moths.

Kashkash was not the first Djinn—that poor, benighted soul has no name that any may recall, being the unwanted child of the fires that the Stars conflagrated when they walked through the first lands of the world. Every scorched thing spat out a Djinn like the pit in a cherry, and we had to find our way, even though we burned and burned and could not cool. We are nothing but charred, forgotten children whose birth was utterly unnoticed. I am a child of the Djinn who rose up from the scalded grasses. Khaamil is the child of the seared winds. The Queens kept their counsel and their records, though Kashkash wished all knowledge of our origin destroyed in the fire of his name. Now that you are one of us, we shall have to look into your pedigree. Kashkash was not the first, then, though many might now say he was. For it is not only the common Djinn who pray in the name of Kashkash, but many preening priests and men of rank who know the truth in their boiling hearts, but take delight in telling the tale of a Djinn like Kashkash, who could have any woman, destroy any man.

Kashkash was indeed powerful, and fashioned his smoke into waving, fiery shapes to terrify us in our infancy, colored as no other Djinn had done, in blue and green and violet. To see him was extraordinary, they say, and we do not argue, at least in this. Around his head waved these airy flames, proud and strutting, proud and vain. So too is it true that he was present in the early days of the city which would come to be called Shadukiam. He dragged his flaming heel around the perimeter of that dung-spattered clearing that could hardly be called a shantytown in those days, when the long boulevard on which your Alcazar sits was nothing but a red dust-run. The place which Kashkash marked out in the mud was quickly dwarfed by the endless growing roads and markets of the Rose City. We built nothing, as he instructed us, but stole and wished our first settlement into life. Kashkash told us that no one of the Djinn could wish as he could, and thus wishing which he did not approve was outlawed. The great talent of the Djinn is in wishing, and of it we made a science after he passed from the world, though it has, in its turn, passed out of its keenest use since children have ceased trapping us in lamps and spoons. In those days we were young, we could not do it very well, but he could do little better: He wished for a palace of cedar and horn, and up rose the ramshackle towers of the Quarter. But oh! What he promised us! When he learned better, learned more! When he had made enough Kings his slaves, what he would build us then! How long he could stretch our lives—we would no longer be candles, briefly lit and briefly snuffed. We would be the flame of ten thousand generations!

He did learn, he did become a prodigy of wishes, but never to us were his talents bent. He loved better anything that was flesh and not smoke— the smallest of these things seemed to him more beautiful than we.

We are not meant to tell outsiders that Shadukiam is not in its entirety the right and province of the smoke-wights. Let the shade of Kashkash take us with his beard flying. We do not care.

The Quarter Kashkash dragged out for himself became a slum, a place where fire ran in the alleys and crimson teeth flashed in the shadows. Rickety towers were built high through the Rose Dome, until the black tips pierced the spaces between the pale pink petals, and so pressed were we in those turrets that our smoke squeezed through the very walls, our fire shot out from floor to floor, and while Kashkash ate grapes in the governor's house and counseled him to save his coin when the scaffolders came clambering down from their work, the Djinn suffered and wept in their black hovels. He danced on the crumbling tips of the towers with his fires wreathing his eyes and sparking in the stinking wind and cried poetry to the blood-riddled sunsets, cried ho! For the thousand-year holocaust of the Djinn! And far below the tenements screamed their adoration through the squalor.

We lived in this way because Kashkash told us we must, and twirled his beard when he said so. He had the longest beard of any of us, after all. This is why monarchs are determined by such strange criteria. Each of the thrones demands its favorites: the hottest fire, the sweetest voice, and so on. Kashkash claimed his beard gave him sovereignty—should we choose differently? He brandished his beard and with it crushed an entire race into six thin towers. He told us then it was only the beginning, that we would rest soon on carnelian and brass and silk like blue fire, but day and night smeared their way across the Quarter and still we could not breathe for the smoke of another on our faces.

Finally, we could bear it no longer; the terrible smell and the unburied bodies and the decrepit buildings were close all around us. Some few remembered the open grass. What the clerics will not tell you is this: Kashkash was strangled in smoke on the steps of the tenements and his body burned. The towers were torn brick from brick and within a winter no charred stick of the Djinn Quarter could be scried out among the pretty new marble and hanging tapestries. We buried him at the crux of the crossroads of a new city, as far from Shadukiam and the memory of our shame there as it was possible to go. And we wished for nothing, but with our own hands built up a city of carnelian and brass, with couches of silk like blue fire, and paved out in beryl a long boulevard, along which we raised six Alcazars, one for each of the horrid towers that were.

But guilt rode us like a bull-tamer, and the Djinn built statues over the place where Kashkash had been buried. They swore in his name. They made a secret of what had been done, and named the new city Kash, hoping to avert the anger of his shade and lure some part of the beauty that had been his. To the world we say he was great, and only to ourselves do we whisper: *We are glad rid of him.* We have never seen the furious ghost of his long beard haunt the streets, but no one can say if this is because we keep his name spit-polished. But we wish to be safe in all things, do we not?

Do you understand, little long-hair? May we go now to our luncheon? And if we hear you swear by the name of that thing again we will cut your tongue from your mouth and that will be that.

I BLINKED AT THE KING AND THE QUEEN, WHO peered at me like teachers saddled with a particularly dense student. "I...understand," I said. "I suppose a Queen must be ready to hear a great many things she would rather not."

"Quite." Kohinoor snorted.

They showed me through the Alcazar of Embers with a brusque efficiency, eager to leave me alone. Finally, we came to a small room full of statues in every imaginable stone, from lapis to tourmaline. I gaped, I did not know what to say—there were hundreds upon hundreds, each of them draped in glittering shawls and intricately carved with faces, men and women, human and otherwise, Djinn and else, each different from the other as a rose from a turtle.

"What are these marvelous things?" I cried.

The Hearth-King snickered a little. "They are your wives," he said.

Kohinoor rolled her eyes. "Don't be a child, Khaamil. In the years after Kashkash perished, the six monarchs looked to other races to learn the shape of a reign. Human Kings had many wives—why should we not? Are we not greater and wiser and lovelier than men? Yet it had also been long decided by worried priests that no King or Queen of the Djinn should ever be allowed to marry or have children, for the lineage, as you should well know, is not counted from parent to child, and should we bear children like an apple tree bears apples, surely some one of us should be tempted to wrest the throne for their little ones. Thus this rather pretty compromise was reached—we commissioned their carving long ago, and they are passed from monarch to monarch, both Queen and King, for if the humans count their power with wives, should any Queen of ours be counted less? We have the most delicate, pliant, and quiet wives in the world, more beautiful than flesh, and easier to transport. And more than any human ruler could dream of." She sniffed. "We treat our stone wives with much more care than they treat their warm ones, anyway. I personally dust mine once a week, and I know Khaamil gives them presents when I am not looking. These are yours—they are in your care, and you must be faithful."

With that, they left me alone in my bedchamber, braziers of white-hot coals casting shadows on my hands. I crawled onto my bed, and listened to the breeze through the arched window, trying not to feel hundreds of stone eyes on me until I fell asleep.

I was Queen for one day before I was asked to lead an army.

The Hearth-King sailed into my Alcazar at first light, his smoke trailing behind him like a cape. "It has been decided!" he announced. "We are headed across the nine deserts to Ajanabh, and woe to them when we arrive!"

I poured my hair into my baskets and tried to clear my eyes, to be ready for my first day as Queen. "What?" I put on my best imperious tone. "Why was I not told? Why must we go to Ajanabh?"

"Because of the war, of course."

"We are at war with Ajanabh?"

"Not yet, but when we arrive we certainly shall be."

I clutched my head. "But why? What have they done to us?"

Khaamil smiled, his dark features rippling, streaks of fire playing under his skin. "You must understand, my newest sister, that Ajanabh is a dead city. The spice fields died and it is easy fruit; only a few folk even remain within its walls, and it is a lovely city with a seaport and a river and any number of things. We will make it magnificent again with only a few short and graceful battles."

"But it is so far away! What use is it as a colony?"

Khaamil's smile faltered slightly, his flames flaring white. "There is also, ah, the matter of a holy object which lies in there and which they have refused to give up to us as we have so politely and often asked. Now that the city is dead, there is no reason not to root through the corpse for our property."

"What is it?"

"That is none of your concern!" said Kohinoor, her voice deep and rolling, echoing in my hall like a golden ball tossed from wall to wall. "You are too new to understand, and besides, it is hardly necessary that you know every little part of our minds. The five of us will look after you, never fear. And wait until you see the army we have assembled!"

I was nervous to put on the general's sword so soon after my Ember-Crown, but I could not show them. "Where is the army, then? On the boulevard? In the square? I should like to inspect the troops."

The King and Queen laughed, their expressions delighted and cruel, like children who have played an especially good joke. "They are on the field already, little firefly! Our wish has been approved by the Khaighal, and when the others have arrived, we shall wish ourselves in their midst, and woe betide the Ajan Gate!"

The other three monarchs swept into my Alcazar before I could draw myself up to my full height and demand an explanation: the Tinder-Queen with her long, high-collared orange robes, modest to the last; the Kindling-King with his belt of driftwood; and the King of Flint and Steel, his endless beard tucked into a golden pouch at his waist. Behind them like ghostly winds the six priests of the Khaighal blew in, holding in their hands a fiery book, whose pages were pure white smoke. Their own smoke was equally blanched, and I did not like the look of it at all. These were the men who determined the way of wishing among us—

for not a Djinn in the world could wish a thing which Kashkash had not in his time wished; this is hubris which would bring his wrath upon us. In their books was every wish the famous Djinn had ever committed or granted. They were consulted whenever a wish was desired, be it for peasant or lord, woman or Djinn. I do not know of any case of a shade's wrath descending, but the wrath of the Khaighal is terrible, and their hearts toll like bells when a wish not in their books is uttered. Their punishments are fell and feared, and there is no dark corner where a Djinn might utter a wish they do not countenance, where they will not hear it. They must not know the truth of Kashkash, I thought. They must believe it all, or they would wish for whatever they liked, and who could stop them?

"It has been determined," droned the head priest in a bored tone, "that our lord Kashkash many times wished himself on the field of battle before hostilities began in order to stymie his enemies. Therefore you may wish in his Shadow and his Stead." The new wish was recorded in a different book, old and dusty, with wooden boards and lazily cut pages. It did not flame even a little.

The Kings and Queens of Kash gripped my hands and before I could blink we stood on a wide red plain before a city whose walls were so tall clouds wisped at their heights.

I had never seen such an army. My flames caught in my throat, banked in wonder. Every soldier, if they could be called such, was armored in fabulous metals that glittered in the bloody sun. Their shoulder-plates were flared and fluted, edged in antlers and diamonds, their helmets topped with feathers from birds I could not begin to name. They sat astride war chargers whose chests bulged like boulders, and carried swords that no doubt had endless lineages and cost more than whole towns. The supply carts and pages stretched off in the distance—including six vast carriages carrying our wives like cannonballs behind the artillery—like the audience at a circus, and the hot wind blew back the hair from thousands of craggy, stern, proud faces, faces forged by generations of select nobles courting their select cousins.

In the Bay of Ajan floated dozens of long black ships, and on the beach were dragged dozens more. Campfires glittered on the floor of the plain, which spread out below the high hill of Ajan like a woman's scarlet skirt.

"We have had to call in every wish we have ever granted to gather them," Kohinoor said, her own face set to the wind, the smoke of her skin billowing gray and black. "An army of Kings and Queens; not a pauper in the lot. They owe us, or their father owes us, or their grandmother. Their aunt became eternally young, their foster mother promised her firstborn to pay for the life of her lover. And now they are all here, paying their debt as good breeding will, and never has an army of more beauty been assembled. Some of them are unused to battle, having sat upon cushions and not upon horses, but they have the finest military minds in the world, and they will find a crack in those walls for us."

"Please. Your Majesty," I said. "Tell me what we seek in this place."

Kohinoor rolled her eyes. "It is a box of carnelian, and in it is a thing which is mine and no other's, which they have no right to keep from me. More than that I will not share with a young upstart with no military experience. Matters of state, you know. Suffice it that we wish to have it. The priests of Kashkash have determined that it is not righteous that we simply wish it out of its hiding place—for what fool hid a thing from the fire-tyrant? But fear not! This city is so weak that you will doubtless hardly know the battle has begun before it is over. Sit back, drink your brandy, and enjoy the sun."

She passed me a vial of brown liquor and I sniffed at it, but did not drink. Instead I drifted down from our little cliff and through the ranks, where Kings and Queens of unpronounceable places groused about their conscription and cursed the Djinn under their breath, or bragged about how much better they would prove at killing than their layabout knights had done. I trailed my smoke behind me and let them choke on it. Why should I be kept out of their councils, kept ignorant of their ridiculous box? Was I not Queen as well as they? So far my throne had gotten me little but a vast, empty house and a closet full of stone wives.

The sky was growing dim as I approached the massive Gate of Ajanabh. The stone of it was red as a girl's hair, red as my own ribs, and as blemishless as any wall I had seen. I wondered if Kohinoor had examined it this closely, closely enough to see it was not easily broached, closely enough to see that the Gate itself was a huge pair of arms crossed over each other, with a worn and weathered face frowning down at the adorned throng.

"Go away," the face said.

I saw what she did not: There was no Gate at all anymore, just this *gargantua* whose shoulders spanned the breadth of what was once the Gate. His belt grazed the rocky earth. His eyes were old and cracked at the edges, bronze-green, his brow beaten leather, his jowls deeply stained with wind and sun, his great arms and hands the red rock of the wall, huge and dry and barnacled, a petrified giant. Moss grew on his knuckles; birds nested in his ears. His voice was slow and slurry as old snow.

"I am sure you think I am impressed with your brigade of strutting swans. I have been here since the pepper plants were taller than stallions in the fields. You will not chisel one flake of stone from me."

He glared at me and tightened his arms.

"Who are you?" I gasped.

He seemed to consider for a moment. "I am the Guardian of the Gate. I had a name once, but it is no use to call me by it. I am Ajanabh. I surround it and contain it and feel its barges on my back, and so I have become it. It is better to call me Ajanabh than to guess at what my name might have been before I laid my limbs down around this place…"

The Tale
of the Giant
Who Stayed

ONCE AJANABH HAD SAD AND CRUMBLED WALLS,
with a gate like a crease in a cheap linen curtain, when I
came to work the fields, as my folk often did during the
harvest season. The pay is steady, and my shoulders
bear those tiny yokes far better than poor, feeble
horses—why, I hardly feel it! The streets just began
somewhere in the middle of this rocky red plain, and
sooner or later if you followed them you came to the
spice plantations and then to the city proper.

Lawlessness doesn't mean there's no law, you know, it
just means that there are a lot of different laws slugging
it out in the streets, and none of them have come out on

top yet. Anyone can dole out stocks and nails and a right tap in the gut for infractions of whatever law they take a fancy to, even ones you never heard anything about, so you just learn to watch yourself. Ajanabh was lawless then, which is as good as a wall twice my size.

And so I worked in the red-pepper fields, the black-pepper fields, the green peppers and the pink, and the cinnamon groves, and the coriander fields, and the saffron fields, and the cumin farms, on the salt flats combing and drying the crystals like hard, cutting snow. I pruned and tended the mustard plants, the paprika bushes, and cut vanilla beans from the vine. I crushed them all, endlessly, with my feet in a mortar the size of a galleon. I was happy with my work. Then, Ajanabh smelled so rich and sweet and smoky, all her spices puffing from one window or another as they were rendered, pulverized, and mixed. During the long, warm harvest, when the sun turned the bay into a great glittering mirror, I pulled spices from the earth—for who does not want their food well flavored? And during the spring I put my back to the plow, and drew furrows deep as a man's legs in the rich soil.

But soil does not stay rich. Who can say why land which gives and gives like a mother with endless sweets in her skirts one day shakes her finger at her babes and denies them?

In my own country we are so careful, we plant only every other season, and we are so large that we digest but slowly, and need only to feast like bears through the summer long every second year. But those feasts! A whale would be embarrassed by our plenty. Goblets bigger than camels' humps, plates the size of shields.

But in Ajanabh they were not so careful, and greedily ground into powder everything the earth could throw up, until she put her hands on her aproned hips and shook her head sadly. No more, she sighed. And there was no more. But such things do not happen all at once. For a long while no one noticed, and the sacks of saffron went out into the world as they had always done. I kept at the plow, even though my heart told me to rest, that there was no use in it. But I loved Ajanabh by then, roving laws, stolen coins, spice-smog and all. I would not leave her. But slowly, in clutches like wild rabbits, the Ajans began to go.

Carrying bags on their backs they went across the plains with squinting eyes, or to the harbor with rum flasks at their hips and oranges to hold against the rotting of their teeth. The bargers went first, since moving downstream for them is as easy as eating. Then the other giants went, following the promise of better fields in the east where they could pull up strawberries and turnips like red and white bouquets. They begged me to go with them.

"The feast is almost here!" they cried. "Where will you find enough mule meat and coconut-wine to satisfy you?"

"Ajanabh will provide for me, and I will sup as well as you," I answered.

Well, I did not sup nearly so well as they, and I cracked my own co-conuts down by the bayside, and drank the raw, unfermented milk. It did not really compare. But I did find a mule to roast, left behind by one of the sea-bound families, and I sat on the beach with my driftwood fire snapping like a housecat, and gnawed my mule bones, and sucked my coconuts dry, and it was not too wretched, really. At least I could still smell that sweet, smoky air, the cumin and the turmeric wafting over the broken walls.

Once while I plowed a near-dead field, I saw a couple clutching a lit-tle girl in their arms, and her hardly old enough to walk.

"Simeon!" they hailed me—for everyone knew me by that time, the Giant Who Stayed.

"Hello, small folk," I said warmly, and squatted down so they would not have to crane their necks so much.

"We are bound for Muireann, where the whale fur thatches the roofs, and the roads are paved with mother-of-pearl." Their girl giggled and reached up to me—I gave her my pinkie to hold, as big in her arms as the trunk of a tree her own age.

"I wish you well of it," I said.

"This place is dead. There is nothing for us now; our pepper plants withered and died, and there are no corns for our little girl to grind when she is grown. She will spear seals and narwhal instead, and sleep in a bed made of their spiraling horns! We will bounce our grandchil-dren on knees chilled by snow and sea—won't that be something!"

I smiled at them. Ajanabh was so warm and wet, it tended to make one forget what snow was—I only dimly remembered breaking through the frost with a shovel to get the bulbs in back home. They walked off, down toward the harbor where the ships bellied up to the dock every day, and left the city that loved them. Sometimes I imagined I could hear Ajanabh weeping, a poor lady distraught that her babies abandoned her when she grew old and dry.

Finally, I put my plow aside, and sat on my last field, knees drawn up to my chest, looking at the city. There were no lights in the houses piled up like red beehives, and no sounds of laws being worked out in the streets. No bells tolled out the hours, there being no one to ring them. My city was empty, and so I decided that no one should really mind if I were to take up my residence there. No one could tell me I was too big anymore, and I would sleep under a blanket of spice-smog, as I had once or twice dreamed, snoring after the giant-feasts of home.

I stepped over the rotted gate, long since claimed by mold and sea air, and into the steep hills and alley-dells of a city which was built up and up, with streets that jackknifed sharply down and diagonal and straight up and any way they pleased, the cobbles being as lawless as anything else in Ajanabh. I walked with my hands in my pockets, sniffing the air, still delicious and dark as ever, save that the sour smell of people had gone, and left only the spices to scent the night. I grinned, my big teeth like a moon above the city. I tried not to step on anything that wasn't meant to be stepped on—but I had to squeeze, sometimes.

I thought, again, that I could hear my girl, my city, weeping, lost and lonely.

"I'm still here, my lady," I whispered.

But there was something—there was a sound. It wasn't my fool head playing games as it does when the plowing is boring and the sun is high. It was high and piercing and sad as anything, like a voice but not a voice. I had never heard anything so beautiful in all my days—and the giant-esses can play the bassoon like nothing you've known, when the mules are fat and the coconut-wine has a good head on it. I followed the sound, careful not to crush anything too much, up and down the weird maze of streets that makes Ajanabh seem all alley, and finally to the center of the city, a little courtyard all humped up in the middle, with a fountain that has green water shooting about like vines and all manner of vines shooting about like water. It's got a little figure in the middle of it, too, which I think is supposed to be the Cinnamon-Star all cavorting in the stream, but her eyes fell out a long time ago, and her knees aren't so good, and I never could tell if she's got the Bark of Plenty in her hands or some old toys the children stuck in there when they got bored with them.

In front of the fountain was a lady, and I was six kinds of shamed to see I was wrong, and ten kinds of tickled that I wasn't the only one who stayed. But she wasn't like any lady I'd seen before. She had a red dress on, not much more than a slip, and she was dancing—but that wasn't too odd. Ajanabh never was poor of dancers and singers and that sort. It was her hands, well, her hands and her hair, but without the hands the hair wouldn't have struck me. She had no fingers at all, but violin bows, fiddle bows, strapped on where her fingers ought to be, and the strips of leather went all around her forearms and up to her shoulders, to keep the bows on tight. Her black hair was stiff as catgut, and she danced so quick and light that it flew out in all directions, long and wide enough that I swear to you that woman was playing her own hair with each hand, five bows together, whipping her head from side to side to change the length, like a fiddler presses on his frets. With bare feet she slapped the cobbles, her toes all bound in copper rings, and the sound of her playing was the sound I had heard, swift and terrible and lovely.

When she stopped her scales for a moment to oil the bows, I cleared my throat. "I thought you had all gone."

The woman looked up, her eyes green as palm leaves under the ecstatic shocks of hair. "Not all," she said mischievously. "Some of us will never go."

I looked at the beehive-houses, and indeed, in some of those round windows, faces peeked out, looking for the violin-girl, wondering why she had stopped her song.

"My name is Agrafena," she said, and put her bows very gingerly into my great hand. "I am the song of Ajanabh. I am staying, and so are they."

"But who are they?"

The woman spun around on one heel, sending her hair flying again. "We are those who loved this place enough to hold her hand through death, and watch her come out the other side. We stayed to record her dying, each in our way, painters and poets and calligraphers, singers and dancers and violinists, sculptors and acrobats, jewelers and jugglers, glassblowers, pantomimes, orators, and toymakers, novelists and layers of mosaics, mask-makers and players of scenes. We stayed. We wrote and painted and chiseled and sang her death, and we have found, now that the crowds have gone, that like a fallen tree, she has enough for us, we mushrooms and mosses, we spiders and glowworms. The dancers tamp down the seeds in our little city gardens, and there are carrots and blackberries enough to feed us. The lion-tamers find little clutches of cattle preposterously easy work, and there is meat enough to fill us. We take empty houses and apartments, parlors and sitting rooms, and there are more than enough—there are few locks in Ajanabh these days. An empty city is a paradise, and here all Vstreychas now end. There is even a wine-maker who stayed to press out the last vintage, the famed cardamom wine which is now ours alone to savor."

I hung my head. "Then I am sad, Agrafena, for I stayed, and yet I know no art but the pounding of paprika and the cutting of vanilla beans. I can give nothing to the new Ajanabh, except my bulk, which is not welcome."

She turned her head to one side, as if sizing me for a new pair of shoes. "Poor Simeon! Our last giant! But if you are willing, and if you love your city, I know a thing you can do which is harder than any of the little acts we perform in her name."

THE TALE OF THE CAGE OF IVORY AND THE CAGE OF IRON, CONTINUED

"SHE TOLD ME," THE GREAT GATE SAID POINT-edly, "that now that Ajanabh had not so many laws prowling her streets, and not so much wealth with which to throw on armor when needed, sooner or later, folk would come who did not juggle or sing, but carried things bright and sharp, swords and arrows and others besides." He glared at me with his brass eyes. "She bade me stretch myself as far as I could and lie around my city so that she would be safe. I worried about my skin, as surely these sharp things will be flung at me in the hurly-burly, and I should not make a very good wall then. But she calmed me with her sweet bows and called to her side stonemasons and brass-workers and tanners, and directed them to shore me up on all sides with red rock and brass buckles and leather straps, so that I should be a proper Gate, and safe withal. I went to the outside of my city, and kissing her topmost turrets, bent back my legs as far as I could, and stretched up through my ribs as tall as I could, until my ankles met and my head cast a shadow on the courtyard, and not a few pelicans dropped fish into the salt sea in surprise at such a sudden mountain in their midst. Then I crossed my arms, and closed up the Gate of Ajanabh, which is who I am now, and not Simeon any longer."

I bit my lip. "But if there are only artists inside—"

"They will all be slaughtered. We have an armorer, an old water rat living in a leaky garret with dozens of empty suits lining his wall—but what are dozens to your assembled horde?" His smile was hard and cruel. "But never you worry about it, you drafty old thing. No sword will pass my fingers, and they will be safe. Ajanabh will provide for them."

"I did not want to come," I muttered sullenly. "No one asked me, they just whisked me here and put a cup of brandy in my hand."

"That will hardly make us feel better," the Gate huffed.

I turned the flaming rings on my fingers. Something within me longed to see the corkscrewed streets of Ajanabh, longed to hear Agrafena's bows slide through her hair. I had been Queen only a day and seen nothing at all but my own house. I did not want to put a torch to that place, any more than I had wanted to hear that Kashkash was wicked or that I was only Queen because of my hair.

Suddenly, I reached out and clutched at the Gate's massive stone finger, which was like a long temple pillar in my hands. "Let me in!" I begged. "Let me see the city. Perhaps I can convince them to leave. Perhaps if I can find that ridiculous carnelian box, they will take it and go, and be glad to lose no one to a battle."

The Gate squinted, his brass eyes crusted with verdigris, suspicious. "How do I know you are not intent on some sabotage? You are a Djinn. I would sooner trust a starving crocodile who wishes to mind my mule than a Djinn."

Color and flame flared in my cheeks. "How should I trust a giant not to crush me in his fingers because a fly was buzzing at his ear?" I banked my fires. "But come, you must see that I am young. I was only made Queen yesterday; I know nothing of this place, or this war. Let me in, and I will try to find what they want, and bring it out to them with no bloodshed. If I am lying, I will wish it all back for you, and damn the Khaighal."

The Gate frowned, his mouth lines deep and clogged with clay. "I will let you in. For one night. You must be again at my fingertips by dawn or I will not let you out, and you will discover that actors and singers are often forced into rather more unsavory lines of work, and they are not out of practice. No one who lived in Ajanabh-of-old lets their muscles soften for even a moment." I nodded furiously. "Swear by your wish-wrangling King, swear by Kashkash the bold and his brazen beard, and I will believe you," he grumbled.

I could make that promise, but it would mean nothing to me, not anymore, not now. Slowly, I gripped the sides of my silver hip-baskets and said, "I will swear by him, but also by the Cinnamon-Star, and the Snake-Star, and the Seven Sisters."

Grudgingly, he nodded, and lifted his forefinger from his middle finger, exposing just enough space for me to gather my smoke and seep through. "Go to the fountain, and find Agrafena. She is always there this time of night, fiddling up the moon. She will take you to a room with rafters so high you will think it is open to the night, and an ivory cage, and a flame like your own."

I thanked him and, holding my baskets close, drifted through his fingers and into the red city.

In the Garden

THE BOY STOPPED.

"You're doing fine," said the girl warmly. She put out her hands to take his, and opened her eyes. They sparkled in the firelight, and the snow in her hair had melted to dew. "Shall I bring you dinner tonight"—she laughed—"and run to escape my sister?"

"It feels strange, to speak to you, when I am so used to listening. This is how it is in the stories I knew before you—a beautiful girl sits at the feet of a boy and treasures his every word. But it does not seem right."

"This is still my story," said the girl, drawing away. "My last story. It is not yours simply because it sits in your mouth awhile."

"I know! Oh, please do not be angry. I know. And I am afraid. I shall read as slowly as I can. It is your story, and it will take you away from me at the most beautiful part. Just when I want nothing more than to read it forever, it will be over. I know it."

She smoothed his hair, but could say nothing. "At least I can rest. I had become so tired, like a little place had opened in me and all of me had fallen out of it."

"How can you be so tired by only reading? Are you sick?"

"No, but that is the way of it. I told you it was my story. Even now you draw it out of me like a fisherman draws a carp from a lake. It thrashes and bucks as it is dragged from the water, but the sun on its scales is so golden!"

The boy's eyes widened, and he looked at her again, how flushed her cheeks in the cold, how thin her arms, how the black of her eyes seemed to burn like pitch. He was a little frightened of her, and she was so strange—he had almost forgotten how strange she had seemed to him in the beginning, how strange she was still, and how unlike any of the girls whose black hair he had chased around the trunks of trees.

"Are you tired now? Would you like me to leave you?" he whispered.

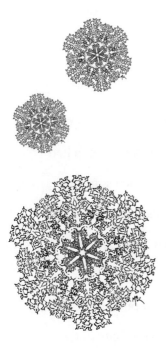

And she came back to him, her face warm and wide and winsome as an eager cat. "No, please. I want to hear more. I want to hear how Scald found the city of artists. How odd it feels to not know what happens next!"

He laughed ruefully and passed his braceleted hand over her eyes, closing them gently. The letters danced. He read, slowly as ever, his uncertain voice sounding in the snow like a hare's footprints.

"I followed the Ajan streets as I was told, and they were steeper and sharper and narrower even than I had imagined. But they whirled inexorably toward a center, and the moon was not even above the brow-ridge of the Gate before I found the fountain, and the dancing, fingerless maid..."

The Tale of the Cage of Ivory and the Cage of Iron, Continued

SHE WAS YOUNGER THAN I HAD THOUGHT—SHE must have been little more than a girl when Simeon had first found her. She was full-grown and then some now, just over the crest of life, laughing lines at her eyes and a deep, weathered color to her brown skin. She played with both hands upon her stiff, wiry hair and her red slip snapped crisply around her as she plied her practiced steps. The song was not the dirge for a city that the Gate had heard, but something sly and serpentine, staccato and sure, something that wound and writhed, something knowing, something hidden to all but her. I waited; I would not interrupt.

She finally stopped, bent at the waist, her foot pointed and poised in the air. Without moving any other muscle so much as a twitch, she turned her head to the side and winked at me. The Gate was wrong—her eyes were far greener than palms, glittering with a weakly burning light I thought I recognized—but no, it was not possible. She looked me up and down, and a secretive smile unfolded on her lovely face.

"You're Djinn!" I cried, pointing like an accusing child. "No wonder that hair can play! How do you get it to stiffen like that?"

Agrafena laughed, a gravelly sound like coals raked over. "No more than a quarter, I'm afraid, and on the paternal side—more's the pity." Her eyes flashed their dim fire at me. "We do not all lie on silk cushions in the vaults of Kash, you know. And like me, the hair is only a quarter smoke. Enough to be reasonable when I treat it nicely."

"But how? It is absolutely forbidden to mate with humans! After Kashkash died they forced us to agree to it—so many were crushed into spoons and lamps that day! There were too many ruined maids and inoperable boys for them to countenance. There has not been a half-breed for centuries! Longer!"

"Thank you for using such a generous word for me. But as I said, I am not half-anything, I am a solid and smoky quarter-breed, and if you wish to arrest someone, you shall have to dig up my grandparents, and I am sure they would be very cross about it."

I did not know what to say. She was an impossibility. At home she would be burned immediately and that part of her which was inflammable sunk to the bottom of the sea. Such was the contract the Khaighal witnessed; such was the contract men made us sign with regard to their prettiest children. I finally settled on the simplest thing I could summon up.

"The Gate sent me," I said.

"Simeon? It will be time for his mules soon, I should think. Is he asking you to call him Ajanabh yet? Silly old farmer, but a better soul you never knew."

"I am from the army outside. The army of Kings and Queens that is waiting to flatten this place."

Agrafena's face darkened, and even a quarter-Djinn can go very dark. "Yes, I know which one you mean," she rumbled.

"I came within the walls to find what my siblings seek: a little carnelian casket, no larger than my arm."

"Your siblings?"

I drew my smoke up and the jewels of my waist flashed. "I am the Ember-Queen."

Agrafena just laughed and scratched her scalp. "And what is in this box?"

"I...I don't know."

"Well, the Queenship of Kash is not what it used to be."

"I have been Queen for a single day!" I protested. "They tell me nothing! I was lucky to learn there was a box at all!"

"Well enough, well enough. I have no idea where such a thing might be. I have seen nothing of the sort—carnelian is common to your country, not ours."

"The Gate—Simeon—told me you would take me to a tall room, and an ivory cage, and a flame like mine."

Her eyebrows arched. "Did he now? Well, I suppose I know what he means. I doubt you'll find your box there, though. More likely bird droppings and an earful of prattle."

"Nevertheless."

"Of course—who am I to shirk the duty of entertaining visiting royalty? Follow me; it is not far."

We moved quickly through the angled alleys, and the shadows were deep and scented below the rounded towers of Ajanabh. I thought I could smell that spice-smog that Simeon had loved so, or the ghost of it, the faintest sigh of cardamom and cumin and cinnamon breathing through the night. As we passed windows and doors, I could see jugglers throwing candelabra high in dimly lit rooms, and hear heartbreaking soliloquies delivered earnestly to tall mirrors. The night was full of voices, and every now and then, a lone and tamed lion would pad by on the cracked road, his collar kept clean and crisp. Surely there was a great ring somewhere, a great stage, and I was missing even now the Ajan carnival in its full waxing. We passed through a wide square peopled with red sandstone statues, each face precise and perfect in scarlet stone, clutching granite mirrors and marble parasols. We wound through them on tiptoe, for I was certain one of them would reach out at any moment to grip my arm. But the violin player walked tall and did not err in her steps, even when the stone crowd was far behind us. Agrafena's hair stood straight out behind her even when she was not whirling about, and I could not see her face for its mass. I suppose I was not one to talk, with my ungainly baskets.

Shyly, I ventured: "Your hands..."

"Yes?"

"How did you come to have your bows? It must have been very painful."

"Not so much as you might think." She stopped and though we could not fit through the alleys abreast, she looked over her shoulder at me. "We have time yet in your night before we reach the roost, if you are genuinely curious—"

I nodded eagerly. She drew me out of the little alley and sat me beside a persimmon tree caught up in a rusty iron trunk-gate, to protect it from climbing children.

"Well enough, then. I have told you already that my grandfather was a Djinn..."

THE
VIOLINIST'S TALE

HE WAS BORN IN KASH, LIKE THE REST OF YOU.
His cradle was carnelian and brass. His smoke was bilious and soot-riddled, even as an infant, and his eyes
dripped orange flame when he cried out for his mother.
My grandfather, whose name was Suhail, was dissatis-
fied by the silent finery of Kash, however, and chafed
against the Khaighal, which was the life charted for him
by the best astrologers. He wanted to find a princess
with a wicked wish for a dark and handsome stranger to
whisk her away and sing to her on a balcony surrounded by swans and imps.

So that is just what he did.

My grandmother had a long braid the color of fire, and very green eyes. As all folk know, this coloring indicates a deviant and difficult disposition, and indeed, she spent her nights at her tapered window, wishing for a dark and handsome stranger to come and whisk her away from a boring life of embroidery and afterbirth, and sing to her on a balcony surrounded by swans and imps. She was not entirely sure what she meant by singing, but in her books, suitors always sang to their ladies, and she was determined to hear a song for herself, even if it did seem a little dreary. My grandmother, whose name was Glaucia, laced her dress very tightly and sighed loudly at her window, just as the woodcuts in her books always depicted such ladies.

My grandfather, lately run off from Kash with a silk sash like blue fire, heard her sighing and needed no Khaighal to grant her wish. He obliged her most vigorously, and the swans trumpeted, and the imps snickered, and Glaucia discovered that singing was not so very dreary after all.

As it tends to do, time produced a child, a daughter with green eyes and very polite, soft black hair that never—not even once!—snaked out to strangle a parrot in flight. Suhail did not know what to do. He could not send her to be educated properly in Kash, for they would burn her and drown her in short order, and universities tended to also ask for pedigrees. But she was a mild and sweet girl, to the astonishment and consternation of both her parents, and she found a mild and sweet boy to build her a house, and was happy enough for someone who couldn't even strangle a parrot properly.

Her only unhappiness was that her marriage could not be consummated. Whenever her husband drew up the covers over them both—oh, how Glaucia rolled her eyes when her daughter recounted that!—and reached for her, the poor girl's body melted into black smoke, every bit as oily and soot-riddled as her father's. Her husband fell right into her and found his face pressed into his own pillow. There was no end to the weeping and storming in their little house.

But it seemed not to matter, for she came down with child just like any other woman, and in the usual span produced me, whose hair immediately throttled the nearest turtledove, to the relief and joy of my grandfather, who burst into grateful and incendiary tears at the sight.

My parents settled in Ajanabh and put down a modest basil field. Everything in my childhood smelled of basil, soapy and green. But I did not love basil, nor the few small squares of garlic my father put into the ground. I loved music, and I sang before I spoke. This delighted my grandmother when she visited. She did not mind that my voice sounded much more like a rabbit roasting alive in a crackling hearth than sweet tiralees. But I would not give up, and when my grandfather brought me a fiddle of lava rock with a long, thin blue flame for a bow, I threw my arms around his black and bilious neck and squeezed until he could not breathe. I learned that fiddle like some children learn their figures—it was as simple and easy to me as adding up a column of numbers and presenting the tidy, graceful sum at the bottom of the page. My mother said I played too fast, and my father said that true virtuosos certainly did *not* dance that way while they played, but I would not stop, or slow.

At last, when the basil fields were still high and bright and green, I reached the limit of my abilities. I could not play faster, or sweeter, I could not move my fingers in more complex patterns. My parents thought I would be satisfied then, to be the best I could, but my grandfather winked at me on his winter visit, and I knew my hands were not yet happy. Once the family had feasted and were snoring in four-part harmony I crept from the farmhouse and into the city proper, which was then as lawless as a ship without a brig. I sought out the cottage of Folio, who was the author, so they said, of every wonder in Ajanabh.

Her door was a menagerie of locks. Every possible type and size, from huge brass bolts to tiny, intricate silver keyholes no wider than a needle, wooden locks with gaping slots and golden locks with birds carved into their faces, iron locks and crystal locks and copper locks and locks so old and worn that only rust was left where the metal might once have been, bronze locks and locks fashioned out of antlers, crude slate locks and locks in the shape of open, staring eyes blown from purest, clearest glass.

I had no key, and there was no spare splinter of door left on which to knock. Being a clever child, I pressed my fingers into ten varied locks, no two of the same stuff, and heard a dozen little bells cascade their chimes through the hunched hut, alone among the campaniles of Ajanabh a short, squat, stairless shack. The door creaked open in just the manner one would expect a mysterious door to creak, and the light within was rust-colored, reeking of oil and copper and burnt air. I stepped gingerly inside; the door behind me swung closed, the locks merrily going about their slotting and turning.

Folio sat at her workbench, an old fig-wood plank with vises set into it and open books lying brazenly a-splay. There were sketches on the walls, and scraps of metal in various states of molten and hard leaning against chairs and baseboards or puddled in molds; loose gears and pendulums and countless clocks, their innards violently exposed, metronomes endlessly ticking away; and many things whose use I could not guess: machines of metal precious and cheap, black with oil or draped in cloth, metallic wings and pens which wrote hurriedly with no hand to guide them, little clock-work lumberjacks who chopped ineffectually at iron stumps, and a spinning wheel whose spindle whirled contentedly all on its own.

Folio had a hunchback and skin the color of fig seeds, and her spectacles— for it is well known that all inventors wear spectacles—were fashioned from clock hands which stuck out every which way from the round glass. Behind them, her

dark blue eyes, the color of good dye, were luminous and calm. She was rather old and her white hair, braided in tiny strips, hundreds upon hundreds of them, piled onto each other like bridge ropes. Her lips were thin and almost blue from pressing them whilst deep in thought, and her hands, those famous hands, had eight joints each. Her nails were very short, but her spidery hands were so delicate, plying gently a little copper sphere that spun over a fountain of steam.

"It's a pretty toy for a dull child, but I've been thinking about a mechanical horse," she said happily, her voice crisp as clockwork. "But you surely do not care much about horses, even if they could be made of silver and weep fire from their eyes."

I shrugged. "My grandfather weeps fire."

"Well," she said archly, looking up from her spinning ball, "it wouldn't be the same thing at all. My horses would have a weeping switch that you could turn on and off. Young people are so hard to impress these days."

"I am sure they would be wonderful. They say you make all the wonderful things in the world."

"That is certainly a lie. Such strange birds folk are—make a few flying machines, purely by commission, and everyone starts telling stories about you. Which is of course what brought you here—come to buy a wonder, I presume."

I blushed a bit. "Not to buy, I'm afraid. I haven't any money."

"To beg a wonder, then. And what sort of miracle am I expected to produce for free from behind my ear?"

"My violin, madam. I wish to play it as no one has played a violin before."

"Practice," she humphed.

"I can already play better than a Satyr plays her pipes," I said hotly. "But *you* should understand. What does the world need with a mechanical horse when every farmer has his own old gray nag? Who needs a horse made of silver, weeping fire? No one—but you'll make them anyway, one day or another. I would be to other violinists as your horse will be to a bent-back dapple with flies in her nose!"

She glanced at my fingers. "Very well said, girl. I think perhaps we can do something for you, but we will have to consider it for a while. I did not think of the horse until I watched the ball spin—who knows where I may find your wonder?"

I swallowed hard. "I should rather stay, madam, and help where I can."

"I do not need an apprentice, nor am I a hospice."

"Of course not! I didn't mean to say—"

There was a rummaging, clanking sound from behind a large stone furnace, and what spit a girl whose blood is a quarter fire can claim dried in my mouth. An extraordinary thing emerged from behind the furnace: a woman all of silver and bronze, whose body was a mass of gears and bolts and plates, with no flesh at all on her, only metal, endless metal, and her eyes were two rolling balls of gold. She had no hair, silver or otherwise, but an oblong head all spiked with joints and gears. Her hands ended in long, many-knuckled fingers, just like Folio's. The inventor turned to the creature and smiled fondly.

"Hour, darling, you know you're not supposed to come out when company is present."

The silvery woman turned and began to burrow behind the furnace again, pulling a dropcloth over her head and piling scrap on her shoulders. Folio laughed.

"We can still see you, Hour."

"All right, Mother," came a muffled, curiously flat voice. A bronze hand flashed out and dragged a large wing of tin plates over itself.

"No, darling, come out; you've spoiled your hiding already." There was a great clatter as she emerged again and the scrap fell to the flagstone floor. She stood there, hanging her head. Gears whirred softly.

"I am sorry I came out. But she has bad hands," said the bronze woman, and her unmuffled voice was peculiar, something between a clock chime and a whetstone spinning.

Folio turned her eyes, but none of the rest of her, and looked at my hands. "Not everyone can be so blessed as we," she demurred.

"She has bad hands," the woman repeated. "Fix her hands. Violins and bows go together, not violins and hands."

"Interesting!"

"Madam Folio!" I cried in alarm. "What is that thing?"

"She is *not* a thing, thank you very much! She is to a person what my horse will be to a nag, what you would be to a violinist. Kindly show a little respect—and don't you go telling anyone either, or there'll be no end to the outlandish strangers who will come fingering my locks for miracles."

"How can you have made such a thing, that talks and walks?"

"You believe with all your smoky little heart that I can make you a virtuoso, but you wonder at this smallest of things? I made her; she is my daughter. There is nothing simpler in the world than that..."

The Tale of the Rooster-Maker's Daughter

WHERE I GREW UP, THE SEA SOMETIMES FREEZES.

Just the edges, mind you, like a puddle freezes, from the edge-side in. The waves would go so cold that their foam came tinkling down in a shower of ice, and the beaches were hard and clear as glass. When I was a girl, I would collect the foam shards like shells, but no matter how quickly I hurried back to my house with its wide porch, I would come to the door clutching a pail of water and nothing more.

My father had a very fine house. The whole dwelling was full of white curlicues and delicate fluting, breaking over the face of the house like frozen foam. But the walls were thick and solid, as they had to be, for it was cold in Muireann, as often cold as Ajanabh is hot.

When I was not trying to ferry ice from the sea to my bedroom, I was *fiddling,* as my mother called it. My father did not think there was very much odd about a child *fiddling,* as he was a *fiddler* himself, by trade, and *fiddling* had bought our curlicued house. He worked with four other men and women in Muireann at a peculiar export which, not being fish, was not much noticed among the other products of the great seaside city. Between the five of them, they produced the most extraordinary clockwork roosters that crowed out the morning with golden beaks. This was their summer crop. In the winter they trolled the oyster beds and carved the tropical birds of their dreams from the pearls. My father made the eyes, which flicked open and shut— not by any mechanism, you understand, simply by eyelids that rolled back and forth as you turned the little golden bird in your hands. His was a simpler trade than mine—but that is the way of parents and children.

My mother was a poet, who wrote long, dreamy stanzas about broken masts and hungry seas. Once she spent a year recording every shade of gray that the palette of the Muireann sky produced. She cried out her poems at the harborfront, and young girls threw pennies at her feet. She threw up her hands like pennies when I *fiddled,* but once, just once, she held her hands in the freezing well water for hours and hours, and then, running to the sea and back again, brought me in her blue and shaking fingers one perfect shard of foam.

My father let me have a few of the finished roosters, and I took them apart in my room when I ought to have been sleeping, until my floor was full of broken birds—but I put them back together again, too, learning how the crowing sound was made by a tiny bellow in the breast, and piecing the poor fellows together in ways my father would have found horrifying, making great, huge cockerels with four or five beaks crowing in harmony. I read endless books with onionskin pages concerning the great fiddlers of old: the Kappa and the Lizard-Breeders, who made such things as I could never dream to touch, who wrote out the whole universe in scales on an iguana's back. Where had they gone, that no one could now see much on an iguana but ill temper? Where had they gone that the world was now so slow and dark, when turtles once grew trees of light in their skulls? I pondered this for hours, alone as I was content to be.

Eventually I exhausted the practical lessons of roosters. My parents wanted to introduce me to society, and served lavish teas with silver plates and watercress and costly oranges so that the white-wigged, whalebone-necklaced girls of Muireann would come and think highly of me, and introduce me in turn to their brothers. More than a few of them I induced to remove their wigs so I could count the hairs sewn into the cloth. Beyond that, I had no interest in them, as they were neither made of gold nor able to crow out the morning hours, nor did their eyelids roll back and forth if you tilted their heads.

Then, of course, there were my hands. It is true that my mother had an extra joint on her smallest finger, but that seemed no good reason to have a daughter with fingers like the legs of grass-spiders. They were very good for fiddling, hopeless at pouring tea, and excellent for making rich young women scream. The glove-makers shuddered in horror and turned me away. I did not care—who can feel a bird's toothed guts with gloved hands?

Finally one of the rooster women died—the one who made the red tails—and I humbly submitted my petition to take her place. I had my own little house then, with a few small curlicues which my father assured me would reproduce in time, and from my uppermost windows I could see the crumbling sea. And tails are easy enough. I had generous portions of my days left over when those golden feathers were lined up on the shelves like red candles. And so I set aside a rooster in my sitting room, and set about fiddling with it. I am sure a Kappa would have found my wonders tawdry and plain. But I am here and they are not, and I have done the best I can.

First, I taught it to crow not only the morning but every hour of the day. This took quite some time, for I first had to teach it what an hour was. Once it reliably marked the time, I taught it to crow a great many melodies, like a little music box, and to sing a different tune for each hour. Intricate minuets for morning; slow, sighing sonatas in the afternoon; and rolling nocturnes, naturally, for the evening. Then, because I was lonely and even my father did not often visit, I taught it to sing words as it had sung tunes, and this took a very long time indeed, for there is a great difference between a note and a word.

After many lessons with which I will not bore you, the rooster marked the hours with little, nervous words: only the number of the hour at first, but then "hello" and "mother" and "ice." I found it pleasant to be with, but I also found that in my thirtieth year I was quite tired of roosters, and quite lonely for people. Muireann is a glowering and recalcitrant place where folk do not much like to speak to one another outside tea and watercress and oranges, where the rules of conversation are fixed and true as the heavens, so that no one need tax themselves overmuch. Thus I began the process of reshaping the rooster's outside as I had done its inside.

I had not nearly enough gold to build her in style—for I had decided to make a hen of my rooster, and to call her Hour, for the first things she ever knew. There was enough, only, for the eyes, my father's famous eyelids, but no more. But I had a great many rooster pieces, and broken clocks, and broken armor, and fishhooks, and such. I took away her little three-toed legs first, and fitted her with bronze bolts and calves and plate. She was like a siren then, a bird's body sewn to a woman's legs. I gave her a new torso of silver and bronze from the armor shards, and then arms, and then the throat—a new voice, lower than the chirping birdsong—and a face, my beloved girl's face that I know so well, now. Finally I gave her hands like mine, and why should I not? A child takes after her parents. For a while I used one of the old white wigs for her hair, but this only made her look ridiculous. Every day I wound her like a pocket watch, and set her going: click, click, click.

She was as curious as any child, and I brought her to my parents' teas, where she learned the words "watercress" and "biscuit" and "speak up, no one can hear you," where we misused our egg spoons together. When we returned to the house and the moon was beaming through the frost-foam, I sat her down on a chair—she had not quite gotten the trick of sitting on her own yet. She asked me, as it was the midnight hour and she did not yet speak between her alarums:

"Good children are given stories at nighttime. Am I a good child?"

"Of course, darling, you are the best child that ever used her salad fork on her snails."

"Then I should be given a story."

"All right," I said. I did not really know very many stories, though I knew a great many poems. But these are not the same thing, even if one takes the newer fashions of verse into account. I settled back in my own chair, and the moon curled up in my lap like a cat. "Once upon a time there lived a maiden in a castle—"

"What is 'Once upon a time'?" Hour interrupted.

"It means a very long time ago, or at least, long enough ago that it would be impolite to reveal the actual number of years involved."

"What is 'lived'?"

"It means to walk and talk and eat biscuits and watercress and use one's fork improperly, and also to sleep inside a house rather than out on the stones in the cold."

"What is a maiden?"

And so I had to explain about virginity, and about dowries, and marriage contracts, and hymens, and paternity, and primogeniture, and the various expressions of royalty, systems of rank, and court etiquette. After that, I had to sketch a castle for her, and explain about buttresses and moats, drawbridges and portcullises, dragons and invading armies, knights and feudalism and a general history of both architecture and comparative political systems. Then she wanted to know about weddings, and how a dress would be made, and feasts, and how food should be prepared, and rituals of pair-bonding, and what a maiden turns into after she is married. It was very tiring, and took many months.

At last, when summer had come again and the dandelions had turned to white gauze, I had just finished explicating the various methods of quarrying stone and in what countries what stones were common. Hour, with her great, eight-jointed hands on her knees, nodded her head with great effort—we had only begun to address nodding and shaking one's head—and said:

"I think I understand now. Thank you. That was a very good story."

The Violinist's Tale, Continued

"MY FATHER DID NOT LIKE HOUR MUCH. HE felt that she never got the crook of her finger quite right when she sipped her tea. I did not have the heart to tell him how difficult it was for her to sip tea at all, how many catches and sieves I had to fix in her throat before every luncheon, so that he might love her, just a little. He did not. And so, having exhausted the amusements of whalebone harps and watercress, we set roosters aside entirely and came south. We did not intend Ajanabh, but sooner or later most folk of a certain temperament find themselves here. In a city of artists and thieves I am not entirely out of place, and Hour mends the clocks. I am a good mother; I wind her every day. She is precise and perfect, and so too the bells of Ajanabh are as accurate as the sunrise, and never fail."

The old inventor took Hour's hand, which looked as though it had been cut from a soldier's metal fist, in hers, and patted it fondly, like a grandmother proud of her cleverest child. The automaton knelt with a strange and awkward grace and laid her head on Folio's shoulder. My mother was right. All the wonders of Ajanabh were authored in that little shack.

And so too they authored my hands. Following Hour's suggestion, ten long bows were fashioned, not only of fine wood both red and dark, but within each stalk Folio laid a strand of her wiry hair and a trickle of quicksilver. No mere horsehair was strung from tip to tip, either, but Folio sent a boy with a coin to find the circus-master and ask after his mermaid, who had died of the most unfortunate gout. Finally, ten slender bows lay on the table, torchlight flickering on their polished surfaces.

"I am no musician, but I daresay these are the finest bows made."

Being somewhat more dense in those days than I have since become, I did not quite understand, even then, what she intended. Folio laughed at my perplexed expression.

"Didn't your mother ever read you stories about little girls who make deals with the devil for the sake of a violin? I've told Hour dozens. What then, should we make of a devil who makes deals with an old woman? I think we should say that anything worth doing is worth shedding blood over."

Folio laid my hand flat on the table, and gently closed a vise around my wrist to keep it in place.

"I am sorry," said Hour, her throat clicking and whirring, "this will hurt very much. It will be like the time that Mother gave me a new arm in place of a wing."

There was blood, a great deal of blood, and a little dribble of fire, but not much, not very much at all.

The Tale of the Cage of Ivory and the Cage of Iron, Continued

I PULLED A PERSIMMON FROM THE TREE AND roasted it lightly for her on my thumb. Agrafena smiled beautifully, her teeth gleaming slightly orange—or perhaps I only wished to see them so. She allowed me to feed her the fruit, its skin brown and bubbling, as her own hands were indelicate.

"She took my old violin as payment," Agrafena said when she had swallowed the last morsel. "The lava-and-fire fiddle that my grandfather hoped would serve me all my days. I watched her as she fit the fiery blue bowstring to whatever strange object it was that allowed Hour to talk. She took it out—Hour was mute for days—and opened it up on her workbench, spooling the string inside. It looked like a music box fashioned from the red stuff of a rooster's coxcomb. But Hour's voice was much better after that."

We rose and walked deeper into the city still, the streets inclining downward, like water swirling toward a basin drain.

"My parents were horrified; my grandparents roared with delight, and my grandfather's fire-beard was never so bright. But I found that if I did not play every day, if I did not dance, if I did not oil my hair and tighten the leather that lashes my fingers to my arms, I would shake and shiver like a starving beast. I knew peace only when I played, and so I went into the city, where a playing beast can earn her supper. Such is the fate of devils who bargain for their fiddles." She stared ahead of her, into the murky distance. "The basil died first, you know. So fragile. My parents went to plant medicinal wildflowers outside of Urim, and I stayed. I stayed with Ajanabh, to watch her die and hold her old red head in my arms."

We were passing through a section of town which was at once resplendent and shabby, spangled and torn. Every house's door had a curtain of some deep red or purple or green shade drawn over it, tasseled in gold. Where the drapes were drawn aside, there were ornate knockers, a griffin or a lizard or an open mouth whose tongue clacked against its lip. But the velvet was worn through in many places, even burned through, and the tassels were unraveling, and the finish on the knockers was rubbed away by countless fingers. Every window had a cascade of flowers, lilies and roses and honeysuckle—and each was wilted and fading, brown at the petals, slumped over the sill. The air was full of dead sweetness. The whole quarter was full of trilling songs, scales sung up and down by tenors and mezzo-sopranos, bombastic arias shattering goblets in every parlor.

There was a little square where the road split, and on it was a stage with long, tall supports and a checkerboard floor, long strips of turquoise satin undulating along its rear edge to represent the sea, and a red ship carved ornately and bobbing upon it. The silk was threadbare and the ship had lost one mast already, but in the torchlight one could hardly see these things. There were two men on the stage, singing fit to burst barrels, their voices punching holes in the night air. There was no audience, but in the wings, a chorus was hurriedly pulling on tights and rouging their cheeks, urgent and excited.

"Who are they performing for?" I asked.

Agrafena smiled sadly. "There are no audiences in Ajanabh. We all act; we all observe. Yet it is no less vital that the theater be perfectly timed, that the songs be on key, that the sculptures breathe as though living. This is the Opera Ghetto—poor things, the opera was always such an expensive profession. I can play my songs whenever I like, but where are they to get more rouge? Where are they to replace the shoes of the ballet corps? But they are brave and true, and there are performances every night, with matinees twice weekly. They are as faithful as husbands."

We watched the tiny opera for a time, and the women danced like no women I have seen, their parrot-feathered dresses more stalk than feather, a few strands of blue and green trailing behind them as they leapt across the stage. A girl in stilts and horns embraced a high tenor in an outlandish seal's head with one eye missing, and I was ashamed to watch their passion. I wanted to give them peace and privacy, though that is surely silly, and so I fixed my eyes at the foot of the stage while her voice spiraled up to the moonless night with the torch sparks.

At the foot of the stage was a little mound capped with a stone plaque, littered with ginger roots with faces whittled wetly into their yellow flesh and rough bouquets of violets, sheet music burnt at the edges and the satin laces of cast-off stage shoes. While I studied this diminutive monument, the show ended and the dancers stepped lightly from the stage into their homes, scraping their rouge carefully into little wooden pots, saving it for the next show.

The tenor sat down on the edge of the stage and grinned at us through his tottering papier-mâché head.

"Brought your country cousin to see the sights, Fena?"

"Hardly. And take that stupid thing off, Arioso. I never liked that story."

He lifted the seal head from his shoulders and tossed it lightly aside. Several whiskers fell out onto the stage. Under the mask he had the head of a great brown bear with yellow teeth and a torn ear. I caught my breath.

"Don't look so shocked, burnt-face. A head is a head." He put his hands to his chin and lifted off the bear's head, under which he had the clapping, flapping beak of a pelican. Cawing gleefully, he wrenched the bird head off by the throat pouch with one hand. Beneath it he was a very handsome young man, with a curly white wig and penciled eyebrows. Unceremoniously, he ripped his curls away. Beneath that, he had the long-eared, sleek-furred head of a jackal with a small black nose, and his jaw was very fierce. I waited, but he did not remove that one.

"Is that all?" I ventured.

"Maybe," he said, still grinning.

"We haven't time for this. Come, Scald, a night does not last forever, even in Ajanabh."

"Wait, wait!" the jackal-headed man cried, bounding off the stage. "She was looking at the grave! She wants to know the tale! I know she does, I can feel it in my ticket-burdened bones! It has been so long since we had anyone to talk to who didn't know our every libretto and score, Agrafena! You can't keep her all to yourself!"

"I *do* know your every libretto and score, Arioso, and besides that I know there is an army camped outside Simeon this very night, an army which contained this one, until recently. Now, do you think you can leave me in peace?"

"An *army*? Think of the full seats!"

A glare from the violinist silenced him for just a moment. "But, Fena darling, you must let me have her for a few moments. Don't be selfish! Do you know why the fields died, smoke-bones? Let me tell her—"

"The fields died because they were farmed dry for century upon century," grumbled Agrafena, scratching her shoulder blades with a long, slender bow.

"Ha!" His small black face was alight with eagerness, his pink tongue panting in and out. "That's what *you* say! But what kind of opera would that make, hm? I have never been one for *verismo*. Let me tell her the better tale, let me tell her about the Duchesses…"

The Tale of the Two Duchesses

IN DAYS GONE BY, WHEN THE PALMS WERE GREEN and high, and the saffron threads were stitched into the aprons of young girls with milk still on their breath, Ajanabh was a Duchy. This is not to be wondered at! No city so absurd, beguiling, and barbaric as ours would tolerate a King. Dukes are far more likely to lose their daughters to enchanted forests or to find themselves shipwrecked on sinister isles. This is a keener expression of the Ajan character than a dotard with a crown teetering on his bald head.

It so happened that the Duke had a lovely daughter, as Dukes are prone to do. Her hair was golden as a rooster's breast, her eyes bluer than the bay tide. It was clear enough that the Duke's wife had been a foreigner, but no one ever saw her. The Duke had it put about that she had died in childbed, and this was common enough that no one suspected otherwise. The child had such sweet pink cheeks and a laugh like silver falling from a sparrow's mouth, and all loved her. She was called Ulissa.

Now, it so happened that in the poorer quarters of Ajanabh, in the slosh-slough of the Vareni, which flows through the left-hand side of the city like a giant's tears, another child was born on the lowest floor of a red and pockmarked tenement, which is to say lower even than the street itself, for such buildings house the poorest folk below the grates and below the ground. This child also had golden hair and eyes like the sparkling of the sun upon the sea, and a laugh like gold coins falling from a grackle's mouth, and all in her sad little rookery doted upon her. Her name was Orfea, and in every way she was identical to the Duke's daughter, though Orfea's mother was nothing but a seamstress with needles in her mouth and dirty blond hair sweat-plastered across broad cheeks, and Ulissa's mother's body was carried through the streets in a closed casket all of mother-of-pearl. Think not that this is strange, for in the theater we see it happen as often as not, and are undisturbed.

Now, as these children grew, the Vareni flowed thick and rich as the rents, and Ulissa had the best tutors to ply her fingers on glass harpsichords, while Orfea sang her own little songs in the morning while she folded her mother's work, and both were as happy as girls can be. Of course, Ulissa sang as beautifully as any flute may play, and longed to walk upon the stage jeweled in glass instead of rubies, and sing of unfortunate love and tame bears and a life on the sea. She sang arias until her father prayed her give him peace, for he did not approve of opera, and even then she whispered them to herself beneath her blankets. And of course Orfea, who sewed the garments of others as day dawned and day set, longed to have enough silk and trim to fashion something of her own. But even her mother's scraps were too fine and precious for a young girl to be allowed to touch, and were resold at market to buy their milk. Instead, Orfea, quick and clever, caught the vermin of her tenements and skinned them, boiling mouse stew and rat stew and mole stew, possum stew and chipmunk stew and weasel stew. Her best dress was made of these weasel skins, and it was softer than anything her mother mended.

And when they were grown as two swans with their heads bent heartwise, they happened to meet upon the roadside, Orfea on her way to fill her basket with turmeric and blueberries at the market, and Ulissa to have her best boots mended.

Can you not see this scene in its proper regalia, staged and sung? The two sopranos in their golden wigs! The glorious set-pieces! We perform *The Two Duchesses* once a year in their honor—you must come!

So it was—and you must, in your mind, see it as it is rightly shown, with Ulissa in her ermine and black bodice, with a little crown of netted silver over plush blue linen, and Orfea in her weasel rags, her plump calves showing, her feet all bare and humble! You must imagine it, how they each dropped their burdens in shock and surprise, how they touched each other's peculiar curls, how they exclaimed in wonder!

"Why, you could be my mirror, walking the streets like a girl!" cried Ulissa.

"Why should I be your mirror, just because you can afford glass! You could as well be mine, and how dare you walk strumpet-proud, bearing my face?"

"Let us not be enemies!" said the Duke's daughter. "For what fun we might have if we were allies!"

And so it was decided. Ulissa would go into the slums and sing for her supper, and Orfea would wear ermine and laced corsets. Neither was entirely sure that she would be as happy in her new life as in her old, but it seemed too good a trick not to play it at least once, and besides, Ulissa had seen many an opera in which this sort of thing turned out reasonably well. Once a month, they would meet and exchange clothing again, and go to rest in the arms of Orfea's broad-cheeked mother, and Ulissa's white-coated father, for a single day before separating again.

For a long while, this was a very satisfactory arrangement. Ulissa rose quickly among the actresses of Vareni-side, for her hair was golden and her eyes were blue, and even in these parts it is well enough known that this is the proper masque of an ingénue. Because of her high bearing and her cultured voice, she earned for herself the nickname of The Duchess, and laughed to herself every night in a shabby bedroom where bottles of perfume stood dusty and dear, where Orfea had boiled water with rose petals and rose hips floating pink and red until some thin scent could be gleaned. Ulissa would touch these bottles and smile, and think of her far-off friend.

Orfea, for her part, learned to dance in very complicated ways, and in very complicated dresses, and though she liked the Duke very much, thought he was odd and haggard about the eyes. She did not dare ask about the golden-haired woman who had once lived there, but on her lace-covered table there were costly oils of frankincense and rosewater and ambergris, and she touched them with wonder, thinking of her far-off friend.

Each month they met in a courtyard far from the center of anything, peppered with persimmon trees and coconut shells. Orfea would take her weasel-skin dress in hand with joy, and help Ulissa into the black gowns she loved so well, and arrange her familiar hair under the glittering snood. But one month of all months, as sweet little Orfea was skipping home, fur-clad, thinking of her mother's caterpillar pies and stone tea, she was stopped by a curious sound in a nearby alley, and paused, as girls ought never to do, to listen.

It was a clacking and a dragging, and a chirruping and a moaning. Orfea, with her curls close around her chin, twisted her weasel-tail belt and peeked around the corner—only to glimpse a Basilisk, his head bloodied and baleful, clambering up the cobbles. She gasped and hid herself, for even poor girls hear stories, and our Orfea knew well that the gaze of the Basilisk turns flesh to stone. But oh! Foolhardy Orfea! She had to look again, to have a thing to tell her mother, to have a thing to tell her friend, who knew well enough all the wonders of the Duke's residence, and needed nothing less than to hear once more how much better her own shoes were than a pauper's.

It was smaller than she had imagined, the size of a wildcat or a large pig. It was a four-legged serpent covered in a cockerel's feathers, all black and red and pale gold, and its face twisted into a scaly, peeling, greenish brown beak. Upon its head was fixed an iron miter, which pinched terribly; that the young girl could plainly see. Trickles of blood had dried around the bands. It moaned and pulled itself up the steep turn, its jaw broken and scabbed. Its feet were red sandstone, pocked and prickled, the very stone of the streets and walks and campaniles of Ajanabh. They scraped along the road, sending up the occasional spark.

Now, it is well known that young women with golden curls and blue eyes are afflicted with a certain fatal innocence. Thus it is that in Ajanabh, where the local coloring tends toward the dark and coppery, there are so many clever, cunning girls. But in pity, as her folk are compelled to do by some inner song which sings not to others, Orfea cried out and went to the poor beast—imagine the aria floating high and pitiful!—wrapping it in her arms and loosening the miter and rubbing its shattered jaw.

The creature looked at her in horror, glaring and gazing with all its might. Yet Orfea lived, warm and sweet.

"Why do you not turn to stone? I demand that you turn to stone immediately!" roared the Basilisk. But his voice was rough and sibilant, as it too was all of red sandstone.

Orfea's gentle brow furrowed. "I do not rightly know—but is it not fortunate for you that I do not? I can clean your wounds and make you well. It is as simple to sew flesh as organdy."

The Basilisk sniffed her from neck to ankle, and when his beak grazed her hem, he recoiled. "What sort of creature goes swathed in weasel skin? I am *quite* sure that is not the height of fashion." The girl understood him well enough, for many of her friends and uncles in the tall tenements were often as drunk and slurred as a mutilated Basilisk.

"I am not the height of fashion, myself." She shrugged.

"Weasel is the enemy of the Basilisk, forever and all time. It is but the thickness of a dress which protects you from me."

"Then I am thankful for it, and I will make you right again. But what has happened to you, poor beast?"

The Basilisk squirmed out of Orfea's arms, nipped her briefly, just to see what she tasted like, and sighed his resignation. Whipping his tail around him in an oddly feline gesture, he began, his tongue-stone wagging pitifully.

The Tale of the Tongue

The tongue of a Basilisk is a valuable thing—the thin veneer of skin, thinner than a manuscript page, hides a muscle all of fire, and with this we hunt, and eat tasty hens and seabirds and pretty little finches. You might think it is wicked of the Basilisk to eat hens, but we will eat what we like, and if what we like is you, woe to your bones! In the lands where the sun is hotter than a thrice-struck blade and the earth is parched as a throat, it is known by even the smallest child that the Basilisk were born when a hen, her feathers warm and golden, saw a clutch of serpent's eggs whose mother had been eaten by barbarous, base, blackguard Weasel, and being kind in her chicken's heart, sat upon the eggs until they hatched.

Hens ought not to sit upon things which are not theirs. One of the little brutes ate her right up, with bits of shell still clinging to her pate. And then, being a wise beast, she began to look for Weasel, who had chewed on her mother's backbone. Ah, but Weasel is tricky, is he not? She could not touch him, when she found him in his filthy hole, though she lashed her fiery tongue at his tail and reached for his furry throat with her throttling claws and glared and glared until the grass itself had turned to stone.

"What have I done?" cried Weasel, trickster-cunning. "I was only hungry! I have my own babes to feed!"

But we were not fooled. Weasel may seem sweet—so may anything. Weasel had eaten our mother, and she must have been a great serpent—cry Woe and Harm! How shall we know her now that Weasel has taken her from us?—for her green meat in her murderer made him by some dread alchemy immune to the tricks of her children.

Weasel is wicked; we shall not forget.

But here we are, feathered and scaled and delighted to turn things to stone and burn birds into supper in midair. We make it our business to search out Weasel in all his horrid haunts, but in these degenerate days, this is more a hobby of the Basilisk than a Quest, for Weasel breeds quickly and is wretched, while Basilisk breeds slowly, and is noble. Instead we take great joy in our art—for who in the wide world can sculpt in better fashion than we, who need but glance at a thing to make its likeness in stone, perfect and fell?

We are each of us capable of casting a certain stone—my eye is prone to red sandstone, plain and sorry though it may be. I have in my time glanced at Kings and Queens, maidens and youths, soldiers and farmers, corn and wheat and peas and melons, dogs with bells on their collars, horses with fringes on their reins, cows with wet noses, a few lions and many lizards, and Weasel, always Weasel, wherever he lies. Of these I have made many fine works, statues where sparrows rest in the eye sockets, a *pietà* that babes still come from far and wide to see. Only Weasel escapes my gaze—but then, perhaps one ought not to immortalize a rat and a coward.

I took the miter after a war widow lifted her daughter from the wreckage field and, weeping toward heaven, was caught in my stare. In me she became art, and her bleeding child with her, and it is true what I tell you, that even now she stands in that mud-mire as a war memorial, and children pile up roses and scallions and peppermints at her feet. My brothers saw this was worthy and good. They wedged the miter onto my head and oh, it hurt, but I was proud that day!

Thus it was that I was not afraid when three women approached me, shading their eyes and singing a dirge. I would make of them graces and goddesses cast in sandstone, scarlet and shining! As they came close, however, I revised my plan, and decided to make them demons, for they were terribly cut and bruised, their breasts severed and bandaged, black blood staining their white frocks, their hair a mass of writhing snakes which seemed exhausted, their forked tongues lying on their mistresses' shoulders, their green skin flushed an unhealthy black. Out of the mouth of each maid trickled a half-dried spit of blood, and they would not look at me, being cunning maids of no gold locks. No matter—I still had my tongue, and I flicked it at their feet experimentally. I am interested in the varying taste of humans, as I have heard in many ways it is similar to Weasel's. They stepped back quickly, as though from the frothing edge of the sea. Still they shaded their eyes and would not look at me.

I shook my feathers. "What is it you want? You are too clever by half, so you might as well speak."

But they would not. They closed their eyes and opened their mouths as one and I saw that their tongues had been hacked out so far back that I could not see the stumps.

"Has Weasel done this to you?" I said. It must be here admitted that we Basilisk are often somewhat narrow in our understandings of horrid deeds. There is only Weasel, who is wicked, and Basilisk, who is noble.

They shook their heads and shuddered. From their skirts they drew a little mirror, and I recoiled—but they chased me with its tiny glass, and I caught my eye in its rim. But only one eye, for the women had only a small mirror, a circle of silver, and I could not see all myself. But I was rooted to the spot nonetheless, and I could feel the beginnings of stone tickling at my claws. Do you know, it feels something like your foot falling asleep, the prickles of blood drifting away where you cannot reclaim it. I watched my one rolling eye in the glass, its iris and its white, and I could not look away.

And so I stood there while they cut my tongue out of my head and, bloody and dripping, shoved it into one of their waiting, empty mouths.

The Tale of the Two Duchesses, Continued

"IT HURT SO MUCH," THE BASILISK MOANED. "And there was so much blood, blood and fire. I stumbled and retched for days, the taste of my own tongue still slick in my mouth. Finally, though there was no art in it, I found a lumbering lizard, turned him to stone, and took his tongue, which faded into sandstone even as I closed my beak over it. The fire still in my blood fused the stone to flesh, but it is a weak join." He shuffled from one stone foot to the other. "That was a long time ago. But it still bleeds. The stone chafes the skin."

"What vile women!" Orfea cried. "Why would they have done such a thing to you? What possible reason?"

"All creatures have their reasons which no other creature divines. But in these later evenings, I wonder if they were not part Weasel, with their fur hidden away."

Can you not see this pair, walking through the early evening light which is so famous, the cool blues which fall across the crimson stones? It is here the flutists play an interlude in a minor key, and all folk weep.

In the months to come, Orfea washed the Basilisk's wounds and rubbed salve into the places where his miter cut the scales, and ground his tongue to smooth on the whetstone near the stables of the Duke's Palace. In time, the Duke died, and still Ulissa did not desire to return to the Palace, and Orfea did not desire to return to her mother's shop. And so Orfea, too, became a Duchess, and a blue sash was strung from her shoulder to her hip, and a bonny sword appended to her side.

Yet the Duchess of Ajanabh did not tell her friend Ulissa about the beast, for she longed for a thing which was hers alone, which she did not have to share with the beautiful soprano, whose name rose and rose, as she sang the greatest parts yet written for the stage: Sigrid, Zmeya, Dapple, Diamond, whose part is so high and sorrowing that only the most discerning can hear the notes. The two women were as dear as ducats to one another, but each did keep her own things, and where Orfea had her mangled beast, Ulissa had a butcher's boy who made her meat pies every Tuesday morning and once killed a stag just for her.

The Basilisk, for his part, was fascinated by Orfea's stubborn refusal to turn to stone. At first he tried to catch her unaware, but she was always so careful to wear her weasel-skin dress, and though the smell of it distressed him, he learned to catch the smell of her underneath the weasel, something very like damp lilies crushed beneath a cart wheel. After a long while he stopped trying to taste her, and finally, began to look for her coming to his little courtyard full of persimmons and coconuts, waited and leapt into her arms when she arrived, rolling in the dust with her and biting her playfully about the arms. He told her terrible, outlandish tales of the misdeeds of Weasel and glorious genealogies of Basilisk and their great sculptures. She told him about her advisors, and her suitors in their silly suits of armor, and her vials of perfume, and how many owners her sword had known before her. She fed him crickets and squirming squirrels, and once he brought her a stone stag, just for her, tall antlers flashing red and rough.

But even these merry duets cannot last forever—though you ought to hear the castrato we have to play the butcher's boy!—and a day dawned stormy and flat, as skies will be when rain is near, so near as to smell it, but not quite yet arrived. The Basilisk was rolling on his back, snuffling the wind, reveling in the wet-mud smell of the coming shower. And he saw, in the corner of his eye, a woman running through the persimmon trees, her hair flapping behind her, golden as apples, her dress dark and thick and furred, her smell like damp lilies beneath a cart wheel. He chortled in his beastly joy and waddled happily toward her, his ambling gait stomping heavily, stone on stone. He could not quite catch her, and her hair teased him, streaming bright as lightning in the dark clouds.

Finally, he clamped the edge of her trailing dress under his claws and hooted triumph in his reptilian way. The woman stumbled and turned to look at him, at what had caught her, golden hair framing her face like a fine fur—and turned to stone. Her eyes went last, closing into sandstone with a hurt and puzzled expression. We can only imagine her final cry, the voice which set the opera of Ajanabh alight—then silence.

The Basilisk was frightened and baffled—the woman looked just like his Orfea, smelled like her—but where was her dress? Why would she wear stoat fur instead of Weasel? Did she not love him? Did she not call him her best and only beast? Her beloved monster? Had he not let her grind his very tongue against her stone? She had abandoned him, betrayed him! Perhaps she had meant to send him away, but thought so little of him now that she had forgotten. She was Duchessing about without him and cared nothing at all for how he might miss her. What had he done? How had he given offense?

The Basilisk wept. He howled in the storm and the thunder quailed. He called her name over and over, but she did not come. His tears streamed fire into the cobble cracks, and he struck his stone claws against the trees until the ground was wet and slick with fallen fruit. He had done nothing! He had loved her better than she deserved! Perhaps it was not a dress after all, but she herself, her wicked, Weasel self, seducing him into complacency so that she could feast on his backbone! Well, he had shown her!

The Basilisk wept. But he had loved her. He had eaten from her hand. She had told him how stupid the suitors who came bearing flowers and baronies were. She had stroked his pate beneath the miter. He had laid his head on her lap. The Basilisk lay on the earth and keened, in rage and grief and loneliness, keened until his stone tongue fell from his mouth and he could keen no more.

Holding his grief before him like a lamp, the Basilisk left the city of Ajanabh. And holding his rage before him like a pike, he stared hard at everything he passed: fence posts, stables, windmills. Basil fronds. Garlic patches. Red-pepper fields and black-pepper fields, the green peppers and the pink, and the cinnamon groves, and the coriander fields, and the saffron fields, and the cumin farms, the salt flats with their crystals like hard, cutting snow, the mustard plants, the paprika bushes, and the vanilla beans, thin and dark on the vine.

"It is said that somewhere beyond the blasted, stone-struck fields of Ajanabh, there is a clear mountain pool with the most extraordinary figure crouched over it: a terrifying stone serpent covered in stone feathers, with a miter on his head and tears in his eyes, staring into the water like a mirror. What you see at the foot of the stage is our memorial to the greatest voice ever to grace the Opera Ghetto: Ulissa, who was Duchess twice over, sweet Ulissa, dead for the lack of a dress!"

Arioso finished with a flourish, and bowed deeply.

"You know that isn't what happened." Agrafena rolled her eyes.

"Who is to say it isn't?" the jackal-headed tenor said indignantly.

"I am! No Basilisk could have blighted every field, yet every field perished."

"Ah! But the root systems, Fena dear, the roots! The stone would have spread, even if you could never see it in the withering leaves. And no city garden was touched. Only the wide and ox-tilled fields." He crossed his arms over his chest in satisfaction, and turned to me. "When Orfea discovered what had happened—for of course, Ulissa had been caught in his gaze, and mistaken for her friend! Ah, without tragic mistakes of identity, where would the theater be?—she went mad with grief for both of them, and for her city which was blasted and broken. And perhaps, just perhaps, the mad Duchess wanders the city to this day, mourning by the riverside! Is it not a marvelous tale?"

I agreed that it certainly was.

"If you are finished, we must go, Arioso," the violinist insisted.

"Yes, yes, to the roost and the river with you—you *are* taking her by the river way, aren't you? It is the best and loveliest route. But promise you'll come back and play for the Duchesses this year. Swear it! No one can play the Basilisk's Dirge like you! And bring your audience with you—she is a pearl among empty seats!"

Arioso kissed both of us noisily on our cheeks, though his kiss went straight through my smoke, and returned to the stage, where the beautiful sea set was being struck, and a forest raised in its place, with leaves all of ladies' cast-off spring veils.

Agrafena did indeed take me by the riverside, the Vareni, which flowed through the corners of the city, cutting deep into the layered streets, as though Ajanabh had always been there, and the river, a latecomer, had had to make do with grinding down avenues and boulevards instead of hills and mountains. The thoroughfares arched out over the water like battered cliffs, their undersides curving sharply away from the current. Leering lanes had long ago crumbled into little red deltas, where ramshackle fishing huts and lock-houses had been built onto the ruins of what might have once been a grocer's alley.

The water of the Vareni, which rushed and burbled, was of every conceivable color. In Kash, everything is more or less fire-colored: red and golden and black and white and the occasional blue. But here was crashing, waving water in rose and emerald and cobalt, stark yellow and depthless black, white and scarlet and orange, indigo and silver, gold, and flashing, peaking turquoise. Even in the inky, starless night, the colors gleamed. The whole thing whirled by, eddying and swirling, sending up a rainbow of spray against the docks and finger piers which jutted out into the water, for the Vareni was a warm, swift-flowing river, treacherous and deep.

Agrafena watched it go by for a moment, and chuckled at my astonished stare.

"Up northside"—she pointed—"is the Dressmaker's Parish. For centuries upon centuries, they ran their cloth through the headwaters of the Vareni, the final wash of the dye. All those colors leeched into the water, and even though there is but one lonely spider there now, weaving her ball gowns still, the colors are fast, and the Vareni is bright."

She led me down to the waterside, to a tall and spindly bell tower which had no bell, though several suspect shards of bronze lay shattered around its base. A warm light seemed to flicker inside, but I could not be sure. Water like blood licked the stairs.

"This is where I leave you," Agrafena said, drawing out one side of her long hair and playing a few slow, jagged notes. "When you will, find me in my courtyard again, and I will take you back to Simeon's hands."

She walked away, her red dress swaying, and her feet kicked a few swift, dancing steps as she disappeared behind a thin little chapel with a kicked-in door. I turned to the bell tower, the roost, I supposed, and sucked in my breath. The Vareni smelled like fish and linen. The door was no more than a gaping arch, and I ducked inside, drifting up the long, curving stairs, my smoke behind me like a shadow.

In the upper rooms, by the light of my own flames, I could see a great ivory cage, burned black by the blazing tail of a Firebird, who lay sleeping within, his wings folded gently over the dozing form of a young girl, whose toes stretched and curled lazily as she dreamed. The ceiling spun away overhead, into the broken bell hook and beyond, and the night poured in.

THE TALE OF THE WASTE, CONTINUED

THE VEILED WOMAN PUT HER HAND ON THE leopard's head, and the great cat arched her neck to meet the peeling palm, purring as her ears were thoroughly scratched.

"She does not sicken you?" the Djinn asked.

"She does not repulse me, no. She is mine. The leash goes both ways. And her hand can do little to me by now that is not already done."

Surprisingly dexterous, Rend pulled a little pack with her soft, spotted mouth from her mistress's voluminous black robes and opened the flap, gently drawing a water flask from its depths and a few strips of dried meat and crusted bread. Curling her lips away from the food so as not to moisten it, she pushed it into the cage, where Scald chewed it gratefully. She refused the water, however.

"That I do not need. They mean for me to starve here, not die of thirst. We do not thirst. What fire longs to be quenched? Either way, it will not be long."

The leopard shrugged her spotted shoulders. The evening was deeper now, and the scent of weeds and mouse bones was thick on the wind.

"We find it interesting that you speak of Ajanabh, for that was the home of my lady, before she was stricken. She knows little of what has passed there since she left the red towers for the black spires of Urim. Did you betray your people? Did you do something to keep them from the carnelian box?" Rend asked, her whiskers twitching.

The Djinn-Queen frowned, her orange-lined eyes narrow and angry. Then she laughed, harsh and hoarse, golden tears showing at the corners of her eyes, where the fire made filigree patterns, as she shook her head. "That silly box. If only they had told me what was in it. But then, I suppose generals are always foolish, no matter how dazzling the host they command. But I would not call anything I did betrayal, no more than it was betrayal to tell no Djinn but the highest about Kashkash's true nature, or to keep a Queen ignorant of her own war."

"I meant no offense," the cat said, and the Djinn glared, not at her, but at the woman with black veils, whose cool, sad eyes returned the gaze. She did not move, and after a long while, the Djinn sighed.

"I think you and your mistress are both impatient. I will come to the box and the cage in time, if you will give me leave to meander in the Ajan alleys of my tale..."

THE TALE OF THE CAGE OF IVORY AND THE CAGE OF IRON, CONTINUED

THE FLOOR OF THE CAGE WAS PILED WITH cushions trimmed in fused tassels and rich gold thread. The child was resting on a lovely blue brocade, and she turned in her sleep, pulling up the Firebird's wing over her shoulder like a blanket. His neck was curled protectively around her, banked and glowing, his beak polished brass, sticking out between the blackened bars of the cage. The door swung open and free, and with the breathing of the pair, the whole thing swayed back and forth on the frame that held it up a ways above the dusty floor.

"Hello?" I said softly, but my voice echoed like a

scream against the red walls. The bird stirred and his eyes slid open lazily, shimmering eyelids drooping. The child moaned softly and her aviary caretaker hushed her.

"Go back to sleep, dovelet, it's only a Djinn come to see Papa." I saw her head fall back to its pillow, and soon enough the contented sounds of a child sleeping drifted out of the cage.

The Firebird gently extricated himself from the child and hopped out of the cage. He was huge, the size of a young elephant, his plumage all the familiar hearth colors: deep red and orange forefeathers down to creamy sear-white underfeathers. And his tail was aflame—unlike the Djinn, the tail of a Firebird is the only thing which is truly afire—long tailfeathers like those of a peacock, tipped in curls of fire and marked in intricate, blistering designs. As he woke the flame wound up from sweet ember to soft roar, and I thought him beautiful in that moment, for fire, as ever and always, speaks to fire.

"You must hush," he said, his voice like a green branch falling into ash. "My daughter needs her sleep."

"Your daughter? But she's human!"

"The ways of the world are strange and dear, my little flint-strike. My daughter she is, doubt it not."

"Simeon sent me to you. I understand now what he meant: a flame like my own."

"Now why in the world would he do a thing like that?" The great bird put his head to one side, as if considering a pile of seed.

"I am looking for a box of carnelian—"

"I'm sure I haven't anything like that, but if you care to look, just keep soft on your feet."

"No, no, I'm sure it would be hidden. But Simeon seemed to think I should see you." I looked down, already a little ashamed of what trespassed outside Simeon's embrace. "Did you know there is an army outside? They will attack tomorrow, or the day after."

The bird fluffed his wings. "The whole city stinks of them. Even Kings and Queens sweat, and their swords weep, and I can smell the cannon even now. And you have their mire all over you, so I am reasonably certain I know you, too. I am sure Simeon means for me to tell you a great many things, in hopes that you will think well enough of us not to smoke us out like rats. But I am not sure at all that I care to speak to you, and I certainly know nothing about your ridiculous little box."

"Please," I whispered, "I only have until dawn. I have been Queen for no more than a day. It is not my fault. Tell me why you are in a cage with a little girl, and perhaps in your tale I can find their box."

The Firebird glowered, and finally settled down onto the floor, his flaming face very close to mine.

"Are you lost?" he whispered.

"Yes," I said fervently.

"Poor lost things are a specialty of mine . . ."

The Tale
OF THE
Cloak of Feathers

CALL ME LANTERN—AND DON'T LAUGH. I WAS
always gentle, always. I was a sweet little flame in a glass.
I was never a devouring blaze. That is for you, and your
kind, and your army, and your cursed box.

That was for him.

The Wizard was holding my feather when I flew into
the turret room—I knew he would be. I had felt his
hands on my fringe for years, waiting for a need. The
moon was a slash on his collar when I alighted on the
sill, pale and sharp. Need stood in the corner, with a

great, round belly swathed in an elaborate yellow coat, the color of daffodils with the first sunlight of all sunlights on their petals. It was epauletted in gold, and spangled in gold, and buttoned in gold, and belted in gold. The lapels were fringed in a green so bright it wearied the eye, and his stockings and high-heeled boots matched to the toe. He had a thin, long sword with a graceful basket looped into his belt, festooned with ribbons, the expensive, poised kind of sword that lets one know immediately that the bearer doesn't mean anything by it. He had a black wig that glossed and curled opulently to his waist, and over his face he wore an angular dancing-mask, painted with gold leaf like a manuscript, with extraordinary peacock feathers fanning out from the hollow eye sockets, their dazzling fronds bedecked with violet eyes. The mouth was a hard little slit.

In his green-gloved hand was a sack of spices, so rich and fragrant they had wet the bag through and filled the room with heady scents.

"Listen well, my young partridge. This is Kostya of Vareni-side, and he will shortly be the possessor of your feather, and you must be a good little parakeet and obey him as well as you have obeyed me by flying all the way here in the dark and cold, and leaving such a lovely, lithe goose crying in your wake."

"There is no need to gloat, Omir," said Kostya, his voice hollowed by the slit in his mask, but still eel-soft and insinuating. "It is poor form. I'm sure he is quite wretched enough without your help. I shall take him, and keep him dry, and feed him so many charming things to eat. All the mice he could hope to gobble up, served on platters of glass and gold. You'd like that, wouldn't you, Lantern?"

The man in the yellow coat put his hand on my wing, and it seemed to writhe beneath the glove. I shuddered, and my colors flared worry and warning, blue on white. I said nothing.

But the deal had been struck, and the Wizard took his bag of spices, inhaling with delight. Kostya of Vareni-side stroked the edge of my feather with an intimate little sigh, his breath ragged and rattled as he fingered the fringes—and then opened the door of a tall ivory cage, and gestured inside.

What could I have done?

The journey to Ajanabh was a long one, and to the rim of the desert, the best route is by river. Being a river man of long acquaintance, Kostya chartered a lavish barge the colors of pumpkins and blood, and I was set in my cage at the prow, to watch the foaming green rivers of the mountain country gurgle by. The barge teetered under my weight, but held without too much complaint.

The river was wide, wider than I had expected. I could see the far green shores, lit up with fireflies and spackled with mosquitoes, but they were not very near at all, and the water foamed brown and weedy around the barge. Beside me on the deck sat a large glass goblet set into a firm wooden hold, and in the goblet was a fat goldfish, snapping her veil-thin tail around her. Her scales caught the river light and her black eyes blinked slowly, one after the other. The cut crystal turned her skin into prisms.

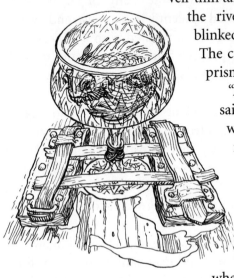

"Are you enjoying the river?" she said, her voice bubbling in the water. "I could speak to the pole men, if the flow is not smooth enough."

"I barely feel the motion of the river," I said gloomily. "It is as smooth as I could ask for, but I did not ask, and I do not wish to go where the river wends."

"I am sorry. It is the nature of animals to be caged and cupped whenever a curious man happens by. This is tragic, but one must take a philosophical outlook. The river is long; the glass is fragile."

I ground my beak. "Ajanabh is wide, and the cage is strong."

The fish brightened; her scales shimmered with pleasure. "Are you going to Ajanabh? I am only taking you so far as the river wanders. How lovely! I have relatives in Ajanabh, you know."

"How wonderful for you. I am not looking forward to it. The peacock-man in the yellow coat says he will feed me mice there, but I think a man with a longing to feed mice to birds may pursue that interest anywhere. If he wants to take me by river to a city I have hardly heard of, there will be more than mice when we arrive."

"But the river there tastes like palm sugar! I do love these cold mountain routes, but when the night is very blue, I think of the Vareni, and how it would have felt in my mouth." She turned lazily in her water, brushing the glass with her fins. "Every morning, they pour me out into this river, and I taste the water—it is like frozen moss this far up in the heights—I taste its current and its depth, the direction of its flow, I find the safe channel, I discover whether or not the trout are spawning this month. And they scoop me back up into my glass, and I chart their course through the flavors of the river."

"They might have given you a bigger glass."

"Men are inconsiderate. I am sure they believe my wine goblet to be an ocean bounded in glass. But I am the pilot of this barge, and they can do nothing without me." Her face, such as a fish's face may be, turned mischievous and sly. "But once, you know, I was a dragon."

I laughed. The sound rang out over the quick water. "You must have been the smallest dragon ever to pick a maiden's apron from your claws."

She colored angrily. "Don't laugh! I *was* a dragon! And bigger than you are, by far..."

The River
Pilot's Tale

I WAS SPAWNED IN A GROANING LOCK ON THIS very river. It was an accident—the water swirls up, the water swirls down, and every so often a handful of gold specks are caught in the sucking whirlpools, and make do in the pockets and eddies beneath the algae-slick walls. We are the lock-children: I and all of my brothers and sisters are called Lock, and it is only confusing in mating season.

The mountains here hunch and bow like old men's shoulders, and everywhere there are clouds and mists and trees bent low to the water, so low that they grow and grow beneath the tiny waves until the river floor is nothing but trees from either bank tangled up in each other, threshing the mud between their leaves. The water is cold and fast, and in the crags where ice creeps in along the sand, seizing the bowing trees, leaving only the middle of the river to run and chase as it is accustomed to do, there is a waterfall.

I do not rightly know where the first goldfish heard that this waterfall was anything but an unfortunate drop in the river table. But gossip travels among us quickly; this is the nature of fish. And some red-finned fellow had heard it whispered by the trout, who had it from the pike, who had been assured by the thorny-boned catfish, who had listened rapt to the drumfish's clacking tongue, who knew the eel would never lie, who was in awe of the adventures of the bass. And all of these agreed, that if a goldfish could but leap over this waterfall, she would become a dragon.

Many of the Locks disbelieved this: what a preposterous idea. Dragons are made from eggs and fire and in far-off countries which no polite fish has ever heard of, and besides, who has even seen a dragon in these days, let alone heard rumor of smoke or scorched maidens dipping their blackened hair in the river to cool it? But then, we Locks were born separate from the other goldfish, and are a recalcitrant and ornery breed. I alone went with the goldfish who were born in the open water to the foot of the fall, to stare into the mist and the pounding, thumping water, to wonder how a goldfish could ever manage to leap so far, if anyone had done it, what it would feel like to have hard green scales instead of soft gold ones, what it would feel like to breathe fire—would you choke on your own smoke? Would it burn your tongue? What does fire taste like? Most important, we gathered in orange and white and red clusters and wondered what it would be like to fly.

We had heard that dragons had wings. The sunfish and the walleye had assured us that they had seen hundreds of dragons in their time, and each of them had lovely leathery wings, sometimes brown, but more often outlandish colors, like our own skin. They were graceful, they looped and corkscrewed in the air, they tasted the wind like we tasted water and everyone, just everyone knew how beautiful a dragon was. Flying was like a long leap, the sunfish explained. So if you could leap over the waterfall, you would just keep soaring and rising, and bony wings would unfold from your back like fishing poles.

This sounded far better to us than to be small and unremarked fish, known only for a color we could not help. We wanted to fly, and scorch things with our breath! What would the fishermen say when we were dragons, and could roast them mightily? If we could put their little ones into glass bowls and feed them whenever we pleased—or not at all, if that amused us!—and laugh at how small a grown man will be if you raise him in a bowl and never let him out, not even on holidays. They would not say very much, we all agreed. And we wouldn't listen to them if they did.

But it is one thing to agree that a thing sounds fine, and another to accomplish it. We waved our tails at the foot of the falls and looked up at the mossy crags. They were so far. Some tried; every day a goldfish or two screwed up her courage and her tail muscles and shot out of the water like a flaming dart, higher and farther than any goldfish had done before—and she always fell back to the frothing pool, nowhere near the crest and just as much a goldfish as she had been a moment before.

Naturally, I wondered if a Lock might be superior. Every day we fought to stay in our homes as the water drained. We swam against the sucking flow, our muscles were tight and golden and we were bigger than the others, with all our constant struggle. But a child loves its mother's breast, and so we loved the lock.

I made my attempts at night, when the others were off feeding, so that I would not be ashamed to fall. But I leapt so far, farther than any of them, and with every leap the crest was nearer to my fins. I could taste the wind and the fire in me, swollen and ready. And then, one night when no one was looking, and even the eel and the drumfish were nosing in the mud, I leapt up, waving my tail in the wind as much like leathery, bony wings as I could imagine—and cleared the falls.

I fell with a great splash into the upper river, and had to right myself quickly to avoid going over again. I was awkward in the water, floundering as I had never had to do, with a fish's instinct for swimming being such that we have never in all the lives of fish had a word for "swimming." There is no need. I dragged myself up by a bent oak branch and lay gasping on the soil, air burning my chest, gill-less and finless and goldless, coughing and spitting and cold.

I was a dragon.

But what kind of dragon I could not begin to say. I had no wings at all, and my flesh was not scaled and green but pink and soft, and I had two legs and long, wet hair that stuck to my arms and all that came out of my mouth was bile and river, and no fire at all. But, I thought, no one has seen a dragon for so long. Perhaps this is what a dragon looks like. Everything that lives outside the water looks more or less the same, anyhow, and sunfish and walleye were often mistaken. Perhaps a dragon does have little dainty toes and blunt, sleek teeth. Who was I to argue? I had leapt the fall; I must now be a dragon, however strange a dragon that may be.

I walked down the mountain shakily, my dragon's feet soft and pale and unused to rocky jags and pebbles. I came upon a village, as dragons are wont to do, and—just like the stories!—their eyes widened and their jaws went slack and they sputtered and ran from me. But they came back with trousers and a long, loose shirt and a belt and a hat, and told me that I could not simply walk around naked.

"Dragons may do whatever they wish," I said haughtily. "And nakedness is no worry for me. I am sorry if it is a worry for you."

But they pulled me into a little house and showed me a long, oval mirror. In it I was, I presumed, a dragon. A dragon with long hair the color of goldfish scales, and small, round breasts, and eyes blue as a river in summer, and a mole at the base of her throat. I saw nothing the matter.

"That is what dragons look like." I shrugged, sounding more sure than I felt. I cleared my new throat. "I'm surprised at your provincial ignorance. But if the color of my scales bothers you, I will take your silly clothes."

They laughed nervously and eyed me from the corners of the room—as well they might!—but I dressed, and with great, hard-soled shoes, walked at my leisure down and out of the mountain.

Summer wound golden around me as I ventured into the world. I ate rabbits and rats, breathing on them until they just stopped running and stared at me while I puffed out my cheeks and became very red in the face. I sighed and snatched them with my hands. I was very disappointed in a dragon's lot. In my darkest moments, when the night was damp and the wolves crooned ballads to each other in the far-off hills, I allowed myself to consider that perhaps I was something slightly less than a dragon, but certainly more than a goldfish.

One morning when the sun was thin and bright on the blackberries, a hunting party came into the valley and caught no hart, but snared a dragon. My face was stained with blackberry juice and I did not know what to say, but the leader of the party was handsome and dark, and though I snarled at him, he did not seem bothered.

"I am a dragon." I sighed, almost pleading with them to believe me. "You ought to run and scatter like ants."

The man looked at me quite seriously. "No," he said, "you are not. My father has a dragon head in his hall, and though it is quite dusty and one nostril has a mouse living in it, I should never mistake it for a maiden."

"But I leapt the falls!" I hissed desperately. "No one else has ever done it! I! A lock-fish!"

"I'm sure I have no idea what you're talking about, but a young girl like you should not be out in the wilderness with nothing between you and the brambles but some uncle's trousers."

"My uncles don't wear trousers—"

I protested, but his fellow hunters surrounded me in a moment like hares around a fox, and ushered me firmly onto a horse, and the horse galloped through the dilapidated gate of a city all of red towers. As we rode, he told me of the glory of Ajanabh, the greatest city which had yet graced the earth, great in all things, including the currency.

"Did you know," he said, his gray eyes flashing like a minnow in an eddy, "we have the most extraordinary coins! Each coin, blue and bright as your own eyes, has two perfect holes in its center! It is such a marvelous country—you could be happy there..."

THE TALE OF
THE AJAN COIN

LONG BEFORE EVEN MY GREAT-GREAT-GRANDFATHER'S
day, the coin was whole, and solid yellow gold, and
prized as all coins are. There was no Duke in those days,
and Ajanabh ground along like a clock: more or less on
time, hoping someone will think to wind it, but unable
to be truly concerned. Currency was what had been
stolen from other cities, or brought by the river bargers.
Nothing was minted here.

In this raucous place lived a man by the name of
Amilcar, and this man was a fisherman on the Vareni.
He caught pike and carp—Why do you look so pale, my
dear?—of the most fabulous colors, bright yellow and

deep green and eye-aching blue. Now this fisherman was wiser than the fishermen of the degenerate tales of the north, and he spent his evenings with a horn of brass and bone, whose rim he used to rub with oil and light, to chase away the river insects. He played the most delicate, lovely music in his little hut, lighting the banks of the many-colored river with his flaming horn.

Now, Amilcar was quite lonely, and even a clever fisherman still reeks of fish. Beyond the local prostitutes, his prospects were few. And so, each evening, he would wet a sheet of music in gloss and place it against his rocking chair. As time went by, the tea-and-sturgeon-stained sheets with their notes like spider's legs thickened and grew into the shape of a lovely wife, all of music. And each evening Amilcar would sit opposite his prize and wish for it to open treble-clef eyes or eighth-note lips and live for him. He played the music of his wife with his flaming horn of brass and bone, but it did not wake.

And if this were a perverse northern tale, it would, eventually, and love him all its days. But we are more practical, in the country of palm and cinnamon.

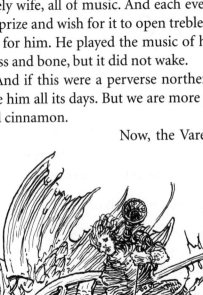

Now, the Vareni, being more or less made of dye, attracts very strange sorts of fish, and very strange sorts of other things which are not fish at all, and so it was that a Lamia called Vachya watched Amilcar at his music, and loved him. He was not unhandsome, and as a Lamia is more or less a sea serpent with three blue breasts and the head and arms of a woman, she was not over-concerned about the reek of fish.

One early morning, before the sun had set about setting his cloud-lures, Amilcar caught a great carp, the greatest one he had yet snared. This carp was all spangled silver, having once swallowed a great quantity of expensive thread. The carp was most displeased at having been caught—Why do you laugh, my dear?—and rolled over in Amilcar's net, a baleen hook stuck into his lip, and said in a frothy, gurgling voice:

"Amilcar, who soothes the clapping clams with his radiant horn, whose flames flash over the water! Hearken to me! If you should let me live, I shall tell you of a great treasure which crouches by your window every night!"

Amilcar thought this was very fine indeed, and was wise enough to know the ways of such fish. He agreed immediately.

"Vachya watches you, Amilcar, and besides being a sure sight better than a rocking chair full of old paper, she is a Lamia, and the gills of a Lamia are full of gold."

The fisherman let loose his carp, and when he returned home that night, he played his flaming horn as he was accustomed, peering at the breasts of his paper-wife for his song. But just when he was playing so beautifully that even the tone-deaf eel was leaning out of the water to hear, he leapt from his chair with his horn in one hand, and with the other threw open the window, where Vachya was curled, her many-fringed tail as blue as dye, and her piscine eyes blinking in surprise.

"I have never seen a Lamia before," said the fisherman. "Why do you come to my window?"

"I heard you, on the open ocean, where the ships break the spume like whales' heads..."

The Tale of
the Blue Serpent

DO NOT GO TO THE RIVER'S MOUTH, THE mother-Lamia say. *It will gobble you up, and then where will you be?*

On maps they always mark us, the hoops of our blue tails humping out of the sea, demarcating the places where you must not go. But who will tell us? The Lamia were born in the beginning of the dark of the world, when there was nothing but a great black sea. Some will say there was always green land, just as there was always black sea, but these are the lies of the landlocked, and we who breathe it know that the sea is greater than the land, ever and always, and cannot have been anything but the primeval blood of the world. The Lamia are old, older than salt. Our three breasts are called morning, evening, and midnight, and we encompass the heavens in our coils.

In the land of the Lamia, all things are blue. The waves lend their own color, and I cannot recall a time when blue was not the sum of my sight. Fields of blue coral where turquoise fins flashed, wavering fronds of cobalt seaweed and blue-black undersea mountains tipped in the last sapphire light where the moon pierced deepest into the water. The Lamia were the bluest of all blue things, our fins snapping bright, our skin like an ink spill, our lures glowing ghostly, blue light in the blue dark. When the tides were shocking and new, and the Lamia sucked the blood from the fat blue fish of the sea depths, my grandmother many times floated on the water, bathing in the moonlight, letting it turn her skin to silver and azure. From this vantage she saw a terrible thing, and her cerulean heart froze in her breast.

It was a ship, and it was bleached brown and white, riding high on the waves, and it was in no part blue. Fascinated, my grandmother followed it, her thick tail looping through the water. She spied on its decks creatures of no tail and no lure, whose skin was dry and salt-cracked. She followed until the ship wrecked itself, for if one watches a vessel long enough, one is surely to witness catastrophe sooner or later. And from the waves she pulled a single sailor, whose eyes were properly blue. Being a fish, she did not moon over his handsome features for too long before fixing her mouth to his throat and taking her supper. We are practical creatures, who live on the sea, and know that serendipitous food is to be savored, for it may not come again. In his thin blood she tasted the green land and sheer rocks which were new in the world, and shuddered.

She returned to the blue depths, and there, in the usual time, discovered that she was with child. She was disgusted and afraid: There are no male Lamia, and the old mothers, long-lived as they were, had given little thought to children. But when she was delivered of a happily wriggling sea serpent, the blue elders decided that it was the new blood, the rocky, grass-riddled blood, which had quickened her. Thus it was that ever since, when a Lamia felt the pull of daughters, she sought out a sailor and devoured him.

In this way was I born, from the slashed chest of a rum-wrangler.

*   *   *

Do not go to the river's mouth, our mothers say. *It will gobble you up, and then where will you be?*

Do not go there. There are monsters there, their harpoons curving up out of the deep, black places. But I was young and foolish as a tadpole. I rejoiced in the soft blue-black water, the cold at the ocean floor, the light of my lures glittering in my hair, drawing my luncheons to me. We are deep-water fish, the Lamia. We drink blood and eat sand, and our skin does not see sun. I was strong; my tail whipped through the water. When I was grown, I went before the oldest Lamia, who is crusted with barnacles so thick it is as though she is no flesh at all, but hoary rock. I sang to her as the young ones will, a recital to please our common grandmother, my voice filled the waves with quivering delight, with my desire for the river and the rock, my curious tail drifting toward their foreign currents.

The old Lamia yawned. Pieces of coral fractured off her jaw and floated up to the surface.

"Fine, fine," she croaked, "but could you not sing something *blue?*"

Why should I not go to the river's mouth? I thought to myself, furious, as I snapped away from her grotto. *Why should I not see the grass and the clearer water, with pink fish and gold fish, and the sun like a great burning clam?*

I went to ask my mother, who was sleek and so dark in her blue scales that she was nearly black, curling around a rock at the bottom of the world, gnawing on its stony roots: "I wish to see the river," I said.

"Do not hurt your poor old mother so."

"I am quite fierce enough to brave the river!" I cried.

Children must have been invented to vex and defy by turns. "Ask the swordfish, then; he will tell you where to go."

I went to the swordfish, silver and blue, his horn glinting in the shallower sea.

"Swim until the water turns warm, and tastes of cod, and then seek out the carp," he said.

I swam and swam, and finally the water became warm, and tasted light and flowery, like the white flesh of the cod. It was then that I heard the first thin, fiery tendrils of a song playing somewhere far off, like a beckoning. I sought out the carp, and found him chewing krill by an overturned galleon which had three sharks living in it.

"You must go until the water changes color," he said. "It will become so many things other than blue, and it will be warm as an otter's skin.

That is the river. But I would not recommend it. There are monsters in the river."

With a trumpet of glee I sought out the green water, and found it flowing into the sea like silt. I leapt into the green, rolled in it, my starry lures waving in their eddies. The song was so loud, then! I sang with it, exultant. I slithered onto the shore and left a long lock of my blue hair waving on the grass, to say that I was there; alone of Lamia I was braver than any forbidding map. The water warmed my flesh, and I found I was not so dark when the ocean did not chill me—I was turquoise and silver and cobalt, all at once, and this was delightful to me.

But then there was the singing, and I remembered what my mother had said about Sirens, but I could not help it. I swam upriver, through violet and gold currents, green and red and orange currents, and I played guessing games with the eels, and rhyming games with the osprey, and I tried to pretend no one sang. But each day I inched up the river, and each day there was singing rippling the water like a wind.

Until I came to this hut, and saw that no bird or Siren sang, but a horn, and the horn flamed white and red, its reflection gleaming golden on the water.

Do not go to the river's mouth. It will gobble you up, and then where will you be?

The Tale of the Ajan Coin, Continued

"WHERE WILL I BE?" VACHYA SAID SHYLY, AND the fisherman helped her up into his house, where her startlingly blue tail wrapped his walls three times and then began to climb up through his chimney flue.

And so Amilcar was happy, for a time. He would not set fire to the sheet-music wife, as Vachya asked, but in the spirit of marital compromise, kept her politely in a closet. But Vachya was a wild thing, and though it was true that her gills were made of gold, it was a foreign gold with an eerie blue tint to the metal. And they could not very well sell her gills at the market. She thrashed her tail at the good china, and though her kisses were sweet as sturgeon eggs, they were hard and violent and Amilcar quailed in her embrace. But he loved her yet, and she sang with his horn so passionately that the eels fell dead in a swoon, and the river moved toward their hut to hear. She sang of sailor blood and blue milk and great blue eggs; she sang of the moon beaming with such strength on her breasts that she felt ice form on her cobalt nipples. He looked on her with wonder, and she smiled.

Now, as husbands sometimes will, Amilcar was seized with an unfortunate folly as some men are seized with leprosy. You may think this is an overstatement, but not so when one's wife is a Lamia. Amilcar traded often with the river bargers, his fish for their pots and pans and tinkered scissors, for their spice and their tales. It so happened that Amilcar desired the wife of one of the bargers, whose hair gleamed like a great store of all the spices of Ajanabh. She looked on him fondly, but was pregnant with her fifth child, and had no time for amorous fishermen. Amilcar loved her as he had once loved his music-wife, but she did not want him.

One evening, Amilcar returned to his hut with the day's catch—a bundle of carp which did not speak or promise wives—and Vachya sat very quietly in the chair which had held the mute and voiceless wife of music. Her hair was deep blue, and tiny light shone in it, like stars, though Amilcar knew them by now for her dark-water lures, meant to catch wary fish in their enchanting lights. Her tail coiled around the entire room, huge and thick and ridged with silver-blue fins.

"How many wives do you wish to have, Amilcar?" she hissed.

"Three," he confessed, his hands shaking. "I wish to have you in my house, and the barger's wife in my bed, and my glossy wife of paper by my horn when I play."

In a rage, Vachya rose out of the roof of the house and flew in a blue streak to the river bargers. The lures in her hair shone bright as lamps. She found, in the great spice barge, the woman Amilcar loved, sleeping on her broad back, her belly barely showing. Vachya had never asked for a child, and when she saw the little swell of the spicer's belly, she thought in her heart that Amilcar had put it there, opening his throat to the brazen woman and letting her suckle at his grass-scented blood. Her tail burned white with shame and rage. The woman did not wake, for a Lamia's lures lull even whales to slumber, and Vachya in her fury pressed her hands to the woman's gravid belly, leaving two livid blue handprints that had faded by morning. The child was crushed to death beneath the sea serpent's palms.

Now, in some tales it is said that the child did not die, but was born deformed, a Lamia's half-breed, with three breasts and a very difficult life ahead of her, but this is surely fanciful.

When Vachya returned to her husband, she scrabbled at Amilcar's neck for the marks of his adultery, and it was not long before she could not tell the difference between the wounds of her hands and any mark the barger's wife might have left. Her sobs hitched like sailor's knots, and she threw open the closet, where the bedraggled, neglected paper-wife lay. She tore it into pieces with her hands before her husband's eyes, and swallowed each bit of music, each bit of wife, in grief and bitterness. Amilcar was shocked, but what can a man do who married a serpent? And this tale would have ended there, with perhaps a more loyal Amilcar and a more kindhearted Vachya, had the Lamia not, just then, coughed with the last mouthful of music.

Out of her turquoise mouth came a golden coin, tinged the color of a drowned sailor's throat.

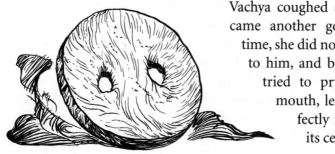

Still reeling, Amilcar stared dumbly at the coin. "Do it again!" he cried.

Vachya coughed again, and out came another gold coin. This time, she did not wish to give it to him, and bit into it as he tried to pry it from her mouth, leaving two perfectly round holes in its center.

The River Pilot's Tale, Continued

"Amilcar became very wealthy, and kept his wife in cold rooms, so that her throat was always a-rattle. Eventually he built a great house on the river, and kept her in the lower rooms, near the water, where there is always a chill to rattle the chest. And thus Vachya became the first mint of Ajanabh, and Amilcar its first Duke! Even now our coins are tinged with blue, and bear those two distinctive holes in their center!"

I looked, horrified, at my captor. He beamed, having told what he considered to be an excellent story.

"I am a dragon, not a bank," I said softly.

"I keep telling you, lovely girl, you are neither."

He took me through the gate of a house with as many rooms as a river has branches lying on its floor, and he sat me near a great fire grate with a dragon's head nodding over it, stuffed like an elk's.

"Now," he said, taking my hand in his and kneeling on a spotless marble floor, "that is a dragon. It is very old and very dead. You are very young and very alive, and a maiden with hair the likes of which I have never seen. I think you are marvelous, and radiant as coins in the sun. And if you are not entirely mad, I would be happy to keep you in this house and dress you in something other than stained breeches and a shirt far too big for you and feed you soup and make you my wife."

The other members of the household seemed to think this was rather sudden, and all the city was dutifully scandalized. But I am a fish. I lay my eggs twice a year by the dozens, and it is none of my care if they survive. If food is scarce, I will even nibble on a few—this is the nature of goldfish, the nature of rivers. Mating is easy—it hardly takes as long as lunch. I have had so many children, and I have forgotten them all, so they their own children, and their grandchildren. A goldfish has a golden heart, and with all that gold, there is no room for sentiment.

And so I married him. It seemed a rather lot of fuss just to spawn. I wore a dress like a thousand spiderwebs trailing over my maiden's body. Perhaps, I thought, a fish becoming a maiden is nearly as extraordinary as her becoming a dragon. Incense swung in censers and bearded men anointed foreheads. But then, maidens did seem to take more fuss over things than fish, and there was a wedding bed with an embroidered coverlet where there ought to have been a nice clump of twigs and a bit of shade. And instead of glistening little eggs I never had to think on again, stuck to the side of the lock, there was a big belly, and it went on for months, until I thought I would spawn forever.

But as my belly grew, my skin began to peel. I had become used to the pink and the soft, and was alarmed. I went to the doctor who lived ensconced in his rooms in the great estate, and lay on his table. He plied me with leeches and poultices for a long while, but still my skin peeled. At last some piece of my foot sloughed off its last shred of maiden skin, and beneath it, gleaming and glistening on the spotless marble floor, were three long black claws, and green scales like emerald shavings.

The Tale of the Cloak of Feathers, Continued

"I UNDERSTOOD IN A MOMENT." THE GOLDFISH laughed, a stream of bubbles breaking on the surface of her goblet. "After all, an infant goldfish looks more or less like a golden eyelash floating on the water—nothing like the full-grown fish. I leapt over the falls and began an infant's life. Once I had spawned, I was mature, and therefore I entered my adult phase—scales, wings, fire, and all. Did you never wonder why the old books are so full of dragons chasing after maidens? The serpents think the girls are orphans, and long to get them away in a lair so that they may grow up strong and tall."

"What happened to your child?" I said gently.

Lock shrugged, rising and falling slightly in the water. "I am afraid that during its birth I completed my molting and rose immediately from childbed and out of the great country house, my long green tail corkscrewing behind me. I bellowed fire at the moon in sheer joy—and then bellowed fire at the house, at its lowest rooms. And as I flew faster than a river barge, I glimpsed behind me something great and blue disappearing into the river.

"I flew as fast as my fishpole-wings could carry me, up into the mountains and back to my river and my lock. I thought nothing of the child. I do not even know if it was a boy or a girl. I thought nothing of its father, either. Mates do not last more than one season; that's obscene. And eggs will survive or fail in their own way. The best a mother can do is keep the males from eating them for a time, and then leave them to the river. I came here, to the other goldfish, to show them how it was done, that it could be done. I

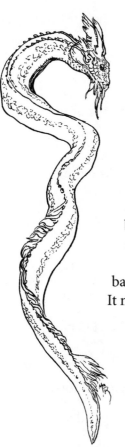

soared over the foaming, frothing edge of the falls, my tail snapping like a green flag, my nostrils flared to taste the wind—oh! It tasted like brine shrimp and broken stones! My spine ridge ruffled white and blue, blue as the poor Lamia. I called out to them, the lock fish, the goldfish, the trout, the pike, the thorny-boned catfish, the clacking drumfish, the eels who would never lie, the bass.

"And as I cleared the waterfall, I felt my scales squeeze in, and my claws seize up, and I snapped back into a goldfish, just as quick as the flick of a fin. I fell into the pool with a loud splash."

I could not help it. I laughed, cawing against the bars of my cage. "I'm sorry, I don't mean to be cruel. It must have been very sad for you."

The fish gave her piscine shrug again. "They laughed, too. But they saw me, some of them, pike and eel and trout and lock-fish. They saw that I was a dragon."

"Couldn't you leap back over?"

"I suppose. But it was not long after that that the barge men came scooping fish up in their goblets, explaining to them what they would pay and how large the glass would be, and it seemed to me very satisfactory work, tasting the river. I travel as far as any dragon on these routes. And I don't think I should like to go through the infant stage again—it was not nearly so marvelous as the last part, and I do not really like the color pink."

Lock and I had many fine conversations on the deck of the river barge, but all rivers end. This one was very long and its passage took a great many months—and it was not even half the journey to Ajanabh. When the water had finally narrowed so far as to be impassable, I had nearly forgotten I was in a cage, so kind and piccolo-cheerful was her voice, so bright were her scales in the crystal goblet. I thought often of my goose, her flapping orange feet, her hooting cry. When I wept, Lock was kind enough to look away. But she bade me farewell with a slosh of her water, and only looked sad for a moment when Kostya loaded me onto a cart, and though I bounced and flashed my tail, scorching the bars, the lock, and Kostya's hems, there was little I could do to keep myself clear of the red city. I had only to wait.

The Vareni was quite as splendid as Lock had promised, and the bridges rattled under our cart, tossing red dust into the current. But I hardly saw the colors in the glare of Kostya's yellow coat, in the gray mire of my own misery. And when he steered his cart through the Dressmaker's Parish, I was certain I knew where he had gotten that coat.

Every window and hovel door was slung with clothes, the dyes glossy and intense, even the simplest apron glowing goldfish-bright. Troughs of dye lined the streets like gutters in scarlet and yellow and blue, and a few merry folk, far too few for the number of troughs, dipped in their skirts, their trousers, their hats, their fine, long coats. Spools of costly thread stood like lampposts here and there, with a child selling lengths with her own pair of shining scissors. There were few enough people, but clothes there were in plenty. Far off there sounded laughter and screaming and jostling and spilling, the crunching of bones and the tearing of silk, the singing of songs and the dancing of feet—Ajanabh was only lately dead, and the wake still raged on. Kostya did not look at me, but stood straight and tall and proud with his prize, as a child or two stopped and stared up at me in mud-cheeked wonder. His gait was awkward—he limped, as fashionable noblemen often do, and until we came to the bell tower by the east bank of the Vareni, far from the crowd and the dresses hung up like curtains, I thought nothing of it.

The bell was whole, then, but much of the rest was as you see it, as many things are on the banks of the Vareni, following their natural inclination downward, sliding slowly into the river. Everything was boarded, broken, dusty, dim. The bell never rang and the floors creaked, and my cage was set just where you see it, and never moved again. Kostya opened his arms expansively, as if presenting me with a very great gift, wrapped up in a bow.

"This is where we shall work, my good friend. It is a lovely place, with a great many corners for hiding things in."

"What work is it you wish me to do?"

"Nothing, nothing! Sit very still while I do what I must. I should have no use for a slave of such a very great size."

And Kostya, with his gold mask gleaming beneath its peacock fringe, bent low, and plucked a single long feather from my tail. I screamed, the sudden, short pain of it; only Ravhija, my pumpkin-dear, my gardener-girl who caught me stealing and plucked her punishment, had ever dared such a thing before. I bled and stared at him, hurt and uncomprehending. He already had me in his grasp. What could another feather avail him? It smoked and hissed against his glove. He quickly threw it up into the belly of the bell, and it remained there.

"So bright!" he cried. "Bright as Stars in the heavens!"

So it went every morning, like a clock chiming dawn. He came and plucked a feather from me, dripping scarlet blood in a circle under the bell, from whence they never returned. His glee increased with every feather, and with every feather I was weaker, wept more bitterly, until I could hardly stand in my cage, and had to be given cushions on which to lie as my tail depleted, morning by morning. The space below my cage was stained with blood and golden tears, as though someone had left a ghastly cup there on the boards.

What Kostya did with his nights I could never say. He went into the city, I presumed to drink and sing and whore as men in wigs will do. But my own nights were dark and damp and full of river sounds, the sloshing currents lapping at the stairs. There were clicking sounds in the bell, but they were no company. My tail was half plucked, my heart half dead. I longed for the glimpse of a silver feather through the tapered windows, a long neck speckled with moon. But she did not come—it was foolish to think she could come.

In my thick and knotted despair, there came a scratching noise, a clattering and a scraping. Out of the bell floated a few of my feathers. I sang happily at them, so overjoyed was I to see them again. Their flames had gone out, of course, long gone from the heat of my body, but the gold sparkled still. After them came a long length of pale thread, and along this came a quiet brown spider, the size of a child's fist, whose legs were eight delicate, glittering needles, their eyes jutting out sharply at the joints where they met her thin true legs, and in each eye trailed threads of scarlet and gold.

"Good evening, oh fabric of mine, oh spinner of my best silks," said the spider in a voice like pages rubbing together. Her manifold eyes regarded me seriously.

"You must be mistaken, for I am quite sure that you are the spinner of silks between us."

"On the contrary," she said, swaying a little on her silky lead, "Kostya has asked me to make him a cloak of feathers, the brightest the world has seen, and you are my cloth, my model, my thread, and my pattern all together."

I looked at her in horror. "Why would you agree to such a thing?"

She shrugged. "Kostya has always paid me well—and well he might. We have known each other since I was barely out of my egg sac and he was adorned in whiskers and fur. I am Sleeve, the Bell Spider, famed the Parish over for my gowns and jackets. Who would not come to me with such a commission? Who else would do the materials justice?"

"I am not materials," I said quietly, my eyes cast to the ring of tears and blood.

"This is Ajanabh," she answered, her voice stitched thick with apology. "Everyone is materials." And at this she waved four of her needle-legs.

"Did Kostya do that to you? Did he make a little bracelet of your legs?"

"How funny you are! No, of course he didn't. I am a recluse spider. It is an apt name, and indicates the poisons of my body, besides. No one could sever my legs did I not ask them to . . ."

The
Dressmaker's Tale

ANOTHER CREATURE'S TALE IS LIKE A WEB: IT spirals in and out again, and if you are not careful, you may become stuck, while the teller weaves on.

Did I become stuck in Kostya's tale, or did he become stuck in mine? It is confusing, and so I will begin with mine, and perhaps somewhere along the strand we will snare him.

The first thing I remember was glass. I was caught under glass with a few dozen others as brown and small as I—perhaps siblings, perhaps not. One cannot really smell the egg sac after a few days, and though we might have been brothers and sisters, we easily might have not. Who can say? But what I saw from that squirming, thronging glass was a long table with a tall cup standing on it, holding up a stack of books, a cup of horn, all twisted red and black and yellowed white.

Each day he would scoop some of us out and crush us in his mortar, mixing in rose and snake scale and whatever else he could think of. He would pour this mixture into the cup and drink it down, savoring and considering each concoction. Now, even as an infant I was a clever thing, as spiders must be to find their web rafters and their suppers so soon after their mother crawls back into the dark. We are born with the knowledge of poison beating hard in us—we taste it; of course we taste it. Do you not know the taste of your own mouth, your own spit, your own blood? So do we, and know it well. He could have been at no other trick than poisoning, with so many of us crushed in his bowl, twitching legs brushing weakly at the rim.

I have no grudge against poisoners, being one myself, but nor did I greatly desire to become a tool of his trade. And so, when he came for me, with his dry, thin fingers groping under the glass, I was ready, and scurried up his reaching arm, all the way to his neck, and sank my fangs in him as quick as a snapping web strand, before he could even cry. When I am very angry, I sometimes have a second bite to give, and this too I gave gladly to him, with a high, whispering shriek of triumph, and two red points of blood on his cheek.

I am quick. I am merciful. He thrashed like a drowning man, and out of his skin came snaking vines—I have since been very careful, in case all men have these whipping things hiding in their skin. Out snarled holly and thorn apple and ivy, reaching to find and strangle and save. But I am too small for such blunt limbs, and they never touched me. One lashed out, a blackthorn branch, and shattered the cup of horn, which had held so many spider broths—and a terrible, sorrowful sound filled the room, like the last gasping note of a song that had once dreamed of forests, and storms, and lightning brighter than love. I shuddered as it died away in the room's stale air. But I cannot really mourn a cup.

Away from his purpling corpse I and some few others ran, into the world and the light. Having been captive since as near to birth as makes the difference of one strand of thread to another, I was not properly socialized, and unsure of what a spider ought to do with her time.

I asked the crickets in the Glassblowing District, and they said:

"We suspect it is proper and right that a spider should rub her legs together and make a very nice sort of music which fills up the night air and draws mates from all corners, green and black and handsome!"

I tried to rub my legs together, but no music of any kind came from them, only a dry sort of scraping. I asked the moths in the Bird-keepers' Ward, and they said:

"We suspect it is right and proper for a spider to seek out the flame wherever it lies, and bask in its light."

I went then to the Candle-makers' Quarter and there found more flame than tallow, but I found it very hot and uncomfortable, and when a foreleg began to smoke, I in my wisdom retreated.

I asked the flies in the Calligrapher's Close, and they considered for a very long while, keeping far back from me—I did not know why.

"We suspect it is proper and right for a spider to eat flies," they stuttered, "but we do not advise it. Perhaps it is more proper and more right for a spider to weave beautiful alphabets, as a calligrapher does, or beautiful dresses, as a tailor does. We do not know, but we seem to recall that weaving is the essential thing. Now please leave us alone."

I shrugged, and set about locating a calligrapher who would take me as an apprentice. I suspected the flies, like the moths and the crickets, were silly, flighty things who knew no more of spiderhood than I did, but without a map, all roads seem equal.

I asked the squid in their tanks, all a-flush with ink.

"We have no use for a spider," they gurgled. "You are extremely drownable, and it would be impolite of us to ask you to work in our element. Try the humans."

I asked the man in the high shop with a hat of blue and buckles, who penned careful manuscripts all through the night.

"I have no use for a spider," he coughed. "You are extremely crushable, and it would be impolite of me to ask you to work beside my careless hands. Try the Sirens."

I crawled beneath the door of a room at the highest floor of the highest tower in Ajanabh outside the Duke's estate, a drafty, cold place—cold! In Ajanabh! But there it was, the tower so high that the air itself shook with a terror of the heights. Within the rooms, the windows creaked and trembled with their own dread of the sheer walls, and three women blinked at me in wonder and hunger.

They had women's legs, and so I call them women, but from the waist, brown feathers overtook the skin, and the upper parts of them were sparrows, great, tottering beaks and long page-brown wings tipped in black folded neat as elbows at their sides. Their huge, wet black eyes regarded me with an early bird's right to breakfast, and I tucked my legs in quickly.

"Please! Do not eat me! I come to learn the art of letters—I can weave and spin as well as any, and I will stitch whatever words you ask me!"

The birds looked at each other and said nothing. Instead, they extended their wings and began to turn, a strange, hopping, sinuous dance that looped each one out of the embrace of the other, ducking under one wing and hopping with bare, grimy feet over the pirouetting leg of another. Their backs arched and bent, their wings dipped down low and fluttered wide, tracing circle after circle. I watched them in awe, their sure steps, their constant touch—never was there a moment when one Siren did not have her wing or her toe on another of her sisters. When they stopped, they looked expectantly at me, as if they had spoken, as if I was now sure to answer, if I was not a very rude creature.

Then I looked at the floor.

It was covered in paper from wall to wall, fine, creamy paper soft as silk rugs, and upon it, with feet and wings which I could see now were dark not with mud but with ink, they had written:

But we find spiders delicious.

"I find many things delicious, but if I were to eat all of them I would be as big as a baker's pan."

The trio danced again, their beaks turned up to the ceiling and down, their wings whipping, snapping, flicking at the paper floor.

This is wise. But do you really think you could dance with us? Your penmanship would be so tiny, so intricate, only the very dedicated would wish to read it.

"I have been told it is proper and right for a spider to weave—either alphabets or dresses, the flies were unclear—and dresses are so very big."

We have never heard of a spider-calligrapher.

"I have never heard of Sirens who do not speak."

The women blinked again, one after the other, six eyes sliding closed and open again. And then they began to dance in truth, a swift, urgent dance that bent them close to the floor, their wings tapping and flipping at the paper, letters forming like shapes in water, long and lithe and exalted, their toes gently tipping an *i* here and a *j* there, their leaps elongated and graceful, sometimes spanning the room entire—but they never broke with each other, staying as close and tight as a flock of migrating birds, racing over the page, their movements alien and aching and radiant.

This is what they wrote:

The Tale on the Floor

WE SANG TOO LONG; WE SANG TOO WELL. WE are sisters in silence now: It is our vow and our penance.

Once we had a nest in the open wind, on the open sea—how gray was that sea of our youth! How soft and thick was that nest we built! How long ago it was, how long ago it seems to us now, how much we have seen since we walked on our spit of stone and called each other sisters! But we are old now, we are old, and there is no sand anymore between our toes. How long since we sang innocent ballads on the shore, sharp and well turned, how long since we opened our throats in the rain and called it harmless.

Our nest was then threshed of straw and juniper and loose, waving cotton flowers, driftwood and scallop shells and sandpiper bones. Long dune grasses crisscrossed themselves within, and there we slept in each other's arms, heads tucked under our wings, and were warm, and were not wicked, no matter what they say.

And in our joy, as we picked our way among the tide pools, sucking the orange flesh from mussels and closing up the anemones with our wing tips, as our legs grew blue and goose-pimpled with the ocean spray, we sang. We sang dizzy waltzes about the moon who breathes so deeply that she draws the whole sea into her, and blows it out again. We sang dirges for our mother, buried at sea when we were chicks with pink toes. We sang dirges for our father, whom we never knew. We sang tarantellas and danced them on the coral boulders until our feet bled. We were happy together in those days, and knew nothing of the world, innocent as mice, slurping fish from their bones and looking at the sky through our joined feathers.

Do you know what it means to sing? Are there songs of the spiders, gossamer and glissand? It means to open up your mouth and unstop your chest and push your heart, your blood, your marrow, and your breath out of you like children. We opened up our mouths and unstopped our chests and pushed our hearts and blood and marrow and breath out of us, and the songs were all our nieces and daughters, lying among us and giggling at the wind.

Then she washed up on our spit of stone. How beautiful we thought her! How blue her lips were! How strange her skin, how odd her hair, seaweed-strangled! How we watched her, how we prodded, like a dolphin beached, our drownèd girl! She had a sailor's clothes, her shirt torn open, and—we did not know humans were made so!—there was a large compass needle waving northward in her navel, pointing up toward her chin. There was rust at the tip, like blood. Her boots were full of water—there were barnacles on the heels, and we pinched her and nudged her and rolled her over, and we sang to her—how we sang to her! What did we not sing to the drownèd dear? Warm, skipping minuets, thrilling ballads of narwhal hunts and octopus cities under the waves, crooning lullabies of children well held and tears never shed, all those we had from our mother so-long-dead!

Wake up, girl! we sang, but blue she stayed.

The tide is coming in! Now is no time for sleeping! we sang, but cold she stayed.

Wake up, sailor-love! Ghadir has you, Ashni has you, Nyd will not let you drink the whole sea down! we sang, and she coughed, she groaned, she made the sounds a sailor does when it does not want to wake up. Her eyes opened, and they were miraculously blue. We had never seen anything with blue eyes, though Mother's songs said that such things might exist very, very far away. Her hair was black and plastered to her back, wet as a fish's fin, and her face was ashen, tired, drawn as a crone's.

"Why do you sing me back, you awful old cat-bait, when first you sang me down?" she croaked.

"What do you mean?" Ghadir chirped.

"It was your song I followed, your song that filled up my mouth with salt and sea..."

THE
NAVIGATOR'S TALE

I STEER THE SHIPS BETWEEN AJANABH AND THE
northern passage, I chart their way between the shoals,
between the shallows and the deeps, between the sunlit
sea and the darkest tide. I am their true beacon, a lighthouse the ship carries with her, never trusting the shore
to give one over when it is most needed. My sextant is
their chapel altar while we are at sea, and at its brass
wheels and at its inky angles they pray as fervently as
they have prayed in all their days.

Which was never too fervently in Ajanabh.

It is easy work, now. We go north so often, to the floes
and the fishing villages and the whales blowing the sea

into a mist over their singing heads. I know the route so well, as well as I know my own body—and that I know as well as I know the sea, for it was mapped and charted like a peninsula buffeted by storms the day I became a compass.

There is a woman in Ajanabh who will do this sort of work. Her workshop is difficult to find, but I can navigate a street as well as a strait. And when I say she does this sort of work, what I mean is that you will tell her what you want to do, and she will tell you what to pay, and then she will grant your wish in the strangest way she can think of, usually having to do with cutting into some part of your body and fashioning you into the tool of your desire. This is how the mind of Folio clicks along in its way: better a golden limb than a flesh one which may fail.

What did I ask? The navigator's prayer: that I should never be lost. Hers is a Djinn's interpretation, I'll grant you. What did she take from me in return? She listened at my navel for the first things my mother said to me while I lay in a cradle of ships' prows—she said you can hear it like the ocean. *I will never let you set foot in the sea,* my mama had whispered, *or you will leave me alone and crying, as he did.*

And then the surgeon took my sextant, and the new compass in my stomach spun, unable to find north for shock and grief. My sextant was to me brother and lover and trusted guide, and it was gone, into her shop like a piece of junk metal.

I had another easily, but it was long and long before I liked it as well. I looked at it on my cabin shelf with disgust and suspicion, until it seemed no longer so alien and the scabs of my stomach peeled away, and then I took out my maps again.

It is easy work, as I have said. The immigrants are thick as oranges on the winter trees these days. They say the fields are failing, holding on to their green shoots like jealous bankers, and those who are wise will go. I am not wise, but the going and the leaving are my profession, and Ajanabh simply the port where my pay is held in my name.

We set out for Muireann-port two weeks ago, our hold full of rum and lemons and little books with pictures children ought not to see—

and families, huddled and shivering-sick, who had never heard of a coat of fur, soft with southern sunlight. I have seen so many like them. Did one couple have a little daughter, wide-eyed and silent in the rocking waves? I am sure one did. Did another have a parcel of boys, wrists tied one to the other to keep them together? I am sure of this, too, but it does not mean I can remember their names.

My map covered my table like a dinner cloth, and all those continents and islands and fjords and bays were my salad and soup and supper and scallion, and I was well pleased, my stomach peaceably north-pointed, my sextant safe on its shelf. I had charted so safely and so well, my equations were neat as bride-clothes, and we would not go near the Sirens' shoals, nowhere near.

Some few of the men talked of hearing those songs when we sat out on watch with the stars like a school of minnows overhead, and the creak of the boards and the splash of the sea against the old strong hull. We smoked pipes of silver, and baleen, and plain corncob, and played dice for the lemons and the rum rations. Sturgeon-sour, the first mate always lost, and had a head full of empty tooth sockets for his pains. But still he played, and still did I, and still did we all. And the helmsman said through his juice-sticky beard:

"Galien, I swear to you, I heard it once! I was a-mending the mast, and it came over the waves like the beam of a lighthouse, sweeter than nothing, singing of my sister and her new baby they all say looks just like me, toddling around with a wooden ship in his fat little hand! They were singing of the time my sister said she was proud of me, that even though our dad said I was a shame to him, what with me not being married and not being rich and not being sober and not being much of anything but an old rot holding a wheel, still I was no shame to her nor her boy, and every time I come home she'd have me a chicken roasted crisp, because I was her brother, and she loved me dear as diamonds. How do you like that?"

"I don't like it, you lying fisherman. How did they know a thing about your sister?"

"How should I know? But I know what they were singing, and I'll tell you more: It was my sister's own voice come over the waves. I jumped after it—you can't hear love singing on the wind when you've been at sea eight months and more, you can't hear it and not go after it, your heart breaking like a jib mast all the while—I jumped after it and got my leg tangled up in the rigging, and hung there for an hour before Captain caught me out, and no rum for me for a week. But I heard them. I heard my sister singing and the chicken roasting at home, and I know what I know."

"Boys," I said, laughing, "I think I can say safe as salmon run that the helm is drunk and ought to be relieved of his lemons immediately."

There was laughter of the kind that haunts ship decks after midnight, and the helmsman shook his hoary head.

"You got no soul in you, Galien. Take us close again, so I can hear my sister sing."

"Your sister is teaching her son his numbers in a hearth-hot house. She's not out here in the dark and wet, bless her."

And so I charted well away from the shoals. But the sea is a funny thing, you know. Sometimes she wants you somewhere and it doesn't matter what your maps say at supper, she'll carry you where she pleases. And if you are not properly respectful of her, or call her names she doesn't like, or give away your sacred tools like they're scraps of paper, she'll drop you at the very place your sextant was quite clear about having no desire to go.

The mist came up like a hand in our faces, and we could see nothing around us. I went up to the crow's nest to try to get a clear sightline of the shore, but it was no good at all. I saw nothing but gray and the occasional gull—which told me we were not too far out—but beyond that I and my sextant were lost as children in a wood.

And then I heard it.

I heard my mother singing. I heard her hushing, quiet-darling voice, off-key as it had always been, lowered by pipes and beer. I heard a baby murmur in her arms, and I heard her rock it to sleep. I heard her sing about the sea, how blue and bright, how much like the body of a wife, and how all lovers leave when they see the whitecaps foam. I heard her sing about my father, who had red hair—imagine it! Red as a heart! Who would think such a thing existed in the world? About my father and his tall ship, and his sextant, and his lilies at the door, about the necklaces of coral and bone he brought her from savage lands, and about his salt skin under her mouth. I heard her sing about the empty dock and the empty bed and prayers for safe passage. I heard her sing about a ship that never came back, and a woman standing every day at the dock for years and more. I heard her sing about a daughter who would grow up to bake bread in a shop and never see the blue or the bright, a daughter who would hold her old gray head and tell her she had been a good mother to her all her days and nights.

I heard my mother weeping—*I heard her*—and you can't hear your mother weeping and not go to her, you just can't. I dove into the water, well clear of the rigging, and the splash was like a hanging, so cold and so hard, and the fish scattered in horror at the woman dropped into them, hook-sudden.

I could still hear her, echoing and dim, under the water, under the mist.

"Mama!" I cried, and water stopped up my voice.

But there was an arm around my waist like a mother's arm, and a hand on my hair like a mother's hand, and a voice in my ear nothing like a mother's voice, but sweet and sad and deep.

"Why do you folk always listen?" it said with a sigh, bubbling up to the waves above.

We broke the water far from my ship, fading in the distance, and a great, huge seal held me on his belly like an otter, looking at me with depthless black eyes.

"Let me go! My mother is calling, my mother is crying!"

The seal wrinkled its muzzle. "No, she's not. She is drinking herself dizzy somewhere you cannot so much as guess. You are wet and pitiful and lost, and I have found you, but that is only luck, and luck rarely holds. Now, I will take you to dry land, for I am a kind seal and a good one. But you must answer me this, as I have been answered by every foolish sailor who finds himself overboard: Do you know of a Satyr who serves on a ship, with very big green eyes and curly hair?"

"No, friend, I have heard of no such beast."

The seal heaved a sigh and squinted in the fog. "That is to be expected. I am always answered the same. I ran from her, and that is the truth. I do not deserve to find her again. I ran from the forest and the gold slanting through the oak and the yew and the birch and the pine, I ran from the giggling streams and the grapevines fat and purple, I ran from the hoof-worn paths and the mushrooms sprouting in the shade, I ran from the loam and the leaves, I ran from her. I said a great number of foolish things which seemed wise then and I clutched my skin to my chest, and I ran all the way to the sea, smiling and singing and my feet weren't even tired, all the way to the sand and tide. I leapt into the froth and the wave, the sea beating me back, the waves pulling at my waist. I shouted to the wind and the pelicans, I was so full of salt and my skin was so slick and eager!

"It all seems rather silly now. As soon as I tasted the sea I knew it was no good. I had too much of her in me. It only tasted of tears. And one day a red ship sped by overhead and I knew it for her; I knew she was above me, stomping the boards with her hooves. I followed, but the ship was so fast. I followed all the way to the edge of the Boiling Sea, and there I could not go. But I am patient; I waited. I followed them to the Skin-Peddler's Isle and I followed them into the icy seas where they were swallowed whole. And there too I followed. I beat the sea with my hands for weeks before the turtle-whale came up and gobbled me down with her. But his belly was so wide. I looked and looked among the old wrecks but I could not find her. I lay down on the liver of the beast and prayed to die. Time passed in the dark and I did not mark it. When the

great fluttering of birds came and his mouth opened, I did not even look up, so far was I from those curtains of baleen. It was only when the awful old beast caught his belly on a reef and retched most everything in him up onto the tide that I escaped. I looked among the flotsam for the shard-planks of a red ship, but found nothing.

"But I have heard rumors of that ship in the harbors and ports again. I know she is alive; I know she crests the waves." The seal smiled softly. "Who would have thought she would go to sea? If I had known, if I had been a cleverer beast, if I had been older, less silly, I would have built her a house on the shore, and fed her black bread and sardines, and we might have been happy. There are many ways of being happy. We might have found ours."

"I am sorry." I gently touched his face. "I have heard of no such ship, no such beast. Even the Boiling Sea has dried to a long, white, dry bed with no water in it at all now. We must steer around that wasteland, where shark skeletons litter the blasted seafloor."

He nodded miserably. "Well I know it. But still I ask. There is no shortage of sailors flying off their boats like great ungainly albatrosses. One of them will be from her ship one day. I know it."

The Tale on the Floor, Continued

"He was a Selkie," our sailor finished, "and a Selkie dare not approach the shore. He dragged me as far as he could, and pointed my body at the land, and told me to swim. But"—she coughed, and seawater sprayed from her mouth—"I have never been a strong swimmer. I sail; I do not swim. I swallowed the ocean, and deep in the dark, in the bottom of the bottomless dark, I heard my mother singing again. I heard her telling the baby in her arms to wake up."

We looked at each other, blinking, perplexed. "Your mother is not here. Our mother is not here. This is a motherless place."

Galien sat up with difficulty, propping herself on her elbows. "Of course she isn't. You're here. Didn't you listen to me at all? You sing, and we hear. We hear everything we long for. Do you know how many of us have died diving into the brine after your voices? On every map your isle is marked as danger, as wicked, as a place never to dream of going."

Nyd's beak began to quiver. She tried not to cry. "That's ridiculous," Ashni said, stamping her bare foot. "We sing to each other. Every creature is allowed to sing. The songs were not for you. We did not go fishing for sailors, dropping our voices into the sea like barbed hooks. We push out our hearts and blood and marrow and breath—"

"You dash out our hearts and blood and marrow and breath on these desolate rocks, and no one survives your song," the navigator whispered.

"But we did not mean to. We did not intend it. Our songs were for us alone," Ghadir said, her face ashen.

Nyd fell to her knees, and her sobbing echoed over the shoals. She laid her feathered head on the rocks and cried over and over: "I'm sorry. I'm sorry. I'm sorry."

We carried Galien home. In the tangle of our legs she flew as no woman has ever done, and in Ajanabh we left her, to collect her pay and buy her mother beer and see her old helmsman's sister with her roasted chickens. Her eyes were bruised and her lips were broken and bleeding, and the high, thin air did not help her. She was hollow-eyed and bent when we set her down trembling on the red rooftops. Her navel-compass waved erratically, and she slapped it into submission.

"We will never sing again," said Nyd, her voice shaking, as we stood with Galien among the chimneys and the steam pipes, the tiles and the pigeons' nests. We held her between us, wing to wing, and the navigator's eyes had no grace for us. "We will never speak again. This is our vow. We will call to no one, not even ourselves, and in years to come perhaps the drowned will call us forgiven." Her black eyes overflowed with tears; her beak began an anguished clattering. "But I doubt it," she finished.

The Dressmaker's Tale, Continued

THE SIRENS STOPPED THEIR DANCE WITH THE three of them spinning in unison over the final characters. They were bathed in sweat, their feathers sticking wetly together like newborn butterflies' wings. They panted, stretched their exhausted feet, mopped one another's brow. The floor was black with writing, and I finished reading some time after they finished their dance. The one I presumed was Nyd was hitching her chest, nearly weeping again with the memory of it.

We never meant it, she wrote by herself in a small corner. *How could we mean such a thing? We were just singing.*

"I think," I said hesitantly, "that a Siren sings as a cricket does."

No one drowns in a cricket's song, Nyd scribbled hurriedly.

Besides, wrote another of the sisters, *the silence helps us to work. We see the world in our calligraphy now, and if we were forever squawking and cawing, we should not know the song of silent letters.*

The sisters allowed that if I did not scurry too quickly, and therefore look to them like breakfast, I might be permitted to work on the marginalia. I stepped into their inkstone, wetting my feet in the black iron-gall, in the sepia, in the costly blue. I tried very hard, as hard as a spider may try. I danced masterpieces of tiny points in their corners and frontispieces. I wove my silk into pages so strong they might never tear, and they marveled at how soft the webbing was beneath their callused feet.

But I was not happy. I was often underfoot—a dangerous place for me—and they looked at me sidelong when supper was scarce. The silence clawed. I wished for the buzz of flies and the splash of water and voices, just a few harried voices to break the thick quiet. I did not feel that I was a weaver so much as a very poor painter, and the heights made my head hurt.

It seemed to me time to seek out a truer expression of the flies' commandment. While the sisters slept, I dipped my legs in blue ink and spun in the margins of their latest manuscript a panorama of farewell against a calm and easy sea: sailor after sailor, standing safe on the shore, whole and singing.

In the Garden

THE BOY FELT HER EYES ON HIS BACK AS HE WALKED BACK TOWARD the Palace and a bed which had no snowflakes in it, no cold and no hardnesses. His vision was so full of her, full of her dark eyes dancing, full of the words he could now taste in his mouth like cakes.

"Come to her wedding," he had said.

"I can hardly avoid it," she had answered him.

"I will come away from the crowd, and I will find you, and how clever we shall be, to meet with all such folk about!"

"Be sure that in your cleverness you come far enough away."

But a thought had begun in him, like a flame which smokes and sparks before blooming into gold. He was not sure he dared—but how the smoke filled his chest! How it prickled and burned and billowed! He felt his heart catching; he felt himself beginning to burn.

And so it was that the boy who would one day be Sultan went into his sister's chamber the night before she would become a wife and a foreigner in one blow. Dinarzad sat at her mirror, and her hair was all unbound, falling around her like a desert tent, and before her on her little mahogany table were cloths stained with red and gold and dark blue. Her eyes were tired; her lips were thin.

"I am so tired of all this paint." She sighed. Her nightdress was laced tight around her, like armor. "I cannot breathe for its stink."

"I am sorry," the boy said.

"It is not your fault. Are you not glad? Another night and you will be rid of me."

"If you are glad, I am glad," he answered carefully.

"It does not matter if I am glad."

She was quiet then, looking at herself in the mirror. "You may brush my hair if you like," she finally said, awkward and hushed.

The boy went forward and took her bone-handled brush. He ran it through her hair, afraid at first to snarl it, to hurt her, but she made no sound. He smoothed her black hair with his hands, amazed at the heat of her scalp. He had never touched her so before.

"What..." Dinarzad cleared her throat, her voice faltering somewhat, like a bird who has not enough breath to finish a song. "What do you think happened to the Papess? Was she happy, do you suppose, in her tower when the war was done? Was she bitter? Did she rip books apart with her teeth and plot against the others? Did she rail like a caught tiger in that place? Did she throw herself from the tip of the tower? Did she go to sleep and never wake up? Did she wake up one morning and find that her heart was as white as a silkworm, and the sun was golden on the sill, and did she then believe that she could live, and hold peace in her hand like a pearl?"

The boy started. "I...I do not know. She has not told me."

"If she does, when I have gone," Dinarzad said thickly, "come to me in whatever Palace I live then, and tell me how it was with her."

It was then that his sister crumpled into his young arms and wept. "I am afraid," she whispered, over and over. "I am so afraid."

He stroked her hair as he had seen their nurses do to the children, and in his heart he cursed his own unkindness toward his sister, poor lost beast that she was. Her shoulders stopped their jerking and shivering after a time, and she looked up at him with red and wretched eyes.

"Tell me, my brother, tell me a story. Tell me a tale in which a woman is wed, and her husband is kind to her and no cold stranger, and the other wives love her as they would a sister. Tell me a tale in which a woman is wed and her children are beautiful and whole, and live a long while, and her sister-wives teach her to make bread in the fashion of their country. Tell me a tale where she wakes one morning and finds that her heart is white as a silkworm, and the sun is golden on the sill, and she then believes that she can live, and hold peace in her hand like a pearl. Tell me a tale in which a woman is wed, and she is happy."

The boy's lip trembled, and there was pity in him like a strangling vine. He knelt at Dinarzad's bare feet, and held her hands in his.

"I do not know any stories like that," he whispered.

"Neither do I." She sighed. "But it is not impossible that such tales are told."

Brother and sister sat with their heads together, and after a long while the boy told her of the thing which smoked and sparked in him, and she did not strike him or tell him he was foolish, and he loved her in that moment, his sister with her beautiful hair and her cold, thin fingers.

The morning of the wedding came white as a silkworm, and the snow drifted lazily down, unconcerned about the occasion. A skeletal sunlight shone pale through the flakes, and all the court wondered at it. The boy escaped, his arms full of boiled quail eggs and chocolate, and found the girl at the wrought Gate again, her cheeks lashed red by the cold. He told her nothing, but they smiled and laughed like old comrades, and he passed his hands eagerly over her eyes to close them.

"There are hours and hours before the wedding!" he said excitedly. "Let us find out how a spider changes her profession!"

The girl closed her eyes and lifted her chin, her breath fogging in the chill.

"It took me a great many days to walk to the Parish," the boy began. "Eight legs are no guard against distance, and I am, in the end, so very small..."

THE
DRESSMAKER'S TALE,
CONTINUED

THERE WAS A PLACE IN THE PARISH IN THOSE
days which you might have thought was a church, if you
were not careful. It had a carved door and a frescoed
ceiling, and in the pews were parishioners, after a fashion. Where the nave should have been was a spinning
wheel, and a loom, and a raised dais not unlike an altar.
The windows were cast in fabulous colors, but this was
not a church, and the woman who stood between the
wheel and the loom was not a priest.

This was Xide's house, and even to a spider with
eight legs to her name, Xide was extraordinary and grotesque. Her arms wheeled around her, one for each

of mine, and there were rings of petrified wood and plain gray stone on each of forty knuckles, and each of forty fingers was occupied with needles and thimbles and cords, spindles and pedals, bolts of fabric and strips of lace, bustles and whalebone, tassels and cuff links. She was a wheel and a whirl, and I was frightened of her. In the pews were cedar boxes and in each of the cedar boxes was a silkworm busily spinning away, the thread draped over the benches, flowing up to the altar, through copper bowls brimming with dye of every shade, and to her.

They looked up at their mistress from time to time in the mute adoration of which blind worms are capable, and, satisfied that their goddess remained yet among them, exuded another tiny length of precious, wet thread.

I passed through all of these fragrant boxes unseen and unmarked, up toward Xide whose face shone among her arms, whose web-white hair was bound severely back. I watched her weave and my legs twitched in unison with her—they longed to touch such cloth, to make such miracles of cotton and silk. I was rapt; I was held.

On the dais at that moment was a woman whose nose was very long and highborn, and Xide was spinning a red dress around her even as I watched, culling silk from the rows of cedar boxes and spinning it into fabric faster than my vision could catch. The woman was naked beneath the growing dress, holding up long strands of black beads in tented fingers so that they would not be caught in the rushing skirt.

Everywhere I had asked where I might learn to weave properly, I heard Xide's name, whispered, murmured in reverence. I called her name out then, and two of her hands ceased their motion, shading her eyes as she gazed into the distance, trying to find the sound.

"Xide, it is I, I am here, on the floor," I cried.

"Hello, Spider. I am afraid I do not know any patterns for your body, but if you wait, I will try."

The woman in her half-built dress laughed. A pearl fell out of her mouth. One of Xide's hands caught it deftly, and tossed it into a bowl already half full of white gems.

"No, I do not need clothes. I wish to be like you, to learn to weave. I have been told it is the proper profession for a spider. I wish to be proper."

"My silkworms might be jealous," she mused. "And I suspect, not being yet a proper spider, you know nothing of weaving beyond base instinct."

I hung my head. "I am sure that is true."

"Come closer, Spider."

I crawled up to her knee, which seemed so great and hard beneath me. Her face loomed huge above, young as a bride's, her eyes full of laughter and light—but they had no pupil and no iris, being all white, smooth as a statue's.

"Fate," she said, putting her head to one shoulder as her arms wove on, "is a blind weaver, they say. Did you know that? Have you lived long enough in the world to hear how she cuts and spins and stitches, how she never ceases, even for a moment?"

"No, Lady."

"It is a very silly story. For one thing, I have never cut a thread in my life..."

The Weaver's Tale

I SPIN EACH THREAD TO ITS NATURAL LENGTH, and when it is ended it is ended, and I exhort it to wind no farther. I do not sever it before its time, simply because it would make a neater sleeve. Everything I weave is neither more or less than what it longed to become.

I was the last to step down out of the Sky. They went down like a rain of light, and they changed in their going, and I did not wish to change. I saw nothing there I liked so well as the hole the Sky had made for me, its cool edges and its darkness. I wandered in the dark after they had gone, an orphan in an empty house. It had once been so full of light, and now the Stars that stayed hung like lanterns, far from each other and silent.

Far off in the reaches of the black there is a field of grass. I could tell you that it goes on forever, but only a child believes that anything goes on forever. But there is a place where the dark becomes speckled with light, thicker and thicker until there is nothing but light, on and on and on. These are Stars, too, these speckles, Grass-Stars who lie over the dark like blades and wait for the part of the Sky that bellied out the world to wander through and nose them, just once, just a bit, just the slightest brush of her skin. There are so many of them who chose this. I suppose you cannot blame them; they are not the only orphans who have told themselves that if they make up the house very nicely, Mother will come home.

I went walking there once, long after the bright ones left. I was lonely—can I be blamed if in the dark I went toward the thing which was brightest? I went walking, through the first swirls of Grass-Stars, their tiny faces beaming with anticipation that never wanes, never for a moment. I walked through the fields, into the marshes and the rivulets of pooled light, where the Stars were nearly to my waist, waving in nameless winds, waving in the dark. And I tried to step carefully, I tried, but they are so thick and so wide, sometimes I did step onto the grass. For that I can say I am sorry. It crumbled beneath me, falling in brilliant shards out of the Sky, sharp and screaming, falling out of the Sky like glass.

And when the shards broke—shall I say I should not have gone? Shall I say I was punished, a little lost girl who has been told not to walk in the gardens, not to ruin the flowers with her muddy feet?—when they broke their light splashed out and into my eyes, and my eyes were washed away in it, and I saw nothing but light.

I have seen nothing since but light.

But in that light I could see a kind of shape, a shape which seemed to me something like the world, and a world which seemed something like me. There were things which wove, and I could not see them, but I could see their weaving, how tiny and diamond-strung, how intricate and perfect. And I wanted to weave that way, I wanted to weave bigger things and greater things, and as this wish formed in me like a spindle gathering flax, my arms opened up into eight, and silk pooled in my belly—but I did not want to become a spider. I only wanted to weave. I stopped before I could grow small and black and many-eyed. What use are many eyes to the blind?

And so at last, I too came down from the heavens, blind and wet and small, cut through with the grass-rain, and in the place where I lay I began to weave with all my fingers, with anything I could find, with grass and leaves and branches and my own hair and mud and silk and cotton and wet wool and flax and rose thorns, stones and river water and stripped bark and tall trunks and evergreen needles: Everything I could touch I could weave.

And as I wove I could see. I could see what I wove, and no more; with all that light boiling in my eye, I could see what I wove, I could see where every stitch began, in rose-seed and flax-flower, and where it would end, rotting to dust on the dead body of a witch laid out on her bier or cut into strips for a child's swaddling clothes in a city which did not yet even have a name. I could see the threads, I could see the warp and the weft, I could see every day a thing I wove would live. It was so big I wept, and with my weeping and my weaving my light went out into these webs, these webs which became stones and streets and cornices and bridges and alleys, towers and bells and doors and churches, cutting into each other at all the sharp, cruel angles of a web, turning and twisting around me, who sat at the center. And after a while there was no light left, and my blood went out into the weaving instead, and all the stones and streets and cornices and bridges and alleys, all the towers and bells and doors and churches ran red as they wound out of me. How it hurt! But how it sang as it came!

I have always been here. I will always be here. The red city is my weaving, and I rest in its center. Every stone and plank knows it was once in the palms of my hands. I can see where it all will end, all the way through the wind-wracked dust and red stones worn to grains of red sand. And I will be here then, too. I knew that folk would come, eventually, and marvel at this empty city, all ready for them, all laid out and beautiful as a dress. I knew that they would be hungry and cruel as little spiders, that they would walk on grass they were told to leave be, that they would weave and weave and weave, until all their days were spooled out before them, red, and bright, and bloody.

THE DRESSMAKER'S TALE, CONTINUED

"THEY CAME BEFORE THE PEOPLE DID," SAID the Weaver-Star, indicating the silkworms in their cozy boxes, "how far they must have come! Crawling on their weak, white bellies over tearing, chewing rocks! My darlings, my courtiers, who knew only that that which is woven longs for a weaver, and here lay one waiting."

The worms wriggled in ecstasy that their mistress deigned to speak of them, and the current of thread redoubled itself, singing through the bowls of dye and into her hands.

"I have no more light, and no more blood, and my silk is rare and thin these days, but they make enough for anything I might wish to weave, and we are family, they and I. I am the Empress of the Alleys; they are silk dreaming of the Stars."

I thought I would burst for love of her, then, and her white eyes filled my vision. "But if you wove all these wonders, how can you be content to weave a woman's dress? A dress is nothing!"

Xide looked at the woman on the dais, nearly dressed now, her waist swathed in crimson, crisscrossed with black ropes to match her beads, the skirt clinging to her legs and falling all the way to the floor. "I do not understand you, friend Spider. How can you say a dress is nothing? Look at her. This thread begins in my silkworms and will end in the mouth of a Manticore, who will come to every window in the Woven City and sing until she is hoarse, and her voice will sound like a flute and a trumpet playing together, and at one particular window she will sing the saddest song she has ever sung, full of failure and sorrow and love thwarted, and searches which end in dust. It will be so terrible to hear that the whole city will weep. How can this be nothing? Tears in every flower bed, in every filthy sink! But this particular window will open and this woman will be wearing her crimson dress when she leans out, her smile so wide it would break your heart to see it. Her hair will hang down around her face, and also her beads, and when she calls out the name of the beast, a shower of pearls will fall from her mouth. The Manticore will break three stairs bounding up to her, and will bite her ever so gently on the shoulder when she knocks this woman to the floor in kittenish delight. They will grow very old together, these two: The muzzle of the one and the hair of the other will go quite gray. And when this woman—this woman, right here, whose dress you call nothing!—dies, as die she must, the Manticore will sing over her breathless body in such mourning that the city will shudder and groan and remember its first weeping, and seven suicides will fling themselves from towers in unbroachable anguish in the wake of the lion's dirge. And in grief, the Manticore will pull all her mistress's dresses from her armoire, and one by one she will tear them to pieces and eat them, for they will still smell of her, they will still taste of her, and the poor beast will not be able to bear to be apart from anything which recalls this woman whose dress was nothing."

Tears rolled down the face of the woman on the dais, her mouth hung open and she could not speak, her tears salting the dress, the beads, her breath ragged and hoarse. Yet through it she smiled, and clasped her bead-strung hands to her lips.

The Tale of the Waste, Continued

THE BLACK-VEILED WOMAN AND THE LEOPARD lay curled together on the cracked earth, listening. The spotted cat lashed her tail back and forth.

"In the place where we come from, which is called Urim, no one may go clothed in anything other than the black robes and veils you see draped over my lady. We cannot, between us, imagine such a dress."

"Nor could I," said Scald, her smoke calm and flowing slowly in a circuit that began at the crown of her head and flowed all the way around to the tip of her mere-tail. "Djinn sometimes wear outlandish things, if they are Kings or Queens or Khaighas, but we can bank our flames into any sort of clothes we should desire, and more often than not this will outshine even the richest cloth. But I cannot see where the cloth of my body will end, and that would be a useful trick."

"In Urim, we know each other only by our eyes, and every window is also curtained in black."

"That would seem to me dreary and morose," the Djinn said.

"It certainly seems so to us—but then, Urim is the Funereal City, and we cannot act against our character."

The Djinn said nothing, her eyes flashing flame. She put her black hands to the bars of the cage. "Yet you are not dead, and you flee that black-slung place."

The cat smiled, in such a way as cats will smile. "The tales of the dead are all the same. We are interested in yours, who live and burn."

Scald shook her head. "You are very strange, Rend. And your mistress is stranger still."

"So says a fire-fiend caged in iron she could surely melt anytime she wished," answered the leopard smoothly.

"Quite so," the Djinn said chuckling.

THE DRESSMAKER'S TALE, CONTINUED

I CANNOT UNDERSTAND WHY SHE LET ME STAY.
I am a spider and no more, yet she bade me sit beside her
and tell her of the glass, and the poisoner, and the poor
Sirens. She never ceased her weaving, but she laughed at
the right parts, and caught her breath at the right parts,
just as though she heard me and could have a care for the
travails of spiders.

And she called me Sleeve. She meant for me to learn
the value of dresses, she said. And so I did, and I listened
to her tales of each garment: the green stocking for the
Monopod who would tear his sock to emerald shreds
on the thorns of the saltberry trees of the Antipodes,

the black coat for the Ajan undertaker who would marry the day before he died, and be both wed and buried in this coat, the wispy white dress woven almost entirely of my own silk, my humble spider's silk, for the Duke's wife who would burn it all up into ash the day her child was born, the wings woven of horsehair and rose petals for the mask-maker's son who wanted to see what Ajanabh looked like from above—these he would hide from his father under the floor, hide them for so long they would turn to dust and brown petals beneath a green carpet. I listened to the stories as carefully as I studied the patterns, and in the company of a Star I learned all that it is right and proper for a spider to do.

In the church which was not a church, there were mice. This is not really surprising, as all churches are so plagued. Outside the radiant seat where Xide wove, and the rows of silkworm boxes, the place was terribly dusty and ill kept. Dust covered everything, turned it gray and dun and dull—after all, it is a rare celestial who will notice the state of the floor. Only I, who walked upon it, noticed. And in the corners where the mice lived, the dust was so thick and deep that if I was not careful I would sink into it like soft ash, and never be heard from again. The mice were much bigger, and walked through this fog of dust as though it were air, and saw little at all but the varying shades of dust, and became like roving drafts of dust themselves.

I spoke to them from time to time, for they were in awe of the Weaver-Star, and her worms, and her spider, and dared not approach her—but they longed to touch her, how they longed to touch her!

One was very large, his muscles trained on dust-wading. Deep in the summer evening he said to me, stroking his whiskers with gray paws:

"She is so bright!"

"I suppose she is. Imagine what she looked like in the beginning, though! All that light!"

The mouse frowned. "She is brighter than anything we know," he said.

"She is no brighter than you or I. Her light is spooled out, thread by thread."

"She is bright on the inside!" the mouse snapped irritably. "We have been talking in the dust, and we think we would like to eat her."

I could not speak for a moment, my voice closed up in horror. "Is this what becomes of living in the dust? You cannot eat her!"

"If we all bit her at once, we could."

"I will not allow it."

The mouse grinned. "You have enough poison for five, perhaps six of us if you are very angry. But the rest of us would get to drink all of her! How bright! How sweet! How bright we would become!"

"Please! You cannot! What would we be without her?"

"You may be what you like. We will be bright, bright as no mouse has dreamt!"

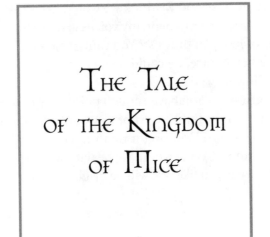

THE TALE
OF THE KINGDOM
OF MICE

IN THE BEGINNING THERE WAS DUST, AND IN the end there will be Dust, and in the middle there is Dust, Dust, Dust!

The Church-mice know that Dust is the substance of all possible things. We have heard that in the impossible land beyond the Church-door there are folk who believe that fire is the substance of all things, or water, or ether, or tiny specks of light no one can see. We cannot believe such folly exists.

Though there are some of us who have heard—ah, if only they had never begun to imagine such a thing!—

there is a burning ball outside these walls called the *sun,* and it is the brightest thing there is.

We will eat that, too, if it exists.

In the Dust, nothing is bright. There is only the gray and the dun, and the soft, ashy smell of it brushing your whiskers at every moment. We hate it, but we did not know, for a long time, how it could be escaped. When I was a pinkie at my mother's teat, I heard the old gray uncles talking about Baldtail, who was the Viceroy of Mice in days gone by— for there can be no King of the Dust, which is all there is, which gives us life and death. The Dust is King over us all. Baldtail was brave, the bravest mouse the Dust will ever allow. He, cloaked in Dust, went forward from the Corners, as Viceroys sometimes do, being valiant rulers who do not shirk adventure. He saw the worms in their boxes— perversion!—and the threads waving, and the copper bowls which sur-round the Weaver. He rose up on his hind legs to peer into the bowls, to see what they could contain, and his whiskers whickered back and forth, showering bits of Dust into the bowl.

As I have said, Baldtail was brave. And so he rashly rose up onto his tip-toes, and pulled the copper bowl over onto himself, and the dye which is the magical and alien stuff the Weaver keeps by her side soaked him from his paws to the end of his bare tail. He was Yellow from eyeball to ear-twitch, a brighter Yellow even than this thing they call the sun could pos-sibly be. The dye washed away the Dust, and alone of all mice, Baldtail was free of it; Baldtail shed the substance of mortality and became golden.

Baldtail returned to the Dust-pillowed Corners, and told all the mice what he had seen and done. At first they recoiled from his yellow body in revulsion and terror. He hurt their eyes, which had never seen any-thing but Dust, and their fellow mice roving in the Dust, lumps of gray among the gray. But there Baldtail blazed! Yellow! Can you imagine the uproar, the consternation? There were now *two* things in the universe: Dust and Yellow!

The more the mice looked at Baldtail, the more they envied him. One or two ventured to lick his gleaming fur with their pink tongues flash-ing through Dust-covered teeth. He tasted so bright, they said. So bright, and so warm. For his part, Baldtail exhorted us to go forth too and discover the bowls for ourselves.

"The Weaver sees nothing but her thread and her worms!" he argued. "She will not hurt us! Become bright! Become other than Dust!"

But we were afraid of the Weaver then. She seemed so very large and cunning. But it was decided that we should become bright, after all, and so we all agreed in the corners of the Corners to eat Baldtail all up, and then we should all be Yellow, and triumph over the Dust. We way-laid the Viceroy in the thickest, dankest mires of Dust, and with our teeth tore him haunch from long, bald tail. He tasted like any other mouse.

But oh, how it felt! We could feel his brightness in us, his Yellow. It slid in our bellies like butter, like we dreamt the sun would slide. Those of us who ate of Baldtail were exalted among mice, and we began to think as no other mouse had done before: What if there were more than two things in the universe? What if there were more than Dust and Yellow? We could not begin to calculate what these things might be, but we hungered for more brightness, for more light, for more Yellow! Those mice who had not tasted Yellow mourned their loss, and they were more eager than any of us to find these other things.

Some few of them went out from the Corners and tilted her bowls over their heads. They came running back, scampering with glee, to show us that a thing called Green existed, too, and also the almost un-fathomable Purple! We gasped, we choked in awe and ecstasy, we could not believe the universe had room for these things and also Dust. And we leapt upon them and slurped Green and Purple from their fur like meat from bone—of course we slurped meat from bone, too. Those were heady days—I cannot begin to tell you of the Feast of Red!

But we do not wish to waste any more time lapping at her bowls. Why beg for crumbs when the roast is in plain sight? We know that the Weaver is the source of all Yellowness, all Greenness, all Purpleness, all Redness, all that is not Dust, and we will eat her up as we ate up Baldtail, and Blackwhisker, and Dustbelly, and Manglepaw, and how bright we shall be then!

THE
DRESSMAKER'S TALE,
CONTINUED

THE MOUSE LICKED HIS CHOPS AND WRUNG HIS gray paws. "What will she taste like? Will she taste like mouse?"

I trembled under his hungry stare. "I have seen the sun, and the streets, and the world outside the Church-door. Why do you not go into it? I will wedge the door open for you, and you may go in all your numbers into the light, and see for yourself what the universe is made of, how many other things than Yellow and Green and Purple and Red. Do you know what Blue is?"

"No! Would it be difficult to chew?" The mouse grinned, his dusty teeth showing.

"Yes, very." I tapped my hind legs desperately, my belly pained and anxious. "But come, friend mouse!" I said with as much joviality as I could manage. "Xide is hardly worth your effort! She is all wrung out, an old cloth! Come with me, into the world outside the Church-door, and all your brethren, too, and I will show you the very brightest things there are! I will weave whatever you like into beauty and color and light! And you will find that you can be brighter than lamps without eating anything untoward. There are so many roads to brightness."

The mouse looked doubtful. "I have heard that in the world outside, it is easy to become Stepped Upon, or Swatted with a Broom. We wish to be bright! We wish to be bright and great, so that no one may Step Upon us, or do anything to us with Brooms!"

I considered this for a long time, tears forming in my manifold eyes. "I think I know how you may have all you like, and still leave the Weaver in her place, uneaten and unknown."

I went to Xide and rested in the hollow of her elbow, as full of sorrows as a web of flies—for now I knew, being a proper spider, what flies were for, and webs, and I understood why the flies had not wanted to speak to me. I told her all I had heard, and all I intended. She smiled sadly, her white eyes gleaming, and let her lips fall—ever so gently!—onto my back. It felt like moonlight, and I was at peace.

I began to weave many things in preparation for my leaving, for the exodus of the mice kingdom. First I wove green stockings, and soled green boots in pew-wood. I wove a long black wig of glossy curls. I sent to the Mask-makers' Slums for a mask of gold and peacock feathers. And because they begged for it, I wove, over days and weeks and months and years, for a spider is still small, and no Star, a long jacket all of yellow, with gold thread at every seam.

The Tale of the Cloak of Feathers, Continued

"THEY PRACTICED WHILE I WOVE, PRACTICED piling one mouse onto another in extraordinary shapes: first a cat, because they are perverse, and then a dog, then a wolf, then a lion, and then, when they could open a mouth of mice and roar in such a way that it terrified the rafter doves and sent a rain of white feathers to the floor, they carefully built themselves into the form of a man, and on their squirming shoulders I helped them arrange their yellow coat, and around their crawling head I strapped their mask of gold, and onto their wriggling legs I pulled stocking and boot. They elected the mouse who had struck the deal with me to be the voice of their golem. He asked me to give them a good name which had nothing to do with whiskers or tails or paws. I suggested Kostya, the name of the undertaker. Perhaps this was wishful on my part.

"'But you will leave Xide be?' I asked desperately.

"'If you keep us supplied with diverting brightnesses, we will surely let her live,' Kostya allowed magnanimously.

"And so I keep them in colors, and they leave the heart of Ajanabh unmolested. I give them a cloak of your feathers, and beg your forgiveness, but I cannot let the smallest tooth nibble at her hand."

Sleeve sniffled a bit and pulled one of her needle legs upward sharply, tightening a golden thread. "As for my legs, you must have guessed by now. Folio did it, who authors all the wonders of Ajanabh, of which I am but a small and secret member. I asked her to, I begged her to, to be worthy of Xide—and in this you will find a common tale in every quarter and Parish of the city. I paid her with more of my silk than I have ever spun out of my body—I was near dead with the effort, but she needed so much, to improve her daughter's joints, you see." Sleeve clacked her forelegs together merrily. "It is strange to think how much of her child is made from the beloved possessions of Ajans! She grants wishes like a Djinn, but oh, she takes and takes in return. Which is, I suppose, also like a Djinn. I wanted to weave more than webs—she obliged me. I was such delicate work, she said."

"What will he do with me when my tail is gone?"

The spider said nothing, clicking her needles together wretchedly. "Perhaps you should remember my poisoner," she ventured hesitantly.

"Where do you find this loyalty?" I cried. "I cannot remember your poisoner! My cage is fast, and the feathers he owns bind me; not so your little glass of days gone by, not so your needles! Do something, if you hate him so, unlock my cage, bite him, do not serve him pitifully, as though you can do nothing else!" I rattled the blackened bars in frustration, but Sleeve simply regarded me coolly, her threads waving.

"Do all large creatures think this way, as though their travails are the tragedies of the world, and the suffering of the small is nothing compared to their own? Certainly Kostya thinks so, now that he casts a long shadow. He does not mark me any longer—I am an eight-legged machine with no other purpose than to manufacture brightness in his sight. From where he towers, he cannot even see me. But he told you there are corners here, and where there are corners there are mice, and all mice live in awe of what he has accomplished, he who walks among men in such beautiful clothes. He does not need to watch me; they watch. They hear. A bell is a cage as sure as your own." She shook her head. "I am not so bright as you, but still I bleed and bear up under him, for her sake."

Abashed, I lay back on my cushions. The cage rocked and the rafter groaned under its weight. The night pooled black on the thin floor-boards. Sleeve's voice echoed again from the bell, thoughtful and rasping.

"The thread I use in your cloak is not from your feathers, you know. It is the reddest of red-golden silk, and I helped Xide to spin it out from the worms in their boxes. And she told me—she always tells me—where the thread will end. Would you like to know?"

"Yes," I said weakly.

" 'Little Sleeve,' she whispered—she is so considerate, not to hurt me with loudness, as so many others do—'you would not believe where this thread will wend! All the way through your little body, through to a cradle in the night, into swaddling clothes and a child's only comfort. But it will not end even there—it is a gift from sister to sister, and there is so much fire to come, so much fire, and light!'

"And so I think again you should remember my poisoner, and take heart."

There was no more from the bell, though I waited and waited and strained to hear the smallest thing. But there was nothing. The bell tower was hushed and still. In due time, the mouse-man returned to snatch another fistful of feathers from my tail. He sang and pranced in glee. I did not scream, but whimpered, and wept, and the circle beneath the cage grew. And so my days and nights went, with a spider at my ear and mice at my cage door. Once or twice I thought I saw the flash of gray fur or tiny black eyes behind the gaping eye holes of his mask.

I am very large, but a cloak is thick with layers, and when my tail was gone, and I naked and shamed, it was still not enough. Thus I had to wait, and so did he, until it grew back, and could be plucked again. Sleeve, being but a little seamstress, could only weave so fast, and be-tween these two happenstances, the weaving of the cloak spanned more than two years. I felt myself growing dim and old with loss of blood and flight and sour, golden tears. Three times he plucked my tail, and in the meantime the bell tower became piled with shining things, with jars of silver and braziers of copper, with coins and endless jackets, all of yellow and each brighter still than the others, with bolts of cloth that seemed to glow, with fruit that sparkled in the firelight—and the remains of this I was allowed to eat when Kostya had finished: apples and pomegranates and plantains and slick, wet dates. Occasionally, true to his word, there were mice, snatched from the corners of the tower and dangled into my cage: Why should he weep over mice who had not eaten Yellow or Green, who had not been reared in the Dust, who did not live in his casing of silk?

Finally, when I had no strength left, so often had I been plucked and stripped, so often had my joy and my will gone floating up to the bell, Kostya came home from his evening sport shaking and giggling with anticipation. I could hardly lift my head without his ordering me to do so.

"Lantern, perk up! It is ready, I am sure it is! The brightest thing I have ever known! I shall be brighter even than you!"

I thumped my sparse red tufts feebly. A few sparks crackled against the bars.

"What a sullen brat you are," he admonished, adjusting his golden peacock mask. "Sleeve! Sleeve! Is not my cloak ready? Send it down! I have waited so long! You promised! If you do not present it immediately I shall run at quick speed all the way back to the Church-door!"

Out of the rim of the bell came a sheen of gold which grew and grew. Even I was stunned, dazzled by it: the cloak of feathers, finished beyond imagination, so long that it would flare out behind the wearer in a regal pool of feather-silk. It shone with gold and red and orange and white, each feather layered upon others, the eyelets almost too bright to look at. It had a little, stiff collar of my shortest feathers, which would cuff the face jauntily, and it glowed with my own light, my own colors, fringed and lovely, lovely beyond the dreams of the highest-born tailor. I could not imagine a Queen, an Emperor, a dandy who would not be made small and mean and dark in that cloak. It was like the very sun woven into the shape of shoulders.

Kostya squeaked in ecstasy. But as he examined it closely, he began to frown.

"It was brighter before," he groused.

Sleeve ran down the length of the hanging cloth, still wavering from the bell. "His feathers will only flame when they are attached—he is the fire, not they. But he is too big to wear as a shoulder brooch—no cloak has ever been made which could be its equal, Kostya, my friend." She clicked her needles and swallowed hard. "You are brighter even than *she*," she spat finally.

At that, Kostya leapt into the air, dancing a jerky but joyful little step, clicking his emerald-booted heel against his emerald-stockinged calf. "Help me!" he giggled. "Help me put it on!"

He stepped into the cowl of the cloak, and Sleeve, with her needle legs and a great deal of struggle, heaved the shimmering thing over Kostya's squirming shoulders, ignoring his chirps of lust and the wringing of his gloved fingers. It lay on him like a huge, fiery hand, and in the moment that Sleeve pulled the left side up onto his body and fastened the clasp of my own talon, clipped and carved, the man of mice began to scream.

He writhed in the cloak, but his mask kept his face impassive, the little slit of mouth neither moving nor twisting. Terrible and high the first voice came, and then hundreds, thousands, shrieking tinny voices, a chorus of mice in agony—and they began to pour out of the eyes of the mask, out of the mouth, out of the wig, chewing through the green stockings, the boots, rushing from the brocaded belly, tearing the yellow coat to filthy shreds. The mice poured out of their body, but as they ran, blind, desperate, they began to die, two by two, falling onto the floorboards with small, wretched thumps, one by one. Sleeve ran among them, piercing them with her needles and crying in her own hoarse, thready way, terrified and triumphant. It took a long time for her to make sure they were dead, dead as dust.

When she was finished, she hooked the cage key from his polished belt onto one of her legs and dragged it to me. I am not so dexterous with my beak as a rule, but I certainly had the grace to let myself free of that thing which had kept me for years on end.

"I have been thinking," panted the spider, "that perhaps mice ought not to be indulged. Perhaps a Star does not really need a spider to look after her. Perhaps I have lived in a bell long enough."

"I do not understand," I said in wonder, stretching my wings from wall to wall.

"It took me two years to infuse every feather with my poison. I am only one spider, after all. It steamed with the stuff by the time I was done, though you could not see it. They breathed in my vapors, and in their panic—one can always depend upon the panic of mice—chewed through their clothes and the bottom layer of feathers, and swallowed

all my poisons as eagerly as they have swallowed everything else. My poison is not bright, but it is quick."

Weeping and laughing together, Sleeve and I walked through the wreckage of mice. I crushed them underfoot, one by one, making little rings on the boards like ghastly cups. She sat on my shoulder, stroking my feathers as my breath heaved in grief and relief. When we had finished, I let my sparking tufts light the cloak, and we watched it burn, the poison leaping bright and green in the flames. We watched it burn until it was clean, and then Sleeve asked me to break the bell.

"I cannot turn that lock," she said. "Surely you will do this thing for me."

I looked up into the disappearing rafters, so broken and high that the sky poured in like a bottle of black ink. I gave a few flaps of my wings to meet it, and though without my tail I was awkward, I managed to shiver it to bronze splinters with a blow of my beak.

"Thank you," Sleeve said, and began slowly to walk down the staircase, her satisfied needles clicking all the way down.

The Tale of the Cage of Ivory and the Cage of Iron, Continued

"Obviously it grew back again," I said, eyeing his full, thick tail, glowing cheerfully in the dark. It lit the room like a hearth.

"Obviously," he said.

"But this place has hurt you so—why would you stay? And in that same cushioned cage? What a morbid beast you must be!"

He laughed quietly, so as not to wake the child. "At first I was afraid to leave, to go back into this strange city, with its empty streets and alien sounds. I cowered here. I kept eating mice. But finally I peeked out of the door, and saw the Parish overtaken by all these saints of

Ajanabh, who stayed, and danced in the ruins. I know something about that—and so I went to dance, as well. In the Carnival of the Dawn I am the sun's best blaze, and in my flames the city sees each day born again. I am not a phoenix, but I do my best."

"You act as though you do it all by yourself!" The child sat up suddenly, long hair tumbling around her face, her arms crossed over her chest, glaring at the great Firebird.

"Well, I did, my dark-eyed darling, before you came along." Lantern looked up at me, his golden eyes bright with pride. "Children change everything, don't you know?"

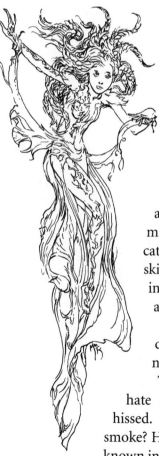

The child, as I could see her clearly now, was extraordinarily beautiful. Her eyes were wide and clear and brown as good kindling, her hair braided loosely, long and soot black, her nose fine and flared, her chin cut sharply as a gem. I do not know very much about human children; she was certainly no woman grown yet. But she was not a baby, either, and I saw corded muscles in her arms—I could certainly believe she danced. Winding up her right arm and one side of her chest, covered in minimal fashion by scraps of red cloth, were intricate tattoos, painstakingly pricked into her skin: the long, forked black outline of a dancing flame, painted all the way up to her neck and licking at her cheek.

"Still," I mumbled, "she cannot be your daughter. Those are not true flames; she is no true child of yours."

The girl narrowed her eyes at me, full of hate and disdain. "What do you know?" she hissed. "Who are the parents of plain, smelly smoke? He is my papa, as true as anything you have known in your life."

Lantern looked uncomfortable.

"Perhaps it is time," he said miserably. "Perhaps I have indulged you like a little mouse." The child looked stricken, her eyes filling with tears as easily as a child's will. "She came back, you see. After all that time, she came back to me..."

THE TALE OF THE CLOAK OF FEATHERS, CONTINUED

I HAD LEARNED TO DANCE IN THE CARNIVAL, and all my feathers were full again. The cloak was closed safely away, and I owed fealty to no one. It was almost as though none of it had happened, almost as though I had never seen the world through a cage. But I could not quite bear to take the cage down, to dash its bars in and tear up the blue cushions. I told myself that it reminded me of what happens when a thief is not careful—for did not all this begin in Ravhija's orchard, when I was so careless as to be caught with my mouth full of cherries? But I think in truth I was afraid of it, as though it were a living thing that had swallowed me up for all those years, and was still too dreadful to approach.

So it was that I was roosting in the ruins of the bell when she came.

I heard her coming up the stairs, a slow shuffle, a panting. When I think on it now I know it must have been so hard for her to climb those steep and winding steps. But climb she did, and stood before me, radiant and sorrowing and old, older than I had imagined, being but a silly bird who thought she would be just the same as when I knew her, just the same as before. This is the folly of all lovers, I suppose.

My goose was there, with silver hair and a little coat of goose feathers, and long gray skirts. My Aerie, whom I had loved so long ago, when she was a spellbound goose and I did not know what a cage was. My Aerie, so long lost. She did not need to speak; I knew her, even walking in that ridiculous woman's body—but what was not ridiculous about that moment? An old woman and a bird: as though a goose and a Firebird were not impossible enough. She had passed beyond all possibility of touch, of nesting, of flight, of the sky and of me. I laughed, a hoarse, barking, anguished sound. We stood facing, each swallowing slowly how far we had come from the other.

In her arms she held a baby, wrapped in gray cloth and scraps of fur. I hardly saw it for seeing her.

"I'm sorry," she said finally. "I didn't ask to get old, or grow arms and legs. I would have been happy just to stay with you. But you wouldn't let me."

"My feather—"

"I know, my darling bird, I know. We could neither of us help it. Ours was a very sad story—perhaps the bedraggled opera down there will perform it one of these days. But being a woman is not so bad, and if I had stayed a goose, I would not have lived long enough to find you. Geese are brief creatures, and often silly."

She told me then all she had done since we parted, how she had known Stars and passed out of the world and in again, how she had delivered the Star's child and borne it out of the dark. I told her of the spider and the mice and the Star at the heart of the city. We would have let our adventures pool between us all night, but the child in her arms awoke and began to squall. She gave it her knuckle to suck and it quieted a bit. She looked up at me through her wispy hair, which was, in her old age, not unlike long, thin feathers.

"I brought her for you, all this way," she said.

"A child?"

"You wanted chicks so much, when I flew with you. You wanted them more than you wanted me. When this little thing first tugged at my hair, I knew where she would be safe, I knew you would look after her, I knew you would want her. She is not a chick; she has no feathers and no beak and she will never fly. But then, neither will I, any longer."

I looked at the swaddled girl, her big dark eyes blinking sleepily at me, her shock of black hair like burned grass. She was not very much like a Firebird, but my heart was always gentle, and when the tiny thing reached out with her chubby red hand to clutch my warm bronze beak and I heard her laugh, I remembered all my cousin's orange eggs, I remembered the ash-nest and the desert trees, and I knew that poor orphan for my own, my solace, my hatched egg, my girl.

"I would have come looking—" I began.

"You would never have found me."

"She is beautiful."

"I know."

Aerie, businesslike and brusque, sniffed a little, and began to root through the broken planks and bolts of silk and shining things the mice had left to find enough shards to make a cradle. While she searched, I sang quietly to the child, and she gurgled along with me, after a while.

It was nearly morning when the cradle was finished, a ramshackle but strangely pretty thing resting on two long, golden cello bows and rounded shards of bell, built of red wood and stone, bedded in the Weaver's cloth and hooded with the lid of a chest that had once held piles of coins which had caught the mice's magpie glance. She laid the child inside and went back to the cloth to cut a blanket.

"Wait!" I cried suddenly, and dashed up the rafters, making the whole tower creak and shake. I pulled out my cloak of feathers from the space in the wall where I had closed it away, unable to look at it, unable to remember without terrible pains in my tail. I flew down, the golden cloak trailing behind me like kite cloth. With this we swaddled our girl, with this we tucked her into her dreams, and that black-haired dear slept in my down, all those golden feathers gleaming around her face like sunbeams.

I missed the Carnival that morning. Aerie lay in my wings as she had once done, and we listened to the sounds of a sleeping daughter. I struggled with tears that I absolutely would not let fall on her slender shoulders.

"But you will not go for a while, will you?" I whispered thickly. "I could not bear it. This is such a lonely place. Given time I could learn to hold this child so dear, dear as flames. Dear as any duck has held her chicks. But not without you. You must stay awhile yet, for me. We shall be a family, for a while. Just a little while."

Aerie turned to me and smiled dazzlingly, like a dozen noontime suns. "Of course I will stay with you, my only love, my own."

She did stay. For a little while.

It was summer when she asked me. I had carried her up to the topmost rafters of the tower and she sat there happily, kicking her feet in the air, looking out over near-empty Ajanabh, pointing like a little girl at the landmarks she knew: the Vareni with its colors blazing, the Opera Ghetto faintly singing in the distance, the square of the Cinnamon-Star, and little Agrafena dancing, tiny and dark against the light.

"Would you give me a feather?" Aerie said suddenly, squinting up at me, shading her faded eyes.

"Why? What could you ask me that I would not do in a moment?"

"I want to be able to call you whenever I wish, when I need to."

"Just cry out; I shall be here. Do I not jump whenever the child cries?"

Aerie laughed. I did not like how dry and brittle her voice was, like crackling wood. "Even so."

I thought about it. The sun was so bright and so red, that merciless southern sun I had come to know well. "For no one else would I ever lose a single feather, but to you, I would give them all, and more: my burning heart, given over flaming into your hands."

I craned my long neck, and the sun was caught in its loop for a moment, its glare and mine blazing together. I pulled a single long feather from my tail, tipped in sparkling blood, and let it fall into her wrinkled hands.

And do you know? It didn't hurt at all.

The Tale of the Cage of Ivory and the Cage of Iron, Continued

"In the morning, she had disappeared as though she had never been, and I stood alone in my bell tower, with a hungry daughter to feed." The Firebird ruffled the girl's hair with his massive wing. "I called her Solace, for so she is, my solace for an empty nest, my solace for a lost goose."

Solace was crying, her little shoulders heaving horribly, her head bent low.

"I thought . . . I thought . . . I thought I was yours," she whispered.

"You are, little pumpkin-seed!"

"No, I thought . . . I was really yours. You came from a

tree, but you're a bird. The Manticore comes out of fruit, and looks nothing like fruit. A dragon looks like a girl when it is young. I thought...I thought I was a Firebird. I thought I would sprout wings one day and fly with you, so close to the sun! I thought: Nothing in this world looks like its parents. I am no different."

She put her arms around the great neck of her papa, and wept bitterly.

"I am sorry, poor dear. I ought to have told you. But I loved you so well, and you were so happy. I could not bear to tell you otherwise. Do you know," he said to me over the shaking head of his daughter, "that when she could walk and jump she ran straight to my old cage and made it her bedroom? She loved the old thing, how it swayed and swung! I piled up more cushions for her, and the minute she was bouncing and laughing inside, it did not seem so dreadful after all."

"I am just an orphan," the child whispered to no one in particular.

"No, Solace, never that."

I watched the two of them, burrowed into each other, and casually patted back some of my smoke-hair that threatened to overflow its basket. They slowly recalled that they were not alone. Solace hopped out of the Firebird's tail and sat on the rim of the ivory cage, looking at me intently.

"You are a very good listener," she said shrewdly, kicking her legs back and forth. Her right leg was blazing with the same flame tattoos, all the way down to her toes. She wore a short little skirt of the same ragged red cloth as her shirt—a dancer's fluttering scarves. "I can't go nearly so long without asking questions when Papa gets on about the dragon-girl and old Sleeve. She comes to see me sometimes, you know. Says I'm just like her: feral, not properly socialized. I asked her what proper girls do once, and she said she didn't know, but she thought that dancing like I do was probably not on the list."

"Probably not," I allowed. "Among my people I'm considered a matron, though I'd wager I'm no older than you in years properly counted. I don't know what a proper Queen does, either, but I'm reasonably sure they don't go behind enemy lines and listen to stories, so I think we're about even in our wickedness." I smiled. Solace flinched a little at the wisps of flame between my teeth.

"I could tell you a story, if you like," the girl said, a deep blush rising in her cheeks—but she did not cast her eyes down. I didn't imagine Lantern had taught her how to do that.

The Firebird nudged her a little, pressing his warm head to her back. "There's time before dawn," he said, proud as any father of his precocious girl. "Tell the bad old devil a tale if you like."

She giggled, a sound that from another child might have been precious, but hers was genuine and dear. "Very well! I shall tell you how I learned to dance..."

THE
FIRE-DANCER'S TALE

BY THE TIME I WAS OLD ENOUGH TO DANCE,
Ajanabh was well and truly dead. I was weary of the bell
tower, but even in a city of artists, I was not brave
enough—not quite yet—to go down into the streets
without my papa to find out what it is that a girl ought
to do. Even a dead city has ghosts, and I could hear
them at night, howling and singing and dancing on this
great red grave.

I only came out to watch Papa dance at the Carnival
of the Dawn. He was so beautiful, with his tail waving
high and low, fluttering like a rain of stars. I wanted to
stand in his tail while he danced, stomping his big claws

down on the courtyard, throwing his plumes back in the first light, flaring that tail like a lady's gown. I wanted to stand there and see all that fire moving around me, and listen to the sound of it—fire makes this great, roaring, snarling sound when it spins and leaps, did you know that? I hear it in my dreams.

One day when I was roasting a mouse and a few dates for breakfast, Sleeve clattered up the stairs as she will sometimes do, grumbling and grousing as she often does.

"Lantern, you are raising this child to be as wild as a kitten lost in the jungle! You must let her find other little girls and learn what it is that girls like, what they eat, what they do when they are happy, what they do when they are sad! Would you have her be like me? The other spiders think my webs are strange, even now."

"I don't like other little girls," I piped. "They are silly and taller than me and they have no flames at all." I chewed a mouse bone and Sleeve gestured in righteous indignation.

"See? She's a wolf-girl."

"I'm a Firebird!" I insisted. I suppose I feel a bit ridiculous about that, now, but you let me believe it, Papa, so I cannot be blamed for having done just as you told me.

"Lantern, let me take her down into the city. If she is to live here, she must learn an art, or she will be shunned, and a shunned girl cries very much, and you will never hear the end. I shall take her to the calligrapher in the high shop, for that is the closest thing to a little girl I know—he has similar parts, at least—and we will find out what it is that is right and proper for a girl to do."

"I am *not* a girl." I frowned. Oh, Papa. You should have told me. I should not have made such a very big fool of myself otherwise. Poor Sleeve!

But true to her word we went first to the calligrapher in the high shop, with his hat of blue and buckles, and his ink-stained fingers, and his many podiums with beautiful books open to beautiful pages of writing, with pearl-handled magnifying glasses resting in their spines.

"What is it, Master Calligrapher, that little girls do in the way that spiders weave?" Sleeve asked primly.

The calligrapher coughed, for his room was very dusty, and there was dust even on his eyelashes, and said: "It is right and proper," he said, "for a girl to read as many books as there are bricks in this city, and then, when she is finished, to begin to write new ones which are made out of the old ones, as this city is made of those stones."

Sleeve beamed at me, pleased that we had discovered the answer in our first try. So it was that I went every day for a whole month to the calligrapher's shop and read his books, which had lovely pictures in gold leaf and letters like swans in flight. I liked the books very much, but it was so quiet in his shop, and all his shutters were closed, so that the vellum would not be damaged by the sun. It was terribly dark and the calligrapher squinted, his face close to his pages. He never talked to me at all. If I stay here much longer, I thought, I shall become as weak and thin as a book's page, and then one flick of my papa's tail will set me alight!

Very politely, as politely as I knew how, I asked if I couldn't take a few of the books with me—the very sturdy ones, mind you, with not so very many golden pictures—and read them myself in the sunlight, or in the bell tower, or anywhere at all but that dark, dreary, dusty place. Besides, I knew to be wary of dust. My papa told me so. The calligrapher agreed, glad to me rid of me, I think, and I ran from his shop with three volumes clutched to my chest, my favorites of all his collection, the ones

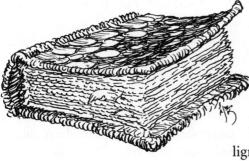

about lost girls and lost beasts and grotesques. And so I was sitting up against a mangrove tree reading about saints and centaurs when Sleeve came clattering up.

"What are you doing! You should be with your calligrapher!"

"It was dark, and he never spoke to me. Lantern speaks to me every day! How was I to concentrate on the books in all that silence?"

"But he was a man; he could have taught you all you needed to know about being a little girl!"

"But he is not a little girl," I pointed out, I thought very wisely. "What does he know? His books know more than he does, and I took some with me, so I think I shall be all right."

Sleeve threw up four of her legs in digust. "How am I to become acquainted with real and actual girls? There are not so many little ones left in Ajanabh, and those there are often think it is right and proper for girls to crush spiders."

So we went to the creatures with which Sleeve was acquainted. We came first to the ants, their little mandibles gleaming red and their hill a great mass of straw and stone.

"We think it is right and proper for a girl to enter into soldiery as soon as possible," they said in unison. "No need to shelter the child— winter is coming, lean and toothed."

"But there are no soldiers left in Ajanabh," I pointed out. One very large ant huffed angrily and said: "What nonsense! We are here!"

And so we went to the worms, who writhed and churned in the dry red soil. They turned over in their muck and smiled in their wormy way, white and fat and eyeless.

"We think it is right and proper for a girl to die. Girls must die if worms are to feast, and we think it is *extremely* proper for worms to feast."

I grimaced; Sleeve recoiled. "Thank you for your honesty," I said, "but I think we shall have to disagree." Their faceless smiles broadened. "For now," I added.

And so we went to the spiders. "I did not want to do this," Sleeve groused, "but you are dear to me."

The spiders kept to their webs like acrobats determined not to touch the ground. I thought Sleeve's needles must have made them nervous, but she put on a very brave face and asked her question. The spiders only laughed, high, tinny laughter like the shaking of marsh reeds.

"What do you know about anything?" they jeered. "Spiders don't weave, they *eat*. They spin and hunt and catch and feed. You have always been the stupidest of us. Whoever heard of a spider weaving dresses? Associating with birds? What is wrong with you, Sleeve? You are the worst sort of maiden aunt for this child. *Girls* weave, you freakish, hideous thing! *Girls* make dresses. Girls squeal very loudly and leap about and clutch their smelling salts."

Sleeve said nothing. Her body slumped, as though she had expected no more, and I could hear her sniffling against the dust. Well, I certainly leapt about then, and blew their webs into ruined threads. "What do *you* know?" I cried, kicking their silk in. "Sleeve makes the most beautiful things in the world while you sit about snickering into your ratty old webs! You know nothing! I have never made a dress in my life—she has made dozens! Does that make her a girl, and I a spider? And I have never smelled salt in all my days; what a stupid idea! Come, Sleeve, your cousins are the worst relations I can imagine."

I cannot really say I was a well-behaved child. I cannot really say I have learned much since.

Her back was straight and her steps high as we left them, and as we walked I saw that her faceted eyes had a gleam in them. By gently pricking my toes she coaxed me down into the Clock-makers' Square, with all its clicking and shadows and tap-tap-tapping of hands against numerals. She led me to a door all of locks, every sort of lock you can imagine: huge brass bolts to tiny, intricate silver keyholes no wider than a feather, wooden locks with gaping slots and golden locks with birds carved into their faces, locks so old and worn that only rust was left, and locks in the shape of open, staring eyes blown from purest glass.

I put my hands against them and the door swung open. There was no one inside.

"Hello?" I called, and Sleeve echoed me.

There was movement in the rear of the workshop, a crash and a jangling. Two golden eyes blinked at me in a wreckage of plate metal and gears which had been her camouflage.

"I am not supposed to come out when company is present," the creature said uncertainly, all metal and whirling clock hands.

"But there is no one here to call us company and make us tea."

"Mother is out," the glittering woman said.

"You can answer our question just as well," cried Sleeve, delighted, introducing the woman as Hour, who had spider silk in her joints. "What is it that girls do in the way that spiders weave?"

Hour seemed to consider it, wringing her metal hands. "I do not know," she answered after a long pause.

"What do you suspect?" I encouraged.

The woman looked wretched, as wretched as a face made out of broken clocks and breastplates can look. "I suspect," she whirred tentatively, "that they live in castles. Beyond that it is hard to say."

"A bell tower is *like* a castle," I said. Sleeve rolled her eyes.

"I am sorry, but it is not," said the ticking woman. "It does not have a Prince inside or outside, and there is no portcullis or moat or chapel. Many castles have towers, but a tower is not a castle all by itself."

"I am sure I do not wish to live in a castle, then. It sounds vile," I answered. "And what in the world is a Prince?"

Hour brightened. "If you would like to know I can explain about primogeniture and patriarchal descent systems," she said eagerly.

"There are no castles handy," chirped Sleeve hurriedly, "so I think we shall have to seek elsewhere. Do not worry! At least you will not have to ask the squid. They are ghastly."

"I am sorry," said the machine, slumping at the shoulders. "I will try to have the right answer, if you will come back later."

I put my hand on the creature's shoulder. "It's all right; I don't know, either. But spiders are funny and determined things, and must be treated carefully."

"Yes," she said. "It is the same with clocks."

We left the strange little shop, and Sleeve seemed glad to be away. She took me next up to the high, windy peak of the highest tower in the city. "Is this a castle?" I asked.

"Certainly not," puffed the spider.

And that is how I met the Sirens, who were frightening as fire unchecked, but pretty enough to make me bashful. They nuzzled Sleeve in a very unbirdlike fashion, their women's legs pointing and skipping in joy.

"My old friends, you must help me! Tell me what it is that a girl does in the way that a spider weaves, so that Solace will not grow up to be the wrong sort of girl."

We like the wrong sorts of girls, they wrote. *They are usually the ones worth writing about.*

"Please." Sleeve sighed. "You needn't be a bunch of silly, flea-bitten birds for my benefit."

"I'm a Firebird, anyway," I grumbled under my breath.

We think, went their flowing feet, their dancing penmanship, *that girls ought to sing. They ought to sing, and dance while they're singing. But we are not girls, and so can be almost certain that we know nothing about the matter. But we let you try, so why not her?*

The sisters seized me with their wings—theirs were cool and dry, not like Papa's, but a wing is the right sort of thing, that I knew. Everything good in the world has feathers and wings and claws. They led me to the ink-wash and passed my feet through, and then began to whirl me between them. It was a mess of legs and wings and beaks, but it slowly became a dance. They lifted my feet with deftly turned ankles, moved my arms in time with their wings. We danced together, the Sirens and I, but they never sang, never once, and I spun with them in silence, faster and faster.

When it was over, the four of us looked down at the paper floor, the expanse of swirling ink, trying to read the tale we had written there— something lovely, I hoped, with no castles at all and a great many birds—the tale our feet had dragged behind us in our swift, complicated dance.

There was a scribble, a scrawl, a jagged mess. The sisters had managed a few words here and there, but in their instruction they could not manage both the steps and the tale. There was nothing of note. They leapt up again and fluttered to a fresh corner.

You are hopeless at letters, they wrote, *that is very sad.*

"But the dancing!" I cried. "The dancing! I want to dance like that!"

Try the Dancing-Master, they suggested with a flourish. *We only know how to dance with each other, how to dance the letters. We suspect perhaps one ought only to dance with one's sisters.*

Sleeve sighed. Her poor needle legs were so tired of walking. But she was determined, more determined, certainly, than I, who after all had little interest in the fates of girls. We wound down from the Sirens and into the streets again, the winding, circular streets of my home. This time she led me down, down the tight, thin alleys and down streets wider than Lantern's wings, but we went up no hills, turning and twisting to remain pointed downward, until we came to a little grating in a high wall, the side, I thought, of the opera house, which even the opera singers barely used anymore, since they now had the whole city happy to stand in for any courts of intrigue or enchanted pastorals they could dream of. It was nearly dark by the time we found it.

The grate was small, and it led into a darkness without depth, but I was little then: I could wriggle through the bars, and darkness was darkness, and could not hurt me—Lantern taught me that, blazing as he did against the fears of any crawling shadow.

"Come with me!" I said to my spider, who hovered around the copper bars, and looked suspiciously into the murk.

"No," said Sleeve slowly, shaking her head. "This is where the Dancing-Master lives. There is another entrance by Simeon's knee, but that is farther. I thought this one best, and I brought you, but I know very well how to dance."

I shrugged. I was not very concerned. I walked into the dark with a straight back. The mud was warm on my feet, and as I descended the air became cooler and cooler, and the ceiling higher and higher, until I knew I was nowhere near the opera house any longer, and even if I put my arms straight overhead, there was nothing above me but dark air, swirling and thick.

At last, the mud slackened, and a real path hardened beneath me, lit by a sudden bank of torches which burned low and sullen on the walls. Wider and wider the path grew, until it opened into a vast vault, whose stone walls vanished into bronze domes, arching up and up and up, spangled with painted dolphins with intricate eyes and faded white stars near the peaks of the many domes. The sides were scored with ancient watermarks, ascending the walls like the rings of a tree.

At my feet was a maze. It was low and small and intricate, but no challenge at all, really, for you could jump over any of the walls as easy as you please. The tallest one came up to my waist. They were made of rock and bone, the little walls, Ajanabh's familiar red rock with chicken bones and duck bones and common gull bones pressed into the sharp corners. It angled off into the distance, over the entire floor of the vault, polished bones glinting in the firelight.

"These used to be cisterns," came a voice like footsteps echoing in a marble hall, "when Ajans cared to worry about such things as sieges. There was once enough water here to keep the city drinking tea well into any war, slurping at their scarlet cups while the army outside ate itself into defeat. You used to be able to put your ear to the street and hear the gentle sloshing of the dark water—it was a comforting sound, for so many people. Now it is empty, it is drunk all up, and no one thinks about sieges anymore."

I looked but could see no one. I began to step over the first wall of the maze—and almost stepped on them.

At the entrance to the maze was a pair of shoes. They were twisted out of the roots of cassia trees, curling wildly at the toe and the heel, the red roots snarling and looping like an embroidered hem. The scent of them was rich and dark and sweet: expensive cinnamon floating in a cup of black tea.

"Don't be afraid," came the voice again. "I am for wearing—no one will punish you."

I raised my foot to slip it inside, and stopped. "I am supposed to learn to dance. And find out what girls are meant to do, the way a spider is meant to weave."

"Ah, but not all spiders weave, so your question is a bit foolish on the face of it, don't you think?"

I blushed. "Sleeve wanted to know. It doesn't make any difference to me," I mumbled.

"As for dancing, there is nothing easier. Put your feet in my care. I am not called the Dancing-Master for nothing."

"*You* are the Dancing-Master?"

"Of course. What else could teach so well as I? But I do not teach alone: This maze is laid out such that should you step through the correct path, by its end you will have learned the most extraordinary dance, such that any coronation would be proud to see at the height of its feast, such that any holy dervish would weep and call you his devotion."

"I think this is very strange—"

"All things are strange which are worth knowing. Come, I have asked a third time. Step into me and while you walk the maze I shall tell you how a pair of empty shoes came to be at the bottom of a cistern."

I lowered my foot and sank into the shoes, which were just my size, and felt like sudden fists seizing my feet.

The Tale

of the

Cinnamon Shoes

ATTEND TO ME, GIRL. I AM YOUR METRONOME.
Keep to my voice; I will keep your rhythm true.

I see you go bare-shod. This is most likely extremely
sensible. Shoes are no end of trouble for girls, that tribe
you seek in the dark. How many have danced to death
in slippers of silk and glass and fur and wood? Too
many to count—the graveyards, they are so full these
days. You are very wise to let your soles become grubby
with mud, to let them grow their own slippers of moss

and clay and calluses. This is far preferable to shoes which may become wicked at any moment.

I seem to remember being a tree. A cinnamon tree drank rain until someone pulled it out of the earth by the hair and made a very nice armoire, two high-backed chairs with seats of stiff linen, a round table at which generations of children learned their letters, a post for witch-burning, an extremely expensive book with cinnamon boards and cinnamon paper written upon with cinnamon ink—a Psalter, I think—a carriage wheel, and one pair of shoes.

I remember also a woman's hands, and how she sipped her tea of white leaves, violets, and a single red leaf as she pulled the roots into the complicated knot-work you see now. Her shop was pleasant and dusty and I had very high company to converse with, any number of riding boots and dancing heels, their white pelts stitched with fine blue thread. But they were truculent beasts, and would not speak to the ragged cinnamon shoes. I was not sorry to leave them when I was packed away and sent to the city on the red plain.

In Ajanabh I was the superior shoe. No riding boot could compare to a shoe of cinnamon, the sacred stuff of the city. I dreamt of sweet, slim feet whirling and kicking at festivals of spice and starlight; I dreamt of being kept on a high podium with a rose-colored cushion, my arches cupped by yielding silk. Instead, I was taken to a tomb.

A tomb is like a cistern, you know. It is full of flesh as a cistern is full of water, and the ceilings drip. There are devotional paintings of the virtuous dead etched into the stone with inks that cost more than water or corpses, and voices echo, and the shadows lick the corners clean, and no one would go inside were they not compelled. I suppose he was compelled, the priest who bought me dear and carried me to his daughter's bier like anointing oil.

She had been a good girl when she was alive, he assured everyone who would listen. But what father has ever said otherwise? She was pious; she was kind to the poor. Every morning she would wash herself in freezing water—such an expense, such an extravagance in Ajanabh where they say the glass bubbles in the pane in summertime! And when her skin ached with the cold, she would dust red her arms, her chest, her face, her hair, with cinnamon ground finer than the most treasured dreams of salt. They were a holy family, and had to set an example, her father said. She went to the finest seminary in the city and learned there how to distill both liquor and ink from cinnamon and the light of the Stars—and more important, she learned that each has its proper time and use, and used them as they were meant. No one was more moderate in her dress or her person, her father said. No one lived who was more serious or more studious. No one behaved so much and so often precisely as it is proper for a girl to behave.

And when the fields died, her father said, she was disconsolate, as it is necessary for the child of the Priest of Red Spices to be. She bathed in their icy fountain until her teeth chattered and her lips went blue and swollen. She prayed and studied her own little cassia-cuttings, her own window garden that it is only correct for a priest's daughter to keep, but they were wild and thick with needles and dusty with sweetness. And finally, she stopped lashing her skin with bitter water, and left her garden to walk out among the fields, where she buried herself in the ailing earth.

She left her eyes and her mouth open to the air, but the rest she covered up in red loam like a child pulling up her favorite blanket over her chest. And there—devout girl!—she kept up her prayers, encouraging the earth to learn from her hot blood, her beating heart, her ascendant soul. And so the earth took these things, but, like a man of poor breeding, learned nothing. Whatever withered the roots of the basil and the paprika, the cardamom and the garlic greens, withered her in the soil, and once planted, his beloved daughter never rose again.

They unearthed her form, cold as it had been on any of her sacrosanct mornings in the frozen fountain, and carried it to the family tomb. There it was laid out on this very bier of fragrant cedar, a spray of cassia flowers clutched in her virginal hands, a dress of rarest bark-cloth arranged in precise folds on her body. He wept at her side every day, he said, his tears her icy fountain.

Who knows with what grief's whispering he decided that I would wake her? It is best not to ask, for the tribe of dead girls is infinitely more inscrutable than that of those living, and who knows what their shades insinuate when midnight has long closed up its windows? He believed it, believed in the holiness of the red spices, and perhaps

that was enough. And so the cinnamon shoes were matched to the cinnamon girl, and slipped onto her hard, gray feet. The Priest of Red Spices waited there at her side with held breath, his face reddening with hope and need.

I will not say she woke and threw her hard, gray arms about her papa. I will not say he sang with joy and they danced a filial waltz around the tomb. But after I had clutched her ankles for a fortnight and more, and he had fallen asleep on an empty bier, as fathers will sometimes do when they are waiting for their daughters to be born, a trickle of red mud came dripping out of her nose, and tears of red mud came weeping from her eyes, and a slow stream of red mud came oozing from her mouth. She rolled up from her slab and began to cough quietly, as a polite girl will cough, all the red earth of the Ajan fields heaving from her, wet and dead, bright and thick.

Her father did not wake. Fathers sleep heavily. The pious daughter cleaned her mouth and stood shakily, balancing in me, in her cinnamon shoes, and I could feel her weight, so little, so light, having been dead so long. I felt her sadness and her fear, her urgency, her shivering soles, her need to see the sun again. These are the secret things a shoe knows, for we carry a creature within us, and divine all its self.

"Papa," whispered the dead daughter. "Wake up. It is time to take me home." She kissed his cheek with dry lips.

The Priest of Red Spices opened his eyes and saw his girl, his devotion, his cinnamon darling. Her long hair was wet and knotted with mud and anointing oil and clotted spice, but he kissed her anyway and held her close. She let him touch her, stiff and uncertain, and allowed softly that she would certainly like to be shown at services, and hold a red candle, and be called a miracle. What else should a pious girl want?

But she was not at services when they were held. She was at the Duke's empty Palace, dancing through the abandoned rooms with their ruined tapestries of tigers and terns, their splintered walls and broken perfume bottles. Since she had died they had become a place for endless balls, endless revels, endless frenzied festivals by the light of candelabras dented and tarnished. The young and careless were there, lined up in the dancing line like shabby dolls. Ajanabh was only lately dead; the wake still raged on.

The priest's daughter had only followed the light. Even the dullest creature knows to follow the light, and in her dull, gray state it was all she could manage: go toward the warmth, go toward the fire. I, too, itched to be used well, to be warm. I forced her feet only a little toward that blazing, raucous place. And there we danced, and there we spun, and there we felt the flames on us, hot and golden.

Thus I danced after all, with her slim feet tight in me, at festivals of cinnamon and starlight. I danced every dance you can imagine—and I danced them all twice. How many arms around her waist, how many polished shoes to meet me, how many floors once shining and check-ered, now shattered and filthy with summer dust, did we press beneath us? Too many to count, my friend, too many to count. And as we danced, as each night ran on into the next in the Duke's abandoned es-tate, with all the topiary scorched black and all the roofs turned homes for pigeons and starlings, as we danced her arms became less hard and gray, her blood became less still and black, her cheeks became less sunken and cold. Her hair flew out behind her like a black wind, and her cheeks went redder than the candles, and her eyes became sharp and wild, red as cinnamon shoes. Her skin was less pink than scarlet, her blood so high I thought it might leap out of her. Her heart was nothing but a long, whirling scream.

Her father was delighted, and saw only her high color and her smiles. He did not see her teeth, he did not see how tight she clenched that red candle, how fast she ran when services were done. And the more she danced like that, the less I liked her. I wished to dance, of course; this is the best a shoe can wish for. But I wished to dance courtly dances, at weddings and harvest-time, complicated reels and waltzes as precise as clockwork. This dance took no skill; it was just a constant tempest, a sirocco that went on and on. I was tired.

And so I contrived, as she ran from the estate gardens with their blackened hedge-swans and hedge-giraffes, to slip from her feet and lie in the grass, happy and silent and unmoving. I would like to report that she fell down dead the minute I let her arch fly free, but she did not. I saw her black hair whipping the wind as she bolted home, over the gar-dens and through the alleys, back to that damned red candle once more.

THE
FIRE-DANCER'S TALE,
CONTINUED

"I AM VERY BEAUTIFUL," THE SHOES SAID, preening like scarlet parakeets, "and was quickly picked up by a girl with better taste in dances. She had such green ribbons in her hair! I stayed in the estate for years, until there was no tallow left at all for the candles, and the violin strings snapped and curled, and the marble squares could take no more stomping feet. I was passed from dancer to dancer, and in this way I learned all that a shoe need know. Finally, a girl took me home, and though I was not at all sure how I felt about that, I did not try to force her feet back, but let her take me where she would. Shame of shames! Her mother took one look at the snarling roots I bear so well, snatched me up like a fish which has gone sour and is fit only for cats, marched out into the street, and tossed me through the cistern grating. I splashed, I floated, and, after a time, sank to the bottom, where I might have stayed, drowned as a dog, if not for the slovenly martial habits of Ajans."

I was panting and my hair clung to my ears with sweat by then, so quick and fast had I been forced to leap and turn and step, with the tiny, heel-to-hip kicks the narrow corridors demanded, the elongated, elegant, sliding motions of the long straightaways, with the pirouettes, with the catlike tiptoes. The voice of the shoes kept perfect time, and my body hummed to the dance, hummed with the knowing of it, hummed with the learning of it, as sometimes it had hummed with the books on my lap in the calligrapher's shop.

"Why the maze, though?" I gasped, executing a daring midair turn and landing hard on my heel.

The shoes did not answer for the smallest of moments. "I did not build it. I assume the Weaver made it, as she makes everything else here, and for her own reasons. It was here when I floated to the bottom of the black reservoir, and I discovered its use quickly enough."

Finally, with three full spins and a flourish of my arms, I completed the maze. The shoes clacked their heels against the floor in applause, which is very disconcerting, having your feet move without your say-so. I doubled over, catching my breath.

"Thank you," I wheezed.

"It is my pleasure," demurred the Dancing-Master.

I could feel the sides of the root-shoes squeezing my feet, trying to hold on. "It is time for me to go now," I said uncertainly.

"There is no need to leave me down here in the dark. Think how well we could dance together, in the candelabra halos! Think how beautiful all men would think you, in your cinnamon shoes, with your long legs dancing like a Gaselli!"

The shoes were strangling now, trying to hold on to me, trying to keep me fast inside them. "I . . . I think I should like to feel my own feet on the cobblestones, if it's all the same."

"It is not the same," cried the Dancing-Master, squeezing tighter, like a snake around a mongoose. "I am tired of lying empty in the dark, waiting for girls to come and fill me up for a moment, only to run away when they are finished! I like you as well as I have liked anyone since the dead girl, and I want to dance again, in the Duke's Palace, in the Duke's garden, with perfume in the air!"

I scraped at the shoes, trying to get them off, tears of pain springing to my eyes. "Please! I don't want to dance at the Duke's Palace!"

"But I know, pretty little bird's daughter! I know what it is right and proper for girls to do! I can answer your question!" The shoes ground tighter against my bones. "Girls are meant to dance, and spin until their skirts flare like petals, and look more beautiful than ruby-rimmed roses at balls which never end; they are meant to live for the revels; they are meant to bat their eyelashes and whirl in the arms of handsome men!" Tighter still the cinnamon shoes pinched and pulled. "They are meant to drink bubbling wine and laugh like finches singing and dash into the shadows to be kissed! They are meant to blush and curtsey! They are meant to swoon! But they are meant to dance, most of all; they are meant to dance, dead or alive, cold or hot; they are meant to dance until their bones crack! They are meant to care only for the dance, only for the whirl of shining gowns and the sashes on young men's chests. They are meant to spin in men's arms for all their days, until their heel bones strike sparks on the dance floor!"

The voice of the Dancing-Master spiraled higher and higher, more and more shrill. I was weeping as the shoes wrenched, crushed my feet into the red roots, and my fingers scrabbled against them uselessly. I drew a hitching breath, my chest searing and tight, and leapt up into the air, just as the maze had taught me, a high, strong leap, and came down as hard as I could on the flats of my feet. The landing shivered my calf bones and I bit my cheek in a sharp-edged wince, but the careening voice ceased abruptly, like a door slamming shut.

The shoes were broken into pieces on the stone floor of the cistern, lying around me in sweet-smelling cinnamon shards.

"No," I said simply, and turned back to the long tunnel, back up to the air and the light.

⋆   ⋆   ⋆

When I emerged from the grate, it was nearly light. Sleeve was there, snoring lightly, as spiders will snore. It takes a long time to learn to hear a spider's snore, but by then my ears were keen as an owl's, and I heard her little wheezing, in and out, in and out. She woke with a shudder when I stroked her back, and looked up at me with her glittering black eyes.

"And how did we do this time? Same as the rest?"

"More or less." I shrugged.

"Well, come on with you, then. It's nearly time for Lantern to dance."

As the sun blinked sleepily over the Sirens' tower, Lantern stood in the courtyard with the gurgling fountain, amid the shouting and singing of the Carnival, and danced. His flaming tail tossed scarlet and yellow up into the air and down again like a fan, each frond of peacock-bright feathers wavering as if each one was a separate dancer. His huge feathered feet lifted up and stomped down in a quick rhythm, one I had always loved. A dozen violins and trumpets and flutes played his music, and he turned his face to the new sun, his bronze beak catching the first light, sending it into the fountain in a shower of gold. I wanted, as I have always wanted, to see the world from within his tail, and that morning of all mornings, I stepped shyly up to my dazzling, burning father as he hopped up onto one claw and spun to the delighted gasps of the musicians.

"Papa," I said, and I wish my voice had not wavered; I wish my cheeks had not been so red and hot! "Let me dance with you."

He smiled, as only a bird the size of a house can smile, and I stepped into his tail.

The world through flaming feathers is washed in gold, scrubbed to gleaming by fire, and the sound of it roars ocean-fierce. I moved my feet as though the maze were still red and wide beneath me, I moved my arms like wings, and I danced in my papa's tail like a Firebird.

┌─────────────────────────────┐
│   │
│ THE TALE OF THE   │
│ CAGE OF IVORY   │
│ AND THE   │
│ CAGE OF IRON,   │
│ CONTINUED   │
│   │
└─────────────────────────────┘

SOLACE GRINNED, HER FACE BRIGHTER EVEN than her father's. "*I shall not dance until my bones crack*," she said. "I shall dance every morning until my heart catches on the sun, and I fill up with gold like a crystal cup! And I shall never wear a proper dress, no matter how many Sleeve shows me, all a-spangle with green and silver!" Lantern nuzzled his huge head under her arm and she kissed his burnished plumage. "Of course, my hair burned up completely that first time! It has grown back just like Papa's tail, and I have had to learn since how to dance without catching fire. It is not too difficult, once you get the trick of it." She pulled hard on one of his feathers and the great bird squawked like a common duck. "But you should have told me, you rotten old seagull. What a trial I have been for my poor spider."

"Yes," Lantern said simply, and turned to me as though I had only just arrived. "That is all we have to tell," said the Firebird. "You may go or stay as you like, now. But the sun will be up soon, and we are for the Carnival."

I pursed my smoke-lips. "I am not sure what Simeon meant me to know of you," I confessed.

"Perhaps only that there is a Star in Ajanabh, and beside her, spiders and birds and girls which do not wish to be burned."

Solace hopped down lightly from the scorched cage and extended her hand.

"Do you want to go to the Carnival?" she asked, her tattoos gleaming up at me as fiercely as her eyes.

"Yes," I said, and slipped my black fingers into hers.

In the Garden

THE AFTERNOON WAS LATE AND GRAY ON THE SNOW. IT HAD BEGUN TO melt, and ice flowed everywhere in silent little rivers. The lake in which the girl had bathed—so long ago now!—had frozen silver and smoky. The sun wore a veil that day, and it shone only fitfully through the thick, gauzy clouds. The Gate glittered with hard little knots of ice, and the boy, who had never seen such cold in his life, ran his fingers over them in wonder.

"You must go now," the girl said. "Do not think you ought to linger here."

"I don't," he said, and shut his eyes while he fingered the ice. It melted to water against his skin. "What," he added thoughtfully, as casually as he could manage, "happened to the Papess, do you think?"

The girl furrowed her brow. She, too, touched the ice, and shook her head as her fingers stuck to the hard little globes that clung to the iron. "I do not know," she said, as though he had asked her what the inside of her eyelids looked like. "If there is something more about her written on my skin, you must read it, not I. I did not create her; I cannot arrange her footsteps through the world like a basket of flowers."

"What do you think, though?"

"I do not know, I told you. And it is time for you to run back to the court-yards, where your sister will be saying very serious vows, and eating, and dancing."

The boy smiled broadly, like the moon emerging from the horizon. "You are absolutely right!" he cried, and seized her hand in his.

"What are you doing? Let me go!"

"No," said the boy firmly. "You are a child of the Palace, and that gives you the right to dance at the wedding of Dinarzad, just like the others. In fact," he added with a crooked grin, "as a child of the Palace, you really haven't much choice in the matter."

He led her to the frozen lake, with its icy cattails waving still and shattering against each other from time to time. The ferns were white and shivering, and long naked branches bowed black and deep. From behind a rock crowned with bright mosses he drew a little bundle, just where she had said it would be, and presented it to the girl with all the pride of a cat who has managed, at long last, to catch a blackbird in flight, and brought it back to its mistress. The girl looked blankly at it, and he opened it for her, drawing the strings slowly open.

Inside was a dress. It was red, like her cloak, and overlaid with the most delicate mesh of gold, knotted into elaborate roses and birds soaring past ripe fields. The netting made a little train, and there was a belt of tiger's-eyes and golden chains, and a necklace of garnets, and lastly, a golden circlet which held up a soft scarlet veil.

"I told you not to," she said gently, but he saw her lip shaking.

"No one will know," the boy whispered, his voice as full of coaxing as a mother's who wishes her child to eat. "The veil will keep you hidden, and I shall brush your hair clean of leaves and snow. No one will know, and you can eat at the table, and stand by my side all the night long, and dance, like Solace, like a Firebird."

The girl was weeping, her shoulders quivering as she tried valiantly not to.

And so the boy helped her arrange the netting of the dress. He fastened her belt of tiger's eyes. He laid the necklace of garnets around her neck. He brushed her hair with his own fingers until it was soft and gleaming, and he braided it as best he could manage. He fixed the circlet on her brow, and let the veil fall over her face. He stood back and looked at her, blood-bright against the snow, the gold already catching new snowflakes like threads of silk.

"It was hers, you know," he said, "when she was our age. She let me have it. She is . . ." The boy swallowed. "Not quite so awful as I thought, my sister." He squared his shoulders and shook his snow-dappled hair back. "But I was younger then, and much more foolish."

He took her hand, which was terribly cold in his, and thinner than bones, but he smoothed her hair, just a little, before he remembered that it was not terribly polite, and withdrew his hand quickly. The boy and the girl walked together across the snowy orchards, toward the chestnut chapel, where firelight was already leaping toward the sky.

No one knew. He showed her the table, with its roasted birds and roasted beasts, with its wine and its steaming stews and its chocolates, with its slices of rough, red hippopotamus meat and its shaved camel-hump, wet and glistening. He showed her the crocodile, its sawtooth jaws propped open with silver bolts, and stuffed with sugared pears. He showed her the rhinoceros horn dripping with honey and salt. She laughed shyly, and ate as much as she pleased, and no one took any notice of her at all in all the milling children with their colored plumage.

The girl watched Dinarzad very curiously while she was wed, and she saw the trembling of her, and heard the breathlessness of her. The boy watched, too, but he tried not to see these things, for he did not wish to shame his sister by weeping.

And in the light of a hundred torches, under a sky full of hard, cold stars like ice on an iron gate, they danced. She was uncertain at first, but he showed her easy steps, and led her into the center of the throng, where the laughter and the voices and golden, whirling bodies were thickest, and the boy danced with the demon girl in the sight of all his relations, turning her faster and faster, until Dinarzad's dress was a red-gold blur. He could see the tears fall from her chin beneath the veil, and his hands were wet with them. The boy's sisters and cousins and matronly old aunts spun by and laughed as they spun, their voices thick with wine.

In the midst of the dance, the Sultan gestured from his holiday throne of ivory and plum-branches dipped in bronze. The boy looked nervously to his veiled friend, but could not refuse. He walked slowly to his father's seat with her frightened hand clutched in his. Over the Sultan's black beard he looked at them, his eyes reflecting the firelight like a Djinn's.

"What a beautiful little friend you have found, my son. She is quite striking, just as red as a demon."

"Y . . . yes, Father."

"Is she one of mine? It is so hard to tell, these days!"

"N . . . no, Father. She is visiting the court for the wedding, like so many others."

"Then, welcome, child! Be sure to speak well of us when you return to your foreign court. Tell them how good my son has been to you. Tell them my daughter welcomed you at her wedding. Tell them," his voice faltered slightly, but so slightly no one would have thought it was anything but the good, sweet wine, "tell them we were kind to you."

"I am sure she will, Father."

The Sultan leaned in to the two tremulous children, his long, curled hair wafting its scent of cedar and frankincense into their eyes. "And," he whispered, "look after my son, young lady. A boy can get his head turned quite around on an evening such as this."

The girl nodded, her voice long having fled her throat. The Sultan nodded their dismissal, and the boy led his scarlet friend onto the dance floor again, but the girl could not go on. Her weeping and her shaking was too great, and the boy took her away from the crowds, away from the chestnut canopies, and into the snow again, where she thrust her hands down into it, watching it melt under her heat. She looked up at the boy and he lifted her veil gingerly. Her face was streaked with tears, her eyelids shining like ink.

"If I weep long enough," she whispered, "do you think the ink might wash away, like a painting left in the rain? Do you think I could walk among those fiery people every day, among your drunken aunts, and your cousins, do you think I could sit beside your father and be called beautiful without my veil?"

"No," he answered gently, "I do not think that."

She laughed shortly and wiped her nose. "Neither do I."

He drew her cloak close around her and dried her tears with the corner of his sleeve. The porphyry bracelet knocked lightly against her cheek. She looked up at him with a stare full of red-rimmed urgency, and closed her eyes.

"Please," she whispered. "Please."

The Tale of the Cage of Ivory and the Cage of Iron, Continued

THE FIREBIRD AND HIS DAUGHTER AND I WALKED through an empty city. I saw those places the night's tales had laid out in my heart: the Dressmaker's Parish, the opera house, the Clock-makers' Square and the little house with so many locks, the church which was not a church, the churning river in more colors than I could count if I had a ledger and a thousand years. I thought I could see the Sirens' tower, impossibly high, off on the east end of the clustered red edifices.

We walked a wide and well-kept street, which skewed and counter-skewed as everything else in Ajanabh does, but this one, it seemed, less than usual. In fact, as we went, it widened, until we passed through an ample court peopled with a hundred silent statues, each face frozen and perfect in red stone, fluttering slate fans and clutching snuffboxes of agate and marble and malachite. It was the same one Agrafena had led me through, and once again I was chilled. But the Firebird did not seem to even notice them, and walked around the menagerie as Solace and I, being more graceful of foot, walked through, marveling at the sad, exact faces, each its own,

with flared noses and slender ones, high brows and glowering, lips full and meager. We touched their cheeks, and the stone was full of little flecks of quartz that flickered in the dim predawn light. They were hard and warm and unyielding.

"They look like wives," I said, laughing, and Solace looked at me as though I were well and truly mad.

I would have left that grove of folk and thought no more of it than I had the first time, a wonder in a nest of wonders, if I had not heard her scrabbling in the corner of the square, mumbling frantically, a chisel in each hand.

She was probably beautiful, when she was young. Her hair was long and stringy and white, showered with stone dust, her worn face lined like a discarded map when no one is any longer interested in the treasure it promises. She had a snaggle-edged shawl knotted over her head, and her rags were brown and stiff and filthy. She was missing a tooth, and her feet were bare on the road.

"I suppose we ought to be glad she never grew up!" the old woman barked. I think her voice was fine once, but it sounded now like a harp with a broken spine.

"I'm sorry, old mother, I do not know what you mean," I answered her, keeping my distance.

"He told me once, when there was a shipment of brandy in and it was very, very late. That's when he liked to talk, you know, by the big fireplace, under that stupid, ugly old head. He told me where his wife went, and I suppose we ought to be glad she never grew up, or it would have gone badly for the butcher's boy when she turned up all green and fire-breathed!"

Solace covered her mouth with her hand, her eyes wide. The old woman trundled over and chiseled a bit of a spindle-waisted statue's eyebrow. "I made these for her, all of them. Over the years, you know. I didn't," her voice thickened like cream, "I didn't want her to be lonely, you see. I couldn't bear for her to be lonely. I couldn't bear for her to be like me. She's here somewhere, in the crowd, where she always liked to be. She's here somewhere . . . but I forgot." The crone's blue eyes, filmed and rheumy, were full of tears as she looked around her. "I just forgot," she whispered.

Solace dashed off without a word and I was left with the madwoman, as she scratched at her scalp, her eyes lost and dark. "Where is my Basilisk," she hissed at me. "Where is my baby rock-foot? Why didn't he come back for me? Why doesn't he look at me the way he looked at her?" She stumbled a little on her thick feet and I caught her, though she choked and sputtered in my smoke. She righted herself and set to the sandstone bustle of another figure. "Where are you, you old lizard?" she choked. "Why don't you come back?"

While she worked, I told myself not to touch her, that she would not understand. But all the same I saw my dark hand, my blazing finger-nails, reach out to her doddering head. I stroked her hair, and cupped her head in my hand. Perhaps she was just mad enough not to care, but she rested her head against my palm and closed her eyes, tears seeping out over the deep creases.

"I'm sorry, Orfea," I whispered.

Suddenly, Solace hooted and laughed from far off in the menagerie, and I took the old Duchess's hand and followed the noise as one follows the sound of a pheasant in the brush. We found her standing next to a tall sandstone figure, red of cheek and ankle, long-haired and high-browed, her fur-lined dress whipping sharply around her as she turned to stare, hurt and puzzled, at something on the ground.

Orfea reached out her rag-bandaged hands to the statue's face.

"Good girl," she said with a sigh, "good girl, you found her, my darling, my old friend." She nestled herself into the crook-armed embrace of the red stone, her withered cheek against its rough, stiff face. "Do you think they can hear her singing?" she said. "The others, do you think they can hear her, in their stony ears?"

"Of course," said Solace kindly, stroking the old woman's hair just as I had done. "I can hear her now. She is so beautiful, when she sings up the sun."

The child drew me away then, and we left the two women there, stone and flesh. As we turned our backs, I could hear Orfea singing with her broken voice, and my throat closed on fiery tears that burned to fall.

And as we passed the last statue, the farthest out, a sandstone child in her mother's dress, tripping over the hem, I saw it, clutched in a red, rough hand, what was meant to be a snuffbox but which was not, just like the church which was not a church: a box of carnelian, no bigger than my own hand. I pried it out of the coarse-fingered child, and it was not heavy, not nearly heavy enough.

"What is this?" I said urgently. I grabbed Solace's arm and showed her the box.

"How should I know? Just some junk the Duchess used for her little zoo. She uses everything; you must have seen just as well as I." Solace rubbed her arm, a pale pink hand-shaped scald rising where I had touched her—I had not been careful. I pled her forgiveness. "Surely there are many boxes in all these dead hands. How can you know this one is special?" she grumbled, cradling her arm.

But I knew. I looked at its polished surface, its design of curling, corkscrewing, arching grasses worked into the lid, its tiny claw feet, its minute, gold-speckled latch.

"Well? Open it!" said Solace.

"Should I? Kohinoor said it belonged to her. Perhaps it is not right that I should open it."

"Then I will open it! Come, you cannot resist it—don't you want to know what's inside? They never told you anything a Queen should know. What do you owe them?"

I looked sharply at the young girl with her gleaming black tattoos and bare belly. "I thought you were sleeping," I said suspiciously.

The girl grinned sidelong, her hair hanging down into her wolf-keen face. "Open it," she coaxed.

And so help me, I did. I slid the flame of one thin fingernail into the lock and turned it, listening to the click of the carnelian tumblers. The lid popped up slightly, and I lifted it gingerly. Lantern peered over from behind a statue of a young man slaughtering a stag, and Solace stood on her toes to see inside.

I let the casket fall open, and lying within, no bigger than a finger, was a woman made all of grass, her hair a mass of curled seeds, her form woven reeds braided together, one over the other. Her meadow-eyes were serenely shut, her tiny blade-hands folded over a dress of straw and light. No part of her did not shine with this light, silver and sere, and it pooled in the box as though I were holding a red candle in my hand. The three of us stood staring at her, the little green woman in the box.

"Is she going to wake up?" Solace asked.

"I don't know. I don't know why Kohinoor could possibly want her," I answered.

With infinite care, I put my finger into the box and stroked the side of the grass-woman's face with my smoke. She turned to it like a child suckling its mother and breathed the black of my skin. Her eyes opened lazily; they were green as a pasture. She sat up in her box, seed-hair falling behind her, and looked up at the faces of a Djinn, a Firebird, and a curious little girl.

"Oh," she groaned, "let me go back to sleep…"

"I'm sorry," I said quietly, so as not to hurt her reedy ears, "but it's terribly important. Who are you?"

She turned her face to mine, grassy eyes blinking miserably.

"I'm no one, not now." She sighed like prairies waving in the night winds. "Not anymore…"

The Tale

of the

Carnelian Box

IT IS A LONG WAY TO FALL, FROM THE SKY TO THE earth. It is a long way to fall, in the dark, and the space between is cold.

I do not blame her. It is not in my nature to blame. But I did not want to go. The others all chose, to stay or to fall, to burn or to gutter and darken. I could not choose. A Star walked among us with legs like pillars of fire, before she wove, before the red city, and we were uprooted from the soft black, uprooted from the earth which is the Sky, and I wonder if she even saw us crumple beneath her, if she even saw us fall. So many were trampled and shattered that day, so many fell in shivering slivers, a slaughter of broken rain howling through the Sky like a shower of glass, but I was lucky. I lost only my feet under hers, and fell more or less whole, my ears able to hear all the screams of the Grass-Stars around me, sheared into nothingness, their light splattered across the fields.

I know that if I had been allowed to stay, the black thing that bore me would have come back. Mothers always come back. I chose to be grass for her, I chose to lie at the bottom of the Sky, so that she would see how humble I was, so that she would see that I wanted only to be a thing that would please her. These things I was allowed to choose, and if I could have stayed, I would have felt her gentle face above me, I would have put my hands to her dark cheeks. I would have cried—children always cry—but I would have told her: *See, Mother, I waited for you. I knew you would not abandon us. I knew you loved us still. I knew if I was faithful, you would come home.* And she would have kissed me, and told me I was her best-loved daughter, and I would have known her smell and her skin, I would have known what she looked like, I would have known my mother at the end of all things.

But I was not allowed to choose.

I landed in a great field of sugarcane and my broken stumps burned the stalks. They crumpled and sizzled beneath me; smoke and shadows leapt up from their fractured, boiling leaves. *I'm sorry!* I cried as I walked; I wept as I walked, and as I walked I began to scream, for I walked nowhere that I did not burn, that did not incinerate beneath me, that did not fall into flames at the touch of my skin. *I'm sorry,* I wailed, for I scalded them to nothing, ash and shadows, and they could not choose any more than I. I tried to walk lightly, I tried to run, but shadows and smoke leapt up at my every step, until I stumbled onto mute stone, and huddled against a jagged cliff face, burning nothing, sobbing and afraid. It was there I lived, terrified to move, terrified to sear all beneath me, until even the stone had blackened to a slick, scalded glass, and the light in me was dim and hidden.

That was how he found me. When it was all over, he would call me Li, and if I had a name before that, he spoke the name of Li so many times that I have forgotten it.

His shoulders were draped in a tiger's slashing skin, and from the edges of this hung talons of hawk and lizard. He was a big man, but his face was young, clear, and eager, and his lips trembled.

"He did not lie!" the man marveled. "He did not lie to me! You are here, and real, and alive, and mine!"

"Do not touch me!" I shrieked.

He drew back, hurt. "Of course not, if you tell me I must not."

"You will burn," I mumbled.

"But you are my wish! You could not harm me!"

"I assure you, I can. And what can you mean? What did you wish for?"

The man smiled with such joy and hope that my throat tightened in the face of it. "Why, what else? I wished for a wife..."

The Tale of the Tiger Harp

Is this not a beautiful country? You could be happy here. I would build you a den of wattles and tiles, and bring you sacks of down from the river geese for your blankets. I would do both these things for you, and more besides.

When I was a boy, my father taught me to hunt, how to be very silent on my feet, how to strangle partridges and cut open deer in such a way that it hurts them little enough. When nineteen of my winters had left me living, I killed a tigress. This is very difficult, as tigers are clever, and my father was proud. He dressed her and gave me her heart to eat, steaming red in the snow. It was wet and soft; it tasted of old arrowheads and marrow. Then he gave me her liver, then her bones to suck. He told me to name the tiger I had killed, and remember her taste, how tall she had been, how many cubs watched us from the bracken. He told me to make a thing from her body every day for a year, so that I would know my tiger as well as I knew anything in our house. Soup and coats and sausages and rattles and roasts and gloves and lyre strings. All these I made and more. I worked all the year through, and grieved for my tiger.

I called my tiger Li. It is a common name in this country. After the year of my tiger had passed, I saw in our village a girl fairer by far than tiger-ink. She had hair like black stripes, and eyes black as a cat's, and her hands were soft and deft; she wove beautiful things, and she tasted like lemons, and warm stones. Her mother was a planter of crocuses, and a threader of the priceless saffron culled from their blossoms. Her land was wide, almost endless. Her name was Li. I have told you it was common. Li was so wealthy, I thought I could never wed her, being a boy who knew little but the secret taste of a tiger's heart. But I loved the crocus-girl, even as I hunted silent and kind, even as my father died of chill and my mother of fever, even as I cared for my house alone, and made each tiger I killed last for a year, in soups and coats and sausages and rattles and roasts and gloves.

There came a day when my cupboards were bare and I went into the birch-bracken to hunt. As I followed the tracks of a broad-shouldered tiger, in motions I had practiced as a dancer does her favorite reels, I heard beside me other footsteps, just as practiced. As I came upon the tiger, who snarled as cats will do, the other hunter came into the clearing, and before I could loose my bow, shot a crow-fletched arrow, straight and true, into the tiger's heart.

You will not be surprised to know it was Li. She stood with her long legs apart, her hair flat and straight, her arms cradling her bow easily. She turned to me and smiled.

"What do you think I ought to name my kill?" she said. "Shall I call it Lem? It seems only fair."

"Yes," I breathed, "call him Lem."

Together we cut open the white fur of his belly, and I gave Li his heart to eat, wet and soft. She said it tasted like her own skin. I gave her his liver, and also his bones, and together we took the carcass back to my house, where I showed her how to make tiger soup.

Li's mother was not altogether angry, but she did withhold her crocuses from our wedding, since her permission had not been asked. I accepted this as just, but I leapt over her stone wall and stole a single yellow flower for Li to wear in her hair, my crocus-girl, my tiger-girl. Li made tiger soup in my house, and tiger coats and tiger sausage and tiger rattles, tiger roasts rich as cake, and she played upon a tiger harp songs so sweet and strange that on warm nights there would gather around the threshold wild and striped creatures, nosing the air curiously and twitching their long, white whiskers.

But Li was not happy. After a year she stopped hunting with me; after two she would not make the tiger soup.

"What is the matter, my beloved, my crocus, my cat?" I said, taking her head in my arms.

"Outside our door the tigers come to hear me sing, and I cannot make the stew of their bones, no matter how much saffron, and thyme, and marigold roots I grind into it, without tasting not my own skin, but my own song, which they love well enough to gather around the house of those who sharpen their arrows to pierce striped flesh."

"I need not hunt only tigers, Li. Deer are easier prey, and rabbits, and bear."

My wife turned her wide-cheeked face to mine. "And what will happen when I make the deer soup, and the rabbit soup, and the bear soup? What will happen when I play the harp of deer, the harp of rabbit, the harp of bear?"

And so I hunted still the tiger, and made the soup myself. But Li still played the harp, and still the tigers gathered. One evening, when the sky was as deep a blue as any crocus may own, I brought her a wooden bowl with a soup of thyme and marigold, and no tiger at all.

She drank it, and then took up her harp of bone and gut. She stood and opened the door to our house—I tried to stop her, but she laughed and shooed me back, and so I watched from the window as Li sat on a stump among the crocuses her mother had finally sent to us years after our wedding, and played to the moon and the bracken.

It was terrible, what she played. It hurt me to hear it, the strings plucked in longing, the melody foreign and savage and toothed. She put her head back, and the moon glossed her scalp, and I did not know her in that moment, not really, the woman who slept beside me with her cheek on my chest.

Slowly, the tigers came. There were nine of them, I remember that. Their muzzles were white and ghostly in the dark. Their stripes cut the night apart. Li played, and they listened, their heads cocked, tails stiff. One by one, they threw back their heads and howled. You will say cats do not howl, only wolves do as much;
cats screech or hiss, but do not howl. But you are wrong. Cats can howl, and nine cats can howl like a choir of demons. Their voices joined with Li's strings at feral angles, their fangs gleamed yellow, their throats ululated, and beneath their paws a hundred crocuses were crushed.

Tears ran down Li's face. She stopped playing, staring with wonder and ecstasy at the throng. One by one, they ceased their howls and looked steadily back at my wife. She opened her arms to them, and I understood her—never tell me I did not understand my wife. She opened her arms, pleading for forgiveness, pleading for feline clemency, for what grace tigers can give.

They leapt as one beast into her arms, and devoured her: her heart, her liver, her bones. She did not last a year.

The Tale
of the
Carnelian Box,
Continued

"I AM SORRY FOR YOU," I SAID WEAKLY.

"I ate nothing but crocuses for months. I hunted all nine tigers and boiled their hearts. It did not help. I watched them eat her, and I could not go on." Lem's voice was rough and hard-used, as though he had never known the end of weeping. "But it is all right now. He granted me a new wife, and you are here!"

"I do not know of any promises made to you, but I am not your wife."

"It was not a promise, it was a *wish*. And you are here. You are *here*. This is a beautiful country. You could be happy here. I would build you a safe den, away from the water and the storms. I would make for you the tiger soup. I would be as grass for you, humble beneath your feet."

I started, and met his eyes. I should not have moved from my rock. But I knew nothing of the world, I was alone. I did not know not to look into his face, so eager and needing.

"I cannot walk," I protested. "My feet are broken off. And still you must not touch me, for you will burn."

"My darling, my Li, I will make you new feet of pure, pale silver, and I will not ask for your touch."

"I am not Li. I am not her. Look at me. I am made of grass and light—I am nothing like her."

He looked at me sadly, great dark eyes wrung dry with yearning. "It is a common name in this country."

He would not meet my gaze, and stared at the rock floor, speaking very quietly, his voice tremulous as an infant sparrow. "But I knew that if I waited, if I was faithful, you would come back. Wives always come back. If I chose to become very still, to play the ghost-harp on a stump of hazelwood, you would come to the door, and I would feel again, in my own hands, your gentle face above me. I would put my palms to your dark hair. I would cry—widowers always cry—but I would be able to say to you: *See, wife my own, I waited for you. I knew you would not abandon me. I knew you loved me still. I knew if I was faithful, you would come home.* And you would kiss me, and tell me I was your own husband dear, and I would know your smell and your skin once more after all these years; I would know my wife again, at the end of all things."

After a long while looking at his bent and penitent head, I sighed. "I do know something about that."

But still, I wept as we walked, and the grasses burned beneath my tears.

His house was low and its roof was sound. I stood outside and would not go in, for I would burn his thatch, too; I knew it. I was fallen from my mother, and could touch nothing without harm. But in all the windows and the grassy roof, in the crocuses of the little garden, lizards blinked up at me, tiny lizards of blue and green and black.

"What are they?" I asked.

"Oh!" He laughed distractedly, putting his hand into his thick hair. "They are my lizards. Even tiger-hunting is sometimes tedious, and I learned from one of your uncles—" he blushed "—you remember, darling, the one who never married, and keeps all those skinny dogs—that lizards are pleasant and keep the insects away. But he did not know what I do, that the markings on their backs are strange and complicated. One of them had an incantation written on his scales. He is the only one, so far, but I have hope. It is how I made my wish, how I summoned him."

"Summoned who?"

"Kashkash. He gave you back to me. Bless his beard! One day I shall take my bull-lizard to the Queen and show her the marvels in his skin, but I am not ready." He smiled shyly. "And I have a wife to look after."

And so he went into his little house and began to prepare the soup of tiger meat and thyme and saffron and marigold roots, singing a little to himself, happy as a roosting hen. I stood outside, and shivered in the frost. My hidden silver leached into the earth even then, into the stump, into the lizards, who gathered around me as if around a drinking-hole, and my light flowed out of me over their scales. Before the night was done, I ventured in, burning nothing, never again, to his choking gladness. There was still light in me, but it was cold, then, and thin. I ate the orange soup from a bowl of wood. I could not decide if I was sorry that the hut did not go up in flames. But I was walled up within it, true and tight. By winter, true to his word, he had made me new feet, all of silver, and set my green and broken ankles into their hollows. I tried to make him a soup of light, but he would not touch it, pressing me with his cat meat and his fingers. I tried to believe that it was as good to wait upon the earth as in the Sky.

But I was not happy. I did not wish to hunt the striped cats. I did not wish to learn to make the soup. I did not wish to learn to play the harp—the deer harp, the rabbit harp, the bear harp, even the tiger harp, which Lem would not let me touch. But I did not wish to touch it. I sat ever in the dark corners of the house, trying to feel as I had felt in the endless night-pastures of the Sky. He did not like this, and though he coaxed me toward the hearth, and the knitting chair, and the bed, I would not go. I wept, and scratched at the reedy flesh of my arms, and forgot my name in his grief.

One evening, he touched my face with his big, gentle hands, and his palms grew greasy with light, and he said:

"What is the matter, Li, my beloved, my crocus, my cat?"

"I am unhappy," I said.

"How can you be unhappy? I have made for you the tiger soup and banked the fire so pleasantly, I have crushed thyme flowers into the bed linens so that it smells sweet. I have kept your crocuses bright as little candles in the soil. What else may I do?"

I said nothing, stubborn and sullen. Why did I stay, you may ask me? Why did I not leave him to his muddled soup and his silver feet? I am accustomed to lying still and waiting, I would say to you. But how could my mother see me, down there on the ground, with the crocuses and the lizards?

That very night he pulled his blue bull-lizard from a high cupboard, where the fellow had been gnawing on an old wine bottle, and whispered the words on his back, the black and winding words that the lizard's fringed flesh offered up to him. The lizard's eyes flared, and his scales split open to reveal terrible scarlet embers, and smoke belched from his poor mouth.

"Lem! You are a tedious man! Why do you drag me from my paradise of six towers, where the music of the Djinn twangs stars against the wind hour after hour, and pack me into your foul, stinking lizard once more? This is no fit vessel for me!"

"I am sorry, Kashkash! But I have great need! You were so kind and wise when last we spoke, and you heard my travails, and told me where to find my wife, huddled against the cliff! I have done so, and she is here, bedded into my house!"

"Then why do you trouble me?" The lizard licked his eyeball in an uninterested fashion. He grimaced, the taste of eyeball being less than savory.

"She is unhappy, and I cannot make her well. She does not speak, she does not make the tiger soup, she does not love the thyme-scented bed!" Lem rubbed the bridge of his nose and pled wretchedly with his beast. "I wish, I just wish her desires were not so great, that she were not so vast and empty, a pit into which my love pours and yet sounds no echo. I wish her needs were smaller and sweeter." He licked his lips. "I fear she will take up the harp soon, and then where shall I be?"

The lizard considered. "Surely this is easy enough for me to accomplish, who may hold in the circuit of his arms all possible things, even to the crushing of a Star into a house not big enough for her smallest finger. Even this Star. But why should I do such a thing?"

"Because I will keep her safe! I will keep her and love her, I will be as grass beneath her feet, and I will never let the tigers touch her again, I swear it, noble Kashkash!" Lem took the tiny lizard's claws into his hands.

"Don't touch me, you filthy tiger-tanner. I certainly do not care—but very well. And have a care with this lizard. I do not enjoy being summoned. I prefer to appear in regal excitations of smoke and flame whenever I please."

"Of course, Kashkash."

"Go to your wife and see what I have accomplished in your name."

"Yes, Kashkash."

The flames beneath the lizard's skin snuffed themselves out and his broken scales sealed up again with a hiss of steam.

I would like to say I felt it, but I did not. When Lem came rushing to me, his face once more full of eagerness and need, his face once more adoring and stricken, I was no larger than his hand. I waited for him to be horrified, to curse the name of his lizard, but he exclaimed, he exulted, he danced in his rickety house. He clasped me close to his cheek.

"Now you will never leave me, never, and we will be happy, Li, you will see!"

But I was not happy. I hated how small I had become, how impossible it was for me to eat or touch or see anything without the help of Lem, who for his part was pleased as a full tiger. He carved for me a tiny bed of cherrywood and packed it with soft linens. He made for me minuscule knives and forks. I wept, and little more. But as the years went on he began to fear for me, helpless as I had suddenly become. He forbade me to leave the house, to become the quick and thoughtless prey of a passing owl, and then forbade me to leave my bed of cherrywood, in case some cruel mouse were to take me in his hunger. I lay abed and did not move, and this suited me well enough, for I cared for nothing, and stared into the dark, trying to imagine myself home.

So it was that he removed the blue bull-lizard from its perch near the chimney, and whispered once more the incantatory scales which were scrawled there. I lay in my cradle and watched the poor beast swell up with fire and spew his smoke, remembering the scent of the burning grass, remembering the grass I had been.

"Lem, I do not like you." The lizard belched. "Why must you call me again? I told you, I prefer my entrances to be of my own choosing."

"But, Kashkash! Hear me! I cannot bear the state of my life—what if, small as she is, my darling Li, my crocus-girl, my cat, were to be gobbled up by a possum or rat or falcon who knows no better? I cannot watch her always! I have not slept in so many days."

"What is it you ask of me? I cannot follow your gibbering."

"I wish that she would stay with me forever, safe and whole and untouched! I wish I could be certain that she remain unharmed, for all my days and more!"

The burning lizard considered. "In your madness, Lem, you do know she is not your Li, don't you? I never promised you your old wife back, and what I arranged for you was infinitely better than some lackluster flower-farmer."

Poor Lem, gentle Lem, looked at his lizard blankly, without comprehension.

"She is a Star, Lem. She burned the earth when she came, and if you would understand me, I would tell you that I myself leapt from the smoke of her searing grasses. This is why you have this silly lizard, who nibbled rather densely at the scorched prairie where she fell. This is why I come to you when I have no real desire to. Every creature longs to see how his family is getting along." The lizard grinned, fire leaping out of his throat. "But if this is your wish, I shall do what I must—and in this way no one will be able to say I was not the first, that I was not the finest and first of all Djinn! Darling Lem. Good boy. She will be safe, I promise. But this is your last wish."

Lem frowned, his eyes bleary and dim. "Why? Because I have had three? I have heard this is a law."

"No, because I find you tiresome. Go away."

The lizard bellowed out his fire and closed up his scales. He extended

his long, pink tongue, and on it was a box all of
sparkling carnelian, on its edges carved
wheeling, curling grasses, with a tiny
lock gleaming on its side. It was just
the size of my bed.

"Oh," breathed Lem. "Yes."

The Tale of the Cage of Ivory and the Cage of Iron, Continued

"HE CLOSED ME UP INTO IT," SAID THE LITTLE Grass-Star, "and latched it firm. I sat upon his mantel until he died, his finest possession, his art, his beauty: perfect, pristine, eternal. Licked by lizards and fondled by a man whose hands were rough with soup-stirring. When he died, his old mother-in-law took it into her family, and passed it down and down and down, and I suppose someone must have taken it to this red and ghastly city, probably stuck it upon some Duchess's dresser and called it a pretty little trifle—I do not know. I fell asleep. I did not care to know. In the dark I was at peace, and could pretend that I was home, that my mother would see me shining, even through that awful box. That she would know I never meant to burn anything. Let me go back to sleep. Let me go back to the dark. I have been leached dry and shrunk into a ridiculous manikin, crammed in a box and left on the sill for centuries. I have done enough."

I blinked back my awe. "But . . . you could go back, now, if you wanted to," I said.

"I am tired," she said, and her seed-eyes glistened.

"I am a Djinn, you know. I came from, well, probably not you, but from some Star's burning. I am not sure, really; the others haven't cast my kindling yet. But we are distant relations, one might say."

The Grass-Star looked at me stonily and said nothing.

"Scald," Solace said, looking up at me with pleading eyes. "You can't give her to them. The best thing they'll do is put her on another mantel."

"Grandmother," I said slowly, though the Grass-Star scowled at the name, "will you let me carry you? Just for a little while."

"When has anyone ever let me choose?"

"Now. I am letting you. Scald of no particular family, the Ember-Queen of the Djinn. Because, you know, the dark"—I held up a palmful of my soot-riddled hair—"is something of an obsession of ours."

We rose like smoke. My tail trailed after me, and my silver baskets shook, buffeted by the wind. In her carnelian box, Li curled around herself and did not speak. I could see the tips of her silver feet peeking from the hem of her reed-dress. The air grew cold, and I drifted higher, to the tip of the Sirens' tower, to the tip of Ajanabh, where her outstretched fingers reach their furthest. And there I held gentle, green-shouldered Li in one hand, and touched the dark sky, the last gasp of dark before dawn, with one flaming finger. The scent of scorched air flowed out from the puncture, and I cannot say whether it was because my fire is terrible or because I wanted it so fervently, wanted her to rest, wanted her away from Kohinoor and the army of Kings and Queens, wanted her home, that it blazed as hot as a wish might have, but the dark opened around my finger like a square of silk dropped over a candle, and I worked my hand into the flaming night, widening and stretching the dark around me. It felt like skin, and I choked, I wept, my throat froze. But I took her from her box, Li, one of a million seed-blown Stars, and folded her into the night like a child tucked into her bed.

She looked at me, disbelieving, and she did not smile. I wish she had smiled. I wish I knew that I had done well by her. But she simply breathed deeply and closed her eyes, and the dark closed over her.

In the Garden

WELL AFTER MIDNIGHT, THE TORCHES STILL BLAZED AND THE SNOW pooled and watered around their polished stalks, quick little crows hopping forward to drink. The moon had set, and outside the halos of fire, it was dark as dreaming. In the still of the outer Garden, there was so little sound, no frogs, no geese, no hooting wolves. The flowers were dead and icy, the trees naked and hard. The stars were silent on the snow.

The girl opened her eyes. The blackness vanished from the boy's throat even as she did it, and he stopped in midsentence.

"Come away," she said. "Come away from here. I don't want to be near them, your family, your father. It is almost over, I know it."

"We are safe!" the boy said, pointing through the waving branches at the far-off dancers, far-off children laughing and throwing brandy-soaked green grapes at one another.

"No," she said. "Come to the Gate, come to the edges, come to the snow and the iron."

"If that is what you want."

"Yes."

He took her circlet from her and let the scarlet veil fall onto the ice.

She brushed flakes from her hands and lifted her heavy skirts, turning away from the light and the sound behind the chestnut boughs. The boy took her hand.

"Wait," came a soft voice behind them. Dinarzad stood there, in long yellow veils, her every finger ringed in emerald, her waist bounded in red. The children turned to look at her. But again, Dinarzad did not speak. She lifted her own veil and looked with mute pleading at the girl, her eyes dark and desperate. The girl let go her friend's hand and crossed the snow to the older woman. She looked into Dinarzad's face as in a mirror, and slowly took the amira's long, glittering fingers in her own chapped, cold hands. She took a long breath, frightened as a hare who does not know if she has or has not seen an arrow in the mist.

"I think," she said, softer than light, "I think that one morning, the Papess woke in her tower, and her blankets were so warm, and the sun was so golden, she could not bear it. I think she woke, and dressed, and washed her face in cold water, and rubbed her shaven head. I think she walked among her sisters, and for the first time saw that they were so beautiful, and she loved them. I think she woke up one morning of all her mornings, and found that her heart was as white as a silkworm, and the sun was clear as glass on her brow, and she believed then that she could live, and hold peace in her hand like a pearl."

Tears slipped warm and grateful down Dinarzad's lovely face, her lips trembled, and she folded her arms around the girl like a mother, like a sister, and kissed her frozen hair. She let her go, and drew down her yellow veil, and returned to the dais—but every so often, she glanced back over her shoulder, into the dark and the branches, into the Garden.

*   *   *

The girl wound her hands in the iron Gate. She looked into the deep woods beyond the Palace grounds, where she had never ventured. Her fingertips were pale as mushrooms, and she could not feel the ice. Shadows pricked in the trees outside the Gate, shadows and starlight filtering down through leafless boughs and stiff black needles.

She closed her eyes and tried to quiet her heart. She turned to the boy, her black eyelids blazing as though they burned her, and whispered:

"Come, tell me how it ends."

The Tale of the Cage of Ivory and the Cage of Iron, Continued

THE CARNIVAL OF THE DAWN sang with a hundred open throats beneath the gentle shadows of Simeon's elbows. When I returned to Orfea's courtyard, Solace and Lantern had gone before me, and left me to find my way by the sounds of drums and flutes, trumpets and lyres and pipes and shouting, the sounds of so many voices. It was not difficult. I rounded a tall lamppost whose capital was shaped like a fish, mouth flinging a spume of flame into the air, and the cobbled street below the wall was alive with folk, alive with Ajans, and the colors caught my eyes like hooks.

Jugglers tossed iron pokers and scarlet flowers and

the occasional child into the air, fire-eaters swallowed their trade, masks were donned and removed—and there, I saw Arioso pulling the edge of his jackal-face away to the delight of a young boy, but I could not tell what was underneath. Painters leapt madly at Simeon's back, throwing pigment against him with the abandon of mating herons, their hands a bristle of frenzied brushes. The Sirens flicked their wings at the wall, inscribing it with their own blue ink:

Even in penance is beauty; blessed are all the ocean's drowned!

Singers stood in clusters around trumpeters and pipers, voices high and low echoing by, and the howling, and the keening, and the barking of countless creatures. A woman with a parrot's green and scarlet head cawed out the hours, and a man with a tiny wolf on his shoulder howled a duet back to her. And the dancers—oh, the dancers! Everyone danced, a flurry of legs and arms, leaps I could not begin to follow in the throng, and Agrafena, Agrafena dancing and playing amid them all. But she was modest, after all things, and many others played louder, danced faster. Near a fountain that trickled water from the mouth of a fox-faced woman there was a girl all in red dancing with a man in a green coat, whose legs were like those of a gazelle, and she wound her long black beads around his throat while he bit her gently on the cheek. A red lion cavorted at their side. Spiders leapt from lamp to lamp, trailing iridescent webs behind them. Did one have needles for legs? I could not see.

But there in the center of the square was Lantern, his tail flaring and flaming, and within its snapping ribbons danced Solace, her eyes shut in ecstasy, stepping deftly between the orange-red feathers, throwing her arms out, her head back, her black tattoos glowing wet and bright in the glare of her father's light. When Agrafena stopped to shear a frazzled thread of her hair away, the two of them rested, and Solace ran to me. She was soaking wet from head to hip, her hair plastered to her skull, wrapped around it in long ropes. Her skin was slick and slippery. She looked down at herself and giggled.

"Folio made this stuff, so I don't burn. It smells a bit sour and bitter, like old beer, but it works. I'm only a little pink when I finish. I used to blister terribly."

I showed her the empty box, and she nodded. I think I might have stayed there, I might have walked through the Carnival with a child's hand in mine, eaten apples doused in cardamom wine and told her how once, when I was very young, I had seen the old Queen dancing in her lonely hall, her embers red as bleeding, and I thought she was so beautiful, then.

I thought she must be so happy. I might have done those things. I might have even declined to drift back through Simeon's hands and ridden out the siege with the Ajans, cowering in corkscrewed streets—but a deafening sound cracked open the winds, and then another close behind it, shredding the last threads of blue night and letting the sun in, letting the fire in—for the fire did come, bellowing up before the wall, black and scarlet and vast, and a sound like the ocean. All our faces were lit by it, blanched white. Solace hid her eyes in my waist. There was another terrible sound, another gout of fire, shooting up into the dawn like a dragon being born. And then there was a worse sound, a crying, a snuffling, an awful sobbing as Simeon began to bleed, began to weep, began to call out to Agrafena, terrified and alone.

Agrafena took up her bows and began to play a slow, gliding lullaby, all blue and silver and kind, and she did not cry at all, not at all. The Ajans rushed forward to put their hands to Simeon, to whisper and stroke him and press their cheeks to his back. I went to him, too, and put my palms, split by flowing fire, to the inside of his thumb.

"Let me go," I whispered, and his fingers parted for me to pass through.

On the other side of the wall I could see the army with their proud plumes, their raven and their swan helmets, their horses with chests belted and bolted in bronze, their shields with a thousand seals and crests that I would never remember. I could see Simeon's brass eyes lonely and afraid, trying not to weep louder than he already did. Kohinoor stood some ways off from me, astride a great salamander. We have little enough choices in mounts, and salamanders are sweet as kittens, really. They do not mind the smoke, and bear their saddles with grace. His beady eyes flicked between his mistress and me, and his skin glimmered like an oil slick. Beside her were all the others, Khaamil the Hearth-King, his one eye glinting,

and beside him the Kindling-King and the Tinder-Queen with her blazing yellow face, and the King of Flint and Steel with his sparks snapping in the wind. Behind them, I saw the wispy white smoke of the Khaighal, anticipating punishments before the day was done. Catapults lazily flopped forward and back, empty. They were angry; it was not difficult to see, though a Djinn looks often angry, even when she is asleep. It seemed wise not to let them begin the lecture, or the execution, and so I spoke before she could; I spoke standing in a wreckage of shattered terra-cotta, splattered in oily, viscous stuff which burned like a Queen's hair.

"I have it," I cried, and held up the box in my orange-lined hand.

Kohinoor goggled. "What? How can you have it? The Ajans would not give it up!"

"The Ajans never knew where it was, you old fireplace. But I have it, and I will give it to you if you do not hurt the poor wall further, and go home like a cat who has played all night, and now hears the breakfast bell ring."

The Ash-Queen's eyes narrowed to gray and smoky slits. "Give it to me, and we shall see."

I had not been Queen long enough to be cleverer than she was. She drove her salamander forward, her hair streaming behind her like burning trees. I put the red, gleaming box into her hands; she snatched it away and turned her back to the others, as if to keep it for her own, to look first into it, and share the honor with no one.

She did not howl with rage, or scream curses on my name, or strike me with her black fists. She did not even look at me.

"Where is she?" she said quietly.

"She is gone. She is home. She is beyond you, or Lem, or Kashkash, or any snarling tiger. She is safe."

Kohinoor shook her head. "How could you?" she half-sobbed, hurt stitching her voice like a dress.

The
Ash-Queen's Tale

Do you know what you must have to become the Ash-Queen? As you have your hair, and
Khaamil has his low and lovely voice, harmonious as
two nightingales singing together?

Nothing.

You must have no fire at all in you. You must have no
spark, no breath of scarlet, not the slightest shuddering
sigh of embers. You must be cold, and gray, and hollow.
And so I was. I blew on my hands endlessly, hoping for
light, hoping for warmth. I did not want to be Queen, I
wanted to flame. I shivered always, I was thin, an orphan, a burnt, discarded branch.

Do you know that without fire you cannot wish? I doubt you have even thought of it. It is true. I wished so hard when I was a child, I wished for everything I could think of—but most often I wished for fire. Eventually, in my desperation, I wished without letting a Khaigha scribe it in his book: I wished for a bird to love, to hold in my hand, with a blue head and wings of ice. I wished for the briefest life of all Djinn. I wished for a mother, a real mother, with fire in her eyes.

But still I was alone and scrabbling in the ash while other children blazed on the boulevard of beryl like ridiculous, idiotic fireflies. Someone noticed the smudge of black against the carnelian wall and I was made Queen before I was two years old. There was no competition—no Djinn had been born dead of flame in years. I sat alone in my Alcazar, inching closer to the fire, trying to catch a sleeve aflame.

Khaamil was as newly crowned as I. He was entirely perplexed as to what to do with the vast hearth that was the central hall of his Palace, and I tried to help him—those born to fire are so often useless with it. I helped him to keep it clear of ash, to keep it banked and ruddy, to keep the black streaks off his brass pillars. He told me wild stories about his wishing exploits: He loved a woman in the north with horse-hooves, and blessed her with an unfailing orchard of limes; he loathed a man who stole three of the green fruits and cursed him with never-ending hunger. I flushed black with jealousy; he mocked me, mocked my lack. He told me tales about the wind-Djinns and the water-Djinns—and I had no idea what he meant.

"Who raised you, girl? Djinn that come from Star-burned winds, Djinn that steamed up from Star-scalded oceans. We all have our tribe, everyone knows that, and now that we've the libraries to ourselves, we can discover just exactly who is who—imagine! I could know the very name of the wind that bore my grandfathers!"

"No one raised me," I mumbled. "My mother burned out bearing me. My father wished himself after her."

Khaamil started. "That's not approved!"

I smiled wryly. "What can they do to him?"

"Well, let's find out who you are, then! Where you come from! Genealogy is such a lot of fun."

I looked at him dumbly, rather taken aback at the idea that poring through a lot of old books with more dust than pages could be fun. But then, it probably was, for them. The excitement of knowing that at any moment, a stray lock of hair could ignite the whole library. But the pages would stay cold and pulpy beneath my fingers, and I would smudge them black. I followed him into the vaults of my Alcazar, for where else would we keep such fragile records but in the cold and the black, in the halls of my house? We are obsessive about records—how can we be otherwise? We live such a brief time, and it is so easy to forget.

The library was drafty; its ceilings were high as the topmost branches of a sandalwood tree. The rafters were blasted black with forgotten fires, with the handprints of the Djinn who had once hollowed out this place, when Kash was made of dirt and daub, instead of carnelian and brass. Those scorch-marks mocked me, howled their derision in the high, screeching voices of white-eyed rats. There were no shelves, only iron grates which might have held an evening's fire, but instead held books, old and dead. The Djinn do not write fanciful tales or epic poems of valor and sacrifice—what glory is it when one flame consumes another? No more than that which graces any pile of wood and scrap of spark. Kashkash forbade us to write of any exploits but his, and the poets tired quickly of this. Thus our books are few, and precious. I ran my fingers over them, and tried to ignore the insult of the rafters. The pages were fine as ash, made from the skin of salamanders, and the words were charcoal.

Khaamil hovered over me as I read, played with my sleeve. I curled a tendril of smoky hair behind my ear, and looked backward through the books, back and back, parents and grandparents, with names I could hardly pronounce, while Khaamil exclaimed in delight if he saw a Djinn that connected us, that made us cousins a hundred times removed. As I pored into older books, sewn together from ash and soot, I saw my ancestors shrink, become drier, burn hotter. I saw them wither back into the grass they had been, I saw them blow seed and wave in a wheat-scented wind. And I saw a Star fall, with broken feet, and I saw her stumble weeping through a field, and I saw shadows fly up from her footsteps.

Khaamil's eyes widened. Tears trickled down my face—mute salt water, not fire, not flame. I cannot even cry like a Djinn.

"But that's Kashkash's book, it's his line. You're descended from the same scald, the same Star. I think that makes him—"

"Nothing, it makes him nothing! Didn't you listen to the King of Flint and Steel when he told you? Kashkash is nothing; he was the burning scrim of oil on the trash of our Shaduki towers, and I am nothing like him!"

I slammed the book closed. I did not want to know. I did not ask to know. And in the days to come Khaamil learned not to ask me about it. I may lack flame, but I can smother the fire of any of them in ash. Only once did he put his hand to my hair and tell me he had fire for both of us, that he would make me burn. I put my hand into his smoke, and he felt my cold, he felt the softness of ash falling on his heart, and shuddered, and did not suggest it again.

But as I drifted through my own halls, as my pillars grew gray with ash, I could not forget the Grass-Star, how sad she had seemed in the beautiful illuminations, rimmed in fire on the page, her eyes flaming tears, real tears of naphtha and boil, how her poor, broken feet had bled on the grass. Did I come from the blood, or the tears? Did I come from her shattered stumps? Or did I come later, when that man had wrung her out, and she was dark as I—did she touch some insignificant blade of grass with her last pathetic press of light, and did some sickly, flameless shadow issue, and was this my grandmother? In my dreams, the Grass-Star spat at her husband, and her saliva rolled itself into a pale and bloodless baby who cried for her, though she did not hear, and that sodden child was I. When I did not dream, I searched the books of the gratings and the blasted vaults for her—where might she lie now, a deathless Star at the core of the world?

Khaamil was worried about me. His flames make him soft. While I slept on the finger-scalded floors of the vaults, and blind, gray-clawed doves pecked at my hair, he hovered like a grandmother, twisting his beard in his hands.

"Kohinoor," he said one night when I knelt by a grate whose claw-feet had rusted red as heart's fire, "let me help." He swallowed, his flame-eyes wide and dear. "Let me wish for you, and I will take what punishment the Khaighal can find in their white tails." He took my hands and I looked up into his face, bright and eager as a young salamander in his first saddle.

"I just want to know her, Khaamil. She ought to be here, in Kash, with her children, seated on a cushion of silk like blue fire, hearing their voices sing new songs, songs which make the ears glow. She ought to be piled with red jewels, and red fruits, and held to the bosom of so many Djinn who would love her. She would put her hands to me and I would burn, I would have her silver fire licking at my ribs, and we would sing together of the dark at the beginning of the world."

My eyes ran with hideous salt tears, wet and colorless and useless.

Khaamil put his painted palms together and raised his eyes to the rafters. The rats squealed and ran—and on a golden grating we had never seen before was a book of such colors that in that blackened place it seemed a peacock among sparrows. It was bound in lambskin and malachite, and its pages were written in clam-ink—the story of a carnelian box, and a crocus-farmer who kept it in her family, down and down the years. But flowers have poor memories, and the book only knew that the box had passed out of its home country, and into some lowly, unkempt city at the bottom of the world whose towers were red and hideous, and who did not deserve her.

The next day the Khaighal took Khaamil's eye.

The Tale of the Cage of Ivory and the Cage of Iron, Continued

KOHINOOR GLARED AT ME OVER THE TOP OF HER salamander's wide, mottled head. "The Ajans never once answered me. The Duke did not respond to a single missive. When the Khaighal investigated, they discovered the degenerate state of the city, and determined that Kashkash would not have let such a rich corpse lie in the desert, picked over by flies. Though the knowledge came through Khaamil's well-meant treason, they agreed that we should be allowed to invade. I would find her. I would touch her." The Ash-Queen's voice deepened into a canine snarl. "And then the old Queen died, and an ignorant gutter-coal took her place, who could care no more for history than a flame cares for a match."

"It doesn't matter now," I said. "She is gone."

"She was mine," Kohinoor whispered, her gray eyes pleading. "How could you take her from me?"

"She wasn't your mother. Or mine. It was an accident, the Djinn that came from her steps, just an accident. You had no right to her."

"Neither did you!"

I hung my head, made myself as humble in her sight as I could. "Let us go home, Kohinoor. Let us go back to our Alcazars and drink coalwine and sing new songs. Songs of Ajanabh and Stars and the hearts of tigers."

She shook her hair back, and her salamander stamped its dry feet. "This is her city. I will take it, and I will live in her footsteps, held in these red stones as she was held, and I will climb every tower to the sky until I find where you have hidden her, until I can look her in the eye, until I can have my fire, and she her children."

I straightened, and put my hands on my silver hip-baskets. "This ignorant gutter-coal thinks you will not."

"Have you spent so long within that giant's fat knuckles that you have gone mad? This is the decision of the Kings, the Queens, and the Khaighal, and you can do nothing."

I tried to smile, as I imagined a Queen in full possession of herself would. I imagine it came out a sickly snarl, a kitten hissing at a lion. But I could not let the Ajans burn. I could not.

"I can make a wish," I said.

The Khaighal roared. "You may not! It is not permitted! Nothing you could wish is in our books! Kashkash would never wish for defeat; he would never wish to lose a battle, to lose a city! We will shrivel your tongue in your mouth before you can utter a single word!"

"But if I could," I said sharply, holding up my hands, their orange and black flaring in the faces of the crimson Khaighal salamanders, "if I could wish for a thing permitted, if I could wish for something that Kashkash himself would have drawn from his beard with such glee that the heavens would flame in answer, would you let my tongue rest in my mouth, would you let my wish disturb the air?"

"You cannot wish for the salvation of this place," they said. "Nothing in your wish can touch our will."

"Nevertheless?"

"If it is in our books, it is permitted. This is the law of the Khaighal. We are accountants, not senators."

Then I did smile; I could smile. My teeth flared white-hot and I pressed my palms together. "My wish is the simplest thing there is, something Kashkash wished for a man in a little hut so long ago that the trees who witnessed it are dust. I wish"—my smile broadened—"for my wife."

They looked puzzled; their pale beards flushed blue and yellow. Kohinoor rolled her ashen eyes. Khaamil raised his mangled eyebrow. And there was a peculiar sound in the supply train, a grinding, rumbling, inexorable sound, like the wheels of a catapult grinding against the earth. The salamanders stomped nervously, and Kohinoor struggled with her reins.

When they came, I had never seen anything more radiant. The sun caught their brows, their eyes, their shoulders as they rounded the front lines, all my wives, alive and walking to me, men and women of stone: emerald and ruby and turquoise, tourmaline and hematite and granite, garnet and topaz and jasper, diamond and brass, silver and quartz, copper and malachite, and carnelian, so many red carnelian faces glittering in the morning. They came to me one by one and kissed my cheeks, and by the time the fiftieth of them came, and the hundredth, and more and more, I was weeping, my cheeks wet with flame. They kissed me and they took their places along the wall as I asked them to, a fabulous skirt for Simeon, for his poor, bleeding chest, for his poor city.

"The simplest thing there is," I said. "They will not let you in—after all, a wife's love is absolute, eternal, untouchable as breath. Come near them and they will smother your fires in stone."

Kohinoor looked at me, her expression curiously like a child's: hurt, uncomprehending.

"She was my mother. I only wanted to touch her," she whispered. "You could not possibly understand. I searched my vaults for you, for your family, for grass or wind or water or stone. You are not there. You are nothing, and no one. You drifted into Kash like a scrap of trash, and it is only chance which made you Queen. You are smoke, and nothing more."

"So are we all, sister." The hands of my wives tightened on mine.

I would like to say the Djinn dispersed before the day was out, that the army of Kings and Queens was sent to their well-curtained homes and their many-pronged crowns. But it was weeks before they determined that my wives would not move, that the Khaighal would find no precedent for repeal. They went slowly; they went cursing. And on the day when the fields of Ajanabh were empty of all and dry, Simeon opened his hands entirely, and my jeweled wives were let inside, hesitant as infants, reaching for the folk of the Carnival, to touch them and know their names. I let them go; I let them wander. They were not truly mine. They clung to me at first as kits will cling to a vixen, but soon enough they took names, and tried their first, stumbling dances, and asked after lovely fauns and chorus boys they had seen.

When they found Orfea's courtyard they were as upset as a flock of squabbling geese. They put their fingers to the eyes of the statues, they shook their stone shoulders, trying to wake them, they called out to the sandstone figures, they begged them to answer, begged them to breathe. They wept and trembled to see these mirror-siblings; they did not understand. I tried to calm them, but hundreds of stone folk who think they stand in a field of slaughter are not easily calmed.

I held the head of an inconsolable woman of lapis in my lap, and a young man of obsidian lay sickened at my feet. From behind a sandstone bust of a boy with bees' wings, a soft voice sounded:

"Please," it whirred, "listen to me."

The stone wives looked up, eyes wet with sparkling, mica-flecked tears, and before them stood Hour, her head bent, her clock-heart ticking, her armor hands clasped like a girl who has forgotten her lesson.

"These are not like us," she said, "and if you will listen, I will help you to grow up, I will tell you all you need to know of living."

They gathered close round her, many-colored eyes hopeful and curious. They, too, folded their hands politely and waited. The tall, gleaming woman stood very still.

"Once upon a time," said Hour, "there lived a maiden in a castle..."

The Tale
of the Waste,
Continued

"I LIVED IN AJANABH AS WELL AS A GOOSE IN ITS flock. But it was no more than a year, I think, before the Khaighal came. They did not bring an army. They did not bring their books. They brought a cage. Not because I had wished for my wives—they could say nothing on that score—but because I had abandoned my Alcazar, and left Kash without one of her Queens." The Djinn laughed as bitterly as a veteran. "Dereliction of duty. They poured out their smoke over me, white and roiling, and when it cleared a cage was in its place. It is not iron—it is made of Djinn-bones, and I can no more melt them than I can breathe at the bottom of the sea. I cannot slip through the bars. They keep me here, in the wasteland, and until you, there has been but one other visitor to my prison of bone and sand and sage."

The leopard and her mistress waited with the patience of stones.

"She came when I had been here through a full summer, and my heart was as dry as cedar bark. Kohinoor, without her salamander, a pillar of smoke and ash in the desert. She came near to my cage, though not too near.

" 'I am sorry they decided this,' she said. 'But it will not be long. You are old now; you will not last. Nor will I—ash is ever older than flame.'

"We played the scene that angry, soured old women will play: We taunted, we sneered, we threatened. It hardly matters, really. She stood there a long time when the words were done, silent, staring.

" 'Why did you come?' I asked.

" 'She was mine.' Kohinoor sighed, as though she no longer believed it herself. 'Who will fill me with flame now?'

"I understood. I was not Queen long, but I understood. Sisters, even such motley sisters as we, do understand some simple things. The simplest things there are. I extended a long hand from my cage, and she walked into my fingers. Into her smoke, into her throat, into her eyes I reached, and the flame of my palms and my wrists and my fingertips passed into her, lighting the darkness of her bones to a radiant gold, red flames opening like funeral flowers in the base of her belly, streaming from her navel. The roots of her hair glowed incandescent, and in the desert, the Ash-Queen burned.

" 'Oh,' she breathed. 'Yes.'

"She wept then, real tears, liquid fire, dripping to scald the earth. And then her body fell into ash, true ash, and her last breath scorched the wind."

"Thank you," said the leopard, sitting at attention. "We are grateful to hear such things, though we are disturbed—rather, I am disturbed on behalf of my mistress."

Indeed, the veiled woman wrung her hands and looked imploringly at her cat with great red eyes. Scald reeled in a length of her hair and obscured her face for a moment, overcome by the memory of the old Queen. "Why?" she said from behind her screen. "It is my tale, it was not meant to disquiet you, it is nothing to you but a story told by a devil caught in a cage."

Rend frowned and pawed the thirsty ground. She purred softly.

"That is not entirely true . . ."

The Tale

of the Lepress

and the Leopard

IN URIM, EVERY WINDOW IS HUNG WITH BLACK.

This is not so monotonous as it might seem—shades of black differ as greatly from one to the other as oxblood and cobalt. In our long black banners are infinite designs, spirals and mandorlas of ghostly and intricate design. Within tall citadels the people of Urim contemplate these banners, and it calms them.

For Urim is a city of plague.

It is a hopeless place, and those who are hopeless are its priests and its citizens. Lepers and other ailments of as many varieties as spices in Ajanabh by the thousand gather there, treat one another as they can, salve one another as they may, and die in each other's arms. The wildflower fields surround it in a wide, green-rose circle, like the window of a church, where cures of all fashions are bred and planted and culled. Some of them taste sweet as apples, some bitter as banyan root. Most of them do nothing. But we hope, we always hope. In their ailments, Urimites are brothers, and no city is so full of gentle, exhausted, beneficent folk.

They tore out my mistress's tongue when we came, and chained me to her while she lay broken on their streets.

But I get ahead of myself. It is a cat's habit. We bound and leap and leave the tale far behind, when we should hold it between our paws and worry it to the bone. I shall pierce it with two claws: She found me in the grasslands, and I was cold and gray as slush-snow.

Do you know how a leopard is born? We are mules, soft-nosed and long-tailed. My mother was a lion, my father was a pard of many colors; his pelt was like a war flag. On a day of hunting he found her, her muzzle bloody with antelope, and against the custom of both feline tribes they coupled in the long glare of a screaming sun. They went their ways, as cats will do. And my mother gave birth to one cub, dead as an antelope, as all leopards are born. Our mothers must breathe into our snouts, or our fathers roar into them, or we will take no life. But a new lion with a mane of tangled gold had padded into my mother's pride, and did not care for cubs which were not his own. She left me in the saltbush, unbreathed, unroared.

That was how my mistress found me. Little gray paws curled up toward the sun like old mushrooms, spots like specks of mold, a tongue that never tasted light or meat. Even in her extremity, the woman I came to know as Ruin knelt by that bedraggled, infant cat, fur still stiff with birth water, and without knowing what she did, looked closely at my half-lidded eyes, and breathed into my spotted face.

I woke. I saw her. She was not a lion, or a pard. Her veils were parted to show her face: her cheeks flushed, her eyes scarlet as the inside of a deer, and her skin peeling from her like paper, layer after layer, like pages falling out of a book. I gripped her fingers with my paw and pierced her skin in my eagerness—but drew no blood.

"You cannot hurt me, little one," she said, her voice rough as a tongue. "And as you are quite yellow and black and neither peeling to pieces nor turned to stone, I think perhaps I cannot hurt you . . ."

The Tale

of the

Good Daughter

I HAD A NAME BEFORE I DIED. I KNOW I DID. I can taste it on my tongue like the ghost of sugar. But I cannot remember it. Ruin I became and Ruin I am. My father said I was an angel, seraphic, holy as myrrh. It was never so, but I tried so hard, I tried for his sake, but Ruin is the whole of me.

Our house was full of bundled spices, yarrow and cinnamon and paprika, bright red turmeric flowers bunched by the windows. My father wore red robes, and taught me to pour out the freezing water into our carnelian font, and put wild celery flowers in my hair, so pungent in their scent that my eyes itched. Everything in our world was red. Red, my father said, was the color of heaven, the color of Stars falling. Red was the color of piety, and so he swathed my crib in it, and my body when I rose from that crib. I knew nothing that was not red.

Is it surprising then that I kept to red things, in the House of Red Spices? Is this piety, to never step outside the shade of your bedclothes? I bathed in the frozen font each day, and I learned, after a very long while of gritted teeth and chattering, to love the blue feeling of its splash on my skin, which was not red, which was nothing like red. Under my bed I collected green things: grass, jade, green silk, clover. White things: chalk, alabaster, dust, daisies. Blue things: lapis, blue crinoline, scraps of paper from the indigo dyers' shops, ice. The ice always melted, but I kept it in vials of crystal, and in some lights, these too were blue. I would take these things and hold them to my chest in the night and dream about water which was warm as a heart.

And then the fields began to die. I did not understand why—I was so young, innocent of everything outside our house; I could not have even matched my stockings if everything I owned had not been red. But I watched them wither and die from the tower windows curtained in scarlet, and I wanted to see the green and the white and the blue and the gold and the violet of them before they were gone. I wanted to lie down in everything not red and feel them crawling over me as they rushed to escape from the world.

I went from my father's door with prayers weighing my wrists. I pulled the earth over me like a hood. I waited. Roots nosed my elbows, the hollows of my knees—and something deep in me hardened into stone. It sat in me, spreading and chewing, and I closed my eyes in the earth. I saw no red, but black.

It hurt so much. That is what I remember. The shoes were wedged onto my feet and in the place within me which had turned to stone, the place which was pumice and sandstone, wrenched in anguish. My skin softened, blood flowed back into flesh, dragging knives behind it. On my red bier my limbs became heavy, prickling like a forgotten finger. I could not even groan for the sear of it. Even when I woke, and stood over my father, tired and empty of piety, the blood in me bellowed, enraged that it was no longer stone, not black, that it was forced into red once more. Every step in my gnarled, twisted cinnamon shoes was filled with the bright, piercing cries of my blood, blood which remembered being stone, which howled to be stone again.

And the shoes, through the howling, whispered. They whispered of the light in the far corners of the city, they whispered that there would be no pain if only I could move fast enough on my feet, if only I could dance, if only the world could whirl around me, swift enough to carry any stone away.

The shoes lied. I danced, I danced every night, and I went to no services, held no red candle until my father dragged me to the altars and tied my ankles to them under my red, red skirts. I danced, endlessly, and every step, every whirl, screamed. As I danced the stone left me, scouring me empty as it went, but it did go. My hair became long and bright again, my cheeks red, my legs nimble. And on one night of all nights,

when there was al-
most no pain left,
only the nagging,
grinding ache of
my belly, where the
stone had begun, I
lost my shoes.

I did not mean to
lose them: Though they
lied and chose their own path, they
were good and lovely shoes. I did not feel
them when they fell from my heels. I did
not go back, searching through the brush
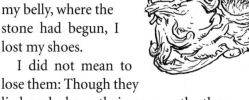
and the ruin of courtly orchids trampled by revelers to find them. Some other girl could have them now, I thought: I was well. But as I lay in my red blankets, in my bed so like a bier, the thing in me which had turned to stone as I lay in the earth pricked once more, and hardened a little, like a fist clenching.

My father told me it was nothing.

"Do not think on it," he said, "and it will go away, just as it did before."

"Before," I mumbled, "I had my shoes, red and dusty."

"Perhaps," said he, stern as stone, "you should take up your ablutions again. Perhaps this is your punishment for such unseemly things as you did in the Duke's old Palace."

"I told you, Father, I only danced."

"I will search the city for the sacred shoe that fits your foot," he announced, and though I protested, he turned his back and called his heralds.

But I did as he said, fearful of the hard thing in me like a pit in a plum. I tried to scrub it away in the clear, hard morning water, frantic to melt it back to blood. My father saw this with pleasure, and held up my hair while I shivered. I held the red candle at the altar, and after a time he removed my stays. In the evening he rubbed red spices into my belly and mixed them with his tears. The spices burned, left blisters, trickled from my stomach to the linens.

And all the while, every shoemaker in Ajanabh, which was, certainly, fewer shoemakers than there had been, came to the House of Red Spices. They brought their finest heels and laces, of the twisted roots of tamarisk with rosettes of aloe, scraggle-toed banyan shoes, cedar and pomegranate-wood, date palm and sandalwood, camphor and wet ginger-shrouded shoes that burned my soles. They brought delicate black vanilla-bean shoes and fragrant maydi-shoes, shoes of nutmeg seeds and shoes of cardamom pods white as pearls. They even brought cinnamon shoes, dusty as my own, but none of these helped, and still my stomach hardened.

And my skin began to peel. Like onion skin, it fell from me. The stone wished to come out as I wished it to wither. I woke in the morning, my flesh sloughed off in the night, the skin beneath new and raw. My father exclaimed—I was healed, I must be healed, such a thing was a miracle of the candle and the altar. My skin lay around me, translucent and dead. But as the days went on, the skin beneath peeled, too, and beneath it was not new skin, red and bright, but more peeling, thin and terrible, like plum rind, sliced away, ruined. My father sent to the Duke's old Palace for every set of cast-off shoes, for every maid that danced, but they were gone, vanished, shredded to flavor some beauty's tea or danced to pieces on a floor I knew as well as my bed.

And still my skin peeled. There seemed to be no end to me, or to the peeling, and my belly was hard and cold, waiting to emerge.

The Tale
of the Lepress
and the Leopard,
Continued

"ONE DAY, MY FEET BARE AMONG A DOZEN PAIRS
of shoes, I said to my father:

"'This must stop. I am dead, Father, I am dead and
you seek to cure it, but there is no cure here. I shall go
to Urim, where all cures reside on shelves of obsidian
and pearl. I shall go to the pale white sea, which
washes the hem of Urim with all the salt of the world.
The dead will walk in the desert—our place is not in
the city.'

"And so I came, little cat, peeling and shedding my
skin like a snake. I wrapped myself in black so that I
would not frighten anyone, and so that the gate of Urim

would know me as a pestilent. The stone in me is so heavy, now. Anything I touch hardens. Anyone I touch becomes art, becomes sculpture." Ruin laughed wryly. "Perhaps I have found my calling. But you pierce my skin, you see that I have no blood left but stone, and yet you are soft and sweet and spotted as ever."

I coughed, a tinny kitten's cough. "You breathed into me. I...I am not a leopard, I am not alive. My mother did not give me her breath. You did, a corpse walking wide. Thus, I think, I am dead, still, dead as I was born, as dead as you. We are dead together. How could you harm me? Do you believe, in Urim, there is a salve for you?"

Ruin regarded me calmly, her eyes red and serene. "No. But we always hope."

I nuzzled shyly into her palm. "Take me with you. I have your breath; I am your leopard. You cannot leave me. You must name me and love me and lick my fur into behaving itself. It is very necessary."

She laughed. "You are not bothered by my eyes, the molt of my skin?"

"How could I be? You are the first woman I have ever seen."

And so it was that we went together, and my legs grew very long, gold and black and wiry. I loved my mistress, and once, just once, when our fire was very low and she looked out across the empty plains between Ajanabh and Urim, I put my unruly head in her lap, and she licked my fur to shining.

We came to Urim in the night, and all things in the city were black. It was a city mourning itself, and how dark were its vestments! We entered; there was no sentry. Urim is not often visited. All things slept, and we sat at the center of the city, waiting for dawn on the lip of a great memorial: a pure white man resting on a bier, his face beatific. On the lip of this slab was carved:

FORGIVE US, FOR WE WERE IN NEED.

Against this nameless man and his nameless bed we huddled; I wrapped my tail around my haunches, and the sky wheeled by over our heads. Sometime before sunrise, a strange creature came walking from a distant road, its footsteps scraping the pale cobbles. It was a woman all of wicker, of brambles and stick, of hazel and red osier, green and pliant willow. It moved smoothly and gracefully for all that, and bowed low to us.

"That is an uncomfortable place to sleep," she said, her voice hard, like branches snapping. "Perhaps it brings you hope, however?" Her eyes were sappy blossom nubs, rose-colored and wet.

Ruin stirred and adjusted her veils quickly, covering her exposed cheek. "We await the day, and the Urimites, to tell us how to live in this place. We are . . . in need."

"So are we all," answered the wicker-wight. "But he"—the woman indicated the statue—"is the answer to need . . ."

The Tale
of the
Cattle Merchant
and the Apple

EVERY POOR, LOST CREATURE OF URIM KNOWS
this tale, gathers around this pale casket in hope so hot
and bright it would burn any who did not know that
Urim itself flames with such hope, that you can look
nowhere in the city without being blinded.

Long ago there was a man with three daughters. This
man lived in a country which bordered a sea so salty it
foamed white on the sand, a country full of rich grass
and cloudy skies. This man was a cattle merchant, and
as all merchants did in those days, he traveled often to

Shadukiam to trade. On one such occasion, when he was in need of such sundries as merchants long for: cloth, jewels, food which could not dream of growing in their own countries, he asked his daughters what they would like from the great city.

"A dress which shines as brightly as the last moon of winter!" cried his first daughter, who was called Ubalda, and who loved such things.

"A golden ball, as lovely and round as the first sun of summer!" cried his second daughter, who was called Ushmila. He frowned at her for a long time before he agreed.

"If it please you, Father," said his blushing third daughter, who was called Urim, "I should like an apple."

"No more?" said the merchant, who had certainly not raised his daughters to ask for such silly, simple things. A merchant expects certain tastes from his children, and he was mightily disappointed.

"No more," answered the girl, whose hair was very red, red as the rarest salamander hide, and whose eyes were very blue, blue as the most costly dolphin skin.

"Very well," said the merchant, and went in search of the meager fortunes which Shadukiam grants to foreigners: enough to snare them, but not enough to make them stay.

Now, as often befalls merchants with one meek daughter and two haughty, fortune did not smile on the cattle merchant. He drove his flock before him, sheep of such fleeces as your mother might have heard of in the oldest stories she knew, and when he crossed into Shadukiam, he was promptly set upon by minor city officials and relieved of his livestock. His throat bled out into the Varil like a sheep cut down for supper, and we would weep for him, save that we have quite enough to do with weeping for our own misfortunes.

As the cattle merchant's body lay drifting into steam below turrets of diamond and bowers of roses, its blood called as it might to a shark, and as the moon rose milk-thick and silent, one of her children approached. He was very tall and thin as a length of paper. His skin and cloaks were the color of the moon—not the romantic, lover's moon, but the true lunar geography: gray and pockmarked, full of secret craters, frigid peaks, and blasted expanses. His eyes had no color in them save for a pinpoint pupil like a spindle's wound—the rest was pure, milk—moon white. He bent over the slaughtered cattle merchant and smiled.

Perhaps you have heard of the Yi. We envy them—how much we would like to shed our bodies when they shrivel to pockmarks and craters. But we cannot.

The Man Dressed in the Moon stepped into the cattle merchant's body like another man steps into his winter coat, and he walked away warm and snug in this new face. And as the Yi are perverse, it amused him to drive the merchant's cart out of the city of Shadukiam with a dress as bright as the last moon of winter, a golden ball as lovely and round as the first sun of summer, and an apple, a simple, silly apple. He remembered these things in the bones of the cattle merchant's legs, in the veins of his fingertips.

His daughters greeted him with kisses and exclamations of delight, for he kept a scarf at his throat and his skin was still more or less whole and pink. The slight gray pallor they ignored as daughters eager for presents will. He gave Ubalda her dress of deep blue and silver, and Ushmila her golden ball, and urged her to run along and play, and he produced with a flourish the silly, simple apple for pretty little Urim, with her red hair like foreign suns and her blue eyes like foreign seas.

"But, Father, this is not an apple," said the girl, her sweet brow furrowing.

"Ah, but in Shadukiam, this is what is called an apple," the Man Dressed in the Moon crooned.

It was a ruby as deep and darkly shaded as a true apple, and at its ebony stem was an emerald leaf, thin enough to flutter in the wind.

"How shall I eat it, Father?" Urim said.

"Put your teeth into it, girl, like a wolf biting into a reindeer's cheek."

And so the girl did. It tasted, she said, of brandy and cider and the reddest berries she had ever known. Because she was a good child, she shared the fruit with her sisters, and all of them agreed it was lovely, and their father the best of all possible fathers. They ate only half, and kept the rest for the dreary winter. But foreign produce does not often sit well with the provincial daughters of cattle merchants, and the girls sickened, the jewels in their stomachs pricking at their flesh, refusing to dissolve.

And all the while they sickened, their father grew gray and silver and pock-marked, frozen peaks appearing on his cheeks, craters on his arms, and his eyes grew white, white as the salt sea of their home. Now, the daughters of this man, though weak of digestion, were not weak of will, and between them were wise enough to know their father was not their own, and that Shadukiam, as often as it gives, takes and takes and takes. Ushmila was overfond of books, and she saw the marks of the Yi on her father. Ubalda was overfond of sharp things, scissors and knives and diamonds, and brought her collection to her sisters. It was decided that Urim of the red hair like apple skins and the blue eyes like moonlight would discover the truth of the matter. And so the clever child brought her father the uneaten half of the Shaduki apple, jeweled and wet.

"Father, I am sick, and close to death," said Urim, her face pale as wasting.

The Man Dressed in the Moon smiled hungrily. "How wonderful," he said.

"Surely you do not mean that, Papa!" cried Urim.

"Of course not, my darling! Forgive an old man—his mind runs away without him sometimes."

Urim cast her eyes down, and mourned her father.

"Will you not share this apple with me? It would comfort me, in my dying, for though it hurts me so, I have never tasted anything so sweet."

The Man Dressed in the Moon's face softened as much as it might, for he believed well in the greed of young girls, and he folded her into his arms. "It would delight me, my darling daughter."

Urim cut a slice of apple for the pocked Yi, and he chewed it with the relish of an alligator sucking the bones of a finch. But soon enough he began to cough, and choke, for Urim had poisoned her foreign apple, and the daughters of the cattle merchant, Ubalda and Ushmila, rushed from the shadows and leapt upon the gray-skinned creature, cutting into him over and over—but never enough to kill. They had no Griffin's talon, and could not hope for death. Urim sliced his cheeks with the faceted edges of her apple, grinning wildly into the face that had once been her father's.

"Let it never be said," she cried, "that the daughters of a cattle merchant do not know how to put an animal down!"

The Tale
of the Lepress
and the Leopard,
Continued

"THEY WERE AS CLEVER AS A PACK OF HYENAS, those girls," the wicker-wight said. "They did not kill the Yi, but opened his skin and took the thinnest shavings of his bones—how they must have shone, like shards of the moon itself!—and these Urim instructed them to place on their tongues. The bones melted to vapor and the girls were healed, the sharp apple-jewels in their bellies melting to nothing. And Urim, wise child, kept her father barely alive, collecting his blood in the glass jars they had used for sheep's milk, and put his body into a casket of white stone." She nodded at the memorial. "A city grew around this casket, on the edge of the white and salted sea, and when folk were in need, shavings were carefully taken from his bones, placed on their tongues, and the casket sealed up again. After one hundred years, the Man Dressed in the Moon stopped screaming." The wicker-wight looked down, ashamed. "Urim, named for that clever girl who wanted only an apple, became famous. More and more came. I came. My branches were drier than the skull of a lion left in the waste when I finally arrived at the gates. My skin was gone; all that remains was what you see. How this came to pass is not important—is the beginning of illness ever remembered so clearly as its boils and blood and broken, aching bones? The moment when you breathe your last clear air? One never remembers it. I am afflicted; so are we all. When first I came I was sure that Urim would hold me in its black-clothed embrace, look on me with her gray and mothering eyes, and brush my brow with her lips. She would give me an apple and a shaving of bone. I would walk from her whole. But there are so few cures in Urim, these days. The Yi's bones are not infinite. They are precious. We do not all deserve them."

I yawned. Of course my mistress deserved all things. "Will you wait with us, for the dawn?" I asked the poor, empty woman.

"Of course."

I have told you what happened. The dawn came. Black-robed lepers came hobbling on canes of ash and hazel, having heard that one of their number had arrived, and they embraced us as sisters. Their hands safe on Ruin's veils, they told us we were loved, that flowers would be rubbed into our wounds, that there were altars ready for our knees. If we were fortunate, if we were worthy, perhaps we would be granted a sliver of bone. A leper with one leg reached out to cup Ruin's face in his rotted hands, his eyes alight with joy. He said:

"There are no veils in Urim, my dear. Show us your affliction—we do not care for beauty."

With a stifled cry of relief, Ruin pulled her veils from her face, and with it came peels of skin like pages torn from a book, and the lepers recoiled.

"You are not a leper!" one cried, covering her mouth with one putrid hand, green mold springy and thick in the webbing of her fingers.

"She is dead," whispered the first. "She is dead, already dead, and her death will spread among us like plague."

A third, his nose a crusted red gape in his face, hissed: "She shall not have the bones! They are ours! She cannot have them!"

A fourth wondered if perhaps she was not Yi herself, with bones for their tongues.

Lepers know well not to touch the sick—they embraced her thinking her like them, but they could not risk contracting whatever other vile illness she bore. They beat her with their canes and slashed out her tongue, so that she could not give their names to the night.

The Tale of the Waste, Concluded

"I SNARLED AND LEAPT AND TRIED TO BITE them, but I am only a cat, and I was not raised to hunt, only to walk with her in the waste." Rend raised a paw over her eyes. "They chained me to her, so that my thrashing would only harm my mistress, and left us battered against the white casket. They took her tongue gingerly, in gloved hands, to see if it could be boiled into medicine. After a long while, she stirred as if dreaming, and I pulled her from the city. She is dead; she did not bleed. I am as near to dead as makes no difference among leopards; I did not bleed. The silver chain suits us, we find. We are bound, she and I, and now we go home, to Ajanabh, where there are red spices and no cures, where she may lie down again in the earth and rest, and I may mourn my mother. When she has gone to stone entirely, I shall carry her on my back into the city, and place her before the House of Red Spices, and sparrows shall live in her hair, and I shall live at her feet."

Ruin wept, and in her tears tiny specks of flesh washed away. Rend looked at her with huge black eyes full of feline grief.

The Djinn looked at the black-veiled woman as well, her red eyes dim with despair.

"I cannot give you back your tongue," Scald said slowly, her hair clearing from her flaming face, "but I could heal you." She cleared her burning throat. "Well, I could try. My wishing days are done, the Khaighal saw to that. But if you would free me, I could try."

"How could we open such a cage?" the leopard said.

"I suspect that if your mistress were to touch the bars, they would turn to stone, and could be as easily broken as any other stone."

"And what would you do, if we were to set you free?" The leopard clawed the ground uncertainly.

Scald looked into the east, across the cracked earth with its ruined gold and scurrying mice. "Kohinoor was right. I am old now, nearly fourteen. I have not long left. I would go home, to Ajanabh, and converse with my friend spider, and dance with the Sirens, and burn in Lantern's tail, and let my hand fall once or twice on Solace's hair. I would watch the Carnival, and listen to Agrafena every morning as the sun graces her bows. I would see how my wives had got on. I would tell Hour such a story, such a story!" The Djinn-Queen closed her fire-rimmed eyes. "I would swim in the Vareni, and hear the bells ring out, and when all was done I would put my cheek to Simeon's fingers, and rest."

Tears flooding her rheumy eyes, Ruin raised her arms and threw back her black cowl. Beneath it was sparse hair and skin like shavings of bone. Her skull showed through black strands, and her cheeks were hollow, translucent. She was made of glass, glass which was fainting back into sand. Her mouth was dry and white and chapped, and though she opened it, no sound came. She reached out with both hands toward the cage, and as her fingers grazed the Djinn-bones, the bone-bars flushed red and porous, Basilisk-bright. Wordless laughter erupted from Ruin's broken mouth, and it mingled with her wrenching cries. The cage shivered red, at the end of all things, as red as Ruin's house, her shoes, her father. And as she released the bars, Scald put her incandescent palms to them, and they sloughed to molten white. The Djinn emerged, her smoke-hair spreading free around her, with no baskets to contain it, like spilled water.

"What will you do to her?" whispered the cat nervously, inching close to her mistress.

"My darling cat." The Djinn smiled. "I shall breathe into her, and bring her to life. There is no stone that cannot be rendered like the fat of a cow in fire—if the fire is hot enough."

"Will it hurt her?" Rend's spotted, gold-furred head lolled anxiously on the earth.

"Very much."

Scald drew a long breath, and the desert seemed to shimmer into her. Her chest cracked, and beneath the black skin embers flushed bright as two suns, then in her arms, and in her cheeks, and how she blazed, then, her face puffed and ready, her breath held, her painted palms phosphorescent. She blew out her breath, and the wind and fire of it was white as a Star at the center of a city, engulfing Ruin in light. Rend cowered and scrabbled away, singeing her tail. Ruin burned, a red candle in the blasted waste, and even after Scald had wheezed and coughed her last flames, the dead girl stood with her arms raised to the sky, her flesh peeling off in blazing strips like the ash that floats from a summer bonfire.

It was hours before she stopped.

Once, in the wasteland between Urim and Ajanabh, three long shadows were cast on the thirsty earth, whose dark cracks forked out in all directions like vines searching for the smallest trickle of water. Three long shadows lay black and sere on that fractured desert. A woman, a Djinn, and a leopard stared at each other over the golden earth, and the woman fell to her knees, her body burned and pink and blistered, but whole. Her hair was burned away, her bald head shone in the last rays of the sun, and she put her living, blood-bright hands to her soft belly and screamed into the ground, screamed, and laughed, and wept.

In the Garden

IT WAS NEARLY DAWN. A GHOSTLY BLUE LIGHT LAY ON THE CHILDREN, stippled with stars. Long shadows lay on the snow, and the fires had gone out in the center of the Garden, and the braziers at the Gate had guttered to smoking embers. The courtiers wandered back into the Palace, full of rhinoceros horn and cinnamon wine, dogs with bells on their collars leaping at their mistresses' hems. The laces which held the chestnut boughs in the shape of a chapel were loosed, and sprang back with red-barked relief into their accustomed fork-boughed shapes. The wood beyond the Gate was dark and deep, and in it nightingales and starlings sang, pecking in the snow in search of the sun. The lake with its frozen reeds was still, as still as the world becomes before dawn, a hesitant hare testing the ice for thickness with its forepaw.

The boy and the girl sat together, huddled for warmth. The world before dawn is very still, but also very cold, and it seemed as though everything had been conquered by blue, even the girl's shivering lips.

"That is all," the boy said. "There is no more."

The girl opened her eyes, her hair wet with melted snow, her scarlet gown black in the dark. "That was a wonderful story," she said, a smile opening like a lily on her face.

The boy frowned, his face suddenly grown-up and very serious. "And there will be no others, no more strange and no more wonderful. It is over."

The girl touched his face gently, putting her cold hands on his cheeks. "Do you wish you had never asked me, that day, why my eyes were dark, like the lake before the dawn?"

"No...but I thought...I thought something would happen. There would be lightning and thunder or a terrible pillar of smoke and something dreadful would come out."

"I don't know," the girl said. "I never knew what would happen."

"Maybe," the boy whispered eagerly, "nothing will happen. I can come to you every day until I am Sultan, and then you can come to me, in the Palace, and sit at my table without a veil."

The girl shut her eyes, and the vast blackness of her lids glinted in the blue snowlight. No letters moved on them, they were dark and smooth and empty, no more than a mark, no more than ink. An owl flew overhead, home from a night of hunting.

"Perhaps," the girl said. "There is always a moment when stories end, a moment when everything is blue and black and silent, and the teller does not want to believe it is over, and the listener does not, and so they both hold their breath and hope fervently as pilgrims that it is not over, that there are more tales to come, more and more, fitted together like a long chain coiled in the hand. They hold their breath; the trees hold theirs, the air and the ice and the wood and the Gate. But no breath can be held forever, and all tales end." The girl opened her eyes. "Even mine."

"Yes, my dear, even yours," said a gentle, rough voice, like the feathers of a goose's wings rubbing together.

The girl turned and saw, on the other side of the Gate, on the other side of the wrought-iron battle with its cannon of ice, a bent old woman with tangled silver hair and a long, hooked nose. The girl caught her breath like a fawn in sight of a wolf, and her hands began to tremble.

"You are here...you are here to judge me," she said, her throat dry.

"That would be a severe interpretation," said the crone with a sly grin.

The girl's great dark eyes filled up with tears, glittering like snowflakes in firelight. She bit her lip. "Am I good?" she blurted. "Was I good enough? Am I a good girl? I am not wicked, like they said. I am not a demon, I swear it. Was I good enough for the spirit? I tried so hard not to be wicked, or angry, or bitter, even when the night was very cold."

The crone tucked a silver strand of hair behind her ear. "Do you remember me?" she asked, as though she had not heard anyone speak.

The girl dried her eyes with the heels of her hands. "Yes," she said, "you came when I was little, as little as one of my brown-backed geese. You told me about the tales. And you gave me my knife." The girl drew it out of her crimson dress, the small, curving silver knife with its handle of bone.

The old woman nodded. "It is my knife. But it was better that you have it. You were more often hungry than I."

"Please," the girl said. "How does it end? How do I end? I have waited so long."

The old woman wound her hands in the dead, dry rose-roots of the Gate. "Oh, my darling girl," she whispered, her voice thick, "I know you have."

THE LAST TALE

ONCE, THERE WAS A FERRY ON A LONELY GRAY lake on a lonely gray shore. It creaked in the storms and the wind, and its tether stretched. A man with a hunch on his back poled it back and forth, clothed all in rags.

Once, there was a lonely island in a lonely lake, and on that lonely island was a woman with green scales glittering on her skin, and she walked the shore, and the eyes that blinked on the gray lakeside wept for her. But the woman did not weep. She wrung her fingers and looked into the mist and considered many things, for her mind *was as vast as the lake itself. From time to time a young man with red skin like fine wood came to find her, and stroke her green-black hair. But she could not be consoled, and finally stepped onto the cracked boards of the dock and opened her throat to call the ferry. She called until her voice died on the wind, dry as a molted skin. Please, she called.* Please come back.

It did not concern the ferryman if the lake folk needed him. But he could not help but hear the snake-woman's cries, and when the day's storms had passed, leaving his bones wet and his lizards irritable, he let the ferry drift as it wanted to—for sometimes in his loneliness the man believed the ferry as alive as he, and he spoke to it, and listened to its troubles, which had mostly to do with barnacles and algae. But the ferry now spoke of a voice pulling at it like a pole, and it longed to go toward that voice, that snake-song which flicked its tongue at the poor ferry in the fog. They floated out to the island with the beach of eyes, and there was the woman with her glittering green skin, her long hair wet and plastered to her hips, her eyes dark and needful.

"I want to see her," she said, before the ferryman had finished his docking.

"That is impossible."

"No, it is not. You ferry anyone, if they pay the toll. I will pay. In the world, in the Sun, in the blood-riddled world, my daughter is breathing and eating her breakfast with a golden fork and laughing at a joke the cook has told her. I want to see her." The woman's eyes softened with depthless pleading. "Just once."

"And what do you think you can pay?"

"You took the huldra's tail."

"I did."

"Will you take my hair?"

The ferryman considered. He did not wish to. It was not right, and not his habit. But he should, perhaps, have refused the child in the first place, and to become priggish now seemed useless, small. The tolls these days were strange, and he had seen more tolls than he had ever seen years in the world. He thought perhaps he had tired of them, the endless coins, and these late, grotesque amputations.

"I will take it," he said slowly, his voice echoing not at all in the thick fog, "but you must agree to my terms."

The woman waited, her green a scream of desire in the gray.

"I will take your hair as two tolls—across, and back. You may not go as the goose-woman went, into the world to live and eat bread and dance. You must come back. You are not like her. Go to your child, just once, and return to me, to the lonely lake and the lonely shore. This is all that is right and proper."

The woman nodded, and gathered her long, shimmering green-black hair into her hand. With the sharp edge of the ferryman's wing-bones, she severed it at her neck, and stepped on board the ferry. It sighed under her, glad in what ways nails and wood can be glad. They drifted into the lake, and Zmeya looked back to the shore, where two young men with red skin like a ship's hull stared after the dwindling raft. She raised her hand, and the mist closed over her.

She stood above her daughter's crib. It was a beautiful room, with a fire in the marble hearth and a bottle of hot wine on a little glass table. The crib was cedar, and the blankets were pure and white as a dove's belly. The little girl had a shock of dark hair and her red fingers were curled into fists, her tiny brow furrowed as she dreamed. Zmeya opened the window, so that the light of the Stars could stream in, the light of the Moon, the dark of the Sky. Dappled silver light fell onto the child's face.

"Sorrow," she whispered. "My Sorrow, my love."

Tears welled up in her eyes, tears of light, of Snake-light and Star-light. Zmeya lit the room like a brazier, her silver self spilling into the corners. She had not known such light in her skin since before the Boar-King had taken her. It filled up her throat so she could not breathe. She had forgotten what it felt like to be so bright. She knelt by the crib, her jagged, shorn hair dripping light like blood, and smiled at her daughter. She wanted to stay, after all. She wanted to put a veil over her hair and take this child downstairs into the spinning world of the court, and watch her grow up. She wanted to make sure that the Moon and the Stars were always on her. She wanted to hold her child to her as she had done on the lonely island, and feel her living mouth tug at her breast.

Slowly, Zmeya reached out a glowing finger, and with infinite care, caressed her daughter's eyelids, the first and last touch of the Star and her daughter in the lakeless world.

The skin beneath her finger curled black and steaming, and shadows leapt from the smoking flesh. Sorrow began to cry. A nurse came bustling in, and Zmeya stepped into the shadows and the starlight, chagrined.

*   *   *

Once, there was a ferry on a lonely gray lake on a lonely gray shore. It creaked in the storms and the wind, and its tether stretched. A man with a hunch on his back poled it back and forth, clothed all in rags. He saw a woman walking along the shore toward him, her hair short and unkempt, her eyes red with weeping. She came to the ferry and looked up at him stonily.

"I only wanted to touch her, with living hands, my living child. Just once."

"Was it enough?" the ferryman asked.

Zmeya was a long time answering.

"Yes," she said finally, and stepped onto the ferry once more.

Out of the Garden

"WHAT SHE LEFT ON YOUR EYELIDS, SORROW, MY DOVE, MY DARLING, my little goose," said the old woman, "was your history, winding and tangling back and back and back. It was your story, the story of your birth, your life, swinging forward and backward like a holy censer, the tendrils of its smoke reaching out and around and into each other like the coils of a snake, pursuing all those strange and varied folk with a Star's tenacity. They are the tales of everyone who reached into silver shadows and pulled you into the world: your mother, who was a murdered Star; your father, a lonely creature who loved a raft that became a tree and a tree that became a red ship; a tea leaf that found its way out of the world and quickened a dead woman's womb, and the girl who carried it there; the boy who paid your fare across the water, the women who pushed your mother back from death, the Basilisk three women mutilated to speak once more before they died, the bear who was turned back, and the flame-hearted Djinn who was born from your eyelids burning beneath your mother's hand, who drifted into the world before you." The crone smiled, her face breaking into wrinkles, her eyes spilling with tears. "And perhaps not least the woman who carried you on the ferry, who was once a goose, who took a child away from her cradle and far away, who left you instead, a magpie's trick, who watched over you, and gave you a knife to keep you from hunger and safe, her own knife, the one she used to kill a Wizard when she was very, very young. Your name is Sorrow, my little bird, my dear-as-diamonds, and you have been loved all your days."

The girl could not breathe. She coughed, and wept, and crumbled into the snow. Aerie opened the Gate and took the girl into her arms. She stroked her hair. She whispered to her and dried her tears. The boy watched, his mouth open, trying to remember every tale and losing them as quickly as they rose up in his heart, golden fish that would not stay.

Out of the wood a young girl came. She was very beautiful, and she wore a wispy red dress that seemed made for dancing. All along her right side ran stark tattoos: a dancing black flame. Beside her were a great Firebird, a black, smoking Djinn, and a small brown spider with glittering legs. The young girl walked slowly to Sorrow, who untangled herself from Aerie and stood to face her. Solace touched the girl's eyelids softly, and looked into the white-hushed Garden.

"So this is where I would have lived, if I had not become a Firebird's daughter," she said. "Did you like it?"

Sorrow blushed. "No," she whispered. "It was cold at night. I think...I think I have paid for your fire with my sadness since we were born."

Solace grew very serious. "I am sorry." She folded the other girl into her dancer's arms, and kissed her cheek. They looked so much alike, the boy thought, standing like that, with their faces buried in one another's shoulders, all that long black hair mingling.

"But now we will be sisters," Solace said brightly, brushing Sorrow's hair from her face. "And you will learn to dance with me, I promise."

The Djinn floated forward, and Sorrow could see, in her eyes, how old she was now, the ancient, guttering fire. She was still as youthful-looking as any flame, her stomach taut and black, her palms gleaming, but she was so tired.

"I think," she said, one red eyebrow arched, "that you are, somehow, my mother. At least as much as you are her sister. Aerie has tried to explain it, but I was never good at history. But it would seem I am the only Djinn of seared flesh, and that is something to know before one is blown out."

"Why did you leave me for so long?" Sorrow cried, unable to

contain herself. "I was so alone! I was so frightened! You could have come for me anytime! Why did you wait?"

Aerie regarded her solemnly. "The world is wide, and the rearing of children is a delicate thing. But, heart of my heart, I knew"—and from her skirts she drew a long, golden feather—"that all tales end. And I, and all, would be here when it was time for yours to begin."

"Come with us," said Solace.

"I . . . I am afraid!" Sorrow said. "I have never been outside the Gate, ever! I have wished for it, so many times, but I am so afraid!"

Aerie bent and took the girl's dark face in her hands. Her laughing eyes were black as a bird's. "Sorrow, come. Come into the world, into the land beyond wishing, where, I swear to you, there are miracles: a multitude of Griffins, and a Papess at prayer, and lost girls found, and a Satyr laughing in a cottage by the sea."

Solace turned to Lantern and the two shared a glittering and conspiratorial expression. The spider said nothing, but clicked her silver legs together. He turned and let a long, glistening cloak fall from his back, and Solace caught it. She wrapped her sister's shivering shoulders in a cloak of golden feathers, and arranged her hair over its collar.

"Come," she said, "I will show you so many strange and wonderful things."

The boy squeaked. He had meant to make a much more grown-up sound, but it came out a squeak. He did not know what he wanted, he did not know what to say, but his face was stricken, his mouth trembling—he tried valiantly not to cry.

"You were not always alone," he managed to say. "Not always."

And the girl, his girl, looked at him for a very long time, as still and strange as she had ever been, her dark eyes showing stark in the first pale light that tipped the trees like snow. She stood there, her hand clasped tight in Solace's painted hand, a Djinn at her shoulder, a Firebird at her back, a spider at her feet, and an old grandmother with her hand resting on her shoulder. He wanted to run to her, but he dared not. He did not belong; he knew he did not belong with them. He would be sent back to the Palace to sit alone on a hard throne. But as the sun rose up like a pearl in the winter sky, Sorrow looked at the boy, her boy, and smiled, her eyes bright as feathers.

"Tell me a story," she said. "Tell me the tale of how we met when we were children, how we walked in a Garden and you were not afraid of me, and how we went into the world, and learned even more strange and wonderful things than we could have guessed at when our walls were made of flowers. Tell me a tale I have never heard, with a boy and a girl in it, and a long, wide road."

Sorrow held out her pale, thin hand, shining in the morning like a promise.

The boy looked back over his shoulder, at the Palace, but only once. He laced his fingers into hers.

As they walked into the wood, Lantern sang out the morning bells. Behind them, in the golden light of a scalding sun, a purple bracelet slowly sank into the snow.

ACKNOWLEDGMENTS

At the close of a book that has presided over five years of my life, there are many people to whom I must tip my now-threadbare hat:

My grandmother Caroline, who read me the Bible by day and *Arabian Nights* and the Ramayana by night, and thus wrought this rough beast;

S. J. Tucker, my fiery sister, who both inspires and makes manifest;

The glittering network of folk from all manner of outlandish places who have offered faith, love, encouragement, and their spare bedrooms, but most particularly Delia Sherman, Rose Fox, and Josh Jasper;

Wilhelm and Jakob Grimm, Hans Christian Andersen, Aleksandr Afanasiev, Husain Haddawy, and all other saints of translation, oral tradition, and manuscript preservation;

Juliet and Michele, the twin ravens who sit forever on the shoulders of this book, wiser by far than I;

And last and always, Dmitri and Melissa Zagidulin, without whose steadfastness and insight this book would simply cease to be;

Thank you.

ABOUT THE AUTHOR

Catherynne M. Valente was born in the Pacific Northwest, grew up in California, and now lives in Ohio with her two dogs. This is her fifth novel.